The Quickening

A Paradise Ours Novel

Susan Beth Cole

Cover art and Design by Meowlayn

Scene Break Illustrations by Jen Wolpoff

ISBN 9781966452027 (paperback)

ISBN 9781966452034 (eBook)

First edition 2025

For my husband. There's no one else I'd rather have beside me to face the hard stuff, to help me laugh through my tears when tragedy strikes, and to [redacted] [redacted] as many times as humanly possible. I love you.

Content Note

Beware!

Spoilers below!

The Quickening deals with the emotional fallout of infertility and raising a child as a single mom. A character also struggles with having trouble discerning her current lifetime from her past lives.

Mina encounters an ancient demonic being who does not care about consent and definitely crosses some lines. The being's tentacle monster shockingly does care about consent, though, and helps temper the being's behavior. Oh yeah. There are tentacles.

There's breeding kink, impregnation, fisting, exhibitionism, bondage, edging, fear as an aphrodisiac, more kidnapping, and sharing. There's period blood, impact play, and at least one large ribbed penis. Expect all gender pairings.

The Quickening is book two in the Paradise Ours series, and is meant to be read after book one.

One

A S FAR AS GATHERINGS to celebrate her surprise elopement to the demonic overlord of Hell went, this one wasn't as bad as Mina had feared, even if everything had ended up a bit sideways. Her family tried to immerse themselves in the delicious spread of Indian food, but the intrusion of their past-life trauma—like an unruly, uninvited guest—proved too distracting. Instead they quietly circled each other in the kitchen and dining nook before finally settling in the living room. Mina and her sister, Dahlia, sat on either side of their mother, Sandra. Tabitha, Dahlia's daughter, sat on the floor and leaned back against her grandmother's legs.

Sandra had barely touched her tikka masala, obviously preoccupied with her thoughts, her eyes unfocused, not hearing conversation. Mina placed her hand over her mother's. Sandra looked up, temporarily pulled from her haze, gave her daughter a small smile, leaned over, and placed a kiss on her cheek.

"Are you okay?" Mina whispered.

"Yes," Sandra said. "I have a lot of questions, and some things I need to tell you. But it can wait until we have a quiet moment alone."

"I think Luci would be happy to answer those questions now," Mina said, glancing at her husband, who had just settled on the edge of the chaise lounge where Bellz, Sindy, and Lilith were snuggled together. Mina had questions, too, and she doubted her mother would be able to vocalize any of her own just yet. But Mina was happy to get the ball rolling.

"Of course," Luci said, standing once more and moving to the middle of the room. He looked nervous, his hands refusing to settle. First, he clutched them before him, then folded them behind his back, and finally slipped them into the pockets of his pants. "What do you want to know?"

"How did we manage to get back to Earth the first lifetime?" Mina asked, giving her mother's hand a squeeze.

Luci sighed heavily. "I'm sorry. I usually don't tell you these things. You were with me for five hundred years, Mina, the first time. There are so many memories from it alone. It's dangerous. I don't want to trigger a mental tidal wave."

"Okay," Mina said, fighting an eye roll. Danger hadn't stopped her yet. But she didn't want to push Luci. "Well, we can start with what we do know. You somehow managed to reunite me with my family. Well, almost, anyway, before God and his crew showed up and got violent."

"We did reunite you. Lilith managed to get Sandra, Dahlia, and Tabitha to us during the skirmish so I could protect you all," Sindy said.

Sandra placed her hand on top of Mina's so her daughter's was sandwiched between her own, silent approval to continue.

"And is that when God set us on this perpetual cycle?" Mina asked.

"Yes," Luci said, nodding. "We had already restarted the reincarnation cycle in Hell."

"Restarted it?" Dahlia asked. "Implying that it had stopped at some point."

Luci bit his bottom lip as if he had said too much and regretted it.

"Luci, please. I have half your soul now. Don't you think that might protect me from my brain melting?"

"I don't know. It might, but I can't be sure." Luci pulled his hands out of his pockets, crossed his arms, and started pacing in front of the unlit fireplace.

"We could ask Berith," Alastor offered. He had found a spot to sit against the wall between the fireplace and TV. "They would be sure to at least have a theory."

Luci nodded to Lilith, who deposited Sindy into Bellz' lap and then disappeared.

"Who is Berith?" Tabitha asked.

"They are Hell's top scientist and scholar," Sindy said as Bellz helped her settle into his lap. "When we found Ha—" Luci cut her off with a sharp reprimand.

"When we found Hades?" Mina asked as a memory began to surface. "Cerberus stumbled across us. And then a few weeks later, or a few years later. . .decades? I don't know. The timeline is confusing. Time is so intangible in Hell."

"Mina?" Luci crossed to his bride, falling to his knees and cupping her calves in his large palms.

"Cerberus came back for me. I remember them scooping me up in their jaws. Their teeth were so large and sharp I thought for sure that they meant to devour me, and yet they were so gentle. They deposited me onto their back and took me to Hades."

"That's all correct, my love," Luci said.

"That's it. That's all I remember. The rest is there, I know it. I just can't seem to access it. Like it's still locked away."

Luci leaned forward, brushing his forehead against hers and hushing her gently. "It's okay. You don't need to remember it all right away."

"I think I can get it. I just need to concentrate."

"The locks are protecting you, Mina," Luci said. "Leave it alone for now. It will reveal itself on its own when it is meant to."

"I'm sorry," Dahlia cut in. "Are we supposed to believe that Hades is real? How does he fit in with Christian doctrine? It doesn't make any sense."

Sandra nodded. "Maybe it's because I've only just learned that my daughter has married Satan himself—who, surprisingly, seems like a very lovely young man who loves her a great deal—but I just cannot believe that Hades is real. At least not yet. My worldview has been turned on its head enough for one day, I think."

"Okay, so skip Hades for now," Mina said. "But you got us back to Earth after making reincarnation a thing."

"Yes," Luci said. "I was ready to take your family back to Hell if we needed, but God stopped me from being able to do so. He struck a deal instead. I could keep you forever if you just once chose to be with me and abandoned your family in the process. With reincarnation up and running again, it was easy for him to tie you four together. Your life cycles always happen in the same way, the same order, the same time frame."

"So I was destined to become pregnant at 18?" Dahlia asked.

"Yes," Luci said.

"And I was destined to face losing my eldest daughter every lifetime?" When Luci nodded, Sandra wrapped an arm around each of her children, drawing them in for support. "And what about my husband? Was his death preordained too?"

"He wasn't part of my original deal with God, but I've come to suspect that your husband and Tabitha's father have both been pulled into this. Mina's history never varies by much. She loses her father around the time Tabitha is two, and Tabitha's father is never in the picture," Luci said.

"But now we know," Tabitha said. "Now we can fight it."

"It won't bring Dad back," Dahlia said.

"Where is he now? Waiting in Hell?" Sandra asked.

"I think God has a holding place for you all between lifetimes," Luci said.

"He does," Michael confirmed from where he had been standing behind them all, lingering in the archway between the dining nook and living room. Mina made a mental note to try to include him more. His knowledge alone made him an asset, but, more than that, he deserved to know he was wanted, accepted, and one of them.

"And we can't take Dahlia, Mom, and Tabby to Hell?" Mina asked.

"We've never tried," Bellz said. "We were worried about the consequences of breaking our deal with God." Bellz practically spit with disgust.

"Fuck that," Oz said. Everyone started, surprised to hear from him. He hadn't been there from the beginning. He wasn't cursed with them. The fact that he felt passionate was proof that he really was on Mina's side. She hadn't expected him to be so willing to fight for her.

"Yes," Sandra said. "I agree with the cowboy. God has no more claim over our souls than you do, Lucifer." Mina reached out and cupped Luci's face, reminded that he had just claimed a big part of her soul, and she his. Nothing could break them apart anymore.

"We'll want to take precautions," Alastor said. "Consult with Berith more."

"Are we feeling more settled?" Luci asked, glancing at Sandra in particular, but only briefly so as not to make her feel uncomfortable. "I'd really like to enjoy our night. Maybe put on some music and dance a little?"

"I like that idea," Mina said, turning to Sandra. "Mom?"

"Yes, I would like that, too," Sandra said.

So they stood up, one of the demons used their magic to start up some music, and they all danced. Taking turns to pass out water or rest their feet, they celebrated for hours.

When Tabitha was too tired to keep her eyes open, Mina offered to take her upstairs as Dahlia happily twirled away with Oz.

There was a queen-size bed in the guest room, across the hall from Mina's art studio, with not much else in the way of furniture. This new home was still very much a work in progress. The room needed a dresser, or at the very least a nightstand.

"Hopefully this will be an okay place to nap until your mom is ready to go home," Mina said as she tucked the covers around Tabitha.

"It's comfy," Tabitha said, settling in against the pillows. Her eyes were already heavy with sleep. Mina tiptoed out of the room, turned out the light, and closed the door as quietly as she could.

She had taken all of two steps before someone grabbed her from behind and pulled her into her studio.

Two

SOMETHING HAPPENED WHEN Oz and Dahlia touched. A zap of recognition reverberated through Dahlia as they twirled in her sister's living room. And as the night progressed, she gravitated toward him, testing to see if it would happen again. Did she want it to? He reminded her of someone—someone she'd tried so hard to forget. He reminded her of who she used to be when she was just a teenage girl trying to enjoy her last summer before she went off to college.

But that didn't fit with who she was now. She was a partner at a marketing firm. She dealt with strict deadlines and unhappy clients. She was a single mother who had worked her ass off to provide for her daughter. She wasn't tempted by a charming smile or a soft nickname. Not anymore.

So why did his touch feel so perfect? Why did his presence pull her inexplicably closer?

To avoid temptation, she said yes when Michael asked her to dance. But soon she found herself back in Oz's arms, unsure if she had subconsciously circled back to him or if he had orchestrated cutting in.

When the song stopped, she tugged away, almost stumbling in her haste to reach the back door. Some fresh air would do her good.

If there were any stars above Mina's porch, Dahlia couldn't see them. The lights from the sprawling cityscape obscured the night sky, so she closed her eyes and focused on her breathing.

She wasn't sure how long she had been out there—not long—before she felt gentle pressure on her shoulder. The air left her lungs in a whoosh as her eyes met Oz's. Those deep, brown eyes. She hadn't known how beautiful they were during that week. All she had known of him she had learned with her fingertips, her ears.

The spirit board had been Tiffany's idea, so she and Dahlia and two of their closest friends, Becca and Linda, had gathered around it in Tiffany's attic. It was their last summer before college, and they were eager to hold off adulthood, even though most of them, Dahlia included, had turned eighteen. Dahlia had cooled herself with a magazine as she waited for the revolving fan to make its way back to her. Despite the sweltering heat, the girls remained. If Tiffany's mother knew what they were doing up here, she would have a cow. But there was no way that the middle-aged woman would bother climbing up the rickety built-in ladder to the small square of exposed wooden boards that made up the attic floor. Dahlia scooted closer to Becca, inching away from the pink insulation surrounding them.

Feeling safe from interruption, each girl placed her fingertips on the planchette.

"Is there anyone here?" Tiffany asked. The plastic triangle jerked over to "Yes."

Giggles erupted, and Linda placed one hand over her mouth in shock.

Dahlia shook her head, eyeing Tiffany with suspicion.

"What is your name?"

Again the planchette moved with little hesitation. It spelled out the name Zozo.

"Fuck no!" Linda said, snapping her hands away.

"Linda! Put your fingers back," Tiffany said. "The instructions say that if it's Zozo, we have to immediately end the session with a goodbye."

"I'm not touching that thing again!" Linda half whispered, half screeched as she stood and made a hasty exit down the ladder.

"What do we do?" Becca asked.

Tiffany removed her fingers and crossed her arms. "One of you two needs to take this thing out of here."

"What? No way!" Becca jerked her hand back as if she had been shocked.

Dahlia, the only one still touching the planchette, felt tingles spike up her arm and imagined a warm breath against her neck. She shivered and shrugged the sensations away. Clearly, her imagination was overacting again.

"That thing is attached to that board. We can't keep it here," Tiffany said.

"Well, I'm not taking it," Becca said.

"Oh my God, guys." Dahlia reached out and scooped up the spirit board and planchette before stuffing them into her backpack. "I'll take it home. You are both being children."

"It can't stay here tonight," Tiffany said. "Take it home, and then you can come back."

Dahlia laughed. She had no patience for Tiffany when she got like this. A quiet night at home watching rom-coms with her mother and sister suddenly sounded much more appealing.

"Nah," Dahlia said. "I'll see you guys tomorrow maybe."

A quick drive later, Dahlia dropped her backpack off in her bedroom before joining Mina and Sandra on the couch in the living room.

"I thought you were sleeping over at Tiffany's," Sandra said as she wrapped an arm around her younger daughter's shoulders.

"She was in a mood," Dahlia said.

"We're glad to have more time with you," Mina said. "Mom's only slightly freaking out about being an empty nester when you head to Chicago in the fall."

"Sorry, Mom," Dahlia said, resting her head on her mother's shoulder.

"I'm excited for you, Dahlia. This is a big opportunity." Sandra squeezed tight.

Halfway through the movie, after too many late nights with her friends, Dahlia could no longer keep her eyes open. Eventually she gave up and kissed her family members goodnight before heading to her bedroom.

She stripped down to her panties and a tank top, tugged on a pair of cotton shorts, and crawled under the covers. Dropping her flip phone on the bedside table, she fell back on her pillow and closed her eyes.

She had just started to drift off when she felt someone touch her face. The caress jolted her alert, but when she opened her eyes, she found an empty room lit by the light of the full moon shining through her translucent drapes.

She rubbed her face, turned onto her side, and nuzzled into her pillow. With her eyes closed, she pulled the sheet up to cover her shoulders.

This time, she felt a fingertip trace her forehead before a strand of her hair was tucked behind her ear.

"What the fuck?" she asked, sitting up in bed.

Again, no one was there.

Whoever or whatever it was had been right on top of her. There's no way they would have been able to move fast enough for there to be no trace of them. She hadn't heard any footsteps, no shuffling of clothes. Her closet door was still closed. It made a terrible racket any time it moved, so she knew no one was hiding there. There were built-in drawers beneath her bed frame, so they couldn't have snuck under her bed either.

Taking a deep breath, Dahlia told herself to calm down. Most likely it had just been a dream. That was the only reasonable explanation. Exhaustion from too many sleepless nights had to be the culprit.

She sighed and lowered herself once more. This time, she pulled the sheet over her head completely. Hesitantly, she let her eyelids shut once more.

A deep, male voice whispered against her ear, "Keep your eyes closed, darlin'."

She could feel his breath rustling the sheet against her cheek.

"What do you want?"

"Shh, I won't hurt you."

Dahlia felt the sheet being tugged down, inch by inch until it sat around her hips.

"Who are you?"

"We only met a few hours ago. Have you already forgotten me, beautiful?" He brushed his fingers through her hair, pulling it aside to expose her neck.

It couldn't be. Had she actually brought home an evil and dangerous spirit? Whoever he was, his nose nuzzled her neck. And she liked it.

"Mmm, you smell good, human. Like chocolate and rain."

"Zozo?" she whispered.

"Howdy." He pressed a chaste kiss to her cheek. "I'm glad you brought me home. There's something about you, little lady—something that I like very much."

"What does that mean?" Dahlia clutched the pillow beneath her head tightly. The stories about Zozo, the ones she had rolled her eyes at earlier in the day, sent chills down her spine now.

"Normally, I find a human to destroy. Mentally, physically. Doesn't much matter how," Zozo said as he kissed along her jaw.

His lips felt good on her skin, and she pressed harder into her pillow in a futile attempt to gain sanctuary from the way her fear fed her desire.

"But that's not what I want to do with you," he said in his thick Texan drawl. "How odd."

"What do you want to do with me then?" she asked as she turned to face him.

He stopped her mid turn with a strong hand on her stomach so that she fell back.

"Keep those eyes closed."

"Why?"

"You can't hear me if you open them."

"But can I still feel you?"

Instead of responding, he dragged his hand across her stomach and cupped the bottom of her breast through her shirt.

She gasped. Nobody had ever touched her like this before. Her sex tightened, and she sucked in her breath, waiting for more.

"The last thing I want to do is frighten you."

"Even though frightening people is what you do?"

He squeezed her breast. "I want a different reaction from you." His fingers closed around her breast and slid to her nipple, pinching tightly, making her gasp. "Yes, that. That's what I want. Do it again."

She couldn't have held in her second gasp if her life depended on it as he tugged at her again.

"Why am I letting you touch me like this?" she asked suddenly, even as she arched her back into him. "I shouldn't let you—" Her sentence broke off into a moan.

"Would you like me to stop?" Zozo's hand stilled.

"Please, no." She couldn't bring herself to ask him for that. In all of her eighteen years, no one had ever expressed desire for her and acted on it. The feeling was addictive. She would cling to it for as long as she could.

His deep chuckle rumbled through her. "Good. Would cost me a lot to stop." He lowered both of his hands to her hips. One descended farther while the other slipped under her tank top.

His calloused fingers were rough against her smooth stomach as he traced a path to her right breast. He covered it with his hand. Dahlia trembled at the skin on skin contact.

"You are so delicate, human," he said. Then he pinched her between his rough fingertips. "So innocent."

Dahlia whimpered then bit her lip and attempted to hide her embarrassment against a pillow.

"Don't hide from me." He cupped her cheek and turned her toward him, gently sweeping his mouth against lips that had never before been kissed. She gasped at the realization that her first was with a specter, demon, or something otherworldly, and he took advantage of it, slipping his tongue into her mouth.

Tentatively, she kissed him back, pressing her tongue against his until he moaned. The sound of it inflamed her, and she rose up and into him. His hand slipped around her back and clutched her to him. Using his whole body, he pressed her back into the bed before breaking the kiss.

"Let me be in control for now," he said, brushing her hair from her face and neck.

"I wish I could see you," she whispered as she ran her hands along his muscular arms.

"I don't think that's possible. You'll have to take my word for it that I'm big, strong, and very handsome."

"I'm just supposed to take you at your word, am I?" She brought her hands up to his shoulders and along his neck on her way to cup his face. Gently, she traced his features, but, other than determining he had no deformities, was unable to picture him in her mind.

She sighed and brushed her hands back through his hair. He chuckled as she unintentionally knocked something from his head.

"My hat, darlin'."

Dahlia groped for it in the dark, but she couldn't find it.

"You can't touch it now that it isn't on me."

"What kind of hat?"

"Cowboy hat, of course."

"So, the accent. You're a cowboy, or you just watched too many Westerns and decided to adopt the persona?"

His chuckle rumbled against her chest and filled her with joy. "The accent does seem to put people at ease around me, but I'm the real thing."

"How does one go from herding cows to single-handedly terrifying people from ever using a spirit board again?"

"That's kind of a long story that involves selling my soul, dying horrifically, and becoming a full-fledged demon."

"Sounds traumatic." She traced the muscles on his back through his flannel shirt.

"Mm, most definitely." He nuzzled into her again. "That feels good, little human."

Dahlia laughed as she realized she hadn't told him her name. But when she opened her mouth to tell him, he interrupted her immediately.

"I know your name, beautiful."

"Then why don't you use it?"

"I haven't earned it yet."

"You can grope me, but you can't say my name?"

"Well, yeah." He flexed the hand that cupped her bare breast where it sat comfortably.

"That's super backwards."

"Is it?"

"Yes," Dahlia giggled. "You are so odd."

"Not as odd as you. I can assure you that."

"Oh, yes, a typical teenage girl, so very unusual."

"I've never responded to anyone this way. Never had anyone respond to me this way, either." He pressed his lips to her neck and sucked on her until she was squirming beneath him, spreading her legs around him so she could thrust against him. "I give you pleasure, and it's like I'm breathing fresh air for the first time."

"I'm not anything special, Zozo," Dahlia said, tugging off her tank top before working on the buttons of Zozo's shirt. He arched his back and helped her unfasten the rest.

Zozo groaned in response as she tugged his shirt from his shoulders and down his arms. He shook it off, pulled Dahlia against him, and let his soft chest hair gently tickle her flesh. His skin warmed hers.

"Not special? Maybe to no one else, little lady. But you are special to me."

"Really?"

"Yes," he whispered against her brow.

"That's the sweetest thing anyone has ever said to me." Her heart leapt into her throat, and she swallowed hard to force it back down. "Now, quick. Help me get my pajama bottoms off."

"Slow down." Zozo chuckled.

"No. I can't see you, so I want to feel every bit of you against every inch of me."

"That's a really bad idea."

"How?"

"I'm not planning on taking your virginity."

Dahlia wiggled underneath him, tugging her shorts down her legs. "You aren't going to take it," she said as she wiggled her penultimate piece of clothing down farther, "but I might give it to you." With one last flick, the garment landed in a heap on the floor.

Zozo drew off the bed. Dahlia couldn't feel him anymore. She grabbed the sheet and pulled it up to her chin then sat up straight.

Keeping her eyes closed, she called out to him in a whisper. But he didn't respond.

Uncomfortable minutes passed in silence. Dahlia almost gave up, almost believed he had truly gone.

"If you want to feel me, that sheet has to go."

Her heartbeat sped up at the sound of his voice, and she quickly flung the bedding aside.

"I'd thought you'd left," she said.

"Just needed a moment to think," he said as he rejoined her on the bed.

"About staying?" She reached out for him, and he clasped her hand in his, using it to tug her across his lap.

"Among other things."

"I'm glad." She caressed his cheek before leaning in to place a peck on his lips.

He cupped her butt in one calloused palm and gave it a squeeze. "Me too."

"I'll trade you the use of my name for the reason you sold your soul," Dahlia said. Wow, would her mom freak out if she knew her youngest daughter was currently sitting on a demon's lap and making deals. At least she was making clever deals. She wanted so very badly to hear her name on his lips and to know more about him. This way she'd get both.

"I sold my soul to be able to talk to my sister again. She died of Spanish flu the night before I came home from the war. I spent the rest of my life trying to contact her, fruitlessly, until I encountered the demon, made a deal. I didn't fully understand the consequences back then. Not when I was just a simple human named Oscar."

Butterflies ignited in her belly, and her chest heated with something very much like joy. "Oscar," she said. "That's beautiful."

"You can use it, if you'd like."

She blushed, overwhelmed with the sudden need to remove herself from the spotlight. "So, somehow your end of the deal was to spend your afterlife haunting spirit boards?"

"The demon made spirit boards actually work, or so I believed at the time. And now it's *my* job to make sure they *don't*."

"Well, at least not in the way we intend them to. I still managed to reach the other side. Unless I'm dreaming you." Her fingers danced across his muscular chest.

"I promise I'm real, but, darlin', you seem like a dream to me as well, if it makes you feel any better," Zozo—no—Oscar said.

"A bit," Dahlia said as she pivoted to straddle his lap. The heat of him hit her center, and she rolled her hips just once to gauge his reaction.

He sucked in a breath and stiffened. Everywhere.

"I'm supposed to be the evil one, darlin'," he said as he took her hips in his strong hands and thrust against her.

"Guess it's contagious." She shrugged, moving her lower body again. He froze, and she took, finding her pleasure.

Oscar's grip dug into her flesh as he growled. Tipping her onto her back, he climbed on top of her, cradled between her thighs.

"How far do you want to take this, Dahlia?" He held his breath while he waited for her answer.

"I want all of you."

"Are you sure?" His whisper was ragged with desire.

"Very sure." She punctuated her statement with a string of kisses along his throat and chin.

"If you change your mind at any point, promise you'll tell me."

"I promise." His concern only reaffirmed her resolve that this was the right choice, despite all the Sunday school lectures, abstinence seminars, and a lifetime of parental pressure to wait until marriage suggesting otherwise.

Dahlia thanked God when Oscar slipped his hands into the sides of her panties and tugged with supernatural strength until they ripped as if they were rice paper.

Dahlia gasped, but she didn't ask him to stop.

Instead, she lifted her hips so he could pull the scraps away. Oscar rolled to Dahlia's side and whispered, "You are the most gorgeous creature I have ever encountered. Your firm breasts, so perky. Gravity's met her match. Your curves, those strong legs, that hair, an intriguing hint of fire."

He sucked in his breath as she slightly parted her thighs, giving him a glimpse of more of her beauty.

He slipped between her legs and held them open with his thighs. Then he stopped moving. He didn't speak. He barely breathed.

"Oscar?" she whispered. "What are you doing?"

His breathing hitched at the use of his human name. "I'm sorry, darlin'. I was admiring the view."

Her cheeks grew hot.

"You're beautiful, Dahlia." Scooting down the bed, he brushed this tongue against her labia. Dahlia's back arched in surprised pleasure. From not just the physical act, but from hearing him say her name for the first time. Had she ever heard anything so divine? And then he licked her again, and all thoughts of sacrilegious divinity fled her mind.

Dahlia writhed under his relentless tongue. Sliding his hand up her inner thigh, he collected some of her moisture on his fingers and slowly inserted one then another into her slick heat. After slowly moving them in and out, he began to thrust faster and closed his lips around her clit. His tongue flicked against her nub a few times before he began to suck.

When she came, she spasmed around his fingers. But it wasn't enough. Not nearly.

"More. I want more, Oscar. Please," Dahlia whimpered.

This time when he moved off her, he assured her that he was just removing the last of his clothing, and Dahlia was immensely grateful for his courtesy.

"Are you sure?"

"Yes. Please don't tease me."

She reached for him at the same time that he descended upon her. When their tongues met, dancing together to a song all their own Dahlia felt every nerve ending come alive for the first time. Goosebumps dotted her arms and legs. He kissed his way down to her collarbone.

"Oscar, please," Dahlia whimpered as she wrapped her legs around his hips.

"I'm going to ask one more time, Dahlia, and I want you to think about it. This is a decision you should not take lightly."

"No one has ever made me feel like this, Oscar. Maybe I'm being rash, but if I don't do this, if I miss this opportunity, I know a part of me will always regret it."

"Are you absolutely sure?"

"Yes. I want to give you my virginity."

Oscar brought his hand between her legs and let his fingertips brush over her labia before stopping at her clit and applying pressure. She trembled in anticipation. Her need for him overwhelmed any reservations she may have had. Should have had. She would die if she didn't feel every inch of him inside of her soon, she was sure of it.

Removing his hand from her, he gripped his erection and guided it to her sex, flicking it against her before placing the tip at her entrance.

She thrust up against him, engulfing him halfway all on her own. Oscar cursed. He was so large, she so tight, yet he slid in smoothly. As if he was made for her, her for him.

"I broke my hymen doing gymnastics as a kid. Don't hold back."

"No, darlin'," Oscar said. "I'll give you every bit of me, fuck you harder than you could have ever fantasized, but first I'm going to love you."

And he did. For a full week and a half, they spent every night together until the first rays of light pierced Dahlia's curtains and she fell asleep from pure exhaustion.

Until one day she came back to her room to discover the spirit board was gone. Her mother hadn't said anything, and she knew her mother. Sandra would have said a lot of somethings if she'd found that board. When she asked her sister about it, Mina had known nothing.

It was gone, and so was Oscar. A month and a half later, she found out she was pregnant. A panicked explanation about a drunken night at a party, and it was accepted that they'd just never know who the father was.

And Dahlia kissed her future in Chicago goodbye. Not keeping the baby never even crossed her mind. Even if Sandra would have been completely against it, Dahlia knew Mina would have driven her to a clinic. But Dahlia just couldn't bring herself to give up the one piece of Oscar she had left.

It had been thirteen years since those fateful nights, and Dahlia regretted none of it. Except for his leaving.

As time passed, as Tabitha grew older, she stopped believing the truth, though. It was just a fantasy she had made up to make sense of the senseless. To regain control. A drunk party, the broken condom of a faceless man, were easier stories to tell herself. Who believed in demons?

"Zozo?" she whispered now, and he stepped closer to her. "Oscar?" The tear chilled her cheek, but his hand on her hip, tugging her closer, sent warmth rushing through the rest of her. He bent to kiss her, and she knew she should pull away, but she really didn't want to, not even a little bit.

In that moment, thirteen years meant nothing. All the struggle, the sacrifice, all the resentment of doing it alone. Or, if not alone, thanks to her mother and sister, then *without him*. None of it mattered. She was whole again. And horny. Holy fuck. Hornier than she'd ever been. But Tabitha was right upstairs, and she owed the woman she had become some answers. So she pushed against Oscar's hard chest until he reluctantly stepped back.

"Where did you go?" she asked.

"I wasn't allowed to return."

"Who stopped you? Lucifer?"

Oscar shook his head. "The original Zozo. He let me have that week, and then he cut me off from you. Told me my task was complete." He pulled off his hat, clasped it in one hand, and ran the other through his thick, brown hair. "I'm sorry, darlin'. I didn't know what it meant. That I had ruined your life by getting you pregnant."

"You ruined nothing," Dahlia said, glancing up at a second floor window.

"You're right. She is perfect." Light danced in his eyes, like the stars she had been missing.

"You missed so much," Dahlia said as she found herself wrapping her arms around him and pulling him in tight. Her anger had already slipped away.

"No longer, darlin'. I won't miss anything more."

She studied his face, looking for signs of insincerity. When she glanced away, she caught a glimpse of her mother through the kitchen window.

"It might be best to keep this between us for now. My mom has been through a lot. And I need time to wrap my head around this again. I wrote you off as a youthful fantasy, Oscar. But you're real. You're here, and you still want me."

Oscar's eyes traveled downward, taking in all her curves. Wide hips, a rounded belly, large breasts. She'd filled out thanks to pregnancy and a busy schedule that often made it hard for her to take time for herself.

"If anything," he said, "I want you more."

In response, she bit her bottom lip and grinned at him.

"How long do you want to keep this a secret? Can I at least sneak into your room tonight?" He herded her until her back hit the wrought iron fence surrounding the porch. "I need you." He cupped the back of her head and pulled her in for another kiss. She let him, but only for a moment.

"I need to get my bearings first before I can even think about sitting Tabitha down to have a calm discussion." Dahlia worked the flesh of her bottom lip between her teeth while she thought. "How good are you at sneaking these days? As good as you were thirteen years ago?"

"Better." One side of his mouth lifted. His cowboy hat left the top half of his face in shadow, giving him an ominous mien that Dahlia felt all over.

She nodded at him, and he tipped his hat back so he could capture her lip between his own teeth before kissing her deeply.

The rumble of the sliding glass door opening jerked them apart. Oscar practically leapt backward.

"Dahlia? Are you out here?" Sandra called, peeking her head out the door. "Oh, there you are." She opened the door wider and stepped through it, shooting a disapproving look in Oscar's direction before pointedly ignoring him. "I was hoping you would help me clean up in the kitchen a little bit so Mina doesn't have to."

"Of course, Mom," Dahlia said, glancing briefly at Oscar before following her mother inside.

"Don't you start mixing with their kind just yet. I need to come to terms with one demonic son-in-law first," Sandra said once they were alone in the kitchen.

"Mom, really?" She mouthed the words, "their kind," to herself and shuddered. Dahlia loaded dishes into the dishwasher while her mother cleaned wine glasses in the sink.

"Well, what were you doing alone with him on the balcony?"

Dahlia gasped dramatically. "Unchaperoned, too. I guess I'll have to marry him to protect my reputation!" She moved to the other side of Sandra and dried the glasses with a dish towel before putting them away.

Sandra laughed. "Okay, I see your point."

"Mom, when was the last time I was interested in anyone?" Dahlia asked, resting her head on her mother's shoulder.

"I can't remember a time when you were ever interested in anyone. That's part of why you telling me you were pregnant was such a shock. Since Tabitha, there has definitely been no one."

"So wouldn't you be happy if I found someone, regardless of who they are?"

"Maybe," Sandra said, wrapping an arm around Dahlia and squeezing her shoulder. "But let's find out if Mina and Luci can have children first. I might need you to provide me with more grandchildren, after all."

Dahlia couldn't help the guffaw that escaped. She had a feeling that Mina and her husband would have no trouble conceiving children, given her own history. But she wasn't about to tell her mother that. Not yet, anyway.

Three

M INA GASPED INTO THE wood paneling of the closed studio door. Lilith fisted Mina's gown in one hand and lifted it above her hip. Fingertips danced along her inner thigh, teasing the elastic of her panties.

"I'm famished," Lilith said, face so close to Mina's that their breath mingled. "I need your pleasure, human." She lifted her right eyebrow in question.

"Yes," Mina said. She held in her moan as Lilith pushed her panties to the side and cupped her hand against Mina's sex. She pressed her thumb to Mina's clit and pumped two fingers into her. Lilith worked Mina hard and fast, breaking her apart in moments.

Lilith breathed her in with a satisfied smile. "That was a good appetizer, little human."

"Another?" Mina asked.

"Most definitely." Lilith stepped back, dropping Mina's skirts and tucking her arms behind her back. She nodded toward the stool sitting in front of the easel. "Please go lean back against that, just enough to support yourself. Don't sit down."

Mina did as she was told.

"Feet farther apart," Lilith commanded.

Again, Mina complied, placing her hands palm down on the top of the stool behind her to brace herself.

Lilith nodded. "Keep your hands there," she said as she approached. Lifting layers of skirts, she tucked them between Mina and the stool then got down on her knees and pulled the gusset of Mina's panties to the side.

Rubbing Mina's labia with two fingers, Lilith gradually spread her lips, exposing her clit, still swollen from her last orgasm. Lilith remained focused on Mina's pussy, but as she leaned forward to swipe her tongue along Mina's slit, they locked eyes.

Mina lost herself in those beautiful, deep-brown eyes for a moment. They robbed her of her breath and her senses. Then Lilith broke eye contact, refocusing her efforts on lapping her way across Mina's vulva, from her entrance to that sensitive nub at the top of her sex. Lilith closed her lips around it and hummed.

Mina had to fight back a scream as her head fell back and she rocked with another orgasm.

When she caught her breath and regained her bearings, she found Luci standing just inside the room, his back against the closed door, hand behind him and resting on the doorknob as if making sure they would not be disturbed. He seemed happy enough to enjoy the show as Lilith continued to torment Mina's now very sensitive pleasure center.

She whimpered under Lilith's continued manipulations, writhing as three fingers entered her. The force behind each thrust of Lilith's hand was enough for Luci to leave his post at the door and brace the stool with his body to keep it from scooting across the floor.

The third orgasm was the largest, and Mina couldn't hold back her scream. Luci wrapped his hand around her mouth at the last moment, muffling the sound so it would not be heard outside of the room.

When his wife was done shaking, Luci offered his hand to Lilith to help her stand. Mina stood up as well, rearranging her skirts and smoothing them until it appeared as though nothing had happened.

"What did you find out, Lilith?" Luci asked as he tucked Mina against his side. He placed a chaste kiss to her temple.

"Berith believes that Mina probably does have a greater capacity to recall and retain her lost memories without compromising her human mind," Lilith said.

"Yay," Mina said, punctuating it with a single clap.

"But," Lilith said, spearing Mina with a glance, "They still think it is wise to take those memories on slowly."

"Did they have any advice for ensuring that they come slowly?" Luci asked.

Mischief lit Lilith's eyes as she grinned. "They said to distract her."

"Ah," Luci said, "and here I thought you were solely focused on recharging your batteries."

"That was but one of my goals," Lilith said. "One of many." Lilith's grin turned predatory as she swept her eyes over Mina.

"Did you not get enough?" Luci asked.

"Never," Lilith replied.

"Later," Luci said, "after the humans go home."

"We have a party to get back to," Mina said, raising on her tiptoes so she could kiss Lilith's cheek. Lilith twined her arm with Mina's as they followed Luci down the hallway toward the landing.

"Oh, hey, I wanted to ask," Mina said. "Did you ever get to talk to Alastor?"

"He keeps dodging me." Lilith paused at the top of the stairs. "I swear he's doing it on purpose. He is so sweet with everyone else, but as soon as it is just the two of us, he turns into such a brat."

"He does?"

"Yes. I'm half tempted to strap him down and tattoo that note idea of yours right across his big green butt."

Mina burst into laughter at the thought of three little boxes next to the words "Yes," "No," and "Maybe" appearing under a simple "Do you like me?" on Alastor's sculpted behind.

"Maybe he does it to get a rise out of you," she said once she had calmed down. "He might want you to mark his ass."

"You think?" Lilith asked, pulling her bottom lip between her teeth briefly.

Mina shrugged. "It's worth a shot. Just make sure to give him a safe word."

Lilith seemed distracted as the night continued, understandably. Alastor was a lot of man—or demon, whatever. Far taller than Luci or Bellz, and all muscle. The thought of him willingly giving himself over made Mina's heart speed up and her knees a little weak, even though her tastes ran pretty solidly toward being the submissive.

Maybe if she asked very sweetly, Lilith would let her play once the two of them had sorted out their relationship.

Mina pulled her thoughts from Lilith. She had a party to get back to.

Hours later, Bellz caught her attention, nodding his head before heading in her direction.

"Come sit with me?" He did not wait for an answer before scooping her up into his arms and carrying her to the chaise where he set her down squarely in his lap.

"What's up?" she asked. "Needing some human cuddles?"

"I just couldn't resist you in this dress any longer. You look like a damsel ready to be put in distress."

"And you were waiting for my family to go home before you did anything?" Mina asked, fiddling with the red lace overlay of her gown.

Sandra, Tabitha, and Dahlia had left an hour ago, midnight having come and gone. Then Oz had begged off, Michael shortly after. Only her core demon family remained, and based on the energy in her townhome, she knew it was only a matter of time before the night degraded into full debauchery.

After Bellz nodded, Mina asked, "So, in regards to the distressing, what did you have in mind?"

Bellz responded by wrapping one hand around her ankle before gliding up her calf.

"Yes," Luci said, approaching from the kitchen. "What did you have in mind for my bride on our wedding night?" He stopped in front of them, arms crossed, a slight frown darkening his countenance. But Mina couldn't help but smile up at him and note the twinkle that ignited in his eye.

"I thought a little bride-napping was in order." Bellz tightened his grip on Mina's waist as his hand slid to the back of her knee. "Bind her, torment her, and keep her for all eternity if you failed to rescue her by the time I had her coming all over my cock."

Luci turned away before dramatically flinging himself back on to the chaise next to them, the back of his hand resting against his forehead. He let out a dramatic sigh. "That would have been a blast. But, tell me, Bellz, how had you planned to do that without any of your powers?"

"For fuck's sake, I forgot."

"You forgot that you swapped spots with a soul-sworn human so you could keep one eye on Hell for me?" Luci asked. He sat up abruptly, concern creasing his brow. "You have been keeping an eye on Hell for me, right?"

For a moment, Bellz only glared in return. "I forgot that I'm powerless."

"Not completely," Mina said, wiggling her ass against Bellz' hard length.

"Mina's right," Luci said, standing again and acknowledging each of his demonic family members in turn. "I have something I need your help with." He reached out a hand to Mina and pulled her out of Bellz' hold.

"What are you doing?" she whispered as Luci wrapped an arm around her shoulders and pulled her snugly against him.

"Trust me?" he asked against her ear, only loud enough for her to hear.

Mina glanced up and tumbled into his green eyes. Involuntarily, her mind flashed back to last night, so full of love, when she had asked him a life-altering question.

"Is it too soon for us to start a family?" she had asked. His arms had tightened around her before he had nudged her onto her back and climbed on top of her.

"Our first lifetime together, you spent somewhere in the range of five hundred Hell years with me, give or take five decades, and then I spent much, much longer—I don't want to think how long; it just depresses me—hunting you down over and over again for a few short, precious days together, and you are asking me if it's too soon? Too soon? Fuck, Mina."

Mina giggled. "What?"

"I've waited an eternity to hear you ask me that question." He pressed a kiss to her forehead. "I've waited an eternity to see you swell with my child." The hand not supporting his weight caressed her flat stomach. "I don't want to wait a moment longer."

"From what I understand, it isn't exactly an instant process, Luci, my love."

"Then we better get started right away."

He had dipped down to kiss her, sweeping his tongue against her lips, and then filling her mouth as he filled her heart with his joy. She had felt it in her soul, her own happiness, yes, but his as well. Their emotions had mingled together, and as they had joined, first their mouths and then their bodies, the euphoria had grown immensely until all she had seen, even with her eyes closed, was green speckled with stars.

"I require your assistance tonight in impregnating my bride," Luci said, jarring Mina back into the present.

"Pretty sure it's just a two-person job, Luci," Mina said, biting her bottom lip. They'd talked about this before with Bellz and Sindy. She wasn't interested in carrying anyone else's child but his. Well, at least until she had carried his first. She could reassess after.

"Only my semen will be involved. Mina is having *my* child. There will be no arguments or further discussion on that. Understood?"

"Of course, Lucifer," Alastor said.

"Yes, my liege," Bellz said.

"I'm serious, Beelzebub."

"I know." Bellz reached out a hand and briefly grabbed Luci's in something between a handhold and a handshake. "It's still fun to piss you off from time to time."

"So how would you like us to help?" Sindy asked. Her bare feet sank into the carpet as she moved to stand next to Bellz, who gave her a nonchalant look before pulling her into his lap. The very edge of his mouth twitched, betraying his true feelings.

"Remember that thing we talked about after Mina summoned us with the spirit board?" Luci asked. He addressed everyone, but his eyes stopped on his second in command.

Beelzebub's eyes grew wide before narrowing in on Mina. His lips turned up in a predatory snarl.

Mina gulped, her knees wobbled, and goosebumps raced along her skin. But then Luci was there, cradling her against him.

"We'll have a few minutes just the two of us first, my love," Luci said as he carried her down the hallway. Kicking the door open with his foot, he brought her into her bedroom before placing her feet on the floor. At his request, she turned away from him. His knuckles brushed against her skin as he unfastened the long row of buttons down the back of her gown. It slipped from her body. He spun her around and helped her step out of it.

His hips made contact with hers as he shuffled her backward until the back of her knees hit the bed.

"Sit," he commanded, and she obeyed.

He placed his hands, palms down, on either side of her naked thighs, bracketing her between his strong arms, the fine hairs catching the light from the single lit lamp on her bedside table. His lips met hers in a quick yet bruising kiss before he knelt before her.

Mina shivered as his hands caressed her thighs, her knees, and her calves. He unlaced her boots, tugging them off, then lifting each foot in turn and placing a chaste kiss to each of her arches.

"Lie back, Wife."

Mina did so, reaching her arms above her head and stretching her back as his lips retraced the path his hands had made down her lower body. When he had finished, he slipped her panties off, gripped her thighs in his hands, and nudged them apart.

The warmth of his breath covered her mound as he dipped his head between her spread legs. His tongue darted out and made contact with the base of Mina's clit, applying only the tiniest bit of pressure.

Anticipation pooled along her spine as she fought her natural instinct to thrust into him or grip his hair in her hands and pull his face against her.

"Good girl." His lips brushed against her labia as he spoke. He massaged his lips against her, slipping his tongue from her entrance to her clit.

Mina whimpered his name and dug her hands into the duvet cover. His assault continued until she couldn't help but writhe beneath him. Her fingers tightened on the cotton of the bedspread in a desperate attempt to keep from touching Luci. But then he pulled her clit between his teeth, tugging on it gently, and she couldn't hold back. She slipped the fingers of one hand through his hair and cupped his muscular shoulder in the other.

In an instant, his mouth was gone. He moved over her, straddling her, caging her face between his forearms. His forehead almost brushed hers. But nowhere did they touch.

"Bad girl. Flip over." Luci stood up on the bed, bent to keep from hitting his head on the ceiling. When she had done as he asked, he wrapped his hands around her hips and pulled them up. "Fold your arms under your head and leave them there."

Positioned this way, Mina knew Luci could see all of her. He was somewhere behind her now, probably taking in his fill. The sweet agony of waiting left her nerve endings on fire.

When he penetrated her with a swift, deep stroke, the teeth of his zipper biting into her labia, she came violently, as if he had ripped it from her. His growl of triumph filled the room. He thrust again and again, and the pain from the metal scrapping against her most intimate flesh, along with the knowledge that he hadn't bothered to do more than unzip and pull it out before fucking her savagely, had her orgasm rolling into a second and then a third.

He came in her, filling her with his potent seed as she broke for a fourth time.

"It's only the beginning, Mina," Luci said against the shell of her ear.

Four

M INA LAY HUDDLED IN the middle of her large bed, clutching a pillow to her chest. She felt raw and exposed in her postcoital comedown. Luci had left with the promise of water only a moment ago. Even though she knew she would need hydration for all that he and her demons had planned, she mourned his leaving.

The bed depressed. A hand caressed her hip.

"There's my damsel." Bellz' deep voice resonated to her core. He slipped behind her and covered her with an arm and leg. "How are you feeling?" He left a trail of kisses along her neck and shoulder.

"Better now."

"I can't believe that husband of yours left you for a second. He knew we were just waiting to swoop in as soon as he gave us an opening."

Alastor climbed onto the bed in front of her. He stretched out on his side, one arm propping up his head. With the other, he reached out and stroked Mina's hair.

"Should we tie you up, my little human?" Bellz asked.

Lilith and Sindy joined them. Lilith leaned over Bellz' waist to lazily play with Mina's breast. Sindy, who sat at the foot of the bed, pulled one of Mina's feet into her lap and pressed a thumb into her arch. She hit the exact right spot, and Mina exhaled any lingering tension.

She was in such a blissful state that she didn't respond to the question. Honestly, they could do whatever they wanted to her and she would not mind in the least.

"I think we let Alastor hold her for us," Lilith suggested. "We'll be able to move her around so much easier."

"I see I have been replaced." Luci's chuckle expanded Mina's lungs with glee.

"No one could replace you," she mumbled.

"No *one* has, but maybe four can." Luci, carrying a very large, reusable water bottle with a bendy straw protruding from its mouth, came around the far side of the bed behind Alastor, who moved down the bed to make space. They all gave Mina room to sit up so she could sip from the straw.

"Thank you," she said as Luci placed the bottle on the nearest bedside table.

"Don't thank me just yet," Luci said, finally undressing. "I've got more for you."

Mina was surrounded by a flurry of motion. Lilith pushed Bellz aside then leaned over Mina so she could whisper a command in Alastor's ear. Mina couldn't make out what the demoness had said, but her tone was crystal clear. Alastor had better do whatever Lilith demanded if he wanted to avoid some serious consequences.

Multiple emotions flickered across Alastor's face—lust, fear, defiance—until only utter contentment remained. He nodded, his focus never once wavering from Lilith. If the grin on her face was any indication, she had observed his internal struggle just as easily as Mina had.

While Sindy and Bellz were busy undressing each other, Alastor pulled Mina into his lap, tucked his arms through hers so they were trapped at her sides, and swung their legs off the side of the bed. He nudged his thighs between hers and spread them to hold her open.

Sitting on her knees behind Alastor, Lilith leaned into him and rested her chin on his shoulder. Even though Alastor's torso was broad, she still easily reached around him and tweaked Mina's nipples.

Sindy and Bellz stretched out on either side of them as Luci stepped between her legs. He stroked his engorged cock, eyes locked on his bride's. The tip brushed against her clit then slipped down between her lips before penetrating her ever so slowly, stopping when he was only the barest amount inside her.

"I'm going to fuck you now, Mina, and my lieutenants are going to make sure that you come so quickly and so often that every bit of my seed is helped along into your fertile womb. And then I'm going to come in you again."

Then he filled her completely. His thrusts were powerful yet controlled. He didn't touch her at all, leaving it to Lilith, Bellz, and Sindy to knead her breasts, tug on her nipples, manipulate her clitoris and vulva, and prod playfully at her anus.

"Does it drive you crazy, my envious demon, not to be able to touch her? To feel her writhe against you, the weight of her ass on your cock, and not be able to do anything about it?" Lilith asked Alastor.

Mina was just a pawn in this game between them. The knowledge made her feel powerless yet significant all at once. It was intoxicating, triggering a hard and fast orgasm. When she opened her mouth to scream, Luci swallowed it with a kiss. He fucked her with his tongue in tandem with his cock until his peak broke his rhythm.

Once Luci's breathing had returned to normal, he offered her the water bottle, allowing her to drink before he satisfied his own thirst. Then he stepped back and flicked his hand at the others.

Sindy slipped from the bed, landing on her haunches before Mina. The demoness lapped at her cunt. Scooping up any of Luci's cum that slipped from Mina's vagina with her tongue, Sindy speared Mina's entrance and deposited Luci's seed as far into her channel as possible.

Mina came.

And then again as Bellz pushed his thumb into her puckered hole.

And a third time when Lilith tightened clamps around the base of Mina's nipples.

The molten steel of Alastor's member heated the top of Mina's buttock and lower back, pulsing angrily. She could hear the hitch in his breath as he fought to control himself, as Lilith continued to torment him with her words.

The air in the room grew heavy with, of course, the smell of sex, but also the sharpness of Alastor's posture, like the slightest provocation would snap his restraint. He was the only one of them fully dressed. The only one denied free participation. Mina wasn't sure how much longer he could last, but she knew that Lilith wouldn't push him too far.

Mina arched her back, pressing her head into the center of Alastor's chest as Luci entered her again. Lilith took the opportunity to slip her hand between Alastor and Mina and unzip his pants, tugging his erection out.

Luci wrapped Mina's legs around his waist and pulled her free of the two demonic lovers. Holding her entire weight as he stood beside the bed, he turned just enough so she could see Lilith push Alastor back and climb on top of him.

"Take off his pants, Sindy," Lilith demanded, using her sharp nails to claw his dress shirt into pieces, leaving faint trails of pink along his green flesh. He hissed in pain or pleasure.

Mina gasped as she watched Alastor's verdant, monstrous length disappear into Lilith's fit form. It didn't seem possible, and yet Lilith sank down on him effortlessly.

Lilith motioned to Sindy, and Sindy climbed between Alastor's legs. Her tongue flicked out to make contact with his balls.

But then Mina was distracted as Bellz stepped up behind her, gripping her ass in his hands. His cock, slick with lube, probed at her anus. He made very little progress before backing off and replacing his dick with his thumb. Slowly he opened her up as her world broke apart. It was all she could do to keep her head on Luci's shoulder as he held onto her, whispering poetry into her ear.

"Stop, Sindy," Lilith said. A moment later Alastor's frustrated cry vibrated the room. "No coming yet, handsome."

"Lilith, you're killing me," Alastor whispered, although his desperation was loud enough to be heard by everyone in the room.

"I promise that if I succeed in killing you, I'll bring you right back. It will be the shortest death ever." She gazed down at him for a moment before bending at the waist and kissing him.

As everyone watched Alastor and Lilith, Bellz replaced his thumb with first two and then three of his fingers. He expanded them as wide as Mina's body would allow before fucking her with them.

Luci moaned audibly at the added pressure. He trembled as he kept his orgasm at bay, waiting for Bellz to join them completely.

Bellz didn't make them wait long, stretching her further with the tip of his dick. His strong fingers rubbed her back as he urged her to relax and let him in.

Once Bellz was fully seated, Luci shifted Mina's weight to Bellz and fucked her mindlessly. The force of his coming dropped him to his knees, but Bellz didn't miss a beat, lowering Mina and himself to the floor so Mina didn't lose either cock.

Bellz helped maneuver Mina as Luci laid back on the floor. Her husband tugged her to him. He cupped the back of her head with his hand and rubbed soothing circles around her back. His gentleness was juxtaposed with Bellz' relentless pounding. Luci slipped a hand between their bodies and rubbed the hub of Mina's pleasure until she orgasmed twice more. Bellz shifting his angle to hit her g-spot through her anal wall triggered the second.

"Keep that pussy clamped on him, Mina," Bellz demanded. "I'm going to fill you so full of my cum, you'll squeeze Luci tight enough that not a single sperm escapes your womb." His words made her inner walls flutter, and Luci pressed down harder on her external nub of nerves while Bellz continued his assault on the internal. She came so hard it hurt, and her whimpers sent both Bellz and Luci over the edge.

Her body, slick with sweat, cramped with her fullness as the room spun around her. Her throat was tacky, the back of her tongue aching, when Luci picked her up and carried her to the bed. Bellz had the water bottle ready, and they both made sure she rehydrated as they watched Lilith finally give Alastor his release, but only after Sindy, who was riding his face, had succeeded in chasing her own pleasure.

Mina found herself in the middle of the bed. Luci wrapped his arms around her and pulled her into his chest. The rest of her demons piled around them, cuddling together. No one was left out as they drifted off to sleep.

Five

DAHLIA HAD A SERIOUS problem. Her demon ex-boyfriend was going to be here in, frankly, who knew how long, and she had absolutely nothing to wear. All of her pajamas were old, stained, or old and stained. Nothing matched. The tops were all ratty t-shirts, the bottoms sporting waistbands that were more band than elastic.

She couldn't just forgo the pajamas altogether. They needed to talk before they fell back into old habits. *Oh well*, she thought as she tugged on an old concert t-shirt that slid off of one shoulder. It was from some show she had gone to her sophomore year of high school. Seeing her favorite bands play stopped being an available option once Tabitha was born.

To be perfectly honest, she probably could have gone to a concert or two. Sandra and Mina had upended their lives to support her education while she had a newborn at home. They had all sacrificed so much, so even though she knew they would have said yes if she had asked to have some fun every once in a while, she could never bring herself to do it.

"Hi, darlin'." Oscar's breath warmed her bare shoulder.

She turned, still surprised to actually see him. She took in every detail. His golden skin, brown eyes and hair, a faint scar that ran from the corner of his mouth to his jawline. He was almost the most beautiful thing she had ever seen, second only to her daughter.

Placing her hands on his hips, she reassured herself that he was really here, and then she let her other doubts creep in.

"I'm not sure we should be doing this, Oscar."

"Why's that? I've warded the room. No one will hear us. If your mother opens your door, she will see the illusion of you sleeping peacefully."

"And my daughter?" Dahlia asked, then corrected herself. "*Our* daughter?" It was weird to say those two words together. She'd never had the luxury of even thinking them before tonight.

"I'll know if she approaches the door. We should have ample time to," he paused, gesturing awkwardly with his arms, "become presentable."

Dahlia stepped around him and sat on the armchair next to her window. She wouldn't sit on the bed. She wasn't sure how she wanted the night to go yet. A large part of her begged her brain to shut up and just enjoy her lover. It had been close to thirteen years since she had had one that wasn't self-powered.

But they needed to be on the same page. She couldn't just sleep with the father of her child and not expect strings. Problematic strings, so tiny she could easily ignore them until she was a tangled mess forever entwined with a demon.

"I'm suspicious of your strings," she said aloud before she thought about how the sentence did not convey her meaning at all.

Yet, somehow, he understood her completely. "I'm a free agent now. No one can keep me away from you. And if they tried, they'd have Lucifer and his inner circle to deal with."

"Oh, God. Do they know?" Dahlia asked. Standing, she paced in front of the window. "That you're Tabitha's father?"

"No," Oscar shook his head. "Of course not. But Mina wouldn't allow them to turn their backs on me now."

"And why is that? What exactly is your relationship with my sister?" Dahlia asked, stopping in front of him and placing her hands on her hips to make herself look larger.

Oscar's whole face turned red. "Maybe we shouldn't talk about that."

"Why not?"

"I didn't know she was your sister until tonight."

"What does that have to do with anything?" Dahlia let his words sink in, horror dawning. Her sister had somehow befriended a whole—what? horde, murder, crew—of demons. How, exactly, had she managed that?

Oscar took a deep breath, closed his eyes, and spoke, "Your sister has magical orgasms. Our paths crossed when she was using a spirit board to try to get in contact with Lucifer. I spanked her until she, you know, and it gave me a ton of power. But also a lot of clarity." He opened his eyes

"You are telling me that my sister recruited you with the magic of her vagina?"

"What?" Oscar's eyes grew large and round in horror. "The only human vagina I have ever entered was yours. The things I did to Mina, I would never do to you. I was mean to her, Dahlia. I'm ashamed to say it, but it's true. And she returned my awfulness with, I don't know, love or something very near to it."

He sighed and sat down on the edge of the bed. Dahlia, sensing his vulnerability, perched beside him. She placed her hand on his knee.

"It hit me like a stampede. She cares for me despite the evil wretchedness that is at my very core. And that feeling of acceptance, it reminded me of you. How you used to make me feel. Only with you it was a million times better. You loved me because of all of me—the flawed parts of me that are still so stubbornly human, but also the evil inside of me, and the good bits too, that side of me that I'd forgotten existed before I met you, and everything that disappeared after I lost you."

"Oh, Oscar." Tears pooled in her eyes. She had never stopped loving him. Even if she had cursed his existence every day for years. "Oh, God. I think I was with her when she bought that spirit board. I tried to talk her out of it."

Oscar smiled sadly. "I almost wish you had bought it instead."

"Oh, there is no way I am ever going near one of those things again. I got very lucky with you. And you left me a pregnant teenager. It could have been so much worse." She bit her lip and tilted her head to the side. "It could have been worse, right?"

Oscar laughed. "Yes. Most definitely, darlin'."

"Like demon possession, heads spinning around, pea soup worse?"

"Why do all y'all humans associate pea soup with demon possession? Did I miss out on some cultural thing that happened recently?"

"*The Exorcist.*" Dahlia waited for Oscar to signal some recognition. "It's a movie, and not a recent one. It's older than I am."

"Oh, well, I definitely missed it. I've been a demon for around one hundred years now. Earth years, that is. A bit longer on the Hell timeline, I reckon."

"The age gap thing is a little creepy," Dahlia said. "I didn't think it was creepy when I was a teenager, but now? Eesh!"

"I think it was your soul I was drawn to, Dahlia. Not your youth."

"Hm," Dahlia said, unimpressed. "That sounds like a line from a teen romance."

"Does this sound like a line?" Oscar asked, slipping to the floor so he was on his knees in front of her. He clasped her hands in his own. "I love you, Dahlia."

Dahlia's heart leapt into her throat. Hearing those words brought back all the exhilaration of being with Oscar the first time. He had just been hers then, and the temptation to return to that arrangement was so strong.

But he couldn't belong to only her now. Even if she kept him a secret from Tabitha, he would never only be Dahlia's again. And she had irrefutable proof that he existed. Tabitha had met him. She would have to actively keep his paternal status a secret in a way she had never had to before, which would be much harder to do if they were also sneaking around.

"Oscar, I will always love you. But I'm not sure whether I'm ready for you to be part of our lives. Tabitha has done just fine without a father. I'd hate for her to gain one now only to lose him if things between us don't work out."

"Okay. What does that mean for us?"

"It means that I can't consent to sleeping with you without knowing what other strings are attached."

"Oh, you meant those strings, too. My expectations."

"Yes."

"I can't lie to you. To be part of Tabitha's future, to be your husband, to have a family with you, there's nothing in all three realms I want more. But I won't force you to accept me. You are her mother. I'm nothing more than a sperm donor."

The sadness in his expression broke her heart.

"If we only ever have this one night, it would be a gift I would cherish until the end of eternity."

Dahlia's mind whirled. He was leaving it up to her. Could she handle only one more night with him?

Could she live with herself if she passed up this chance?

She stole his cowboy hat and put it on her own head. He smiled like he already knew what she was about to say. "One night, Oscar. That's all I am promising."

"Yippee!" He stood up, and she had to hold the hat on as she tilted her head to look up at him.

"You look mighty cute in that." He stepped closer to her, then caged her in with his arms. His face hovered in front of hers before he headbutted his cowboy hat off her head and kissed her.

Flinging her arms around him, her fingers gripped at him as if they needed proof he was actually here. His lips traveled across her cheek and along her jaw before he slipped her earlobe between his lips to suck and nibble. Then he made his way down her neck. Shifting his weight to one arm, he tugged the skirt of her dress up. The palm of his hand ran down her outer thigh, his touch reverent.

"Let me worship you," he rumbled. She reached behind her and unzipped the dress, shrugging out of the top and exposing her lacy bra. Giving him a second to take her in, she waited a beat before unhooking her bra and throwing it behind her.

"Hot Hell." Oscar stopped, completely transfixed by the sight of her. He pressed his knees into the side of the bed and brought both hands up to her breasts. Slowly, he cupped them, feeling their weight. "These have only gotten better."

Dahlia laughed. "They've definitely gotten larger."

"They are perfect." He traced a stretch mark with his finger first, then ran his tongue along it.

"I know," she said with a smirk, but when she opened her mouth to speak again, he closed his mouth around the tip of her breast and she lost her train of thought and fell onto the bedspread.

Oscar kissed down her body, leaving no flesh untouched by his lips, even moving her bunched dress to get to her belly. When he reached the apex of her thighs, he encouraged her to bring her feet up on the bed and knelt on the ground before spending countless minutes bringing her to climax with his talented tongue.

"I need you, Oscar," she said. "Please."

He stood up and removed his clothing while she crawled further onto the bed, discarding her dress in the process. His hands gripped her hips as he positioned himself between her thighs. Big, brown eyes found hers, and she could tell he was holding himself back.

"What is it?" she asked.

"I want to tell you just how much you mean to me, but I'm worried I'll scare you off with another declaration so soon after my last."

She cupped his cheek in her palm. "Show me."

Their mouths found one another again as she hooked her leg behind his ass and lifted her pussy to meet his cock. After slipping a condom over his length, he aligned himself with her opening. With a nod from her, he shifted, sinking into her, and her whole world lit up.

They made love, taking their time, punctuating sensual thrusts with passionate kisses, enraptured touches, and soul-searing eye contact. Dahlia wished it would never end, but her body could only handle so much before her breath was hitching with her release.

Oscar brought his hand between their bodies and massaged the base of her clit in the exact way that made her unravel. When he had discovered that trick during the week they'd spent together, he'd abused it. He abused it now, bringing her to brink again, timing it perfectly so that she erupted when he did.

As they lay together in the afterglow, he nuzzled the side of her head with his own, as if being inside her wasn't close enough. And she relished being so wanted. She had forgotten how nice it felt.

"I know we said only one night," Oscar whispered.

Her heart sank. They had. Why had she agreed to that?

"But I'd like to take you out on a proper date, treat you the way I should have back then."

"It would have been hard to go to a movie together with my eyes shut the entire time," she said. Glee bubbled up with the realization that this didn't have to be the end, and she laughed. "Yes. A date would be nice."

Six

M INA STOOD BEFORE A dais complete with an ornate throne decorated in black and red silks. Jagged walls peeked between curtains like the entire room had been carved out of the surrounding stone. Her slippers provided no protection against the sharp, volcanic rock floor. Despite the warm environment, Mina shivered and wrapped her arms around herself.

A tall man came up behind her and draped a heavy cloak over her shoulders. His hand found hers, and he led her to the dais. He was tall, with pitch black hair and skin the shade of the sky right before sunrise. When he sat down on the throne and pulled her into his lap, she gasped at his glowing blue eyes.

"I am sure Lucifer would not approve, Hades," Mina said.

"He would prefer you to sit on the floor?" Hades asked, raising one eyebrow. "No, of course not, Mina. You are precious to him. So for as long as you are my guest, you will be precious to me."

"Is that what I am? A guest?"

"Of course!"

"There is a different term for guests when they are being held against their will."

"Ah! But I'm not forcing you to stay. We struck a bargain."

"Yes. I will stay here for a time, provided that you make good on your promises to help Lucifer. But so far you have failed to uphold your end of the bargain."

"But that is why I summoned you here." He adjusted her on his lap so that her back nestled in the crook between his chest and his arm.

"I would like to tell you a story. In the space before time as you know it, before there was any use for an afterlife or an underworld, lived two brothers. Their love for each other was immeasurable, and they longed to share that love with others, to express it in a tangible way. So their love would leave an indelible mark on the world."

"They were in love?" Mina asked.

"Oh, no! It was a purely brotherly love. They were asexual and aromantic beings anyway. They just enjoyed being together, exploring the universe. But they struggled to express their feelings adequately. At least until the impulsive brother had an idea."

"Uh-oh."

Hades chuckled. "This story has a happy ending. This part of it does, anyway, at least for the brothers. You see, the impulsive brother decided to turn clay and a bit of his soul into a woman—the very first human.

"But she was opinionated. She saw the dangers this world would pose for her, a being with very little power, and she was vocal about it. The younger brother, the thoughtful one, granted her immortality but banished her from their realm."

"I thought you said there was a happy ending," Mina said. And then, with the knowledge her mother had imparted to her, a truth revealed itself. "Lilith!"

"Indeed," Hades said. "She is the oldest of them. Almost as old as I am."

Mina stared at him in wonder, and she had to fight back the overwhelming urge to hop off his lap and run directly to Lilith to wrap her up in a hug. "Lilith had been banished just as I have been. Only Lilith was entirely alone."

"Not entirely alone," Hades said. "We crossed paths from time to time. Although how much of that she easily remembers, I cannot say."

"So, what happened with the brothers? Did they accomplish what they had set out to do?"

"Oh, yes. The brothers created women and men both. And they kept the secrets of the universe from them, rather than granting that knowledge at creation. They chose instead to reveal them slowly. The experiment worked. Humanity experienced wonder before fear. The brothers were overjoyed, and they started right away creating more humans.

"They saw the humans as a symbol of their undying love for one another, and they vowed to keep humanity safe for all eternity."

"I don't understand how this story fits in."

"Well, there is a lot more to it, but that's all for right now."

Mina sat straight up. She was in her bedroom in her townhome. Luci was next to her, a look of concern plastered to his striking face.

"I'm okay," she said. "I just had a memory—of Hades."

Luci tucked Mina against his side. "What do you remember?"

"He was telling me a story about the creation of man. It seemed kind of similar to the mythology about Prometheus and his brother. Something that starts with an 'E'. Damn. I don't remember."

"Epimetheus," Lilith said from where she lay on Mina's other side. Alastor, Sindy, and Bellz were nowhere to be seen.

"Where are the others?"

"In Hell." Luci said.

"Is there trouble?" Mina asked.

"No, and now there won't be."

"There were rumblings," Lilith explained.

"Will you be going back?" Mina asked them.

"We wanted to make sure that you were safe first. Put up some other protections," Lilith said. She propped herself up against the headboard.

"It's coming on all sides," Luci said. "Demons rumbling about me being extra vulnerable. God poking at the protections I have in place."

Mina nodded. "I have an idea."

"Oh no," Lilith said, resting her forehead in the palm of her hand.

"What if I start summoning demons in an effort to, I don't know, convert them? Like I did with Oz."

"And Michael," Lilith added.

"I don't know, Mina," Luci said.

"I think I've proven that I can handle it."

"You've only done it twice."

"But now you can be here for it or in the next room in case things get out of hand. We can establish a safe word."

"You don't need a safe word, Mina. I was able to feel your distress even from the little piece of soul I had before. Now that I have half of your soul, your distress is my own."

Mina nuzzled into him. "And yours is mine, my love. Let me help you."

Luci let out a long sigh. "Okay, but Lilith is staying too."

"Any ideas on how you'd like to summon these demons?" Lilith asked.

"That's what I have you two for," Mina said.

"We can guide you through it, but you'll have to do the actual summoning. They won't come if either of us summons them."

"Still beats googling suspected demonic hauntings in the San Jose area or taking another Winchester tour. I mean, that place is pretty cool, but there's a tour guide who I think is on the brink of asking me out."

"What's wrong with that?" Lilith asked.

"I don't sleep with humans, Lilith. Not after Victor."

"Yes, so let's go summon a demon for you to fuck. That seems way safer." Angst rolled off Luci in palatable waves.

"You know, Luci, these demons can get me all hot, and then you can swoop in and impregnate me."

"Fuck. Okay, I'm in. Let's do it."

Lilith buried her face in a pillow to muffle her laughter—or maybe a scream.

"Go get breakfast while Lilith and I get set up and decide who you should summon first."

When Mina returned to her bedroom twenty minutes later, she found an intricate pentagram drawn in pink lipstick on her standing mirror. It reminded her of the summoning spell that Lilith had given her to summon Luci. The summoning spell she had safely tucked in the keepsake box beneath her bed.

"Um, Lilith, Luci," Mina called. Her wide eyes stared back at her through the archaic symbols.

Lilith came back in from the bathroom and Luci popped up from the other side of the bed.

"What's wrong?" Lilith asked.

"This is a very intricate summoning. It is safe, right?" Mina looked at Lilith meaningfully. She hadn't told Luci about the spell Lilith had given her. It had seemed silly to risk getting Lilith in trouble for a backup plan they hadn't even needed.

"Yes," Lilith said. "Luci and I have imbued this spell with our power, so it won't take anything from you when you trigger it."

"Why are you so concerned about this all of a sudden?" Luci asked, the quirk of his eyebrow betraying his suspicion.

"It just looks complicated." Mina lifted her palms and shoulders in an exaggerated shrug.

Lilith rolled her eyes. "I gave her a spell to summon you when you got yourself into trouble chasing after Gabriel."

"You did what?" Luci asked.

"Only as a last resort," Mina said.

"Why didn't you tell me about this before, Mina? Is it somewhere safe?"

Mina nodded to her bed, and Luci retrieved the shoe box she kept there.

"You've been keeping it in a flimsy, cardboard box?" Lilith asked, fists on her hips.

"That's where I keep all my most important things," Mina said, shyly toeing the carpet.

Luci stared at the box for a moment, causing it to glow with power. "Perfect, actually." He kissed the top of Mina's head before putting the box back where he had found it. "No one will suspect they'd find a spell to summon The Prince of Hell in a ratty old shoe box, and now it's protected so only the Cadere women can access it."

"Does that mean we are ready to get this show on the road?" Lilith asked.

"Let's invite this dude over and make your legion one demon stronger." Mina cupped Luci's strong jaw in her palms and kissed his lips chastely.

"We'll be in the hall," Lilith said. "Use this." Lilith placed the handle of a decorative dagger in Mina's hand. It looked old. "Prick a finger and put a little bit of blood on the mirror in the center of the pentagram. That should be all it takes."

"I added some protections in your bedroom," Luci said. "They are just a precaution. The protections that are on you already mean that he can't hurt you, but I'm warning you now that he will want to. He will try to."

"Luci, I'd be surprised if he didn't."

"This guy is a nasty motherfucker, Mina," Lilith said. "If we are going to use you as a recruiter, then we are going after the heavy hitters first."

"But we will be right out in the hallway. If you need us, I will know. My soul is your soul is my soul, Mina. Even before we went full halfsies, I could feel when you were having big feelings."

Mina frowned, turning to Lilith. "Don't let him bust in at my slightest discomfort. I will probably get scared, but a little fear can be fun."

"You've got it." Lilith bowed her head. "Come on, boss. Let's leave your bride to it."

After they had closed the door behind them, Mina looked down at the dagger in her hand. It had a bejeweled gold handle. The blade had a wave to it. She wondered at its significance and hoped she would remember to ask. Most likely her brain would be jelly.

Stepping up to the mirror, Mina gulped in a breath before pricking her left forefinger with the tip of the dagger and placing it against the very middle of the inverted star. The mirror pulsed in response. It rippled.

Mina took a step back as the mirror continued to liquefy. A strong red hand tipped with sharp black nails emerged. The long fingers clutched Mina's throat, holding her in place. She grasped at the muscular forearm attached to the hand. A shoulder the color of fresh blood followed. Then a torso, a leg.

Was he wearing a tracksuit? He looked like he had just come from the gym. Except for the horns—one broken—and the wings, the red skin, the missing cartilage of his nose and parts of his ears, and his claw-like fingernails, he looked like a regular Joe.

He snarled at her. Each tooth had been filed down to a point. His eyes matched his skin tone. The only hair on his head was his bushy eyebrows. Anger radiated off of him, and Mina dropped a hand to cover her womb just in case.

He herded her back until she was pressed against a wall. The door to the rest of her townhouse was to her left, and she placed her other hand against the lightly textured surface to remind herself that Lilith and Luci were still there.

Seven

"I LOVE IT WHEN the pretty packages deliver themselves."
The red demon's voice was low and hoarse, like entropy
had begun to claim it. "Your fear is palpable," he said with a
sharp inhale, "and intoxicating."

His pointed nails dug into the sides of her neck, but they
didn't—or couldn't—pierce her skin. He hissed in displeasure,
his face contorting.

"Why can't I hurt you?"

His fingers flexed against her throat, like he was trying to
lift her. When nothing happened, he growled. His large hands
wrapped around her hips, and he tossed her onto the bed. She
scrambled to the headboard, but before she could tuck her legs
under her, he grabbed her ankle and pulled her back toward
him.

"Demons require sustenance. Fear and pain are my meal of
choice. Your fear is a delightful appetizer, but I need more.
Psychological pain will have to do." He swiped a nail through
the front of the black camisole and the halves fell open, exposing her breasts.

Mina lay frozen, transfixed as he hovered above her, resting
his body on four limbs, not touching her anywhere. She felt
him everywhere nonetheless. Gulping, she could only watch

as he dipped down until his mouth hung just over her right breast.

"Whatever protections you have in place, I'm already working my way through them. It's only a matter of time before my teeth penetrate your body." He lowered the last inch, taking her breast into his mouth, sucking deeply before backing off until her erect nipple stood clasped between his sharp fangs. He sawed them back and forth.

The sharp pressure sent tingles into her core. Her toes curled involuntarily, and she stifled a moan. He already seemed so frustrated that she wasn't responding the way he expected that she didn't want to risk making it worse.

Besides, his threat, regardless of how believable she found it—as if he could actually break through Satan's protections—was a bit of a turn on. For a fleeting moment, she wondered at her own depravity. How could the thought of incredible pain replacing her pleasure at any moment be exciting? But then she heard Luci's voice in her mind insisting her perfection, and her doubts dissolved to nothing.

The fear demon switched to her left breast. The feel of his teeth was exquisite, riding the knife's edge between pain and pleasure. Mina couldn't help herself. She placed the bottoms of her feet against the bed and thrust up at him.

The demon's head snapped up, his eyes wide with surprise. "You're enjoying this," he said, his tone full of shocked accusation.

Mina blushed from head to toe. "Guilty."

Tilting his head to the side, the demon studied her for the moment. "You'll feel differently, I wager, when my teeth do some damage." He lowered his head once more, this time biting at the junction of her shoulder and neck. Very slowly, he rested his weight onto her. Grabbing her thigh just above her knee, the demon wrapped Mina's left leg around his hip and ground his groin into hers.

"Your arousal is intriguing. It complements your fear, heightens it."

"Like adding salt to caramel?"

"Mm, exactly."

"How long until you've broken through?" Mina felt the demon's chuckle vibrate in his chest, its deepness reverberating against her clit.

"Why would I tell you that?" He bit her earlobe, and her body broke out in goosebumps.

Those sharp nails made quick work of the flimsy straps holding together Mina's panties. Flicking the fabric away with ease, the demon ran the soft pads of his fingers against the lips of Mina's pussy. His touch was gentle, curious, and thorough, as if he were mapping every dip and crevice. And then he curled his fingers and scratched from her clit to her entrance.

Mina felt a sting, but the sensation was quickly chased away by her heightened arousal. The building orgasm promised to be intense. So long as Luci's guards stayed in place.

The pressure at her entrance warned her of his intentions moments before he acted on them, slipping two fingers inside of her. He rubbed against her g-spot with each thrust in, then scraped along it on his way back out. Once, twice, three times.

Slipping down her body, he brought his head between her legs, never letting up on his torture inside her. He wasted no time in repeating the torment he'd inflicted with her nipples on her clit. When she felt the pressure of his teeth and the sharpness of his claws, she came. The orgasm that had promised utter bliss still managed to blow away all her expectations.

It hit hard, knocking out her breath and almost rolling into a second. But the demon had stopped. When Mina opened her eyes, she found him with his back against the headboard. He stared at the wall across from him.

Mina rolled to her knees and crawled closer, leaning sideways against the headboard and watching him intently. His expression, full of confusion and wonder, reminded her of Oz when she had unintentionally recruited him.

"Are you okay?" Mina asked quietly.

"Fuck no," he said, looking at her fiercely. "What was that?"

"My orgasm. It tends to power up demons."

He nodded. "I feel like I could lay ruin to an entire goddamn city."

"Do you want to lay ruin to a city?"

He shook his head. "That's the part that's freaking me out. It seems like a waste of my talents. But then I'm not entirely sure what my talents are good for. My whole vendetta against humankind never did anything *for me*, other than give me a purpose. But I guess it was never intended to."

Mina nodded. "It's always been to further God's plans."

"Who we thought we were fighting against this entire time. I thought Lucifer had chickened the fuck out, distracting himself with some side piece." He stopped talking to look at Mina again. "Who are you?"

"The side piece."

"Mina." His eyes grew wide once more. "Fuck, fuck, fuck. You're not a fucking side piece. You're the main course. The

God-damning headliner. No wonder he turned his back on everything."

"He told me that I was hope, the first he'd seen in a very long time."

"I can see his essence all over you. Why couldn't I before?"

"Maybe it was part of the extra protection he put in place before I summoned you." Mina bit her bottom lip. "I never got your name."

"Amamemnon, head fear demon and a former lieutenant in Satan's army."

"It's nice to meet you, Amamemnon," Mina said, sticking out her hand for him to shake. He took it, but used it to tug her into his lap. The tender kiss he placed on her lips took her by surprise, and he took full advantage of her gasp to swoop his tongue into her mouth.

"Kindly take your hands off of my wife, Amamemnon," Luci said.

Amamemnon broke the kiss but did not relinquish his hold on Mina. "Of course you fucking married her. Had to mark your claim in every conceivable way."

Mina couldn't help but laugh. "That's not why he married me." Her husband stood next to the bed, hands on his hips. He looked pretty unhappy, but Mina had a feeling it was an act.

"Oh no? Then why did he marry you?" the red demon asked.

"Because I love her," Luci said, rolling his eyes.

"She doesn't make you feel like the absolute scum of the universe?"

"No one could make me feel like scum," Luci said. He bristled a bit at the suggestion.

"Wait," Mina said. "What do you mean?"

"Fear. It's such a dirty emotion. And my only purpose is to foster it, spread it, let it devour humanity from the inside."

"That's not really fair. Fear is a powerful thing, for sure. Corrupt leaders use it all the time. But it's also a tool that's kept humanity alive. On its own, it isn't evil. It's people's reactions to it that matter. You have to let fear motivate you, not manipulate you. Really, it's fear combined with ignorance that's the issue."

The demon hummed, digesting that for a moment before saying, "And you believe that I can use my powers for good."

"Of course," Mina said. "Your destiny is your own, Amamemnon. Not God's."

"So, what? I join up with you guys?"

"I'm not sure I trust you yet," Luci said, pulling Mina off of the fear demon's lap and into his own arms. She draped one arm around his shoulder, resting her head against his chest as he sat down with her in the armchair next to the window.

"What can I do to prove my loyalty? If not to you, then to your bride."

"Bring your fear demons into the fold."

"Um, love, I'm not sure that I'm up for an orgy right now." Mina squeezed her thighs together.

Luci chuckled.

"An orgy isn't needed. They are connected to me. There is a ripple effect occurring already. But they have a fuck ton of questions. I should go." The demon stood, smoothing out his tracksuit and tugging down the hem of his black tank.

"Leaving before you've had a chance to say hi to Lilith?" Luci asked.

"Where is she, anyway?" Mina asked.

"Lilith is here? That bitch hates me." Amamemnon paled.

"Lilith isn't a bitch," Mina frowned. "Take that back."

Amamemnon nodded, kneeling in front of where Mina perched on Luci's lap. "Forgive me," he said. Bowing his head over her hand, he kissed it.

"To be fair, she does hate you," Luci said.

"You were always such a drag at the orgies," Lilith, casually leaning against the door frame with her arms crossed in front of her, said.

"Lilith, can you see Amamemnon out, please?" Luci asked. "I need another round of breeding my wife." Mina blushed at Luci's crude language and buried her face in his neck, her embarrassment fueling a new wave of desire.

"Sure thing, boss." Lilith chuckled as she led Amamemnon out of the bedroom. She closed the door behind her.

Luci stood, cradling Mina in his arms. He deposited her onto the bed where she sprawled out dramatically, draping an arm above her head.

"It's really a lot of work for some foreplay," she said, peeking at Luci from around her arm as he climbed up next to her.

"You're the one who wanted to multitask." He grasped her hip and encouraged her to straddle him with an expressive wiggle of his eyebrows. She sheathed his member in her slick heat and ran her fingers along his muscular chest.

"The stronger your legion, the safer our children will be."

"Children?" Luci asked as he thrust into her, cupping a breast in one hand and teasing her clit with the other. "How many children?"

"Let's see how the first one goes before you hold me to a number, but I think at least two."

"We can do better than two. Especially if we get Bellz involved."

"You want to see me swell with Bellz' child?"

Luci growled, flipping her onto her back. "Mine first."

Alastor's Interlude

F ROM THE MOMENT THAT Alastor first saw Lilith, uncount-
able years ago, he fell in stupid lust with her. He ached
with longing and did reckless things like breaking into her
territory and fucking around with the souls in her charge,
hoping she'd catch him. Aching to feel the thick sole of her boot
against his neck, holding him down while she administered his
punishment with a whip, cane, or flogger.

If Alastor thought Lilith was hot when she was angry, she
was a cataclysmic inferno when she zeroed all her focus on the
flick of her wrist, hitting him as many times and with as much
force as he could handle, not a bit more. Just the right amount
to satisfy his craving. For a time.

Before Mina, it had been easier to prompt her into action.
But he didn't mind the change in their dynamic. He grew
closer to her, got to know the woman behind the whip, learned
to feel things for her aside from lust. He never would have had
the courage if not for Mina.

Nowadays, when he wanted Lilith's attention he'd turned to
other means. Namely, bratting. Lots and lots of bratting. She
was so unflappable most of the time that he couldn't even tell if
his rudeness, childish barbs, or ornery behavior hit their mark
at all.

And then she'd do something like she had at Mina's place. Authority radiated from her, and Alastor was all too happy to obey her every demand.

"There you are," Lilith said after flinging her office door open. Alastor sat behind her desk. "Why are you here?"

"Your view is nicer than mine."

Lilith tapped her foot impatiently and braced one hand on her hip. "They are exactly the same."

It was true. Sindy, Bellz, Lilith, and Alastor all had identical offices overlooking lava, rock, and endless empty sky. Only some small personal differences separated them. The surfaces in Sindy's office were covered with carved animals, and a live cat often slept on top of her filing cabinet. Alastor's was decorated in plants, vines climbing the walls.

Lilith's, however, was mostly bare. Except for a single scented candle she kept on her bookcase—leather and caramel, her scent.

"Yours smells nicer." He stopped himself from saying more. Hell forbid she took it as a compliment. A completely true compliment that he absolutely believed, but he couldn't let her know that. It would ruin this game of his. Then what would they be left with? Alastor didn't know, and it wasn't worth the risk of finding out.

"You snuck out of Mina's the second we all closed our eyes. Why did you leave?" She sat on the arm of one of the two chairs in front of the desk. With only one foot on the floor and the other dangling in mid air, she looked vulnerable. Her expression was open, curious, and a little bit pained.

Instantly uncomfortable, Alastor stood and turned to fiddle with a granite bookend on the shelf next to the window. He thought about turning the tables by asking why she didn't allow him to get her off, but he chickened out. Or maybe his subconscious recognized that it wasn't the time.

"Alastor, don't turn your back on me." When he turned around, Lilith was standing right behind him. She fisted his jacket in her hands and tugged. He was too big for her to move, even with all her strength. It would have been like trying to displace a wall. But he took a step toward her anyway. "Please, talk to me."

A request, not a command, yet Alastor felt his resolve crumble. "I'm scared, Lilith."

"Of me?" she asked. "Because of the whips, the chains, and all those things I did to you for centuries?" Lilith peered up at him, her hand tracing his pecs before cupping the side of his neck. It was as far as she could reach without rising onto her toes. But then she did perch on top of them, and her hand caressed his jaw on its way to his cheek. "I'm sorry."

"No," Alastor said. "Never apologize for any of that. I've loved every minute of it." He swallowed. "I needed every minute of it."

"I never want to do anything to make you feel uncomfortable."

"You haven't."

"I need us to sit down, to agree on rules."

"Rules?"

"To your game, you brat." All the colors in her eyes twinkled with delight.

"I don't need any rules."

"They aren't for you." She blinked up at him.

Then Alastor said the one truth that had been burning through him all this time. "I will let you do everything. Anything you need from me, it's yours already. It always has been. So I don't need any rules, but I will abide by any that you set."

"Rule number one, aftercare is a must." She pinched his cheek. "No. Running. Off."

Alastor closed his eyes and nodded.

"Rule number two, you'll have a safe word."

He scoffed. "I'm not going to use it."

"You'll have one anyway."

"I'll purposefully forget it."

"Then I'll make you repeat it as many times as it takes before we start a session."

Alastor crossed his arms and glared.

"And if you still can't remember it, we just won't play."

He sighed and rolled his eyes. "Fine. Do I get to pick the word?"

"No," she snapped prettily. "Since you won't remember it anyway, I'll come up with a new word each session."

He nodded.

"Aftercare, now. We're making up for your premature departure from Mina's." She pointed to her desk chair. "Sit." When he did, she climbed into his lap, straddling him with her thighs. She wrapped her arms around his neck and buried her face against his chest. "Hold me."

Like this, she seemed so small, nestled against him. Delicate. Completely unlike the warrior who had cut down enemies at his side so recently. And he was in awe of her, this many-faceted being who wanted him, who wrecked him, and who then sought comfort in his arms. She sought to comfort him as well.

He bent his head and breathed in her hair. Leather and warm sweetness.

Too quickly, that grounding scent of hers faded as she retreated. "Stay there," she commanded. She moved to the other side of her desk and dragged the large armchairs there to the edges of the room, leaving the center of the room empty. She then cleared her desk of a few scattered papers and other objects, leaning over the desk to place them in the top side drawer.

"Stand here, in the middle of the carpet." She snapped her fingers at him.

He stood on shaky legs and walked around the desk to stand where she had indicated.

She sat halfway on the desk facing him, again one foot firmly on the ground while the other dangled elegantly from her ankle. She wore strapped, spiked heels.

Alastor cursed under his breath at the sight of the thin leather wrapping around her dark, muscular calf.

"Strip for me, Alastor." The corners of her lips pulled up tightly. It was a threatening kind of smile, but arousing. Everything she did aroused. Fighting next to her in battle was a delight and a danger. Standing before her now while she demanded his nakedness was nothing short of a dream come true.

He wiggled around to the beat of a song only he could hear, attempting a strip tease. But he must have failed miserably, because when he turned back around without a stitch of clothing on, Lilith was doubled over with laughter.

When she looked up at him, she saw his frown, and her laughter died. "Hey," she said, standing up and taking a step toward him. "You're perfect. Sexy. Vulnerable." She took another step. "Mine." She placed a hand over his heart.

"Yes. I'm yours."

Stepping back and to the side, Lilith gestured toward the desk. "Bend over it." She lifted a single brow in challenge, but of course he did what he was told.

The warmth of her body permeated the skin on his bare ass and the back of his legs. As she rubbed her hands along his hips and down his thighs, his fingers wrapped around the far edge of the desk.

"You know I have to punish you for invading my space without my permission, don't you?" she asked.

He gulped as blood rushed to his genitals. As her hand made sharp contact with the meat of his ass, he closed his eyes and soaked in the delightful pain. He would never get tired of this.

"Your safe word is 'gregarious.'" Lilith slapped his upper thigh. "Repeat it back to me, Alastor."

He shook his head. He had behaved, willingly, happily, but now that she dealt out her sweet torture, he wanted more. He wanted harder.

"What is your safe word, Alastor? Her voice growled as she reached between his legs and seized his balls with enough pressure to be threatening without causing harm.

Once again, he refused to answer, closing his eyes in anticipation of her next move instead.

"Give me your safe word right now or everything stops." She gave him the tiniest squeeze, and pain shot up his spine. Fuck. He needed more.

"I think that's the opposite of how safe words work," he responded, voice tight.

"Fine. Have it your way." She dropped her hand and stepped away.

Fuck. "Gregarious." Fuck. Fuck. Fuck.

"Good boy." She cupped him gently this time, her other hand moving in soft circles on his lower back. He watched in the reflection of the window as she brought her thumb to her mouth and wet it. She applied pressure to his asshole, pushing against him without penetration as she tugged on his balls. "But you weren't good earlier. Always egging me on. I bet you want me to turn this green flesh of yours red."

"Please."

"Only," she pushed a little harder with her thumb, "if you promise," until it popped through his tight ring, "to stay for aftercare." She left it there, barely the tip of her inside him.

"I promise."

She twisted his love berries ever so slightly and seated her thumb fully inside him. Alastor's heart stuttered with the knowledge that she filled him. She had let him fill her at Mina's place, and he'd thought at the time that he had never been more complete. But this feeling was just as strong. He wanted to be owned by her so completely, and she was doing that now with a kindness that expanded his soul, but he wanted her to own him with cruelty, too. Not that he knew how to ask for it. That had always been his problem. If he couldn't request it outright, then he'd have to provoke her. But how?

"I thought this was supposed to be a punishment."

"I'm just getting started, my brat." She removed her hand from his testicles and rotated the other, keeping her thumb in place but bringing her fingers forward so she could tease his sex fruit with her fingertips or curl her hand inward and graze him with her knuckles. "I don't think I'll be using any impact toys. I want to make your ass smart with my very own palm."

As she worked over his rear with spanks, she slowly pumped her thumb inside his tight hole. The redder his ass became, the faster she fucked him. His entire world narrowed until it consisted only of the two of them and the desk that supported him. Gratitude radiated from him that she hadn't put a flogger or crop between them. He had erected enough barriers through his games over the centuries.

"I need you to come, Alastor, so be a good boy." She removed her thumb only to penetrate him with it again in one smooth thrust. Moving up behind him so her hips bracketed his smarting ass, she reached around and gripped as much of his cock as she could fit into her hand and pumped.

He came with such force that he fell forward on the desk, a whimpering, crumpled mess. But Lilith didn't leave him there. The warm weight of a blanket enveloped him, and she helped him move from the desk to the plush rug where she held him across her lap and stroked his forehead.

It quickly became clear that their scene was over, yet she had once again not taken any pleasure for herself. Alastor so desperately wanted to ask if he could be the one to help get her there. He would let her sit on his face for hours. But ultimately he lacked the courage to do so, and that truth was crushing. When would he ever be good enough for her? What could he do to be worthy of her?

Eight

"I HAVE A DATE," Dahlia said to her sister via their video chat. Her phone was propped up in the windowsill above the kitchen sink while she attempted to finish washing dishes before Oscar arrived.

It had been his idea to take her on an official date. He'd brought it up after her third orgasm the night before, when she was too weak to see reason and therefore easily pliable. What on earth a demon who hadn't been human in just over a hundred years could have planned, she hadn't the foggiest. She was low-key excited to find out.

But she wouldn't get to go and solve the mystery of what it was like to date an out-of-touch demon if she couldn't line up a last-minute babysitter. Her mother had volunteered to watch Tabitha this morning, but now Sandra was nowhere to be found.

And even though Tabitha was technically old enough to stay home by herself, she had lost her PlayStation privileges Saturday morning when Dahlia had gotten up at her normal time to get coffee going and found her daughter still awake from the night before, glued to the TV screen, her hands contorted—not permanently, luckily—around a controller.

Dahlia had called her mother frantically, only for Sandra to pick up after half a dozen rings to tell her that she "just couldn't deal with it today." Which, you know, fair, but it still left Dahlia in an awkward position. So she had called her older sister in the hopes that she would be up for hanging with her niece.

"You have a what now?" Mina asked, her voice pitched high and her eyes wide. "With whom?"

Dahlia frantically looked around the kitchen, trying to find a believable lie. She almost blurted out Phillip Kenmore but stopped herself at the last second. The lies were already creating a sizable distance between Tabitha and her, because of course her daughter noticed something was going on. Dahlia did not want to have to keep secrets from her best friend as well.

"Oscar is taking me out," Dahlia said. "But please don't tell anyone. I'm not ready for that to be common knowledge yet."

"Oscar? Who's Oscar?"

"Oz."

"Oz? I know you two hit it off at our reception, but wow. A date. With a spirit board demon. You hate spirit boards." A beat. "He told you his name was Oscar?"

"Um, yeah," Dahlia said, nervously tucking a piece of hair behind her ear. "Anyway, Mom was going to babysit, but she bailed last minute."

"What do you mean Mom bailed last minute?"

"I think she's at church."

"Oh," Mina frowned. "I guess something must have come up."

"Do you have a lot of unexpected guests right now or can I drop Tabitha off at your place?"

"Let me check." Mina leaned off camera before yelling, "Luci, did Amamemnon leave again?"

"Who is Amamemnon?" Dahlia asked. Someone had only been half listening to their mythology professor.

"He's a fear demon I met yesterday. Luci and I decided to start trying for a baby, and I thought it would be a good idea to get more allies before we brought along new vulnerabilities."

"You're going to have a baby?" Dahlia's heart speed with excitement. A new little bundle of joy! It had been so long since she had held a newborn. She almost swooned at the notion of smelling a baby's head again.

"We are trying. Just started trying, actually. We decided right before the reception, so don't get too excited. We don't even know if it's possible."

"Of course it's possible. Why wouldn't it be possible?" Dahlia asked, thinking of a very living Tabitha upstairs doing homework.

"Well, it's not exactly something that has happened before. A human and a demon having a baby, that's like apocalyptically big news."

"Oh, right." Dahlia bit her lip to keep herself from confessing everything. Her sister had a legitimate reason to know. Except, everything had worked out very easily for Dahlia and Oscar. So most likely a positive pregnancy test was in Mina's very near future. And Dahlia could tell everyone about Tabitha's parentage in her own time, which was not now, when she was only just starting to make things work with the father.

"I'm trying not to get my hopes up too high," Mina said. "But why don't I come to you? The fear demons just switched to our side, and I'm a little worried that Luci might get some more drop-ins at our place."

"Okay, but please don't let Tabitha convince you that she can play video games."

"Oh no." Mina chuckled. "What did she do?"

"She was up until six a.m. playing video games Friday night."

"No wonder she crashed at the reception so hard."

"Yeah, pulling an all-nighter the same weekend that the universe decides to brain-dump a millennia-old memory and your aunt marries Satan himself will take it out of you."

"Tabitha already knew I was dating Satan, so I think at least that bit came as less of a shock to her."

"Right. She had met Lucifer, Sindy, and Beelzebub the last time I asked you to babysit last minute." Dahlia pursed her lips and furrowed her brow. "Do you think Kathryn is available tonight? She's not mixed up in all this demon business, right?"

"Hey! I want to see my niece."

"Fine, fine. Just leave any demons you aren't married to at home, okay?"

"Says the lady who is going out with one of them," Mina said, her voice loud enough that Dahlia covered her phone with her hand and glanced behind her.

"Shh! Tabitha could hear you!"

Stringed lights twinkled above the vineyard, competing with the stars for attention. As they made their way down a row of grapes, Oscar's calloused hand gripped Dahlia's. At the end of the row, a table for two had been set up. Oscar pulled out a chair for her before taking his own.

"I have to admit, I didn't think this is what we would be doing."

"Where did you think I would take you on our first date, darlin'?"

"I don't know. A rodeo? Traveling side show? A county fair?" Oscar's laugh encouraged her for one more. "A square dance?"

"A square dance?" Oscar guffawed. "I do keep up with modern media, you know. I have seen plenty of romantic comedies. I know what modern women expect on a date."

"According to Hollywood, but I guess that puts you on equal playing field with every other American man."

"That doesn't sound like a good thing." He bit his lip, sawing into it, telegraphing his nervousness. He had never hid a thing from her in the past. That his emotions should live on his sleeve even now shouldn't have come as a surprise, yet it did.

"So you only chose this place because you saw it on TV?" Dahlia asked.

"Well, not quite." Oscar removed his hat long enough to run his fingers through his hair. "Vineyards remind me a bit of the ranch back in Texas. Ya know, before."

"When you were still human."

"Yes." Oscar poured them both a glass of wine. Cheeses, grapes, and finely sliced deli meats sat on the table between them. "It's bittersweet being reminded of home."

"And your sister?"

"Yes, ma'am. But also my parents. My horse."

"You never fully explained to me. You said you made a deal to talk to your sister again after the war. But if you were coming home, why did you need to talk to her?"

"The Great War ended, but before I shipped back home, my sister came down with the Spanish flu. By the time I arrived home, she had already succumbed."

"I'm so sorry." He let her wrap her hand around his, and she scooted her chair closer.

"I had managed to survive the war. It wasn't fair. Keeping her safe gave me a reason to fight. At times, it was all that kept me going." A tear slid down his cheek, and she caught it with her lips, replaced it with a kiss. He turned toward her, chasing her lips with his own.

His mouth was soft yet firm against hers, and she forgot where they were as she tipped his hat back so she could deepen the kiss. He pushed his chair away from the table and invited her into his lap. His hand made its way under her skirt and was playing with the elastic around the leg of her panties when her stomach growled.

He chuckled. "You're hungry, darlin'."

"For a couple of things," Dahlia admitted.

"Let's feed you food before we feed you demon."

Begrudgingly, Dahlia removed herself from Oscar's lap.

The cowboy demon barked in protest, his hands finding her hips and pulling her down, back to his front this time, before she could reclaim her own seat. Plucking a piece of Gouda from the platter, he held it up to her lips, which brushed his fingertips when she took the cheese into her mouth.

As Oscar leaned back, he brushed Dahlia's brown hair from her neck. His hands settled on her shoulders, fingertips kneading her tense muscles. An involuntary moan slipped out, and Dahlia hid her face in her hands.

"Darlin' don't," Oscar said as he dipped his head low so he was level with her. "Let me take care of you."

Nodding, Dahlia lowered her hands and let Oscar resume his massage while she fed him an occasional grape. They spent the rest of the evening that way, snuggled together on Oscar's chair while they finished their food and wine.

After, Dahlia pulled out her phone and showed him every single video and photo she had of Tabitha until Oscar had seen the highlights from his daughter's entire life. His eyes filled with tears at all he had missed.

"Whatever you need from me," he said as he walked her back to her car, her hand in one hand and his hat in the other, "I will give. As much time as you need, but, please, let me be a part of your future. Our daughter's future."

Turning to face him, Dahlia wrapped her arms around his waist and looked up at him. Everything in her screamed to say yes, to hold onto this man and never let him go again. But he wasn't a man. She remembered the way her heart had broken when he stopped visiting her and again when she found out she was pregnant and truly on her own.

In the beginning, she had believed that she would have to raise her child alone. She had been so shocked when Mina and Sandra had offered to help, rearranging their work and school schedules so she could get her degree. But even with all their help, she still felt so alone at times. Alone in her pain. She couldn't even talk to her sister or mother about what Oscar had done. They wouldn't have believed her. Not then.

Mina would believe her now in a heartbeat. But instinct told her to keep it to herself, where she could maintain control over it. Surely Mina would be sympathetic to her demonic friend; however, Dahlia wasn't ready for the input of others just yet.

She needed more time. Time to learn how to trust Oscar again. Time to readjust to a future where she might not be a single parent. As much as she wanted to say yes, she just wasn't ready.

Her emotions must have played across her face, because Oscar nodded before pulling her tightly against him. He rested his chin on the top of her head, a hand making lazy circles over her upper back.

"It's okay, Dahlia. You don't have to say anything now."

She squeezed him in response, kissing his chest, even if he couldn't feel it through his thick flannel shirt. For long minutes, they stood holding each other. But then he cleared his throat, and Dahlia took a half step back, just enough so she could stand on her toes and press her lips to his.

He pulled her against him once more, and she yanked at the back of his shirt, untucking it and slipping her hands beneath the heavy fabric and over his warm skin. They opened to one another and dove deeper. When he pressed her against the driver-side door, she didn't care that her car was dirty or that her coat would need to be dry cleaned. All she wanted was more of him—closer.

As she wrapped her leg around his waist, his hand on her ass propped her up against him so her crotch met his quickly growing bulge.

Was she really about to fuck a demon in the middle of the gravel parking lot of a Sonoma County winery? The way he was nibbling her had her wishing that they could.

"Oscar," Dahlia managed in a breathless voice, "we shouldn't do this here."

"Do you want me to meet you back in your room?" he asked as he kissed his way down her neck, across her throat, along her collarbone. "Or should we rent a cheap motel?"

"Between those two options? Definitely my room."

"Sneaking off to an establishment that lets you pay by the hour doesn't excite you?" Oscar asked, laughing.

"Of course not, but you already knew that." She glanced down at her watch. It was getting late. "I need to relieve Mina anyway, assuming Mom isn't back from church yet."

"Seems kind of late to be at church."

"One would think, but she's been getting home pretty late this week, always with an excuse about the congregation."

"Maybe she's dating someone."

Dahlia mulled it over for a moment, then shook her head. "She'd tell us if she were. She'd be too excited to keep it to herself. No. Mom usually only keeps us in the dark when it's bad news."

"How annoying."

"Indeed." Dahlia couldn't help but smile at him.

"So am I meeting you back at your room?"

Dahlia nodded. "Wanna drive back with me and try climbing up the trellis and through my window?"

"As fun as that sounds, I think I'll be less likely to get caught if I use demonic methods."

"You're no fun," she grumbled, but the smiling lifting her cheeks said otherwise.

Back at home, after she had dismissed Mina and checked in on her sleeping daughter, Dahlia slipped into her pitch-black bedroom. Oscar's strong arms closed around her from behind. Tugging her close, he bent to her neck, which he peppered with kisses. His lips were soft against her skin, but his evening stubble was rough. The juxtaposition of sensations tightened her arousal.

She was already so wet. The whole car ride home, she had replayed their make-out session in the parking lot and how erotic it had felt while he fed her. Not that he had to do any of that to get her going. A growled "darlin'" or a tip of that damn cowboy hat were enough on their own.

Spinning in his arm, she pushed against his chest, encouraging him backward until he stumbled and fell onto the bed. She hopped on top of him, rubbing her sex against the thick crotch of his jeans through her panties. Her hands pressed against his chest, helping her balance and giving her leverage. His hands cupped her ass, encouraging her along.

Sweet holy universe, she could come like this. There was just enough light from the streetlight outside the window to see his heavily lidded eyes. He was close too.

But she needed just a little bit more. Grabbing one of his hands, she put it on her breast. "Be a little bit mean. Be rough. Pinch me."

His lips parted as he obeyed, fondling her through her top.

Lifting her hips slightly, she gave herself enough space to move the gusset of her panties aside. When she lowered herself once more, the thick texture of his denim caressed her labia, adding a hint more friction to her dry humping. Tilting her hips forward, she let her clit drag against him, and he jerked against her, pinching her nipple in just the right way.

The sparks that had started to gather at the base of her spin ignited, and she rode out her bliss. His body spasming beneath her, Oscar came as well.

She collapsed against him, resting her head against his collarbone, and burst into a fit of giggles.

"I haven't spent in my trousers in over a century," he said, chuckling beneath her. His hands rubbed lovingly along her limbs.

"Can I clean you up?" she asked, pushing up and lifting an eyebrow.

"I'm more than capable of cleaning myself up, but that look in your eye is telling me to say yes."

Scooting down the bed, she unfastened and pulled off his jeans and underwear. Then she spent her sweet time licking his ejaculate from his body.

Nine

A FEW HOURS LATER, Mina's phone chimed as she climbed out of her car. Chucking the door closed with her hip, she fumbled to pull her cell out of her pocket. Kathryn had texted her. She must have beaten Mina to her townhome. Kathryn had called thirty minutes before Dahlia had arrived home from her date—her date with Oz. Mina shook her head to try to get rid of the thought. She didn't have the time right now to process that because Kathryn had asked for an emergency cuddle session.

It was one of the things they did fairly regularly. Kathryn had told Mina that before Victor, she had not merely enjoyed sex; it had been an integral part of what made Kathryn Kathryn. She had been discerning with her lovers but had a regular rotation. Nowadays, sex was essentially non-existent, but she still craved closeness with someone she could trust. Unfortunately, that number had dwindled to a small handful of family members and Mina.

Mina didn't mind in the least. They would cuddle on the couch or chaise and binge-watch the newest romance or a reliable classic. Luci knew to give them their space. He'd met Kathryn briefly, but he mostly avoided the human. Mina suspected that he felt guilty for the role he'd played in Kathryn's trauma.

Finally, Mina managed to unlock her phone, and opened the text in the secure messaging app they used. Like every time she saw it, Mina giggled at Kathryn's handle, Kathryn the GR8, inspired by her love for a certain cereal and her low-key obsession with early internet acronyms.

Kathryn the GR8

> **There's a strange man sitting on your porch.**

Mina's phone chimed again.

Kathryn the GR8

> **Do you know any Greek gods?**

"Well, actually," Mina mumbled under her breath as she made her way out of her garage and to the front entrance to her townhome.

Michael was sitting on the porch swing to the left of her front door. He looked up at her, his lips turned upward in an obligatory smile that didn't reach his eyes. His wings were camouflaged, but Mina could make out the barest glimmer framing his shoulders.

"Hi, Michael." Mina leaned against the porch rail across from him. "Are you okay?"

"I'm having a rough week."

Movement at the window behind Michael's head caught her eye. Kathryn had used her key to let herself in and was now peeking out at them.

"Hold on," Mina said. She glanced down to type out a message to Kathryn. "My friend is here too. Before I invite you in to talk, I need to make sure it's okay with her. She's been through a lot."

"Oh." Michael looked down at his lap.

"Not that you haven't." Mina sat down next to him and waited for Kathryn to respond. She wrapped an arm around the angel. "What's going on?"

"I'm just so disgusted with myself." He flexed the hands in his lap, his palms face up.

"There is nothing disgusting about you, Michael."

"I've masturbated every day this week. Multiple times today. It just never seems to be enough. I finish and then something happens that gets me all worked up again."

"I think that's pretty normal when you're starting out. Every little thing can feel erotic."

"Do you know how many books I used to read in a week?"

"No idea. How many?"

"Twenty-one. Now, on a good week, I can maybe manage seven. Seven!"

"That's," Mina paused so she could get a grip on her amusement, "still a respectable number of books."

"That's only one book a day, Mina."

Kathryn opened the front door and stuck her head out, but Mina could see from her collar that she was wearing her pink footed pajamas with little bunny heads on the top of the feet.

"It's okay if you two want to come inside." Kathryn blushed. "I may have been eavesdropping a bit. Your voices carried really well through the window."

Michael stood, eyes wide, and started to stammer.

"Hey," Kathryn said, stepping out onto the welcome mat. She placed her hand on Michael's forearm. "It's okay. This is a safe place. Mina helps me deal with my complicated sexual feelings too."

"She does?"

Kathryn nodded. "Why don't you come inside and we can talk while we decide what to watch."

Mina sat between Kathryn and Michael, shoulder to shoulder with Kathryn—who was flipping through a streaming menu—knees barely grazing Michael's. Coughing, the angel shifted away, and Mina threw him a small smile.

"I can't help it," he mouthed to her, and her smile widened.

"You know you don't have to be embarrassed with me," Mina whispered.

Michael wrapped his arms around one of hers and placed his chin on her shoulder. "It's exhausting. I don't understand how you humans live like this," he whispered, but his voice carried.

"We humans? What are you?" Kathryn asked, her tone jolly and light. "A hairless yeti?"

Michael shot Mina a panicked expression. "That was a joke," he blurted out, so quickly that it sounded disingenuous.

"Oh. Okay." Kathryn cocked her head to the side. "I don't get it."

"An inside joke," Mina said.

"This whole sexuality thing is new to me," Michael explained. "So I've never really felt human before now."

"Oh," Kathryn said. "That makes sense based on what I, um, ahem, overheard." She sighed heavily then handed the remote to Mina. "I went through some, uh, traumatic stuff. Mina is the only person I'm not related to who I allow to touch me these days. Sex isn't even on my radar. Not even self-care. And it's not that I don't want to. I desperately want to feel like my body is mine. But it just hasn't felt right. It isn't the safe space it used to be."

"It felt like a safe space for you?" Michael asked. "How?"

"I guess because I was taught that sex is an expression of love. And I explored it that way by myself and then with others. Sometimes that love was truly no more than friendliness with a side of lust, but it was mine to give. My body to give. I found it empowering."

"Until someone used it against you for hate," Mina said, squeezing Kathryn's hand in her own. Kathryn rarely opened up like this, and not at all since the first few months of their friendship. They mostly just watched movies and talked about family, Kathryn's nonprofit, or Mina's newest project. Sometimes they'd make cookies or cupcakes.

Kathryn nodded. She sniffled, and Michael leapt from the couch, retrieving the box of tissues from the credenza in the dining area. He handed the box to Kathryn, their eyes meeting and holding for a long moment, before he sat back down.

"Sex for me has always been taboo. Something beneath me. Unfit for those I loved," Michael admitted. "But I never had to contend with this lust. It was easy to condemn others for beastly behavior before I was reduced to being one."

"Oh, Michael." Mina turned to him, climbing up onto her knees so she could make eye contact with him. "You are not a beast." She cupped his face in her hands and brought her forehead to his, holding his iridescent blue gaze with her own. "You are a beautiful being who has just opened up a brand new sense. You get to experience a part of the world that was closed to you before."

He blinked.

"I know it's a lot. Like an overwhelming amount of a lot, but you have me to help you through it. Believe it or not, you have the others too. Luci has not forgotten what you did for him."

"I did it for you," Michael whispered.

"You two are so dramatic," Kathryn said through tearful laughter.

Mina pulled away from the angel, plopping back down onto her butt. "Well, we should definitely watch something in this irreverent comedy category then."

"I'm here for you now, too," Kathryn said to Michael. She reached behind Mina to pat him lightly on the shoulder.

Michael's eyes grew wide. "Did I just get accepted into your circle of trusted touchers?"

"Nope," Kathryn said mirthfully. "But I don't mind touching you. So long as you are okay with that being a one-way street?"

"Yes," Michael nodded. "You can touch me whenever, and I will not touch you unless you tell me to."

Mina glanced between them. Kathryn worried her bottom lip between her teeth, Michael was practically panting, and Mina suddenly felt like a third wheel.

"Would you two like to use my guest bedroom? It's upstairs on the right."

"What?" Whatever spell had a hold of Kathryn broke. "No. We are watching a movie together."

"Offer stands. Whenever. Kathryn, you have a key."

The three settled in for a movie, and any residual tension quickly melted away. When the film was over, Mina made sure that her friends exchanged phone numbers.

"I was hoping to stay over," Michael said.

At the same time, Kathryn said, "I don't want to be alone tonight."

"Sleepover!" Mina shot both arms into the air. It was a good thing that she had a king-size bed. But if this became a regular thing, she might need to upgrade to the Beelzebub size.

After brushing their teeth, Mina and Kathryn sat on the bed together while Michael did whatever passed for an angel's bedtime routine.

"He's really cute, Mina." Kathryn leaned against the headboard. "Do you think he'd be interested if I offered to help him navigate his new sexuality?"

"I think there's a good chance he might. There are probably some things I should tell you before you get too involved with him, though."

"Things about his history?" Kathryn asked. "Unless I need to know, I'd rather hear them from him."

"Some things about me, but also things about him too. But I'm not the one keeping his secret."

"He was keeping yours?" Kathryn scratched her chin. "Does this have something to do with that human joke? That was super odd."

"Yeah." Fuck. Was she really going to just spill the beans right now? "If I tell you before bed—"

Kathryn cut her off. "Knowing you are keeping something from me will make it impossible for me to sleep. You know you can tell me anything, right? You saved my life, girl. You are forever my sister."

"Okay, well, you asked for it. Please don't think I've lost it." Mina sucked in her lips, delaying just long enough to gather her courage. "Luci, my husband—"

"The hottie," Kathryn said.

"—is the devil. Crowned Prince of Hell. Satan. Lucifer, the first fallen angel."

"Okay, I can see why you thought I would question your sanity."

"He's the reason that I met you, Kathryn. He used a crossroads deal that that evil prick Victor had made with another demon, but one under Luci's command, to find me and bring me to Hell. Temporarily."

"Your near-death experience on that yacht?"

"Uh-huh. And then when I got back from Hell, I was confused. I thought it was a dream. Went on a date or two with the evil prick. He brought me home, tried to kill me, as you know, but Luci stopped him. Then we heard you, and that's when I called Detective Jacobs."

"We need to take her out to brunch again soon. That was so much fun."

"Kathryn? Did I lose you?"

"No." Kathryn shook her head in emphasis.

"Michael is an angel, newly fallen. He gave me his ability to go to Heaven so I could rescue Luci."

"I'm glad Luci's not the only one doing the rescuing."

"Indeed he is not," Michael said, leaning against the bathroom door frame. "Would you like some physical proof that I am who Mina says I am?"

"Honestly, I believe her." Kathryn crossed her arms over her chest. "It is the only way that it makes any sense that that evil fuck was able to get away with what he did for so long. Of course he had the powers of Hell on his side."

"Luci has been slowly reviewing all crossroad deals to see if there are others out there that evil. Mostly they are pretty harmless. Demons don't usually give deals that good," Mina said.

"Okay. I changed my mind. I do want physical proof, but just for fun!" Kathryn sat up straight and clapped her hands.

Michael hummed while he circled the bed. Then a pink teddy bear filled his arms. It was wearing a yellow plaid skirt and top and a little white hat with a daisy pinned jauntily to its side.

"My Cher Bear-owitz!" Kathryn squealed, launching herself at Michael. "I lost her on a trip to Chicago when I was a kid!" Michael held out the bear so that Kathryn could grab it without touching him, but she scooped both the bear and Michael into her arms. Michael did not hug her back, but his smile was blinding.

Kathryn's Interlude

T HE TRILL OF KATHRYN'S phone filled her too-quiet condo, and she fought the urge to jump for it. But she
couldn't. She was three minutes into mixing the filling for her
French silk pie with her hand mixer, and she couldn't stop for
another two. She really needed to splurge on a stand mixer,
but her grandmother's pie recipe was the only thing she ever
baked. It seemed silly to buy and store special equipment when
she could work on her arm strength and save the counter space.

Her phone buzzed again, and then one more time thirty
seconds later. A minute left on her timer. She told herself she
could wait, shifting from foot to foot. It was probably just a
phone game notification, an email, a text from a political group
asking for money, or some combination thereof.

There was no reason for her to believe that Michael was
texting her.

None.

None at all.

Except.

Except they'd been texting every day for the last two weeks.
She'd get home from the office after a full day of lobbying and
fundraising, and, like clockwork, he'd text her half an hour
later.

His first text had simply stated that a cloud in the park looked like a giraffe. She'd asked for a photo, but what he'd sent her had been a blurry picture of a clear blue sky.

Kathryn the GR8

> That's not a giraffe.

NoFlyList Michael

> I couldn't figure out how to take a picture quickly enough, and he turned first into a pogo stick and then an armchair before dissipating.

Kathryn the GR8

> That's an awful fate for a giraffe. Do you want me to help you learn how to navigate your phone?

NoFlyList Michael:

> Yes, please.

In the time since, he'd sent her slightly improved photos, all of clouds that never looked like what he said they did.

The timer buzzed, and Kathryn set down the hand mixer, immediately reaching for her phone to find three new texts from Michael.

NoFlyList Michael

> This cloud looks like a butt, Kathryn!

It looked like lumpy mashed potatoes. She felt the edges of her lips lift. He was such a cutie, so wholesome and delusional in the most charming way.

NoFlyList Michael

> That picture doesn't do it justice. Join me
> and see for yourself?

Kathryn bit her bottom lip. He was in the park across from her building. They'd discovered two days ago that they were neighbors. He lived in the building next to hers, but it was technically the same complex. They shared a parking garage and amenities like the indoor pool, gym, and rooftop patio on the main building, which happened to be Kathryn's.

Her phone buzzed in her hand. Another picture. This time of two round clouds at the base of a long, conical cloud.

Kathryn the GR8

> Excuse me. Did you just send me a dick pic?

NoFlyList Michael

> What? No! It's a rocket blasting off.

Kathryn the GR8

> Michael, that is clearly a fluffy dick.

NoFlyList Michael

> I would never send you a dick pic without
> permission, so it can't be a dick.

Kathryn the GR8

> A likely story. Anyway, I can't come down
> right now. I'm busy with my pie.

NoFlyList Michael

> Is that innuendo? Are you telling me you're
> masturbating to get back at me for sending
> you an accidental dick pic?

Kathryn snapped a picture of her almost-finished pie filling with the empty store-bought pie crust next to it and shared it via their chat.

NoFlyList Michael

> Okay, now I'm embarrassed.

Kathryn the GR8

> It'll be ready tomorrow. Wanna come over and help me forget it's sitting in my fridge? I have been known to eat it before it has set.

NoFlyList Michael

> Sure. Be right up.

Kathryn barely kept herself from squealing as she added the third egg and beat the mixture for another five minutes. She turned to scoop the pie filling into the waiting crust, slipping the unset pie into the fridge right before there was a knock on her door. When she opened it, she found Michael standing on the other side. He was in slacks and a button down. His jacket was draped over his arms in front of him.

"Come in," Kathryn said, stepping back to give him space. He walked over the threshold then paused.

"You might not want me around right now." He held the door open with the heel of his foot.

"Why not?"

"I may have gotten myself into a predicament when I teased you about the pie."

Kathryn's eyes shot to the jacket conspicuously blocking his crotch. She smirked up at him. "I don't mind." She reached out and took his jacket, hanging it on a hook in the entryway.

"Are you sure?"

"Of course. This is exactly the distraction I require."

The bulge in his pants twitched. "It is?"

"I may have been working on something. I was going to surprise you with it later, but I think I'm ready now."

"You're ready?"

"It was probably the dick pic."

"What?" His eyes grew as wide as saucers—the nonflying kind, probably.

She laughed. "Follow me."

She led him down the hallway to her spare bedroom. The space was largely filled by a king-size bed with a boxy, metal frame. She'd attached silk ropes to the headboard, one on either corner.

"I thought I could help you get past some of your holdups while I worked on some of mine. At my pace." She turned to face him and swallowed at the desire and trepidation she read on his face. "Is that something you'd be willing to try?"

"Yes," he said with no hesitation.

"I still can't have you touching me. That's why the ties."

He nodded. "You'll be completely in control."

"Are you okay with that?"

"Yes."

She moved toward him, stopping close enough to touch. Looking into his eyes, she gauged his reaction as she untucked his dress shirt. With steady fingers, she undid each button. When she moved to push the shirt from his broad shoulders, she accidentally brushed his collarbone, and they both gasped. As the shirt fell to the hardwood floor, Michael clasped his hands behind his back.

"Don't trust yourself?" Kathryn asked.

"Of course not," Michael said. "Not with these hormones coursing through my veins like they own the place."

"We'll take care of that next, then," Kathryn said, flashing him her most charming smile. He visibly relaxed. "Go lie down." She patted his butt when he turned to comply.

She made sure his arms were held in a comfortable position as she tied them. Since neither of them had done this before, she left the ties loose. They were very long, giving her flexibility for lots of holds, but she tied them off to the headboard so his hands rested at ease next to his head.

"How does that feel?" Kathryn asked.

"Fine," Michael said. He could move his hands an inch in each direction. "Maybe too much range of motion."

"I guess you'll just have to work on that self-control, then," Kathryn said.

"Kathryn, please. You've asked me not to touch you, and I will not. I would hate myself if I even did it on accident."

"I won't get close enough, I promise," Kathryn said, brushing a golden lock from his forehead. Briefly, he followed her hand as she pulled it back before resting against the pillow once more.

Kathryn climbed onto the bed, straddling his hips with her firm thighs. She wasted no time in flipping open his fly and tugging off his pants, leaving him in black boxer briefs.

She scooted to the bottom of bed and grasped his right ankle in her hand. The short blond hair on his legs tickled her fingers as she leashed his ankles with more silk ties. Again, she left plenty of slack in the tie and let his legs stay where they had naturally landed.

His comfort was really important. He was trusting her with not just his body but his sexuality as well. This needed to be a good experience for him just as much as it needed to be good for her.

She traced his legs with her fingers as she made her way back to the top of his waist. Hooking her fingers under the elastic of his boxer briefs, Kathryn slowly rolled them down until they sat on his thighs right under his perfectly shaped balls and proudly erect penis

She looked her fill before making eye contact. "How are you doing?"

"A little in pain," he said, and she immediately moved to her knees.

"Was I putting too much pressure on your legs? Do I need to adjust a tie?"

"That's not what I meant."

She smirked. "Oh," she wrapped her hand around his dick, giving him a single pump. "Is that better? Or worse?"

"Yes," he clenched his hands into fists.

Kathryn let out a throaty laugh, but she pumped her hand around him again.

"Oh, fuck," Michael groaned, and his hips bucked. His thigh bounced against hers, but she didn't mind, hardly even noticed. All her focus was on his pleasure. It was exquisite to watch and to know she was the one giving it. She worked him until he was trembling, and then she stopped. "More, please."

"Do you want this to be over already?" Kathryn asked, tilting her head to the side as she peered at him.

"No," Michael said, emphatically shaking his head.

"Then it's my turn for a bit." She moved off the bed and stripped out of her sheath dress. Her panties were next to go, followed by her bra. Michael watched her every movement. She spun away from him and bent over at the hip, giving him a good look at her ass and pussy lips nestled between her fit thighs as she picked up her clothes from the floor and draped them over the chair at the desk in the corner.

When she untied his left bond from the headboard, Michael panicked. "What are you doing?" His wrist was still wrapped firmly in satin.

"Trust me," she said. Then she brought his arm down so it lay next to his body and tied the satin sash around his lower thigh. She did the same thing with his right arm. "I needed to move your hands out of the way, so that I can do this."

Climbing back onto the bed, she placed her knees on either side of his face, far enough away that he could easily see the folds of her pussy. She knew she was flushed and wet. Her hand moved to the top of her mound, and she teased the base of her clitoris with the pad of her middle finger.

He groaned but didn't move. He could easily rise up and taste her. Even with his upper body bound to himself, the abs he was sporting meant he'd have no trouble.

She rewarded him by slipping that middle finger into herself and masturbating until she brought herself to a quick climax. Then she turned around and fell on top of him, taking his cock into her mouth. He was taller than her, tall enough that her crotch rested on his chest underneath his chin. She straddled his chest and rubbed herself against him.

"Kathryn, please, I can't—" he cut himself off with a quiet scream as he came in her mouth. There was no ejaculate, just tiny quivers and trembles as he fought against moving his hips.

Sitting up, she turned to face him, then unwrapped his wrists from his thighs and freed his ankles. Lastly, she tugged his boxers back into place.

"Can we cuddle?" she asked.

"You want me to touch you?" His eyebrows lifted in disbelief.

"Not in a sexual way," she clarified. "But I'd like to add you to the list of people I let touch me."

"Then I think we should both get dressed and go cuddle in a different room."

"That's smart," Kathryn agreed. "Keep these parts of our relationship separate."

"For as long as you need, Kathryn."

When they were both dressed again, she grabbed his hand and took him into her bedroom. They both lay down on top of the comforter, and Michael wrapped his long body around hers. His hand rested on her stomach, but he didn't brush her breast. Not even accidentally. Not even when she nodded off.

When she awoke several hours later, he still held her the same way. He hadn't moved a muscle. And in that moment, with the lights off and her part of the world asleep, she decided that she really wouldn't mind keeping him.

Ten

MINA WAS SO INTENTLY focused as she bent over her drawing table, she didn't notice that someone had come up behind her until they laid their hands on her shoulders. Strong fingers gently worked at the tight muscles there, and Mina sighed in pleasure and straightened her spine. Surprisingly, the smell of sulfur didn't greet her. Just the distant scent of campfire on crisp mountain air. The devil's scent. Her husband's, after he'd spent too much time near lava.

"Luci," she said as she leaned against his firm chest.

"Can we take you out now?" One hand moved to cup her throat, and her whole body relaxed at the same time it strained toward his grip, willing him to strengthen it.

She glanced at the clock on the wall. "It's one in the afternoon. Who's we?"

"Bellz, Sindy, and I," Luci said, but he didn't give her what she wanted. Not yet. "They're downstairs, and this is the perfect time for what I have planned."

"Yes," she whispered. And then his fingers tightened, sliding under her jaw and squeezing for just a moment before letting go. Mina whimpered, and Luci's amusement rumbled through her back. His hands moved to her hips, and he spun her around on her stool so she was facing him.

"Let's go, then." His actions contradicted his words, though, as he blocked her body with his and kissed her. She opened to him, and he deepened the kiss, lingering before abruptly breaking away. "Why are you dawdling?"

"You kissed me!" Mina said as Luci pulled her to her feet.

"I don't see what that has to do with anything. I kiss you often." Luci opened the door for her.

"You were keeping me from standing up," Mina reminded him but was met with a smart smack to her ass. "Hey!"

He pressed up behind her, wrapping an arm around her middle to keep her from progressing farther down the hall. "You know I just wanted an excuse to punish you."

Mina wiggled against him. "And you know that you don't need an excuse for that."

Luci only grunted in response, but he released her.

"So where are you taking me?" she asked at the bottom of the stairs, looking around for Sindy and Bellz.

"Bellz just learned of a nearby demon bar. He thought we should go check it out, dangle you like bait before the locals, see if we get any bites."

"My fertile window has to have passed by now, Luci," Mina said.

"True, but we can either be proactive about building my army, or we can sit around and wait to see if our impregnation attempts were successful in dreadful agony."

"You're right. Let's stay busy." Mina spotted Sindy and Bellz on the porch swing, heads bent toward one another. "How are they doing? Still getting along?"

"Oh, you'll see."

"Well, they look pretty cozy right now." Mina ducked into her bedroom, stripping off her work clothes. The old pajama bottoms and tank top were a far cry from the business casual outfits she wore during her hospital admin days. "What should I wear to this?" Mina called into the other room, only to turn around and find Luci opening the door to her small walk-in closet.

"Hm," he rummaged around for a moment. "How about this?"

Luci held up an outfit that she had never seen before. It consisted of a black corset over a lacy black dress with a cute sweetheart neckline and cap sleeves, but the fabric was transparent, and she'd be lucky if the skirt was long enough to cover her ass. Luci flipped the dress around to reveal its very low back. It would show a lot of skin.

"You did not get that from my closet."

The devil smirked at her.

"Lucifer, my beautiful morning star, what are you up to?"

"I want you to fit in."

"What is Sindy wearing?"

"You don't need to worry about Sindy."

"If I walk out onto that porch and she's wearing a sundress, I'm going to be pissed."

"She is not wearing a sundress. I don't think." He paused for a moment, wrinkling his forehead in thought. "Actually, she might be. I didn't really take notice."

Mina gave him a look.

"What? I was too preoccupied thinking about how great you were going to look in this. I designed it for you."

"Okay. Well, let's see it on, then." Mina blinked and she was wearing it. "Full powers today, huh?"

"Yep. It's easier to do that since we combined souls."

She stepped before her floor-length mirror and was pleasantly surprised. She looked hot. The lining of the dress covered her nipples and her crotch, leaving her cleavage and the bottom of her ass cheeks with only the delicate lace as concealment.

"What type of demon exactly am I trying to attract?" Mina sat on the chest at the end of the bed and pulled on a pair of open-toed, high-heeled boots.

"Okay. Let's go," Luci said, abruptly spinning on his heels and making a beeline for the front door.

"Wait up!" Mina scooped up her purse from the bed. Luci had moved her ID, credit card, and cash into a small clutch for her as she had assessed herself in the mirror. His thoughtfulness continued to surprise her, even though he often handled little things for her, lightening her mental load.

But why he was practically running out the door, Mina did not know. She followed him onto the porch, locking up behind her. When she turned back around, she found three demons gaping at her.

"What?"

"We need to leave right now," Luci said. He took Bellz' hand in one of his and Sindy's in the other.

"Why are we rushing?" Mina asked.

At the same time, Sindy asked, "Can't we just go back inside for a little?"

"No, we can't," Luci said.

"Why not?" Sindy asked.

"Because if we go back inside with Mina looking like that, we may never leave," Bellz said. "This outfit. It's too good, Luci. She's going to attract every demon in the joint."

"Gang bang in the back alley?" Mina asked.

"No fucking way," Bellz growled.

"I was kidding," Mina said.

"We'll be luring them back here to where I have provided added protection. And I want one of us with you at all times." Luci folded his arms across his chest and plastered on a stern expression.

"Won't they recognize you and then realize who I am?" Mina asked as she followed the demonic trio to an SUV Mina had never seen before. Luci opened the passenger side door for her and helped her in. He kept his hands to himself and didn't even lean in for a kiss or look at her more than absolutely necessary. Once she settled in, he closed the door and went around to the driver's side. Bellz and Sindy got in the back.

Fifteen minutes later, they pulled up to a strip mall with a laundromat on one end and a pizza place on the other. Luci drove to the back of the building and parked in a space near a nondescript wooden door. It looked more like an employee entrance than the front of a drinking establishment, but it was the door Luci led Mina to, his hand low around her waist and resting on her hip.

Bellz opened the door for them, and they stepped into an upscale bar full of warm, nicely finished woods, thick rugs, and jazzy music. It was busy, but the owners had obviously spent a lot of money on soundproofing, because Mina could easily hold a conversation with her companions as they found a booth and perused a drink menu.

"Come with me to order drinks," Luci requested. "Let's make sure everyone can get a good look at you."

"I'm not sure this is really my kink, Luci," Mina said, but she went with him anyway.

As Luci talked with the bartender, Mina leaned against the bar. A tall man approached her. The fingertips of his left hand brushed her lower back and the top of her ass as he caged her in from the side. His handsomeness stole her breath. He had striking features, curly red hair, and deep brown eyes that flashed orange when he caught her scent. Mina relaxed a fraction with the proof that he was not human.

"Hello, gorgeous. What's your name?"

"You're going to pretend that you don't know it already?" Mina asked, tipping her head in Luci's direction. Her husband was suppressing a smile as he watched the bartender put together their drinks.

"I had a suspicion, but I suppose you just confirmed it, Mina." He picked up a strand of her hair and worked it between his fingers, brushing her breast with the back of a knuckle. "Why don't you spend your night with me? See how much fun it can be with the real bad guys."

"Oh yeah?" Mina stepped closer to him, slipping her hand beneath the front of his leather jacket. He wore nothing underneath, and she felt his nipple pebble against the palm of her hand. "I fucked Amamemnon a few nights ago. Do you think you can show me a better time than he did?"

"He's all about fear, whereas I'm all about pleasure. I'll wreck you with it, sweetheart, until it's all that you are and there is nothing left of you but blissful release and ashes."

Mina felt the press of Luci's hand on the swell of her ass. He pulled her toward him, and she stepped away from the redheaded demon.

"At least let us enjoy a drink or two before you start picking up new friends." Luci's breath was hot against her ear as his hand traveled downward, his pinky grazing her inner thigh. He palmed her ass once more before bringing his hand to rest at her lower back. The movement was possessive, and the demon didn't miss it.

"I didn't get your name," Mina said, offering him a smile.

"Achilied." He lifted her hand and pressed a kiss to the back of her palm. Her whole arm lit up with tingles, and her body warmed. She gasped as arousal throbbed in her center.

But as soon as he dropped her hand, the spark he had generated dissipated. Oh. He was an incubus. The humming that remained had been there before the incubus had approached her. It stemmed from the anticipation of the night, the torture of waiting for Luci to touch her, and the enticement of knowing he'd eventually give everything to her.

"Why don't you join us?" Mina asked, nodding to the large booth where Sindy and Bellz sat. Sindy was practically in Bellz' lap, while he ran his finger up and down the length of her hip.

At this rate, it would be a miracle if they left without starting an orgy.

"If I'm the one going into the viper's den, then I would like to bring some reinforcements," Achilied said, his eyes flicking toward Bellz and Sindy.

"The more the merrier." Mina beamed at him.

The incubus stared at her for a moment in shocked silence before returning her smile. He made a small gesture to a plus-sized Black woman with warm brown skin and black hair who sat at a stool at the end of the bar. She rolled her eyes then downed the rest of her scotch before joining them.

She wore a slinky black gown that hugged her pert breasts, round belly, and full hips. The sleek fabric accentuated her graceful movements, each more enticing than the last.

"This is Artemita," Achilied said.

Artemita tapped her foot in response.

"I'm Mina." Mina held out her hand.

Artemita glanced down at it before returning her focus to the incubus. "I hope you at least got Lucifer to agree to pay for our drinks before pulling me into this."

Luci tipped back his head and let out a full-bellied laugh. "Of course we'll pay for the drinks."

"In that case," Artemita took Mina's hand in her own and shook it. "It's such a pleasure to meet you." The look of absolute rapture that Artemita performed made Mina laugh. It seemed so genuine that it looped right back around to feeling fake. A twinkle flashed in her eye that looked suspiciously like fleeting approval. "Another round," she shouted at the bartender, with whom she must have been on friendly terms because he only grinned and nodded in return.

When Artemita draped Mina's arm over her own and led her back to the table, that buzz of supernatural attraction was back. It rivaled what she felt for Luci, except for a tinge of falseness, like an artificial sweetener in a favorite dessert. Artemita was sexy as hell, though, and needed no help, paranormal or otherwise, to attract victims.

"What are you thinking about, human?" Artemita asked, stopping in her tracks. Achilied stopped on the other side of her while Luci continued to the table with four drinks. He hadn't even tried to give Mina her drink, and she suspected that he would be keeping a close eye on anything that she imbibed tonight.

"Yes, what are you thinking?" Achilied asked.

"I was wondering whether Lucifer knew we'd be running into an incubus and a succubus when he picked out this flimsy piece of cloth he calls panties for me to wear tonight. It is proving to be completely inadequate."

The fingertips of Achilied's right hand brushed Mina's lower back, and even through the fabric of her dress, her spine ignited with tingles. He nudged her forward, and they joined the trio at the booth.

Mina scooted into the back with Luci on one side and Achilied on the other. Artemita sat at one end. Sindy and Bellz filled in on the other side of Luci.

"Do you know what a tease that wife of yours is, Lucifer?" Achilied asked.

"She told us that the panties you made her wear are useless," Artemita explained.

"Is that so?" Luci asked, steadily holding Mina's gaze with his own. His tone was as authoritative as one would expect from the Prince of Darkness, but Mina caught a glint in his eye. He'd play a role for Achilied and Artemita, but the larger game was still theirs. Always theirs.

Mina nodded.

"Then why don't you take them off, my love."

"Here?" Mina asked.

"Yes. Here," he over-enunciated as he casually draped an arm over her shoulders.

Mina shrugged, then wiggled around on the seat until she was able to hook the side of her panties with her thumb and pull them down. She used the toe of her boot to lift them within reach and then placed them in the center of the table.

For a moment, nothing happened. Then there was a mad dash for the garment. Bellz moved to make a play for them, but Sindy held him off at the last minute.

Artemita, being about a nanosecond faster than Achilied, won. She pulled the soaked panties to her face and inhaled. With eyes closed in blissful repose, she passed them to Achilied. He sniffed in their general direction, stuffed them into his pocket, and growled.

Once again, Artemita downed her drink in one gulp. "So, who wants to get the fuck out of here?"

Bellz chuckled.

"That's how we were feeling before we even left Mina's place," Sindy said, smiling kindly at the lust demons.

"But we promised her a night out," Luci said. "We're trying to keep her mind occupied."

"There are plenty of things I can do to her in a private place that will keep her too preoccupied for thoughts," Artemita offered.

Achilied tickled the outside of Mina's thigh with a knuckle. "I'm surprised you'd let us anywhere near her, Lucifer." More of his hand found its way to her thigh. He slowly lifted the skirt of her dress, exposing more skin.

"There are protections in place," Lucifer supplied.

"Frankly, I'm fascinated to see how the wards react to your abilities," Beelzebub said. Sindy sat fully in his lap now, her head resting against his shoulder, eyes heavily lidded, as Bellz clearly manipulated her under the table.

Artemita pulled her eyes away from Satan's second-in-command and his lover to look at Mina. "You do know how our powers work, yes? You orgasm, and we devour your life force?"

"I am aware, yes," Mina said. Truthfully, she had made an educated guess based on what existed on incubi and succubi in pop culture and what Achilied had promised her earlier that night.

"And you still want to roll the dice on this?" Achilied asked.

Mina's eyes flickered to Luci's, and she found what she needed there. He would protect her. They would win this game, and she'd get to keep Achilied and Artemita. She found that she liked them both very much already. They'd be powerful allies in a civil war or a war with Heaven. That couldn't be denied. But she thought they'd make pretty good friends as well.

"I am." She bit her bottom lip. "The challenge is to not come. With you two as my opponents, I know I'll have a lot of fun even if I'm losing." She couldn't help but wink.

"Let's finish our drinks and go," Luci said.

Eleven

DAHLIA SAT WITH HER legs draped over Oscar's. They shared popcorn from the bowl sitting in her lap while an old Western movie played on the TV. She had taken a rare day off from work and decided to spend it with Oscar. With Tabitha at school and Sandra volunteering at her church, the couple had the house to themselves. Sandra had promised to pick Tabitha up from school and take her out to dinner and a movie at the mall. That meant they'd be alone at least until the mall closed at ten.

She'd slept in and met Oscar at a nearby bistro for brunch. After a little bit of window shopping at an outdoor shopping center, they'd come back to her place. It was four now. They had six hours left to enjoy each other's company.

Oscar took advantage of the placement of Dahlia' feet and wrapped his large, calloused hands around one. He kneaded the pad of her foot, dragging his thumb along her arch, before working his way around her heel. She had to place the popcorn bowl on the coffee table because otherwise it would have definitely ended up on the floor.

When he had finished with the first foot, he moved to the second. Then he worked his hand under her jeans as much as he could to rub her ankles and calves.

"You know," he said after a few minutes, "this would be easier if you weren't wearing pants."

Dahlia did not hesitate one bit before she slipped the button through the hole and tugged off her jeans. Oscar helped pull them off and continued massaging her lower limbs. As he made his way higher, he slid out from under her legs and placed them flat on the couch. His fingers worked the tight muscles around her butt, hips, and thighs.

Dahlia was so relaxed that she could have easily fallen asleep if not for the way his fingers kept coming tantalizingly close to her vulva, fingers dipping beneath the elastic of her panties only to retreat seconds later.

"You are going to kill me," she purred, arching up to press her lips to his in a searing kiss that he eagerly returned. His shirt landed somewhere behind the couch, hers next to the credenza. She fumbled with his belt buckle then the fastenings on his pants. After managing to kick his jeans down to his thighs while he worked on unclasping her bra, she realized the odd sound she was hearing was a key fitting into a lock.

"Fuck!" Dahlia clasped her bra and reached for her shirt, but it was too far away, and with Oscar's weight on her, she couldn't get closer. "Someone's home."

"Fuck." Oscar realized he was in the way and quickly moved to get off of her, but tripped with his pants around his legs and barely caught himself before smacking face-first into the carpet.

"Oh, god. Are you okay?" Dahlia crouched beside him, running her hand over the back of his head.

"I'm fine," he grunted as he reached out, grabbed her shirt, and handed it to her.

But it was too late.

"Mom?" Tabitha asked from the short hallway between the entranceway and the living room.

Dahlia pressed her shirt to her chest as if it could preserve her modesty. "What are you doing home, sweetie?"

"What are you doing with that man?" Tabitha's backpack thumbed against the floor where she dropped it. "Wait. Is that Oz? Mina's demon friend?"

"Howdy," Oscar said, waving halfheartedly. His pants were still around his legs, and he seemed at a loss about what to do about it.

Dahlia pulled her shirt over her head as she stood up and walked over to her daughter. She grabbed her hand and steered her into the kitchen.

"I'm sorry," she said. "I didn't think you were coming home before your date with Grandma."

"And that excuses you running around with some guy—*a demon*—behind my back?" Tabitha crossed her arms over her chest.

"I'm your mother. I don't need your permission to date, and I'm sure as hell not going to tell you about a guy I'm dating before I've made my mind up about him."

"But you'll fool around with him?"

"I—well, it's part of the process."

Tabitha gave her mother a look.

"Don't you dare judge me, young lady."

"You're being safe, aren't you?"

"Tabitha! Of course. I'm more than aware of the consequences of unprotected sex." Dahlia gave her daughter a pointed look.

But then Tabitha surprised her mother entirely by devolving into a pile of giggles.

"What's so funny?"

"Our whole conversation. This sitch. My entire afternoon has been completely ridiculous." Tabitha sat down at the small breakfast table. "Grandma stood me up. I was so sure that she had to be coming that I waited at school too long and missed the public transit bus."

"Why didn't you call me?"

"You had planned for a full day off. You never do that. I wanted to let you enjoy it."

"And Grandma wasn't answering her phone?"

"Nope. Straight to voicemail."

"Aunt Mina?"

"I heard from Sindy yesterday that they were planning something special for her and that she'd be unavailable unless there was an emergency."

"Oh, yeah. I got that text too."

"And I figured if I could get home on my own, it wasn't an emergency. I just had to wait around for the next bus. It wasn't a big deal. I got my homework done already, so free weekend."

"Not if we have to find your Grandma."

"You're going to need pants to do that," Tabitha said.

"Shit." Dahlia turned to head back to the living room, but Tabitha stopped her.

"Do you like him, Mom?"

"I do." Dahlia sighed, closing her eyes briefly. "I was trying to protect you. If he breaks my heart, I didn't want yours to get broken too."

"If he breaks your heart, I'm pretty sure Uncle Luci will rip his out."

Twelve

ARTEMITA'S STRONG ARM BANDED around Mina's middle. Her legs twined with Mina's, holding them open so her incubus counterpart had full access. He knelt between Mina's legs, his tongue pressed against her clit, three fingers pumping away inside her.

Bellz stood awkwardly by the door, arms crossed and a scowl plastered to his face. But Mina could see the bulge pressing against the front of his black jeans.

Sindy sat in Luci's lap in the chair by the window. The placement of his hands was respectful—one on her forearm, the other on a shoulder. They both sat forward, in no way hiding their interest.

Even though Artemita and Achilied had followed in their pickup truck, the drive over had been tense. No one had said much at first. Then Sindy pleaded with Mina to be careful, and Bellz vowed not to leave her side.

Luci, though, had just smiled at her and said, "They have no idea what they are getting themselves into."

Now, Mina arched her back, and Artemita strained to hold her in place. She was right at the edge, her orgasm just out of reach. Achilied pressed his pinky against her anus, and she braced for her pleasure to crash over her in a wave of deadly ecstasy. But nothing happened. It heightened and tightened but failed to snap in release.

Artemita made a frustrated sound in the bottom of her throat that made Mina ache as she tweaked Mina's nipples with her free hand. The succubus traced a path up to Mina's neck, where she grabbed hold and tipped Mina's head back, capturing her mouth in a heated kiss.

Achilied refused to give up, only sharing a very brief glance with Artemita. He teased Mina's sensitive bud between his teeth before pulling it into his mouth and sucking.

Mina was right on the edge again, toes curling, body shaking, but she just couldn't get over the last hurdle.

"If this is your protection, Luci," Mina said, "it might kill me."

Luci chuckled.

After yet another inadvertent edging, Mina tapped Achilied on the top of his head. "Stop. Please."

He growled at her. "I want your orgasm."

"Yes. Me too, but this," she gestured at the three of them on her bed, "is not working."

Artemita dropped her arm. "What do you have in mind?"

"Move, please, Achilied," Mina requested. She flipped over and moved down the bed, burying her head between Artemita's thighs. After caressing Artemita's outer labia, she pulled them apart to reveal her clitoris and flowing inner lips. There wasn't a single part of this demoness that wasn't beautiful, and Mina would happily spend the rest of the evening returning the pleasure that this succubus and her incubus partner had given her.

Mina took her time, utilizing her fingers and mouth to read Artemita's reactions before focusing on the spots that got the biggest responses. Artemita cursed and tore the bedsheets with her perfectly manicured fingernails when Mina brought her to climax.

While Artemita recovered, Mina turned her attention to Achilied. She got off the bed and pushed him onto it, falling to her knees on the carpet and crawling between his parted knees. His cock glistened with pre-cum, which Mina happily licked up before engulfing him in her mouth and creating more. She teased him only a little before bringing him into her throat and demanding his orgasm as well.

Achilied crawled to Artemita, collapsing into her arms.

"Fuck, Artemita," he spoke into her shoulder. "No one has ever done that for us before."

"We don't usually give them the chance," Artemita said as she pet his back.

Mina bit her bottom lip, perching on the foot of the bed. Seeing them with their guard down, she imagined they were this way with one another regularly. How few people ever saw it?

Achilied reached over and tugged her down to join them, and Mina found herself on her back wedged between the two.

"I would like to return the favor," Artemita said, drawing lazy circles on Mina's stomach with her fingernail.

"Yes, but how do we go about doing that?" Achilied asked.

Lucifer appeared at the edge of the bed, behind the incubus's back. "You ask for help."

Sindy moved on all fours from the bottom of the bed until she hovered over Mina's lower half. "We couldn't send you home without experiencing one of Mina's orgasms. You'd miss out on the best part."

Artemita grabbed Sindy's hips and pulled the redhead against her plush body. "Let's let Lucifer do the honors."

"Bellz, please join us," Mina said, anticipating his frustration at not being included and his eagerness to protect Sindy. But he surprised her by only nodding in her direction and holding his spot by the door.

Luci, however, did join them. At some point he had removed his clothes. Sindy was naked too, so maybe they had both undressed before approaching the bed, but Mina couldn't be sure. She had been distracted.

"Achilied, Sindy, please hold her down for me," Luci said as his hands found her hips and tugged her down the bed. She spread herself around him willingly. Waiting for him to fill her was agony.

He tapped the head of his penis against her clit, then pulled back and slapped her cunt with the palm of his hand. She cursed.

"Do you like that, my little slut human?" The edge of his mouth quirked up.

"You know I do."

Achilied bent over Mina's torso and brought his teeth down on her erect nipple. And then he was kissing the pain away as Luci lined his engorged member with her slick heat. He swept through her wetness only once before burying himself in her with one quick thrust.

Had she not been edged multiple times and teased before that, Mina would have been embarrassed by how quickly she clamped down on her demon husband's cock. If it hadn't felt so fucking fantastic, like her very atoms burning into stars, it still might have been. Luci obliterated the very thought of it by immediately following her over her pleasure cliff.

"What the fuck was that?" Artemita demanded.

When Mina finally opened her eyes, she saw that each demon glowed. Bellz had joined them on the bed, and, even though the king-size bed was entirely too small, they had all managed to find a way to wedge in close together, basking in the quite-literal afterglow.

"We should play around with edging more often," Luci whispered against her shoulder. He had wrapped himself around her. The others squeezed in around them, limbs hanging haphazardly off all edges of the mattress.

As much as Mina loved the orgies, there was nothing quite as satisfying as a demon snuggle party. There was safety in being surrounded by what so many would call the root of all evil. But they weren't evil. They were as flawed and miraculous as the rest of creation.

In a failed attempt to suppress a giggle, Artemita lifted her hands to her face. Her elbow ended up in Sindy's boob. To keep Sindy from toppling off the bed, Achilied reached out and steadied her with his arm. A tense silence descended as everyone waited to see how Beelzebub would react. Everyone, that is, except for Sindy, who burst into her own fit of giggles.

And then they all erupted into laughter like they were in the final scene of an eighties cartoon. Somehow, through all of it, no one tumbled to the floor. Not until Mina's cell phone began to vibrate incessantly inside her purse. She'd plopped it down on the bedside table and promptly forgotten about it.

Sindy startled, screeching, and Bellz dove at her, catching her in his arms and rolling underneath her in time to break her fall. With a loud thump, they both ended up on the floor.

Mina had barely wiggled over to the side of the bed to check on them before Sindy popped up and snatched Mina's phone from her purse. She thrust it into Mina's hands.

"You have to check your phone," Sindy said. "I told everyone you wouldn't be available tonight. If they are calling, there's a good reason."

Mina glanced down and saw that she had a missed call from her sister. It lit up again in her hand; her sister's annoyed face, a milk mustache adorning her upper lip, filled the screen.

"Hello?" She held the phone to her ear.

"Mina, sorry to interrupt your big night, but I need you to come to Mom's church."

"What's going on?"

"She never picked up Tabitha from school."

"Wait. What? Is Tabitha okay? Why didn't she call me?"

"She got home just fine. She took a bus."

"Okay," Mina said. "Is Mom at church? Is she okay?"

"She's physically fine, but mentally and emotionally not so much. She isn't making a lot of sense, but she's asking for you."

"I'll be right there."

When Mina turned around, Luci held out a pair of her jeans which she scooped up and hopped into.

"I'm coming with you," he said as she pulled a t-shirt from her dresser.

"Of course you're coming with me," Mina replied.

"Sindy, Bellz, stay here," Luci commanded.

"Artemita, Achilied, please stay, too. If you want," Mina said. She leaned over the bed to give them each a kiss on the cheek. "I'd love to get to know you both more, but I also understand if you don't want to wait around."

"As if we wouldn't wait around for you forever," Achilied said.

"Please, speak for yourself. Some of us have lives," Artemita said, but she winked at Mina.

Luci snatched up Mina's phone and purse, stuffing the former into the latter as he herded her out the bedroom door. Her flip flops were by the entrance, and she slipped them on while she snagged her keys off the entryway table.

"You're not dressed," she said as she turned to Luci. But of course she found that he was, in fact, dressed. "When did you do that?"

"Demon, remember?" he reminded her.

When they were both sitting in her car, she asked, "Could you have done that for me? Why did I bother hopping around like a fool in front of everyone?"

"Because we were all enjoying the show too much to stop you."

Mina inhaled sharply, then blew out her breath through her mouth slowly. "I have to get to my mom. I cannot go back inside and fuck a bunch of demons. I have to get to my mom. I cannot go back inside and fuck a bunch of demons." She repeated her mantra to herself as she backed out of her small driveway.

As she pulled out onto the street she mumbled, "Damn you, Lucifer."

He chuckled and patted her knee.

Thirteen

D AHLIA HADN'T EVEN PUT the car in park before Tabitha had unbuckled her seatbelt and ripped the car door open. The heels of her sneakers almost reached her butt as she ran across the parking lot to the glass doors of the sanctuary, one half of an office building the congregation had cheaply converted into a place of worship.

Dahlia had locked the car and dashed after her daughter.

The church claimed both ends of the u-shaped structure, connected by a concrete courtyard. The half with the sanctuary contained bathrooms, a small conference room, and the mother's room, which had been set up with a one-way mirror so caregivers could watch a sermon with a crying baby or while nursing privately. Across the courtyard, there was a communal space for potlucks, rooms for Sunday school, another set of bathrooms, and offices.

The relief she'd felt finding her mother's car in the church parking lot had dissipated with every room Dahlia checked and found empty. As she crossed the courtyard for the second time, she stumbled into Tabitha, and they engaged in an accidental staring contest.

"She has to be here," Dahlia said, breaking their silence.

"Her car is in the parking lot," Tabitha said.

"Did you look in the mother's room?" Dahlia asked.

At the same time, Tabitha asked. "Did you look in that weird room behind the mirror?"

"No!" they said in unison, practically tripping over themselves to get to the room.

And there she was, sitting with the lights off, her feet on the chair next to her, knees to her chest, head down. She rocked back and forth slightly like she had when she had soothed Tabitha as a baby.

"Mom?" Dahlia asked, walking forward and placing her hand on her mother's back.

Sandra jumped in place. "Oh, Dahlia. You scared me."

"Mom, you forgot to get Tabitha. You had us all worried."

"I'm sorry," Sandra had said. "Where is your sister? I need to see her."

"I'll call her," Dahlia had said.

"Yes, I need to make sure she's still with us."

Shaking off the chills from that interaction, Dahlia had stepped out into the hall while Tabitha went in to sit with her grandmother. She had been pacing ever since, first while she waited for her sister to pick up her phone, then while she waited for her to arrive.

The door to the courtyard squeaked loudly. Mina stepped into the sanctuary. She had brought Lucifer. That was probably good. They needed reinforcements.

Still, it was a bit jarring to see Satan himself standing not two feet from the pulpit where the minister gave her weekly sermons, a cross on the wall behind him.

"Where is she?" Mina asked, and rather than answer, Dahlia just opened the door for her.

"Mom?" Mina dashed into the small room and knelt in front of her mother. "Hey, what's going on?"

"Oh, my darling baby!" Sandra said, clutching Mina to her in a tight hug. "I've been so confused."

"What do you mean?"

"It's been happening for years. I know you and your sister have noticed. I get mixed up sometimes when it comes to you. I forget things, right?"

"Like Victor being a serial killer?" Mina asked.

"Ugh, he was, wasn't he?" Sandra said, placing the palm of her hand against the side of her head. "I have so many false memories of you that I sometimes assume the most awful ones can't be real."

"What do you mean false memories?" Lucifer asked. He stood in the doorway, peering into the room over Dahlia's shoulder.

"I have these vivid memories of Mina dying several different ways." Sandra bit her bottom lip. "Drowning is pretty frequent, or suffocation. A bad fever once. Your heart stopped for two minutes exactly, and then you woke up as if nothing had happened. No fever at all."

"Oh. I remember having to get creative for that one," Lucifer said. "I'm sorry, Sandra." He brushed past Dahlia and went to his knees next to his wife, taking his mother-in-law's hand. "This is all my fault."

"It's not your fault, though," Sandra said, her voice full of conviction. "It's God's fault. He did this to our family—repeatedly, for a thousand years. What kind of a monster does that? I know I have always been faithful to Him. I know that in my bones, just like I know how often my daughter has been taken from me. How much I have suffered every time it has happened, even if she's always returned. And He put us in this cycle. Not you."

"We've broken it now, Mommy," Mina said, her voice small. "It's not going to happen again."

"So I just lose you for good this time?" Sandra asked, anger flashing in her eyes. Her jaw tight.

"No," Mina said. "Not if we can help it."

"I'm just so angry." Sandra's eyes brimmed with tears.

Dahlia stepped forward and placed her hand on her mother's shoulder. "We are in this together, Mom, and we aren't going to let anyone, not even God Himself, tear us apart again."

Tabitha caught her eye, and Dahlia read a question in her expression, but she wasn't sure what the question was. They'd need to talk later, but, for now, Tabitha lay her head on her grandmother's shoulder, and Dahlia sighed.

"We have a whole army on our side," Mina said. "One that's growing all the time."

"We'll burn all three realms to the ground if we have to," Lucifer added.

"I mean, I think we would prefer not to do that," Mina said.

"Yes, let's try not to destroy our planet," Tabitha squeaked.

"I meant metaphorically," Lucifer said.

"Yeah, you have to be pretty explicit about that, brother-in-law," Dahlia said. "If The Prince of Hell says something violent, I'm going to take it at face value."

"Why are you just the prince?" Tabitha asked sleepily. "You're the ruler of Hell. Shouldn't you be king or sultan or emperor?"

"I kept my prince title out of respect for Hades."

"Oh, fuck," Mina said, her eyes going wide and unseeing.

"She's having a vision." Lucifer grabbed his wife by her shoulders and eased her into his embrace.

"This!" Sandra shouted, leaping to her feet. "This is what happens to me!"

"It's been happening to Mina this time around too," Lucifer explained. "She gets glimpses of her past lives. We have been trying to mitigate it. It can be damaging if it happens too often or if she remembers too much at once. No wonder you're confused. She shares my soul, more of it now; we think that gives her some protection."

Sandra nodded. "It's like my brain gets split in two, or three, or twelve."

Mina gasped, her eyes wide as she took in her husband's face. Then she scrambled to her knees to face him, cupping his chin in her hand. "You killed him."

Lucifer swallowed.

"You killed Hades."

Fourteen

A LARGE, ORNATELY CARVED desk took up the majority of the space. The only piece of furniture bigger was the chair that sat behind it. Both featured depictions of centaurs, satyrs, and harpies worked into the wood. A reproduction of Cerberus' three heads topped the back of the chair, crowning Hades' head. His hands sat folded atop the desk's smooth surface.

He smiled at Mina when she stepped into the room, but the smile didn't quite reach his eyes.

"What's wrong?" she asked, stopping a foot past the door. Her eyes dipped to the floor, and it was then that she noticed the frightened expressions on the centaurs' faces. Ghoulish wisps of the dead ascended from the feet of the desk, wrapping around horse and goat legs. Mina gulped and pulled her gaze back to Hades.

"I sent for your lover."

"You did?" Mina tried to temper her excitement, but she could see from Hades' tight expression that she had failed.

"He should be here soon." Hades stood, dwarfing the room with his stature. "Please, take a seat." He gestured to the couch that sat before a fireplace full of flames that burned blue and white around seemingly untouched logs.

After she had settled herself on the comfortable cushions, he handed her a cup of warm tea then draped a soft blanket around her shoulders.

"Hades," Lucifer's voice filled the room. "Where is she?"

Mina's heart soared at her lover's sudden appearance.

"Lucifer," Hades said, holding out a glass for him. "Welcome. Your paramour is right here."

Luci ignored the offered glass and fell to his knees before Mina. He brushed her hair from her face, then ran his hands over the lengths of her arms and legs, checking for injuries.

"I'm unharmed," Mina said, the blanket slipping from her arms as she reached up to cup her lover's face in her hands.

"I just needed time with her, alone," Hades said from his spot near the fireplace.

Luci whirled, coming to his feet and placing himself between Mina and her captor. "You better not have touched her."

"You're more than happy to share her with others." Hades' voice dropped.

"With my loved ones," Luci growled. "And only when she agrees."

Mina shushed her demon, touching the back of his hand with her fingertips. "I'm alright. Hades never made me feel uncomfortable." She chose to wait until later to tell him about sitting on the god's lap in his throne room.

"You may think that she belongs to you, Lucifer, but at least a part of her was mine first."

"Excuse me?" Mina asked.

"The being you refer to as God destroyed my kind. He had been such a gentle soul, before his punishment. But a crow repeatedly eating out your innards will do that to a person, I suppose."

"What are you talking about?" Lucifer asked. "God created everything. Who could be powerful enough to punish Him?"

"No, sweet child. God did not create everything. He only helped to create humanity, then gave it fire."

Mina gasped. "With his brother."

"Indeed. After the gods, my brothers and sisters, eliminated the more troublesome Titans, they grew angry at humans, tossed them from their safe haven. And your god stole them flame. When Zeus found out, he went into a rage. Your god's brother sacrificed himself in a last-ditch effort to save him, but failed.

"God's fate was sealed. For a time. But it seems that Epimetheus' plan had some delayed success after all, and God was freed. But He was no longer who He had once been. And He set out to destroy us all.

"He came for me last, but it became obvious to Him as it had become obvious to others before Him: you cannot rule the domains above while maintaining control of the domains below. They are antithetical and will tear anyone apart. No matter how powerful.

"He needed me, and the only way to control me was through my love. He told me He would keep her alive for as long as I did His bidding. My underworld was transformed into the torture palace you were symbolically left in charge of, Lucifer. But I hold the reins still. This is my realm."

"What do you want?" Lucifer asked. He pulled Mina to her feet and pushed her behind him.

"I want you to kill me, sweet Lucifer."

"What?" Mina pressed into Luci's back. "You can't be serious!"

"He told me He would keep her alive." Hades took a step toward them. Then another. His body trembled with each step, and when he stood right before them, he fell to his knees. "But he lied."

Mina dropped in front of him, and a moment later Luci followed. She reached out for Hades. Hades intertwined their fingers as Luci placed his hand on the god's shoulder.

"I see her in you, Mina." Hades' eyes glowed brighter. "You have a tiny bit of her soul. Large enough, though, for me to be sure that she's gone. Scattered through the universe, a part of an untold number."

Luci's focus shot to Mina, and she read the fear in his eyes. This could one day be their fate as well. To be ripped from one another. Lied to. Manipulated.

"I would be scattered too. It's the only chance I'll have of being reunited with her. In some form."

"How is it possible to kill a god?" Mina asked.

"Lucifer was created by a Titan. He can do it," Hades said. "You'll have to do it, Lucifer, if you wish to obtain my power and remake this realm as you see fit."

"Enough power to fight Him?" Luci asked.

"With the right allies, perhaps."

"Would you like one more good night first?" Mina asked.

"I don't think I'm deserving of that," Hades said, bowing his head. "But I'm not noble enough to turn down the offer, either."

Lucifer nodded to Mina, and her heart warmed at how well he knew her already. He understood the wheels turning in her mind. What she needed to be okay with being party to this decision to end a god.

Mina straightened her back, bringing herself level with Hades as he stooped. She leaned forward and pressed her lips to his. His arm came around her waist and pulled her into his embrace.

Luci pressed behind her, brushing aside her auburn hair and peppering kisses along the nape of her neck.

The three of them slid the rest of the way to the floor, abandoning clothing as they went, Hades and Lucifer, keeping Mina between them the whole time. The two worked her over, bringing her to the brink of passion several times before letting her spill over.

They entered her together, driving into her warmth in a controlled rhythm. Their pleasure building as one, before it fractured into a billion points of bliss.

Mina's fingertips danced along Hades' perfect blue skin. Tears pricked at her eyes as Lucifer rubbed her back in gentle circles.

"Are you sure about this, Hades?" she whispered, dropping her head to his chest as he hummed his assent.

"Don't make me wait any longer, Lucifer," Hades said after several moments of silence. He passed Mina into Luci's arms.

"Shh, don't look," Luci said into her hair. He clutched her to him with one arm and reached out with the other. She felt the heat of his power against her back and heard Hades' deep voice break as it had in pleasure.

And then nothing. It was over. Hades was gone. Disintegrated into blue specks that drifted into Lucifer. What lingered of his soul enveloped the two before dissipating, only a small bit lingering, molding itself to Luci along with Hades' power.

One tiny spec flew into Mina. It made her breath hitch, but then it was as if nothing had happened at all.

"How do you feel?" Mina asked.

Luci's eyes met Mina's. He cupped her jaw in the palm of his hand.

"Thankful," he said, and then he kissed her.

Fifteen

"WHAT DOES SHE MEAN you killed Hades?" Sandra asked, the back of her knees bumping into the chair behind her as she tried to step back. Dahlia jerked in her mother's direction, but Tabitha was faster, catching and stabilizing her grandmother. "How do you kill a fictional character?"

"Not fictional, Mom," Mina said as Lucifer helped pull her up from the floor.

Dahlia struggled to wrap her mind around all that had happened since arriving at the church.

The sound of the sanctuary door opening interrupted whatever Lucifer was going to say next. They all glanced at each other in silence.

"Maybe we should continue this conversation back at our house," Dahlia suggested. While it wasn't completely out of the ordinary for this many people to be gathered in the mother's room so late in the evening on a weekday—no, it was pretty strange—there would be questions asked, and Dahlia did not have the emotional fortitude to deal with worrying about what someone else *thought* was going on. No way they'd be able to guess the truth.

"It's the youth group leader. I'll distract her while you get him out of here," Sandra said, thrusting her thumb at Lucifer. At his affronted expression, she patted his shoulder reassuringly. "It's not that I don't think you should be here. It's just that if anyone found out that Satan had come to the church to rescue me, there would be a lot of gossip."

"I don't think your youth group leader will know who he is, Mom," Mina said.

"Just to be safe," Sandra said before exiting the small room.

Mina, Tabitha, Dahlia, and Lucifer watched through the one-way mirror as Sandra steered the youth group leader out of the sanctuary and back into the courtyard. Quickly, they piled out of the room and to the back of the building where a set of glass doors emptied into the other end of the parking lot.

Lucifer wrapped his arm around Mina's shoulders and tugged her close as they walked back to their cars.

"You are not driving home, Luci," Mina said.

"Why not?"

"Cops." Mina replied.

"I can make sure they don't notice us." Lucifer pouted at her. *Pouted.* Dahlia tried to muffle her laughter against her sleeve, but failed. Her sister and brother-in-law turned to look at her.

"What?" they asked in unison.

"You both just seem like such a normal couple, but then it occurred to me that your husband torments souls for a living."

"I do not," Lucifer said.

"He doesn't do that anymore," Mina said. "And when he did do it, it was because that was what God had demanded."

"Mina stopped all of that," Lucifer said.

Sandra had walked up at some point and was near enough to hear them. "Of course my Mina did. She's doing the Lord's work."

"Gah, I'm sorry. I was trying to pay you a compliment, not put you on the defensive. Let's finish this at home," Dahlia said, herding Tabitha toward the car.

"Can I drive with Grandma?" Tabitha asked.

"Of course, my love," Dahlia said.

They'd settled into the dining room. Sandra and Tabitha had put out a tray of cookies, baked from the tub of cookie dough Sandra always kept handy in the refrigerator, as soon as they got home. Their scent filled both the house and Dahlia with warmth and comfort.

"What did you mean when you said Hades isn't a fictional character?" Sandra asked.

"He was real. I think a lot of the ancient gods were," Lucifer said. "From what we've gathered, anyway, based on what Hades told us."

"God and Hades had a deal, but God didn't hold up His end. So Hades asked Luci to kill him, and Hades' power transferred to Luci," Mina added.

"That's what gave me the ability to rework Hell into Mina's vision and reinstate reincarnation. It also allowed me to bring Mina back to you, that first lifetime."

"Which then caused God to come to some truce with us, I guess?" Mina asked.

"Yes," Luci said. "He pulled you into your own cycle. The fact that we'd shared small bits of our souls at the time was the only thing that guaranteed that I could find you. I'm still not sure if He knew about it when we struck the bargain."

"He either knew, and we've been playing into His hands this entire time, or we got very lucky," Mina said.

"Is Jesus real?" Tabitha asked.

"Sure," Lucifer said. "But no one has seen him in a long time."

Mina worried her bottom lip, and Dahlia narrowed her eyes at her. "What are you thinking?" Dahlia asked.

"If what Hades told us is true, then God is actually the Titan Prometheus."

"From that old stop-motion sketch you kids used to watch?" Sandra asked.

"No, Mom," Dahlia said. "From Greek mythology."

"That's a lot to process," Sandra said, snagging another cookie from the platter and systematically dismantling it. Crumbs fell to her saucer at an alarming rate.

"God not being who He says He is is hardly a big surprise," Mina said.

"I will need to do some research, I suppose," Sandra said. Only a small amount of cookie remained intact, and she placed it down delicately on her plate.

"What does this mean for us?" Dahlia asked.

"That we keep doing what we are doing: amassing an army. Just in case."

"Do you think you could recruit some more angels?" Sandra asked. "That Michael is so handsome. He might be a good match for you, Dahlia, if things don't work out between you and that—um, celibacy?" Sandra tucked her lips in and grimaced.

"It's okay, Grandma," Tabitha said. "I know about Mom and Oz."

"You do?" Sandra asked.

"You are with Oz?" Lucifer asked, his brow scrunching up in confusion.

"They hit it off at our reception," Mina said.

"That was not your reception," Sandra interjected. "We are still going to throw a big party for you two, just as soon as everything settles down." Sandra turned her attention back to her granddaughter. "Now how did you find out about your mother's dating life?"

"I walked in on them this afternoon," Tabitha said.

"Oh." Sandra's cheeks flushed. "I suppose that was my fault. I apologize."

"Speaking of, I think he's waiting for me," Dahlia said. "I should go check on him. Tabitha, will you be okay getting something to eat and heading straight to bed? It's almost bedtime."

Sandra cleared her throat. "I've got her."

"Oz waited around for you?" Lucifer asked, looking even more perplexed.

"Is that odd?" Dahlia asked.

"Yes," Lucifer said. "How long did he stick around after you, um, first met him, Mina?"

"A matter of minutes, I think," Mina said. "But he wasn't dating me."

"He's dating your sister." Lucifer stood up from the table, bracing his arms on the wood surface. "I think I should go have a chat with him first."

"Wait," Dahlia said, flinging herself from the table in pursuit. Mina followed.

Lucifer stopped at the foot of the stairs and turned toward her.

"Are you trying to protect me?" Dahlia asked. "Is that what this is?"

"Of course," Lucifer said, standing up a little straighter. "You're family."

"Well, thank you for the gesture and the sentiment, but I've got it handled," Dahlia said, placing her hand on his shoulder. It was the first time she had ever touched her brother–in–law, and she felt a spark shoot up her elbow. It tingled a bit, almost to the point of stinging before dissipating. "What was that?"

"I'm not sure," Lucifer said, "Nothing bad. Probably just a bit of my power recognizing your connection to my wife."

Mina smiled at him and held out her hand. "Come on, husband. Let's finish reassuring my mother and then get home. Maybe our friends will still be there."

The expression on Lucifer's face was alarming, predatory and full of challenge. Dahlia absolutely did not want to know, so she hurried upstairs.

Oscar was reclining on her bed with the light on, but he had placed his hat over his face to block out the light.

"Why didn't you turn out the light?" Dahlia asked as she crossed to the bed.

He moaned in response, and Dahlia thought he was asleep until he said, "I didn't want to surprise you was all." He lowered his hat, placing it on his flat belly.

Dahlia smiled shyly, leaned over, and kissed his stubbled cheek. "Thanks for staying."

"Anything for you, darlin'."

"I had to stop Lucifer from coming up here and interrogating you—or worse. I succeeded for tonight, but I'm not sure how long he'll stay away."

"I can wrangle him," Oscar said.

"Do you prefer Oz?" Dahlia asked, depressing a spot on the end of the mattress, the heat of him warming her from knee to hip.

"I like it when *you* call me Oscar."

"I like it when you call me darling." Dahlia grabbed his cowboy hat and put it on her head then popped up on both hands so she could swing one leg over him, straddling him between her thick thighs.

She dipped her chin and fluttered her eyelashes, but the too-large hat slid down, the brim bonking her in the nose. He chuckled and tipped it back, finding her blue eyes with his brown. His hands settled against her hips.

"Everything work out okay with your mom?"

"Well, we found her."

"I reckoned." His thumbs tickled her sides in tiny circles, slowly lifting the fabric of her shirt and working their way beneath it.

"She's been reliving memories from previous lives, but she didn't realize that's what was happening until the whole Lucifer/Mina thing came to light."

"Oh." Oscar frowned. More of each hand slipped under her top.

"She's always been a religious woman, so I think she's struggling with some pretty complicated emotions. It's good to know why she's been so distant and aloof lately, but I wish she had come to us sooner." Dahlia traced the lines of Oscar's flannel shirt.

"Do you remember any of your past lives?"

"No," Dahlia said as she dipped her finger beneath the seam between two buttons, teasing a bit of chest hair.

"Do you think it's always been me?"

"I'm pretty sure Tabitha's father has never been a demon."

"But I wouldn't have been a demon in your last lifetime. I'm relatively new to it."

Dahlia undid one button then another. "Mina told me we cycle once every hundred years. So if it had always been you, you would have had to have impregnated me before you became a demon."

"Hm." He stared at her, blinking a few times. "Well, I'll be."

"What?" Dahlia unbuttoned more of his shirt.

"I think I remember you."

"What was I like?" She spread the shirt wide and pulled it down his arms.

"Shy, but deeply funny once I got you to open up to me a bit. Pretty much like you were when I met you in this lifetime."

"Uh-huh," Dahlia said. "I'm cracking jokes all the time." She rolled her eyes then smirked at him.

"You aren't like jester funny. It's subtle. You always hit me with it when my guard is down," Oscar said. "Darlin', I love that about you."

"So you've impregnated me twice."

"I can't know for sure that I impregnated you the first time. If I did, it happened right before I left for the war, but I never heard from you while I was gone. And when I got back, I was preoccupied with my sister."

"And getting yourself demonized." Dahlia scrunched her face. "That word already exists, huh?"

"It surely does."

Her cheeks burned with the force of her grin. This demon of hers was beyond adorable. She hadn't realized just how much she missed him as a person. Not just an extra set of hands or a shoulder to cry on when it all became too much. But him. The way he talked, the way he felt against her.

Actually seeing him with her own two eyes, watching him move—so unlike before, when she could only feel him—was just the cherry on top. Damn, was he sexy. She wanted to explore every inch of him with her hands, her tongue, until even if he left her again, he would be permanently imprinted in her mind.

Leaning forward, she pressed her lips to his neck. The cowboy hat bumped into Oscar's forehead and he laughed as he whipped it off and tossed it aside.

"Maybe we can ask Lucifer," Dahlia said between kisses. She wiggled down his body, stopping to lick at his nipples, before continuing downward.

"Should I bring it up when he corners me?" Oscar asked.

"Mm." Dahlia dipped her tongue into his belly button, and he shivered beneath her. "No. You might tip him off, and I don't want Mina and Tabitha learning about Tabitha's parentage from anyone other than us."

"Us?" Oscar asked, his voice strung tight with alertness.

"I think so," Dahlia said. "Our daughter deserves to know. She's old enough to make her own decision about you."

"Have *you* made a decision about me?"

"I'll let you know when I'm done tasting you," she said as she unfastened his pants. He helped her remove the rest of his clothing but let her remain in control—control she used to torment him, teasing him with soft caresses of her lips on his thighs, his shins, the arches of his feet.

His soft, curling body hair tickled with each pass. When she came to the base of his cock, she lapped at him until he was straining against the sheets, and a trapped growl escaped from his throat.

Then she swallowed him, letting his tip poke at her gag reflex.

"Darlin', please. I'm gonna—" His orgasm cut him off as Dahlia pushed down on him, taking him into her throat. A thrill of pride shot through her that she could so easily slip past his defenses.

She felt powerful in a way she never had before, at least not in the bedroom. After savoring his salty flavor, she swallowed his load and looked up at him. His head was resting against her pillows, eyelids half closed.

"I appreciate the attempt on my life, and by such sweet means, but it will take more than that to do me in," Oscar mumbled.

"You better live," she said as she crawled up the bed to lie beside him.

"My turn." He tugged her to his chest, eyes darting down the length of her body. "You're fully dressed," he grumbled then rolled them over and pressed her into the bed.

"I don't have to be."

He was not as patient with her as she had been with him. Her clothes were gone so quickly that she couldn't be sure they were all still in one piece, but, honestly, she didn't really care. Because his skin was on hers, hot as a sunny summer day. His sideburns tickled her cheek before he dipped down to kiss her.

She tried to wrap her legs around his waist, but he stopped her. "I want to taste you, too." He pushed her legs up and back, pinning her knees to the bed, and moved down her body. "Let me be your wicked demon, have my evil way with you."

"Oscar." Dahlia's giggle was cut off by a moan as he brought his lips around her clit. He alternated between sucking and flicking it with the tip of his tongue, his attention rough yet focused. In about thirty seconds she climaxed, but he didn't let up. Not until she came twice more.

And then he was over her, and sliding into her, and she was coming again around his cock, in awe of this multi-orgasmic state he alone could concoct. He had a talent for pulling them from her one after another, leaving her a mindless puddle, begging for more. For the permission to just live in this moment.

When he fell apart inside her, she came one last time. For a beat after, every thought or worry melted away. He tumbled off of her, and when she rolled onto her side, he cupped her with his form.

"I've got you, darlin'," he whispered into the shell of her ear, and she realized she was crying.

"I'm okay," she said, turning into his arms and burying her face against his chest. "That was just very intense."

"You seemed like you had a stressful day. I was trying to help."

"You did help." She gripped his hip in her hand, squeezing lightly. His unexpected giggle filled her heart with light.

Oscar wiggled out of her grasp, turning onto his back.

"I love that you're ticklish," Dahlia said, rolling on top of him and using her weight to hold him down. "My new, not-so-secret weapon." Her hand hovered over his hip.

"Please don't. I'll give you anything you desire."

"Fine." She went limp, and he gathered her against him, his fingers burying themselves into her hair to massage against her scalp.

"Joke's on you," he said before a deep inhale and a satisfied murmur. Was he sniffing her hair? "I was planning to give you everything anyway."

"Such a charmer."

He verbalized his agreement with a soft hum. They lay in comfortable silence for a little while, the buzz of the overhead fan the only sound.

"Oh, I need to pee!" Dahlia shot out of bed.

"Good to know?"

"To prevent UTIs," Dahlia said, tugging on pajamas as she made her way to the door. "I'll be right back." She darted into the Jack-and-Jill bathroom she shared with Tabitha. Tabitha's light was off. That was good. She was hopefully asleep. It had gotten late.

As she washed her hands, she smiled at her reflection in the mirror. He had stayed. Crisis had arisen, and when she'd rejected his offer to join them, he had offered to wait. Even though she had told him he didn't need to, he had anyway.

Flicking off the light, she closed the door behind her and joined Oscar on the bed, reclaiming her spot halfway on top of him. He tucked his arms around her.

"We have to be quiet," Dahlia said softly. "Tabitha is sleeping. I think."

"Can we," he said, stopping for a moment as if to gather his courage, "can we sneak into her room and watch her sleep?"

Dahlia muffled her laughter against him. "She's almost a teenager. I think at this point it's just an invasion of her privacy."

"Damn. I missed my window."

"If it's any consolation, we sleep the exact same way. If you stay the night, you'll be treated to me sprawling all over the bed, whether you are in it or not. When Tabitha and I fall asleep together, we wake up all tangled like we were playing Twister in our sleep."

"I'd love to see that."

"It's kind of a hazard now. I'm getting too old."

"Well, if you wake up in the morning all wound up with me, I'll unfurl you slowly and massage away any aches."

Dahlia's heart beat a little faster, her core aching a little. She lifted up and kissed him. Lazily, their lips came together, mouths opening to receive the other. There was no hurry or urgency. Just a gentle exploration that ended too soon as exhaustion overcame Dahlia and her arm gave out.

"I was thinking," he said as he nuzzled into her hair. "Maybe I could talk to your mom."

"About what?" Her surprise sharpened her tone, and she winced at how harsh she sounded.

"About the whole losing-her-religion thing."

"Oh?" she prompted with a lightness in her voice she hoped made up for any negativity he may have incorrectly perceived.

"I don't know if I told you that my mom was Mexican. My father always said it was love at first sight. He converted to Catholicism so that her mother would approve the match, and he went to church with her every Sunday, even though, as he later confessed to me, he still considered himself an atheist.

"He loved her enough that he would have attempted to believe in anything, even some old guy in the sky and a bunch of saints. But I believed. All of it. Probably part of why I thought it possible to reach out to my sister after she had passed. And then everything went to Hell, literally."

"I'm sorry," she whispered.

"I got to meet you." He swallowed. "Got to fall in love with you. Be the sperm donor for your beautiful daughter. It was worth it. Fuck, just to have this moment right now, it was all worth it."

She breathed his name against his skin. "I'm in love with you, too. Somehow, still."

"You want me to sleep over?"

"Mhm, I thought we could go get brunch with Tabitha. Tell her the truth."

"I'd like that. A lot." He pressed a kiss to the top of her head. "Thank you for trusting me."

"She told me that Lucifer would kick your ass if you broke my heart."

"Would he really?"

"I honestly don't know, but I'm pretty sure he'd gut you for breaking hers." Dahlia shook her head. "They have a strong bond for having known each other for such a short amount of time."

"Oh." The sadness in that one word broke her heart.

"I'm sorry, Oscar. I shouldn't have told you."

"No." He rubbed small circles up and down her back, reassuringly. "I'm glad you told me. I promise not to murder him for being a father figure to my daughter. It's not his fault I haven't been in the picture."

He could say that, but she could tell that he was vibrating with anger. "It wasn't your fault either, Oscar."

"Of course it was. I let myself get played by that fucker. Again."

"Who?"

"The original Zozo. I don't know his real name. He never told me. Surprise surprise."

Dahlia sat up so she could see Oscar's face. "Maybe we can find him. It's his fault. Not yours. He ripped our family apart."

"What would we do if we found him?"

"We could murder him."

"Demons are tricky to kill, even when you're using lethal methods." He winked at her, and she blushed.

"Not if we had help from Satan and his inner circle."

Oscar tilted his head to the side, watching her intently.

"Or we just point my sister in his direct—"

"No!" Oscar cut her off with a shout. "No," he whispered. "Fuck. Sorry. I hope I didn't wake up the whole house." He buried his face against her hair.

Dahlia listened for any noises coming from her daughter's room on the other side of the bathroom or her mother's at the end of the hall. When she didn't hear anything, she placed her hand on Oscar's cheek.

"Hey, it's okay."

"I don't want you or Tabitha anywhere near that guy. And he is completely undeserving of the absolution Mina provides."

"That's fair." She settled against the headboard, and Oscar laid his head in her lap. She couldn't resist playing with his brown locks. "So maybe we just try to live a happy life together as a big 'fuck you' to him."

"Deal."

Sixteen

D AHLIA WOKE SPRAWLED ACROSS Oscar, his arms banded around her waist like he was trying his best to keep her close. She nuzzled into him, prickling her cheek with the stubble on his jaw. Early morning light peeked through the curtains, and the house was quiet.

"You awake, darlin'?" Oscar asked, pressing a kiss to the top of her head.

"Barely." She rubbed her foot against his shin. "Be honest. How many times did I kick you last night?"

"Enough times that I reckon I'll have some bruising, but not enough that I care." He squeezed her ass then gave it a little swat.

"Ouch," she said, but she snuggled in closer.

"Should we get up and make breakfast?" Oscar asked.

"Or," she said, rising up onto her arms and dropping one leg over Oscar's side, "we could distract ourselves for a little bit and have our brunch with our daughter when she wakes up." She adjusted so that her sensitive bits aligned with his and pressed forward. They'd slept in only enough clothing to be presentable in case of an emergency. Oscar wore thin pajama bottoms that hid not a bit of his morning wood, and Dahlia had nothing on under her oversized t-shirt.

"I love that idea, little lady." He gripped the hem of her top and tugged it off.

Lifting up onto her knees, Dahlia yanked his pajamas down just past his butt. She grasped his erection in her hand, spitting on the head and working the saliva down around him. Then she lined him up and sank onto him.

Her senses exploded as she expanded around him. Their gazes met, and the longing she found in his beautiful brown eyes left her speechless. She could give him what he desired without speech, though, so she rocked against him, working more of him into her, until their bodies met.

"Oh, fuck, darlin', you feel so good." He massaged her breast with one hand while his other stayed anchored to her hip, his fingers depressing the plush flesh there.

She watched him take in every detail from her mess of hair to every stretch mark that painted her breasts, belly, and hips. With the sunlight filtering through the window, there was no way to hide any of it. His throat bobbed and his hips jerked upward, and she realized that she didn't want to. She wanted him to see it all.

"Can I take you hard and fast?" she asked, biting her lip.

"Fuck me with your perfect body, Dahlia. Take from me whatever you need."

So she did, riding him with abandon while he played with her tits and tweaked her clit. She came hard, and he held her through it.

Once her brain had made sense of the world again, she opened her eyes to find him staring at her. With a grunt, he flipped over, pulling her with him so he landed on top of her.

"Up for round two?" she asked, hooking the back of her knees and rolling her hips back so she was completely open for him.

He slid into place. "I'm always up for more."

"Then ride me, cowboy." She giggled as the words slipped past her lips. But his eyes twinkled with delight, and he happily obliged until they both collapsed into a pile of post-orgasmic limbs.

By noon, Tabitha was still sleeping, and Oscar and Dahlia were starving. They caved and made a late breakfast. With a plate each of toast, jam, sausage, and scrambled eggs, Oscar and Dahlia sat at the small table in the breakfast nook, holding hands between bites.

"I'm nervous," Dahlia admitted. "Are you nervous?"

His cowboy hat bobbed. "A little, but I'm mostly excited."

"Everything is going to change. I think it will be good change, but I don't have a road map for this. I don't know how tomorrow will be different, exactly, I just know that it will be."

"We can still try to take it slow. We don't have to tell her yet, if you aren't ready."

"I am ready, though. I think that's what scares me the most."

"Come here." He opened his arms to her, and she scooted her chair closer until she could fall into him.

By two in the afternoon, Tabitha was finally awake, but she snuck past them to heat up a microwave burrito before they could stop her. With plans to share breakfast or lunch ruined, they decided they would take Tabitha out for dinner after hitting up the mall to run some errands.

Tabitha needed a new swimsuit and sneakers. Except for the fact that she was unaware that Oscar was her father, it felt like a typical Saturday for any family.

It felt right.

It was nice for all the reasons Dahlia had suspected having a partner would be nice. Having someone else around to make a decision when she just couldn't anymore. Someone to contribute to the conversation and help entertain Tabitha. But it was more than that. It was nice being with Oscar. The vibration of his frequency complemented hers and Tabitha's. Dahlia felt whole, and, based on her megawatt smile, Tabitha did as well.

When they sat down for dinner at a chain restaurant and ordered their burgers, fries, and milkshakes, they were all pleasantly exhausted from the day's activities.

After the waiter brought their food, Dahlia decided it was time to broach the subject of Tabitha's parentage. Their meals would hopefully help cover any awkward silences and give Tabitha an excuse to stop and process while she chewed.

"There's something we want to talk to you about, Tabitha," Dahlia said from where she sat across the table from her daughter, sharing her side of the booth with Oscar, who took the inside so Dahlia could easily move to comfort or reassure Tabitha.

"What's up?" Tabitha asked around a bite of French fry.

"This isn't the first time that Oscar and I have dated," Dahlia said. She had wanted to come right out and say it directly, but she couldn't bring herself to spit out, "Hey, kid. Oscar's your dad." She was afraid of shocking her daughter—and maybe herself. Better to ease into it.

"Okay," Tabitha said, nodding her head like what Dahlia had said was the most obvious thing in the universe.

"You already know." Dahlia's eyes grew wide. Tabitha always did this. She knew things she could not possibly know, and Dahlia didn't have the foggiest idea how.

"Um, yeah." Tabitha smiled, reaching across the table to grab her father's hand. "It took me longer to figure out than it should have, but I knew we were connected somehow, and then when I caught you two together, it finally clicked. Like, bang. Oz is my dad."

"I'm so sorry, Tabitha, that I missed you growing up," Oscar said, turning his hand upside down so he could grasp Tabitha's hand in his own. "I would do anything to go back and change that."

"I wish you could," Tabitha said, shrugging, "but no hard feelings."

Oscar shook his head. "Nope. I don't buy that for a second. What can I do to make it up to you?"

"I mean, I think you're doing it already," Tabitha said. "Don't break my mom's heart again, for starters. And be here like you are now."

"I ain't going nowhere," he snarled, and Tabitha jerked her hand back in surprise.

"Don't scare our daughter," Dahlia said with a smirk. But Tabitha burst into giggles, and Dahlia stopped holding in her own.

When their laughter had abated, Oscar asked, "What should we do to celebrate being a family?"

"Can we go see a movie?" Tabitha asked.

"That's absolutely doable," Dahlia responded.

For the next few minutes, they ate in companionable silence. Every once in a while, Tabitha would hold hands with Oscar or Dahlia, and they couldn't stop smiling at each other. Words meant nothing when they could sit and enjoy being a family for the first time ever.

"Mom?" Tabitha asked as she crumbled up her napkin and put it in her empty burger basket. "Can we keep this between the three of us for a little while?"

"Sure, but can I ask why?"

"I don't know." Tabitha worried her bottom lip. "I like us being in our own little bubble."

"Okay, but not for too long. It wouldn't be fair to keep Aunt Mina and Grandma out of the loop indefinitely."

Tabitha smiled as the waiter dropped off the check. "Do you think I'll have a cousin or two soon?" Oscar scrunched up his face, and Tabitha snorted. "What's that look about, Dad?"

"Residual Catholicism." He ran his hand back through his brown hair. "My mother is turning over in her grave, her son being related to the spawn of Satan."

Dahlia stared her boyfriend down. "My niece or nephew is not going to be some hellspawn," she reprimanded, maybe a little too loudly. A few heads in the restaurant spun in their direction.

"Um, Mom," Tabitha said.

"I know," Dahlia said, dipping her head and blushing. "That was embarrassing."

"What? No. I don't care about them," Tabitha said, then reached out and touched Dahlia's forearm. "I think I'm technically hellspawn."

Dahlia's jaw dropped, and her mouth formed a silent "oh."

"I can't process that, and my dear old ma has had enough grave-spinning for one afternoon."

"Did she not spin right out of it when you *became* a demon?" Dahlia asked.

"Yeah, Dad," Tabitha chimed in.

Oscar's laugh filled the restaurant. "Oh, I could never do anything wrong in her eyes," he said with a rakish smirk, dropping way too much money in the center of the table and grabbing his hat from a hook near the windowsill. "Let's go see that movie, shall we, ladies?"

"She spun right out, didn't she?" Dahlia quipped behind Oscar's back.

"I bet she's still spinning," Tabitha added, looping her arm through her mom's.

From over his shoulder, Oscar said, "Oh, no question."

Seventeen

S IX MONTHS HAD GONE by since Luci and Mina had started trying for a baby—six months, six cramp-filled periods unmitigated by hormonal birth control, and five and a half heartbreaks.

This month, Mina had taken a pregnancy test a mere hour before her period arrived, and she'd grumbled in frustration at having wasted yet another test. It always happened that way. She would pee on a stick, and in the next few hours she'd be bleeding—even when she took longer to cave to the temptation of knowing, that traitorous voice of hope whispering in her ear.

Mina was slowly learning not to imagine what a hypothetical baby's first holiday might be if she were to conceive this month, or how old they would be when Tabitha graduated high school. She tried to no longer become attached to potential names the week after her fertile window or to linger through the rows of sleep 'n plays, onesies, and teethers when she went shopping.

Between all her internet browsing and her OB-GYN, Mina knew it was a little too early to start worrying about infertility.

"A full year of trying is absolutely normal," her doctor had said as Mina removed her feet, bundled up in thick socks to keep her toes from getting cold on the exam-room floor, from the stirrups.

But medical websites knew nothing about what was "normal" when the hopeful father was a demon. For all she knew, his sperm could be destroying her eggs, even if Luci reassured her that wasn't the case. But he'd never gotten anyone pregnant before either. He was just using his creepy ability to know things he couldn't possibly. An important skill for getting random humans to trust you, Mina supposed. Less helpful when trying to convince a human wife that she wasn't destined to only ever be an aunt.

And then came the guilt. She had already been so blessed with the people, demon and human alike, in her life. She had held Tabitha on a daily basis when she was a newborn, helped her back to sleep when she was a toddler. Most aunts weren't lucky enough to have that kind of hands-on experience day in and day out.

She shouldn't be complaining. She shouldn't be sitting on her couch staring at the blank screen of her TV trying to decide if she should watch a Korean drama, continue working on her current commission, or just go to sleep.

Those comic book pages really needed some of her attention. But if she worked on them now, she was sure her current mood would ruin their cheerful tone. Maybe she could start on something new, something just for herself, something to get these rotten emotions out of her system before she saw Luci.

His heart would break for her when he found out, but it would be better if he thought she was taking it in stride.

Before she realized she had made a decision, she found herself upstairs, a blank canvas set up on the easel. The colors seemed to paint themselves as she worked in a trance-like state.

Hours later, Mina stood under the stream of her shower, washing away the pieces of her art that had made it onto her instead of the thick linen of the canvas. A knock to her right frightened her, and she squealed, turning to see Luci's cheerful face through glass speckled with water droplets. His smile faltering a little at her expression, he flicked a glance at the small trash can in the bathroom and nodded when he saw the pink end of a pregnancy test.

"I'm sorry," he said.

"Come join me?" she asked, stepping further into the shower so he would have space. He nodded, opening the shower door and stepping in fully clothed.

Luci tugged her to him. Her head fell to his chest, fitting perfectly right below his shoulder. The water soaked through his black t-shirt and jeans, but Mina didn't mind because the stream hid her tears as well. Even though she knew he wasn't fooled, it meant everything to her that she wouldn't have to worry about staining his top. He had already chosen to do that himself, and in the process given her permission to feel whatever she needed to.

Her hands twisted the back of his shirt, and he pulled her in tighter, brushing her drenched tresses from her forehead, stroking down her naked back.

"It's not you," he half-whispered, speaking loud enough only to be heard above the rush of the shower. "I'll do more research, but know that it isn't you."

All she could do was nod.

He helped her wash and condition her hair before drying her with a towel. Instead of using his powers to dry his clothes, he stripped them off and hung them over the side of the bathtub against the window to dry.

When they were settled in the bed together, Luci asked, "What can I do to help right now?"

"I don't know." Mina sighed. "I think I need to get my mind off of it."

He rolled onto his side and quirked an eyebrow at her, but she shook her head.

"Not that. Not now."

His large hand covered her lower abdomen, his skin warm against her naked flesh, and when he started rubbing in tight circles, a little more tension fled her body. "Is this okay?" he asked.

"Satan, yes."

"We're you addressing me or swearing?"

Brushing a strand of hair from his forehead with her finger-tips, Mina smiled at her husband. "Yes."

Lucifer's fingers wrapped around her hip, and he bent down to kiss her. Their lips brushed in a gentle caress not devoid of heat, but lacking in urgency. A promise of what they would overcome. Of the bliss that was sure to find them once they got through this. Together.

"Do you want to watch overly dramatic television programs and order takeout?" Luci whispered against her cheek.

"That sounds pretty perfect." She nuzzled against him.

"Would you like to do that with me, or would you like me to call your sister?"

"Yes?"

"You want both?" He leaned back to look at her.

"Can we have a giant slumber party? Invite everyone? My sister, mom, and Tabby? Your demons? Kathryn and Michael? Even Artemita and Achilied?" She paused, thinking of the logistics of inviting an incubus and a succubus to the same party her preteen niece would be attending. "The only rule will be no sex."

"I'm not sure we'll all fit in your townhouse, my love. Where will everyone sleep? Besides, you might kill the demons if you forbid sex."

"Luci, if my niece is coming, sex is a no-go."

"There was sex at our wedding reception."

"Okay, there was, but she was asleep in a separate room."

"So no sex while any minors are conscious or in near proximity?"

"Are we really having this discussion?" She narrowed her eyes at him. "Of course not."

Lucifer smirked at her, and she rolled her eyes. He was obviously teasing. He had a very strict code of conduct that mostly boiled down to leaving kids alone. His distraction tactic worked, at least for the moment.

"We could do it in Hell," Mina suggested, pouting.

"Haven't figured out how to invite your humans down there yet," Luci said, scrunching his forehead in thought.

"A lot of them are your humans now, too." She put her head on his shoulder then relished the feeling of his lips against her forehead.

"Only because they were yours first."

Sighing, Mina had to admit that he was right. A pajama party with all of her loved ones would just have to wait. "But you'll stay if I invite over my family and Kathryn?"

"I'll stay with you for as long as you need me."

"I'm obviously going to ask for forever," Mina said. "Does that work for you?"

"You already know it does." He patted her stomach. "Why don't you get dressed? I'll call your sister and see about ordering takeout."

Wearing a black tank top and a pair of plaid pajama bottoms, Mina found a fully clothed Lucifer in the kitchen with his head in the refrigerator. The smell of egg rolls, fried rice, and dumplings permeated the small space. A paper bag, the top folded over and stapled closed, sat on the counter next to the sink.

"What are you doing?"

"Looking for the ketchup."

"For what?"

"The egg rolls."

Mina blinked twice and shook her head. "Gross."

Luci emerged from the fridge with a bright-red bottle and a triumphant grin. "Then I won't ask you to try it."

"Deal," Mina said, rising to her tippy toes to plant a kiss on his cheek. "No luck with my sister?"

"I'm sorry." Luci plopped the ketchup bottle next to the paper bag before pulling Mina into his arms. "Tonight is no good for them, but they want you to come over tomorrow and invite Kathryn too for a much smaller event."

Mina nodded into his chest. "Then just us tonight?"

"Unless you want to invite my side of the family."

"Are they going to want sex, though?"

"Was your niece just an excuse?"

"Yes and no," Mina said. "I meant what I said about that, but also not sure I'm up for a bloody orgy tonight. Maybe in the morning, though."

"Then let's have a quiet night just the two of us and decide tomorrow."

Mina snapped up the bag of food and headed into the living room, turning at the doorway to say, "Don't forget your ketchup."

"Oh, I would never."

"Heathen."

He came up behind her, wrapping an arm around her waist and pulling her against him. "You love me and my heathen ways."

"I really, truly do."

Eighteen

M INA SAT SNUGGLED UP with a fleece blanket and her
knees tucked under her on the couch, a steaming mug of hot chocolate lovingly brewed by her mother
clutched in her hand, some sci-fi B-movie on the TV. Her
sister cuddled around her. Tabitha leaned against the couch
in front of her. Familial bliss. It was just like old times.

Kathryn emerged from the kitchen carrying two more
mugs of hot chocolate. She handed one to Dahlia and the
other to Tabitha. "Extra marshmallows for you two."

Just like old times except for Kathryn, but she fit right
in. Sandra approached with even more hot chocolate and
nudged Kathryn with her elbow. "Sit down and take your
hot cocoa." Sandra moved to the love seat as Kathryn sat
down next to Dahlia. "Mina, how did you find such an
attractive friend?"

Mina gave her mom a look, and Sandra's eyes grew big.

"Oh. I keep forgetting the serial killer is from this
lifetime." Sandra frowned then made eye contact with
Kathryn. "I'm sorry for bringing that up."

"Hey, it's okay," Kathryn said, pulling her feet up and
tucking her oversized sweater around her knees. "I'm doing
interviews about it all the time."

"I really appreciate you taking up all that spotlight, by the way, so I don't get caught up in it."

"You can continue to pay me in hugs per our agreement."

"You're due for another installment, but after we finish our yummy beverages," Mina said. Her tongue darted out to lick a drip of chocolate from the outside of her mug.

"It's also a good way to raise money for my nonprofit," Kathryn said.

"It's really admirable what you're doing," Dahlia said.

"Well, I've always loved attention. What happened to me, well, it wasn't good. But at least I can use it to help those who aren't as lucky as I was, those who might not get the help they need if not for what I'm doing now. On the nights when it gets too hard to breathe, knowing that I can do something for others brings back the air."

"You know you can call me on those nights, right?" Mina said. "Platonic cuddles are always on the table."

"You'd kick out your demon husband for me?"

"He can stay in the guest room."

Kathryn smiled at her. "Well, I maybe have Michael now."

"That hunky angel?" Sandra asked, her screech rivaling the aliens, who resembled small kitchen appliances, invading the small, rural town on the screen.

"Grandma!" Tabitha fell over onto her side in a fit of giggles.

"What? Do people not say that anymore? Hunk? Because he's totally a hunk."

"Grandma," Tabitha grumbled into the rug, kicking her feet.

"What in the world is so funny?" Sandra asked.

"You talking about hot guys, probably," Dahlia said. "She recently did the same thing with me."

"Oh," Mina said, eyes wiggling. "About Oz? How are you two doing?"

Dahlia tried to hide her smile behind her cup but failed. "No complaints."

"You'll dish later?" Mina whispered, and Dahlia gave an almost imperceptible nod of her head.

Tabitha had calmed down and moved over to the love seat with her grandmother. "Can we watch something that's actually good next?"

"What are you talking about, daughter of mine?" Dahlia asked. "This is a classic."

"If it's so great then why have we talked over the entire thing?" Tabitha asked.

"Because we've all seen it so many times," Mina answered.

"I've never seen it," Kathryn said in a soft voice, almost like she was embarrassed to admit she had never seen this absolutely obscure movie that had somehow been deemed a cult classic in the Cadere household and only the Cadere household.

Mina would fill her in later.

They put on a horror movie that they'd never seen before. It was a haunted house movie that Dahlia verified was trigger free for everyone present via a quick internet search. Three kids, the children of a history professor who had been granted the opportunity to study the home of some ancient earl or duke or something, had gotten lost in the sprawling mansion and had just wandered into a round room with mirrors on all the walls. The door closed behind them with a crash. It too was covered by a mirror, and when they rushed to find the door handle, there was none.

Something banged against the floor upstairs toward the back of the house, and they all jumped.

"What was that?" Kathryn asked.

"It's just my closet ghost causing trouble again." Sandra waved it off.

Mina grabbed the remote from the armrest and paused the movie.

"Hey, it was just getting good," Tabitha whined.

"What do you mean by closet ghost?" Mina asked.

"There's a sloped floor in Mom's walk-in. Things fall off her dresser a lot." Dahlia explained.

"Oh, so not an actual ghost, then," Mina said.

"Of course there is an actual ghost," Sandra said. "It opens the door in the middle of the night."

"I'm sure you just don't latch it properly and that wonky floor causes it to open," Dahlia said.

"I've tried to see if it would open on its own if I don't latch it, but it never does," Sandra rebutted.

"Okay, but maybe it needs the vibration of the garage door opening or the dryer going," Dahlia said.

"Both of those things are on the opposite end of the house," Sandra said.

"Stop it, you two," Mina said. "I'm going to go check it out." She stood up.

"Do you want me to come with you?" Kathryn asked.

"Absolutely not," Mina said. "Just in case it's not a sloping floor or a ghost."

"Should I call Lucifer?" Dahlia asked.

"Nah. I think I can handle this on my own."

Mina found her mother's room in immaculate condition, unsurprisingly. The bed was perfectly made and piled with decorative pillows. Beauty products and knickknacks were lined up along the vanity arranged by size. Every item was placed in an aesthetically pleasing way that Mina never could replicate.

The closet door, however, stood open.

Mina took a fortifying breath and flipped on the light. Everything looked in order except for a dresser drawer that sat askew.

Her bare feet sank into the carpeted floor. It was warmer than the hardwoods in the rest of the house.

The drawer was stuck, so she yanked on it to get it loose before setting it back in its tracks and closing it. She wiggled it a bit to see if it would fall off, but it felt sturdy. How it had slipped out remained a mystery.

It also wasn't likely the cause of that loud sound. Mina turned in a circle, but nothing else seemed out of sorts. Maybe they had been mistaken, and the sound had come from somewhere else upstairs. Mina decided to check the bathroom next.

But the closet door was gone. In its place, only a rough, rocky wall.

"The fuck?" Clearly whatever had taken residence in her mother's closet, because something very fucking much had, was definitely supernatural.

"Now, who are you?" a feminine voice asked with a thick accent Mina couldn't place. A short woman stepped next to Mina and examined her closely, lifting her hair from her shoulders and sniffing. "Sandra's daughter, is it?"

Mina caught a glimpse of the woman's brown hair and eyes and her flawless skin, but as soon as Mina looked away, anything more descriptive slipped from grasp. Definitely a demon, then.

"Oh, I'm much older than that, my dear."

Mina was sure she hadn't said anything aloud.

"You didn't." The being circled Mina, stopping in front of her again. "I could smell it on you. Your thoughts." She tilted her head to one side. "Your despair. It's bittersweet, like chocolate. A delicious dessert after the hearty meal I've been getting from your mother. Her angst and uncertainty is truly delicious, but it's becoming a little one-note, and, if I'm honest, not as satisfying these last few months."

Through the whole speech, Mina couldn't move. Not a twitch of muscle responded, despite her urgings. But when the demon stopped talking, the hold on Mina's mouth slipped. "How long have you been here?"

"Since shortly after she lost her husband. It's rare to find a single human who can sustain me. A pity my time with her is coming to an end."

"What does that mean?"

"Oh, just that it's time to move on, but first I think I'll have my dessert." The woman leaned forward and gathered Mina's hair, piling it on top of her head. She used a pair of small wooden dowels to hold it in place then stepped back.

Something warm and slimy wrapped itself around Mina's head, covering her mouth. It slithered across her lips then wrapped around the back of her neck before looping around her throat in a threatening manner. But it didn't tighten. It only held her, and she relaxed into it the same way she would if it were Luci's, Lilith's, or Bellz' hand.

Glancing down, Mina could just get a glimpse of a pink limb covered in darker ridges, and something pulled at her cheeks and the back of her neck.

She felt more pressure around her middle, but her tank top kept her from feeling anything definitive about what was holding her. Even though she had a theory, she was not about to voice it yet. Not even to herself.

"I don't usually kill my victims, you know," the creature said, her voice coming from behind. "Oh, no. It makes much more sense to just drink in their self-made torment day in and day out. Why destroy a renewable food source?"

Mina focused on the word "usually." Was this being planning to make an exception to her no-killing rule? She could only hope her protection against demons would be enough to save her life from something *much older*.

"Don't worry. I'm not planning to harm you." The woman stood in front of Mina once more. "I could, I think. The wards they've placed on you are," she paused, "intense, but, given time, I could absolutely get through them."

The creature hooked her fingers into the sides of Mina's pajama bottoms and underwear. With a forceful tug, she divested Mina of most of her clothing.

At the same time, two more limbs, covered in a viscous substance, oozed over the skin of Mina's upper arms, gripping and pulling them back, winding down to her wrists to hold her immobile.

"I don't plan to make an enemy out of Lucifer and his lot." The woman placed a hand just above Mina's pubic bone. "And you are essential to him." Her hand slipped lower, caressing Mina's folds with two fingers.

"Maybe one day you'll carry his child." Her fingers parted Mina's lips then dipped into her, probing until they found Mina's menstrual cup. One finger pushed in deeper, feeling along the cup until it reached the top and, pushing against its ridge, broke the seal. The woman hooked her finger into the top of it and pulled it out, flinging it to the floor.

"Don't worry. Abraham has never had any issue with a little blood."

Mina was more worried about trying to get the blood out of her mother's carpet. The woman smirked at her as if she had read her mind, and Mina realized that she had been doing exactly that this entire time.

"Smart girl," the woman said as she backed up once more. This time, she stayed in Mina's line of sight. "Now, you do have a choice. I'm going to take what I want from you, rile up all those emotions you are already having, make them as potent as I can, and feast. My friend here, however, can help you through it with as many orgasms as you can handle. Me, I take what I want. He's a gentleman, though. He needs your consent."

Mina swallowed, her throat bumping against the rubbery limb around her neck. It gave a little, and she nodded.

The ancient entity tilted her head at something behind Mina, and seconds later, more of those appendages wound themselves around her legs, separating them and suspending her into the air, and Mina lost sight of the woman once more.

"I can't see the future," the woman said.

It was made of tentacles. Mina could see it now, the thing holding her, Abraham, as it descended on her with yet another tentacle, tucking it down her tank top. He looked like a mass of rubber, slithering against itself with only a small center to house his mouth and a cluster of eyes. It gripped her breast, winding around it like rope, then placed one of its suckers directly onto her nipple. She felt a pulse against her areola, and her nipple hardened.

"I can't say definitively whether you'll ever carry your lover's baby or not." She hit the word "ever" with such a force Mina felt it in her gut.

The thought of never having Luci's baby was one she couldn't face. Not now. Maybe not ever. If she lived to her nineties without giving him a child, she would still happily delude herself into thinking it was still a possibility. Otherwise, she might as well rip out her own heart and feed it to Abraham as a snack.

"But it might not be possible," the woman said. "Has a demon ever successfully impregnated a human before? Not that I've ever heard."

The tentacles holding Mina's legs began to move, inching their way up to the apex of her thighs. Once there, they pushed into her, and she gasped at the friction of their ridges against her inner walls. The tentacle around her waist elongated until its ribbed tip pressed into her clit.

"But don't you worry." The woman chuckled. "Abraham here is happy to fill your womb."

A sound bubbled out of Mina. It was primal, a combination of a sob and a moan, a conflicted vocalization that encapsulated her despair and arousal.

Her desire edged out her sadness, though, her faith in Luci helping to push those fears to the back of her mind. If there was a way for them to have a child together, he would find it. And if there wasn't, then he would make a way.

Nineteen

IT HAD BEEN TWO hours since Mina disappeared upstairs. The movie they'd been watching had ended. Dahlia paced between the foot of the stairs and the doorway to the living room. It wasn't the longest of hallways, and she'd lost count of how many laps she'd made.

"How long does this sort of thing usually take?" Kathryn asked, and Tabitha covered her ears.

"I have no idea," Sandra said. "We don't ask too many questions."

"Can we call Uncle Luci yet?" Tabitha said, a little too loudly because her hands were still muffling her ears.

"I've already texted him," Dahlia said. "And Oscar."

"None of the others have phones?" Kathryn asked. She picked up her cell from where it rested on her thigh and started tapping away at its screen. "Yesterday she liked a post by a woman she told me was a succubus. I think her name was Artemita. Maybe I can DM her?"

"I can't wait any longer. I'm going up there to check on her myself," Dahlia said.

Tabitha leapt up from the love seat and ran after her mother. "I'm coming too!"

"That's dangerous," Sandra called after them.

"We'll be careful," Dahlia said from midway up the staircase. She reached behind her and grabbed Tabitha's hand in her own. When they got to Sandra's bedroom, the door to the closet was open. But it was dark, darker than it should have been given the small port window that let in light from a street lamp outside.

Dahlia made a beeline for the doorway, but Tabitha tugged on her hand and dug in her heels, pulling Dahlia up short.

"What is it?" Dahlia asked, turning partway to look at her daughter, reluctant to turn her back on the closet completely.

"Don't go in there."

"We have to," Dahlia said, taking a single step closer to the door.

"No, Mom," Tabitha whispered. "I'm getting bad vibes. Seriously bad vibes. We can't help her by going in there."

"What do you mean?"

"Whatever has her, it will just get us too."

"Then you stay here. I can't leave her."

"You have to." Tabitha gripped Dahlia's hand tighter.

Dahlia took another step.

"Mom," Tabitha screeched. "Don't."

Footsteps pounded up the stairs then down the hallway. Lucifer burst into the room, Oscar, Beelzebub, and Lilith right on his heels.

"Where is she?" Lucifer asked, taking in the room. "Never mind." He disappeared into the closet.

Lilith cursed but didn't delay in following him.

As Oscar wrapped Dahlia in a hug, Beelzebub took Tabitha by the shoulders and peered at her intensely. "You okay, kid?"

"Yes," Tabitha said. "Go."

Beelzebub nodded before dashing through the door.

Oscar wrapped an arm around Tabitha and pulled her into their hug. "It's going to be okay. They'll get her."

"And if they don't?"

"Reinforcements are already on their way," Oscar said. "I'm to hold the line here, just in case."

Kathryn peeked her head through the doorway. "I called Michael. He'll be here in the next ten minutes."

When Michael arrived, he took one step into the room and cursed. "I know this energy," he said. "It's an angst demon, an old one."

"How old?" Dahlia asked.

"Old enough to predate the term demon. Who has gone in after Mina?"

"Lucifer, Beelzebub, and Lilith," Tabitha said. "The heavy hitters."

"Lilith is there too? That's good. I believe she has a history with the creature. But if it comes down to a fight, which I doubt it will, those three shouldn't have much trouble."

"What can we do?" Kathryn asked.

"Yeah. I can't just stand here waiting," Dahlia said.

"Mina is *not* going to be in a good place when she gets out."

"She already wasn't in a good place, Michael," Kathryn said. "That's why we were having a girls' night."

"I suspect that's why she was targeted."

"So what do we do?" Sandra asked from the hallway. She must have come upstairs when Michael arrived.

"Up your game," Michael said. "Whatever you were planning to comfort her, it's no longer enough."

"I'll bake cookies. From scratch," Sandra said and turned on her heel.

"What time is it?" Kathryn pulled out her phone. "The bookstore is open for another hour. There's a new romance novel we were both excited to read together. I'll go get it for her now."

"Oh! That manga she's been reading has a new volume out too," Tabitha said.

"Can you text me the title?" Kathryn asked.

Dahlia fished her phone out of her pocket and handed it to Tabitha.

"I put some art supplies away for her as a Christmas present," Dahlia said. "I'll go get them from my closet." She paused at the door, then glanced behind her. "As long as there isn't a demon in it, that is."

Tabitha jumped to follow. "I'll go with you, Mom."

They changed the sheets in the guest room that was once Mina's and set up bath salts and her favorite shampoo on the edge of the bathtub. Dahlia had to stop Tabitha from filling it with warm water since they didn't know how long it would be.

If Mina were in Hell, she had been gone a very long time. As the minutes ticked by, they all gathered in Sandra's bedroom. Oscar and Michael had taken over cookie-making duties in the kitchen, and Sandra now sat between her daughter and granddaughter on her bed.

"What is taking so long?" Tabitha asked as she dramatically fell back onto the pillows.

"From what I hear about Mina and her demons, they are probably having an orgy right now," Kathryn said. Tabitha let out a long sound of disgust and Kathryn's eyes widened. "Sorry! I shouldn't have said that."

Dahlia and Sandra made eye contact, and Dahlia watched her mother struggle to keep a straight face. She could feel her own lips tugging up at the ends. Even though it was hardly the time to laugh, they both failed to contain their mirth.

It broke some of the tension in the room, and even though Dahlia could feel the strain returning, it had given her the fortitude to hold onto hope.

Twenty

T HE TENTACLES INSIDE MINA vibrated as an orgasm rocked her, carrying her through and extending the pleasure until she couldn't bear the pleasure anymore. Abraham slithered under her body, supporting her weight with the mass of his body.

The emotional pain that her arousal had held at bay came rushing back all at once, and she sobbed. The tentacled monster held her through that too, and when she was past the worst of it, the creature began to move its appendages once more. Another crept up her leg, over her hip, and between her butt cheeks. It secreted a viscous fluid against her anus before pushing into her.

The triple penetration between two tentacles in her pussy and one in her ass sent little shocks of desire through her stomach and along her spine, but she couldn't really enjoy it. She wanted Luci. She needed to be wrapped up in his arms, to feel the rising and falling of his chest against her back or his hands in her hair, massaging her scalp. She needed his voice in her ear telling her he loved her.

But Abraham kept fucking her. Eventually, she felt herself succumbing to his ministrations. The pressure built, and she came again, gasping in surprise at its intensity.

"That is quite the power surge," the woman said. "No wonder those demons flock to you."

"That's not why," a deep voice said. A voice that made Mina's heart sing. She strained against Abraham, and tried to speak her husband's name.

"Lucifer." The woman said it for her.

"She's bleeding," Bellz growled. "Put her down now, beast, or I will cut her down."

"It's okay, Abraham," the woman said. Slowly, Abraham began to retreat, vacating cavities and relinquishing limbs. He set Mina back on the floor, and when her shaky legs failed to hold her, Beelzebub caught her up in his arms before she hit the floor. Lilith, weapon drawn, took up a position between Mina and the monster.

"Why are you bleeding? Are you hurt?" Bellz asked, backing away toward the doorway and Lucifer. As he moved, it became obvious that they weren't exactly in her mother's closet. There was no carpet but stone instead. No dressers or hangers with clothes, only fuzzy nondescript grays and browns.

"Just my period." She shook her head, burying her face against his muscular shoulder. Her stupid period. The longing to be carrying Luci's child swelled again, and the demon on the opposite side of the room hissed.

"I'm already too full. Get her out of here."

"Fuck you, Fiona," Lilith said. "Biting off more than you can chew. Do your research next time."

The demon, Fiona, shrugged. "I'll have plenty of energy to thoroughly research my next victim, thanks to that human of yours."

"You come near her or her family again, it'll mean war, Fiona," Lucifer said as he took Mina from Beelzebub. "The Cadere family is protected."

Fiona's smile stopped short of reaching her eyes, which she rolled. "Good luck with that."

Lucifer backed out of the closet that wasn't a closet and into Sandra's bedroom. Only once Lilith and Beelzebub had made it safely across the threshold did he dare to turn and face those who were waiting for them. "Where can I take her?"

"Her old room," Sandra said, already scurrying out the door to show him the way.

"What happened?" Kathryn asked someone behind them.

"Let's not talk about this in front of my daughter, please," Dahlia said. "Tabitha, go help the boys with the cookies downstairs."

Their voices muffled as Mina sank into Luci's arms. Her mother filled the bathtub while he cradled her against his chest. Closing the bathroom door behind her, Sandra left Lucifer to tend to her daughter.

Through the door, Mina could hear the muffled voices of Lilith, Bellz, Sandra, and Dahlia, but she couldn't make out what they were saying. And, if she was perfectly honest with herself, she didn't have the energy to care.

"How are you?" Lucifer asked after he had settled them both into the bathtub. Once again, he was fully clothed and soaking wet. For her. He peeled her tank top from her body and dropped it on the bath mat.

"I'm numb, I guess. Like all those strong emotions have been scrubbed out of me." Her head fell back against his pec. "But it's like they were stolen, and I can't deal with them now even though I desperately need to."

Her bleeding had mostly stopped, as if Abraham had pulled the rest of it from her too.

"I'm sorry she did this to you," Luci said, brushing her hair back from her face. Most of it was still held in place atop her head with the hair picks, but some of it had tumbled down.

"I'll just have to deal with it next month when we fail again."

"Who says we are going to fail?"

Mina shrugged. "It's just too painful right now to hope."

"I can feel it, you know? Your pain, I mean."

"I'm sorry."

"No," Luci said. "That's not why I'm telling you."

"Then why?"

"You aren't alone in it. You'll never be alone in anything ever again."

"Aside from when ancient beings send their tentacle monsters after me."

"Not even then. I could feel it. She had set up traps and roadblocks to keep us from getting to you, and each moment I couldn't reach you was agony."

"I used to have to do it on my own. Face demons, I mean. But I was always facing them for you. I guess I don't need to do that anymore. I can wait for you, in the future, so we can face them together."

"I would appreciate that, but, again, not why I brought any of this up." He peppered her hair with kisses. "You are in no way to blame for what happened. You were trying to help your mother. But despite the protections we have on you, Fiona still chose to harm you."

"I think she was mostly taking advantage of the pain that was already there."

"But she made it worse. She nourishes pain, tenderizing it, before she devours it."

"Why didn't my orgasms have the same effect on her that it has on others?"

"Mina," Luci tipped her chin up so he could look into her eyes. "You did. That's why she let you go. It's the only reason why you're still coherent. She doesn't kill her prey, but she doesn't leave them conscious, either. Not when she feeds on them the way she was feeding on you."

"It was different with my mother."

"Yes," Luci said. "She wasn't trying to get a single, calorie-rich meal from your mother."

"I don't think we can count Fiona as an ally."

"If it comes down to out-and-out war, I actually think we can."

"Abraham was kind of nice, though. Under different circumstances, he could probably be pretty fun."

"If you're good, maybe I'll ask Sindy to monster-nap him for your birthday."

The edges of her mouth tried to lift, but she didn't have the energy. Nevertheless, his humor lightened her heart just enough that she let out one calming breath, and a glimmer of hope that she was returning to herself burst to life in the corner of her mind.

"I miss her. I wish she could have been here tonight."

"As soon as she's finished helping Berith with their current obsession, she'll be here."

Twenty-One

Lucifer's body curled around Mina where she lay on her old bed. It was odd seeing her there again, and Dahlia couldn't help but feel the rightness of having her older sister back under the same roof. Yet she felt horrible, too, being pleased that her sister was home, because of the awful circumstances that had led to it.

"Lucifer?" Dahlia whispered. "Can we borrow you for a minute?"

He peered over his shoulder at her and nodded before glancing in Beelzebub's direction. Beelzebub sat in the rocking chair next to the closet. Lilith stood on the other side, like they were standing guard. Just in case. At Lucifer's silent order, Beelzebub approached the bed and took Lucifer's place as he slipped away.

Mina mumbled something in her sleep and turned into the demon, who helped her settle against his chest. His hand made tight, soothing circles on her back, and Dahlia tore her eyes away.

Leading Lucifer into her bedroom across the hall, Dahlia found Oscar and Tabitha right where she had left them. They were sitting on the bed, huddled around Tabitha's tablet as they watched an anime, one Dahlia and Tabitha had watched together many times. It was nice to see Tabitha including her father in their traditions. There was a lot to get caught up on before the new season dropped in two months.

Tabitha looked up after pausing the episode. "You're here." Tabitha put the tablet aside.

"Hey, kiddo," Lucifer said. "Sorry I didn't get a chance to say hi earlier." He furrowed his brow and cocked his head to the side. He probably didn't expect to find the pair acting so casually affectionate around each other. It had only been six months since Dahlia and Oscar had started dating. Well, if that was the case, he was about to be very surprised.

Tabitha shrugged. "You were busy."

"What is it you wanted?" Lucifer asked, turning his full attention back on Dahlia.

"There's something we need to tell you. About Tabitha," Dahlia said.

"She didn't tell you sooner because I asked her not to," Tabitha interjected.

"Okay," Lucifer said. He crossed his arms over his chest and widened his stance, bracing himself for impact.

"Oscar, Oz, is Tabitha's father." The words tumbled out of Dahlia's mouth all too quickly, like she'd been waiting to say them for thirteen years. She had always assumed that she would tell Mina and her mother first—certainly not her demonic brother-in-law. Life sure was funny.

"What?" Lucifer asked.

"It should be possible for a demon to get a human pregnant," Oscar offered, "because I was able to get Dahlia pregnant."

"So you can stop worrying about it as a species thing," Dahlia said, stumbling a bit on how best to phrase it.

"I didn't think it was," Lucifer said, shifting his weight.

"But you can tell Mina, now, when she wakes up. It might put her at ease," Dahlia said.

"Why not tell her yourself?" Lucifer asked.

"We thought that you would be better positioned to make the judgment call on when she'd be ready to hear that," Oscar said.

"I think it better come from you three," Lucifer said. "In the morning." He turned to go, and, seeing the tension in his shoulders, Dahlia realized that his body had been angled toward Mina the entire time. It was doubtful he had fully processed what they had told him. He was too worried about his wife. "Thanks for the heads up," he called over his shoulder on his way down the hall.

"Well, that went not at all the way I thought it would," Tabitha said. She scooted back, resting against the headboard. Then she patted the bedspread on both sides of her. "Let's watch some more anime before bed, please."

Dahlia and Oscar bookended their daughter, and they all snuggled closer so they could fit around the small screen in Tabitha's lap.

In the morning, Dahlia slipped out of bed while the house was still quiet. Oscar rolled over, reaching for her, but she kissed the back of his hand and placed it over her pillow. "I'm going to get coffee going," she whispered to him, and he grunted, pulling the plush down into his chest and burying his face in it, inhaling the scent of her shampoo.

Dahlia smiled all the way through starting the coffee maker, loading the toaster with pastry treats, and warming bacon in the oven. Her family was almost complete. She just needed a nibling, maybe two, to round it out.

Mina stumbled into the kitchen with Lucifer at her side and Lilith and Beelzebub at her back. All three demons kept their attention on Mina, only diverting it long enough to scan the kitchen for any threats.

"You made my favorite," Mina said as the toasted pastry popped back into view.

Dahlia laughed as she gingerly grabbed the junk food by its edges and plopped it onto a plate before handing it to her sister. "Of course. You had a rough night."

Mina sat at the small kitchen table. Lucifer pulled out the chair next to her but didn't sit. Instead, he gestured for Dahlia to take the seat.

"Dahlia has something she needs to tell you, Mina."

"You do?" Mina asked.

Dahlia sat down with a salad plate full of bacon and her coffee mug. "Yes, and I'm sorry I didn't tell you sooner. I should have."

Mina reached across the table and grasped Dahlia's hand in her own. "I promise to only be a little angry," she said, a smirk tugging at the corner of her lips.

"Oscar is Tabitha's biological father."

Mina didn't let go, but her hand went a little limp around Dahlia's, and her eyes glazed over. "When did you realize?" she asked eventually.

"Your reception. I mean, I knew a demon named Oscar had impregnated me when it happened. There wasn't anybody else who could have done it. I didn't get drunk at a party, just brought home a spirit board from a sleepover."

"It always did seem really out of character for you."

"But I realized pretty quickly at your party that your Oz was my Oscar."

"Why not tell me?" Mina's eyes were as wide as Dahlia's plate of bacon.

"I had to make sure that I wanted him in my life before I opened that can of worms. If I'd already told everyone who he was to me, to Tabitha, I knew it would be harder to part ways. After I was sure enough about him to tell Tabitha, she asked that we not tell anyone so we could learn to be a family with just the three of us first."

Mina nodded. "Okay, I lied about being a little angry."

Dahlia swallowed, closing her eyes and giving herself a small pep talk. She could handle Mina being angry at her. They were sisters. That meant sometimes they hated each other, but in the end, they always found a way back to loving one another, since they never really stopped in the first place. This would be just like that. It would be okay. It had to be okay.

"I'm not mad at you at all."

Dahlia's eyes popped open. "You aren't?"

"No," Mina said. "It's not like I told you immediately about my love affair with Satan."

"This is different, though. I knew you weren't going to freak out about *what* Oscar is."

"Who he is is still probably more shocking. Especially since you've known this whole time." Mina picked up the second half of her pastry, but moments later Dahlia heard it crash against the ceramic plate. "You slept with a demon before I did."

"Just in this lifetime," Dahlia whispered. "And hush, Mom doesn't know yet."

"Oh, she is going to demand that he marry you on the spot."

"I hope not," Dahlia said, panic wrapping itself around her heart. "He'll completely agree."

"I bet he has a ring already," Mina said.

"Who has a ring?" Oscar asked from the doorway. He hadn't buttoned or tucked in his shirt, and the dusting of curly hair on his chest made Dahlia swallow with desire.

"No one," she said. "Nothing." She stared daggers at him when it looked like he wanted to push her on her response.

"I smell Pop Tarts," Tabitha said as she ran into the kitchen, both arms flung behind her in an approximation of an anime character. She circled around the table. "Yum, yum, yum." She crashed into the empty chair on Dahlia's other side.

Beelzebub held out a freshly toasted pastry for Tabitha, who snagged it as she ran past. He then held the second out to Lilith, who sniffed it and gagged, taking a step back and lowering her chin to her chest, her face scrunching in disgust. The horned demon laughed at her reaction, shrugged, and bit into it. Only then did he seem to recognize Oscar's presence. "Oh, sorry," he said. "Did you want one? I can start another pack."

"No, thank you. I'm not hungry," Oscar said, but he plucked a slice of bacon from Dahlia's plate. Her heart grew warm. She loved this casual familiarity they had curated. She wished it would never end, and that it would expand to their extended family.

"What's the plan for the day?" Oscar asked.

"I want to spend my day with family," Dahlia said. "I'll go in early on Monday to make up for not working this weekend."

"I need something to take my mind off of all this," Mina said.

"Can I skip my homework too?" Tabitha asked.

"No," Dahlia said. "You have that history test to study for."

"Ugh, who schedules a test for a Monday?" Tabitha groaned, face-planting into the kitchen table. She murmured a muffled "ow" into the wood.

"What should we do to distract you, my love?" Lucifer asked, sweeping Mina's hair off her shoulder.

"Aside from texting Sindy, which I plan to do all day, should we work on increasing your army?" Mina asked.

"I might actually have a suggestion about that," Oscar said. Everyone turned to him, except for Tabitha, who was busy typing away on her tablet.

"What is it?" Lucifer asked.

"There's a house downtown. Old. Haunted. The usual," Oscar said.

"I know Hollywood is obsessed with turning every ghost into a demon, but that's not really how it is in real life," Lilith said.

"I reckon," Oscar said. "But I just so happen to have traced my old boss, the original Zozo, to this house. I think he's been using it to amass power, grow a following of his own."

"You did?" Dahlia asked. "I thought you weren't going to bother?"

Oscar shrugged. "I had unfinished business with him even before I found out about Tabitha, and a line I'd left dangling a few years ago finally got a bite. Apparently I can't let bygones be."

"Are you up for this?" Dahlia turned to Mina.

"I'm almost always up for this," Mina said. She placed her hand over Lucifer's where it rested on her shoulder. "Especially with my husband and his two best knights in tow."

"Let's fuck shit up." Lilith smirked.

"Seconded," Dahlia said.

"You're not coming," Oscar said.

"Of course I am," Dahlia countered.

"Not with that weak-ass protection you've got," Beelzebub said. "Your doing, I suppose, Oz?"

Oscar bristled. "What's wrong with it?"

"Nothing, except that it could be stronger," Lucifer clarified. "The protection of four demons is better than one."

"How long is this going to take?" Dahlia asked.

"Not long," Lucifer said. "But while we are at it, we should really add Lilith's protection to Tabitha too. Lilith wasn't with us the last time."

Dahlia caught Mina's eye, and her sister gave her a reassuring nod.

"I'm not sleeping with any demons, though," Dahlia said. "Just so we are all on the same page. I'm a one-demon lady."

Tabitha chose that moment to look up from her phone. "Ew." She pushed her chair back from the table.

"Sorry," Dahlia said. "But don't run off just yet."

"I know. Protection spell, or whatever. I heard." Tabitha gave the most dramatic eye roll, and Dahlia's stomach pinched. Her daughter was barely a teenager, but she was already acting like a seasoned expert.

Twenty-Two

MINA HAD EXPECTED A large mansion, maybe Edwardian, that had been turned into a tourist trap with its own parking lot. Instead, they parked on the street in front of a three-story Victorian home, definitely the product of a wealthy family of the time, that was only a little larger than her mother's house. Maybe just a little.

It was starting to look a bit run down, and a sign in the window by the front door read, "CLOSED." Mina waited with Luci, Bellz, and Lilith on the sidewalk as Dahlia and Oz circled the block one more time. Once they had parked, they jogged over to join the group.

"How are we getting in?" Mina asked.

"Easy," Oz said. "I have the key."

"How do you have the key?" Dahlia asked.

"I bought it," Oz said, shrugging like it was no big deal.

"You bought it?" Dahlia stepped back and looked up at the house as if seeing it in a new light. "The house or the key?"

"Both, darlin'," he said, amused.

"Are you planning to keep it?" Dahlia asked. Which explained the expression on her face. Dahlia was imagining a life there. It looked like there was an alley behind the house, maybe even an unused garage. The house was about two blocks away from Dahlia's marketing firm. With a little elbow grease, it could be the perfect home for them.

"Not with a demon or ghost infestation," Oz said, and Dahlia's face fell almost imperceptibly. Mina was sure Oz, at the very least, did not pick up on it.

Dahlia snatched the keys from Oscar's hand. "Can I do the honors?" she asked as she turned for the stairs leading to the front door.

"I'm not sure that's the best idea," Lilith said. "I think I should go first." But Dahlia had already slipped the key into the lock and turned it. The door swung open, and Dahlia stiffened.

"I barely touched it." Dahlia leaned into the door frame, one foot coming off the welcome mat. "Hello?" she called.

"What are you doing?" Lilith asked from behind her.

"Drawing them out," Dahlia said.

Lilith motioned to Oz, who climbed the steps and gently guided Dahlia back from the door. "They ain't zombies, Dahlia," he said, chuckling.

"Are zombies not between demons and ghosts on the monster spectrum?"

"Who are you calling a monster?" Bellz asked.

Dahlia slapped a hand over her mouth. "I didn't mean it that way; I'm sorry."

Bellz smirked at her. "You should definitely call me a monster, Dahlia. Don't be like your sister here and forget what we are."

Mina wrapped both her arms around Bellz' left one and rested her chin against his bicep. "I know exactly what you are, Bellz. I could never forget." She pressed a kiss to the sleeve of his t-shirt, drawn taught over his muscle, before releasing him and following Lilith into the foyer.

"Lilith, keep an eye on her," Bellz said as Dahlia and Oz preceded him into the home. They squeezed into the tight entryway. Luci entered last and closed the door.

"There'd be a lot more space if it weren't so crowded with furniture," Dahlia commented.

"You're redecorating in your mind, aren't you?" Mina whispered into her sister's ear.

"Shh," Dahlia said, waving Mina away.

"Don't get too attached, that's all," Mina said as she worked her way to her husband, who was looking into a small parlor. "Something wrong, my love?" She nodded at him, biting her bottom lip.

"The energy in this house is confusing," he said in reply, wrapping an arm around her shoulder and pulling her into his body. "Stick with me today, okay?"

"Show me the kitchen?" Dahlia asked Oscar, pulling him down the hall.

A groan from Lilith caught Mina's attention. "I really should have asked Sindy to take my place today. There are too many doms." Dahlia had led Oz deeper into the house, asking to see the kitchen, so it was just the four of them again.

Mina stepped forward, putting herself equal distance from all three of her demons. She faced Bellz. "One who's too hard, but I secretly love it." She winked at him before turning toward Lilith. "One who's the perfect combination of soft and hard." Finally she turned to Luci. "And one who's my everything."

They all closed in on her. Three pairs of hands caressing her hips, her stomach, her breasts. Bellz wrapped his wide hand around the base of her throat, and she involuntarily leaned into him.

"Lucky me, I think three is just right," Mina said, her voice breathy.

"Let's go find a more private place, huh?" Luci suggested. "I'd hate for your sister to walk in and see what we're going to do to you."

"Dahlia, Oz," Lilith called into the back of the house. "We are going upstairs. Keep an eye out down here, and stay together."

Luci pulled her up the staircase and down the upstairs hall, opening doors as he went. Only none of the rooms he unveiled seemed to be to his liking. The third floor proved similarly disappointing, although Mina had no idea why.

"Where are we going, Luci?" Mina asked, giggling at the frown on his face.

Finally, at the end of the hall, he opened a door that led to another set of stairs leading up to the attic. His face lit up, and he turned to wiggle his eyebrows at her.

At the top of the stairs, they found an open space with exposed beams running along the ceiling. Perfect for rope play. Bellz growled his approval.

"Oh, very good, Luci," Lilith said, patting her friend's shoulder as she walked into the space. Mina could tell from Lilith's expression that she was plotting something.

"Do you think sex will be enough to lure out the demon from where he's hiding?" Mina asked. "I mean, it works in horror movies all the time, right?" She was rambling a bit. Nervous, but in the best way. Bellz came up behind her and pulled her into him. She could feel his erection against her back, and it grounded her. She released a calming breath.

"What do you need, Lilith?" Luci asked. "I'll get it for you."

"Just some of your gentlest rope," she said. "You two get her warmed up while I get everything set."

"Are we sure it's a good idea to restrain me when we are in enemy territory?" With her head resting against Bellz' chest, and her eyes half closed, her words came out quiet and slow.

Bellz tightened his hand around her, creeping up until he had a firm yet gentle grip just beneath her jaw. "Trust us to take care of you."

Lilith appeared at Mina's side, and the demoness wrapped her fingers around Mina's upper arm and squeezed. "If you aren't comfortable, we won't do it, Mina."

The growl in Beelzebub's chest rumbled underneath Mina's back. "You'd better be sure you're uncomfortable before you call this off."

"That's not how consent works, my dude," Luci said.

Bellz rumbled again, and Mina leaned further into his hand.

"I want it. You know my safe word," Mina said. "Just make sure you have a quick release option in case we need it."

"We're demons," Luci said. "We always have a quick release option." He wiggled his fingers at her.

Abruptly, Bellz pushed her toward Luci, who happily caught her in his arms.

"Right," Mina said, smiling up at her husband. "Your not-magic."

"It's not mag—" Luci cut himself off when he realized that's what she had said, and she beamed at him. With deft fingers, Luci unzipped her dress. He caressed her wrists and arms before tugging the dress from her body. Then Bellz was behind her again, kneeling so he could peel her panties from her hips and down her legs. He placed an uncharacteristically tender kiss to the small of her back.

"You don't have to be gentle with me, Bellz," Mina said as insecurity bubbled up. She'd been so emotional while trying to conceive. They were all walking on eggshells around her. And she wished she could honestly say that at times she didn't need it or want it. But right now, she wanted things to be the way they had always been, at least right now.

"Yes, I do," Bellz said, slipping his hand between her legs and cupping her vulva in his palm. "Because *I* need to be gentle with you, Mina." His lips brushed her hip. "Because you deserve kindness, and, despite what I like to believe, I'm not a monster. Not with you. Not with Sindy. Not with the others."

When Mina sank to her knees, Luci and Bellz fell with her. Then Bellz helped her into his lap, and Luci wrapped his arms around both of them.

"Don't say that, Bellz," Luci said, clearing his throat. "Beelzebub. I need you to be a monster sometimes. With me."

"Please be my monster, Bellz," Mina whispered. "You say often that I've forgotten your true nature, but you're wrong. I see all of you, and I love every last bit."

"And yet you married my best friend instead," he said.

"Luci's my soulmate, Bellz."

"I know, and you can only love me because you loved him first."

Mina shrugged. "Do I need to marry you too?"

"Hello," Lilith said, tapping her steel-heeled foot. "You were supposed to be turning her on, not having a heart-to-heart.

And, no fair. If you get to marry Mina, then there's three other people she needs to marry, too."

Mina smiled up at Lilith. "Do I get to have three husbands and two wives? That sounds delightful."

"No," Luci said. "You're my wife. And I'm not ready to share you on that level." He paused. "Yet."

Mina turned to Bellz. "Future husband." Then she gazed up at Lilith. "Future wife, please ravage me now." She flung her arms up and flew backward into Bellz and Luci's arms.

"I'm not sure I can handle having such a dork for a wife." Lilith sighed. "How do you put up with her, Lucifer?"

"What are you talking about? She's perfect," Luci said as Bellz slipped behind her. "Spread your legs, Mina." Her current husband fell into her center, tasting her like she was comfort food and he'd had a rough day. He teased her clit with the strong point of his tongue, and, using two fingers, separated her folds so he could lick her side to side, first down one outer labia, then up the other, before delving deeper.

As he worked, Lilith wound rope around Mina's ankles and wrists. Then, with Bellz' help, she bound Mina's breasts. Not too tightly. Just enough to form a bra of sorts and press her breasts upward, but not enough to restrict blood flow.

First, the three demons maneuvered Mina into standing, Luci making sure to stimulate her the entire time. But he wasn't the only one. Lilith and Bellz peppered her skin with kisses anywhere their fingers brushed as they tied her to the rafters.

When they were finished, she was suspended, her legs bent and tied, her core exposed, the weight of her distributed perfectly so that she felt light as air. They'd never done this before, and Mina would have to have a conversation with Lilith about holding out on her when she wasn't so immersed in bliss.

Bellz flicked Mina's nipple then stood back and crossed his arms. "You look good like this," he said, licking one corner of his mouth. "All that time I spent with fancy furniture, and all we needed was some rope and something to suspend you from."

"I like your fancy furniture," Mina mumbled, and Luci brushed her face with his palms, shushing her.

"It's okay, my love. Slip into that space. We've got you." She managed to nod her head as he slid his fingers between her lower lips, dipping a finger into her while circling her clit with his thumb. "When I tell you, I want you to come for me. A little one, to get the ball rolling." He slipped another finger into her. "Now, Mina. Come now."

She did. And it wasn't a mind blowing orgasm. No, but it was pleasant. An appetizer of what was to come, and all it did was whet her appetite for more.

"Good girl," Luci said. As Lilith came forward to take his place. Mina gasped at the loss of him as his fingers left her and his warmth receded. But Lilith didn't keep her waiting long.

The demoness brought the flat of her hand against Mina's vulva in a small slap. At first, the slaps were light, and didn't leave a sting. They only tightened the exquisite pressure building in Mina's abdomen. Until Lilith began to hit harder. Sometimes she'd land a blow to Mina's inner thigh or her left or right labia, but more often than not, they landed directly on Mina's clit. And Mina was dripping. The sharp sting of Lilith's beautiful fingers brought her closer to ecstasy.

Bellz still stood behind her, bracing her body and keeping her from swinging. "Would you like me to let you fly?" he asked.

"Yes, please," Mina whispered, and he stepped away. For a while it was just her, gravity, and Lilith's hand. But soon she felt the gentle caress of the soft leather straps of a flogger that Bellz expertly flicked across her butt, thighs, and lower back.

And then Lilith's hand retreated, and he brought the flogger between her spread legs. It snapped against her anus and her clit, and her world exploded in delightful rapture.

Luci had her in his arms at once, whispering sweet words into her ear. She rested her head against his shoulder as he slowly rocked her. Lilith and Bellz joined them, soothing her reddened skin with their warm palms.

Gripping her chin and forcing her to look him in the eye, Luci asked. "Would you like more?" When Mina nodded, he smiled villainously.

His highest ranking generals began to prepare her, stretching both of her openings with lubed fingers. When Lilith stepped back, Luci took her place and fit his cock into Mina's pussy. His moan was one of satisfaction. It deepened when Bellz began to work himself into Mina's rear.

Rocking slowly, they held her as the tension keeping her in midair slackened, and lowered her to the floor. Bellz pulled Mina back against his chest and lay supine on the floor. They lost Luci for a moment, but soon enough he was mounting his bride and fucking into her. Bellz' hand fell to Mina's hips, where he gripped her, grinding against her ass at the end of each thrust.

After freeing Mina's legs from her bounds and rubbing feeling back into them, Lilith climbed on top of Mina, treating her to the sight of her beautiful cunt. Mina strained forward, but Bellz banded an arm across her chest to hold her in place while Lilith laughed.

When the demoness finally lowered herself over Mina's mouth, Mina wasted not a moment before pressing her nose against Lilith's clit and lapping at the moisture that had gathered between her petals.

Mina worked her tongue inside Lilith, searching for her g-spot. When she found it, she pressed the tip of her tongue into it as she worked her face against Lilith's clit.

Luci palmed Lilith's breast, kneading it and narrating to his wife what he was doing as he did it. When he reached Lilith's nipple, she orgasmed. And a chain reaction was triggered. Mina's inner muscles flexed involuntarily as she, too, came, squeezing both Bellz and Luci in the process. Simultaneously, they picked up the pace, before filling her with their seed.

Even after her lovers had removed her remaining ropes and held her between them on the floor, Mina struggled to catch her breath. She was half splayed on Luci and Lilith, and, between them, they cradled her. Bellz leaned against the wall above their heads, idling stroking her hair.

"Are you okay?" Luci asked.

"Never better." Mina closed her eyes. "You?"

Luci's chuckle rumbled beneath her.

"Did it work?" Mina asked, sleepily.

Lilith hummed. "It doesn't feel any different."

"There's definitely still a presence here," Bellz said. "But I don't think we've drawn out the demon."

Mina moved to get up, but Luci didn't loosen his hold on her. "We should go check on Oz and Dahlia," she said.

"We will. In a minute," Luci said.

"You know how important aftercare is, Mina," Lilith said.

"Can I at least get dressed?" Mina asked. "I'm feeling exposed after all that. Hyper aware that an enemy demon could show up at any moment."

Bellz used the wall to stand up and retrieved her dress. He threw it onto the trio on the ground and stared down at them. "You can't be comfortable there anyway. Why don't we rain check more aftercare until we get Mina home."

Mina sat up and tugged her dress on. Lilith and Luci nodded to each other, stood too, and then helped Mina off the floor. As they made their way to the door to the attic, they never once stopped touching her. Lilith smoothed Mina's hair and gently detangled it with her fingers. Luci rubbed her back in soothing circles.

They heard the sound of feet pounding on the stairs seconds before Bellz reached for the doorknob. The door burst open, and Mina found herself pressed between Lilith and Luci. Lilith in front in a defensive position, Luci behind, one hand on Mina's hip, holding her steady, the other held out before him, braced for attack.

Twenty-Three

"**Y**OU DO KNOW THAT I didn't acquire this house so that we could move in?" Oscar asked, his stubble tickling Dahlia's cheek as he caged her in from behind against the kitchen sink. They were looking through the window out into the small patio and backyard.

"I know that, but it's kind of perfect," Dahlia said. "It's close to work, and I know this location feeds into a great high school."

"It's haunted," Oscar said. "And infested with a demon who has already done enough damage to our family." He splayed his hand across her lower abdomen, pulling her into him. He swelled against her.

"I'm sure my sister and her husband can remedy that."

"I bought it blind, as is, so no inspection was done. It could have termites, darlin'. What if there are mice, or bats in the attic?"

"It definitely needs some work," Dahlia conceded. "But that just means when we are done with it, it will be undoubtedly ours."

"That sounds like some sentimental nonsense," Oscar said, but she could see his grin in the reflection of the window.

"We don't have to decide today," Dahlia said.

"Damn right we don't." Oscar chuckled.

"We should take it for a test run, though, don't you think?" She turned slightly in his arms so she could peer up at him.

"A test run? What do you mean by that?"

She eyed the kitchen table behind him. "That looks to be just the right height."

"Yeah?" He lifted an eyebrow as she escaped from his embrace and moved to the table. With a practiced flick of her wrist, Dahlia unclasped her high-waisted jeans. She glanced at Oscar over her shoulder as she unzipped them. Her hands made their way to her hips, and she worked her pants down with a little wiggle.

"Dahlia, darlin', you have family right upstairs." Oscar stepped up behind her.

"And what exactly do you think they are doing up there?" Dahlia asked.

"Good point." He brushed the tips of his fingers against her stomach before gripping the bottom of her t-shirt and lifting it off of her. Nuzzling into the hollow of her neck, he pressed a kiss to her freckled skin.

"No interruptions," Dahlia said. "Unless this place is really haunted."

"Didn't I hear someone say that sex might bring them out?" Oscar asked, snaking a hand under her bra. Her nipple pebbled in response. "Are you sure you want to risk it?"

"They'll most likely be attracted to my sister, right? She's the one with the magical orgasms."

"Your orgasms are magical."

"To you. Not to demonkind everywhere in a charging-demon-magic sort of way." She hooked her thumbs into her panties and pushed them down as far as she could. The table got in the way, and they clung to her thighs, one side slipping a little farther before getting caught on her knee.

Oscar, removing his hand from her bra, laid his hand flat against Dahlia's back between her shoulder blades, encouraging her to bend over the table. It felt stable enough, and Dahlia only had a passing worry about it being able to hold her weight.

Any more disparaging and intrusive thoughts dissipated when his hand found her flesh once more. He knelt down and pulled her ass cheeks apart. His breath hitched, and he let out a pained moan. "So perfect."

He placed his hat on the table to her right, but in her line of sight, and Dahlia gulped in anticipation. His warm, wet tongue slid along the outside of her folds. He circled once, twice, before parting her with his fingers and taking a true taste.

Heat shocked her system, sending tiny lightning strikes to dance along her spine. If he had been anything other than a demon, she would have called his tongue divine. Being what he was, it could only be described as damningly decadent. If it meant more of him and more of everything he made her feel, she'd happily resign herself to damnation.

After Tabitha, she'd chosen a life of solitude, sexually speaking. She had her imagination and had gotten in the habit of using it for a quick release at bedtime. She rarely bothered with fancy toys. There wasn't any point. Her mood improved after masturbating. She found she had more energy and patience to get through whatever the next day threw at her. Her personal ministrations had only ever been pragmatic, not something to indulge in beyond the absolutely necessary.

But with Oscar, it was the exact opposite. Even if the benefits were the same, they weren't the point. He was the point—being close to him and allowing herself to be vulnerable like she had never been with another.

By the time he stood up, she was sopping wet and writhing against the wood of the table. He leaned into her, the roughness of his jeans rubbing against her sensitive skin as he lovingly moved his hips against her.

"Are you ready for me?"

"I believe there is a high likelihood that I will die right now if you don't put your cock inside me," she replied.

"I can't have you haunting our future family home, darlin'." She heard the metal of the fastening of his belt, the rustle of a zipper, and then his cock was sliding against her, picking up her moisture.

"Please," she begged. Before the word was fully past her lips, he pressed the tip into her. Her walls spread for him as his cock impaled her, and once he was fully rooted he stopped and waited for her to adjust. His fingers found her clit and flicked it. He explored her inner and outer labia. Touching everywhere as if he were trying to memorize her. The way she felt on the inside and out.

When he began to move, it was with slow strokes that targeted the bundle of nerves inside her. She pushed back against him, circling her hips to heighten the pleasure he provided.

Dahlia came, and her whole world fell away until there was only them and ecstasy. But he wasn't finished. Not even close. With her first orgasm out of the way, Oscar's thrusts became faster and harder. She had to lift up onto her arms and press against the table to stay in place. The change of angle let him in deeper.

He pinched her clit as the head of his cock pressed against her lowered cervix, and she came again. Before she was even through her second, he leaned over her and bit gently at the back of her neck and shoulder, and her second rolled right into a third.

"Do you want me to finish in you?" he asked, and she felt herself tighten around him again.

"Yes, Oscar. Please," Dahlia said, shoving her ass back at him, pleading with her body that he finish this properly. He moved with a new sense of urgency. He jerked against her, filling her. They collapsed onto the table, Oscar half on top of her.

And she hoped she was ovulating. The thought immediately startled her, and she jerked against him.

"What is it?" Oscar asked.

It was then that she noticed the condom wrapper sitting next to his hat. "You were wearing a condom?"

"Of course." He moved off of her, slipping out and disposing of the condom in the trash under the sink. She tugged her clothes back into place and turned to face him.

He pulled out a kitchen chair and sat down, clutching her hand in his and tugging her down into his lap. "What's wrong?" he asked, breathing in her hair. His arms were warm bands around her, holding her close.

"I just wished you weren't," she said, and at his look of confusion added, "wearing a condom, I mean. I wished you had actually come inside me."

"I'm not going to risk impregnating you again," Oscar said. "Not unless you tell me emphatically that you wish otherwise."

"I don't know what I really want. The thought of having another—it's terrifying."

Oscar nodded.

"But the thought of having your child? That's the opposite of scary," Dahlia said.

"We'll keep using condoms until you've decided what you want," he said. "There's no rush."

"I am on birth control. Maybe we could risk it just a little."

Before he could answer, the kitchen cabinet to the left of the refrigerator flipped open with such a force its hinges threatened to come loose, and Dahlia jumped. Then the cabinet to its left flung open too. The other chairs at the table began to hop on their own as if an invisible force was picking them up and slamming them down on a loop. The cabinets, which were luckily empty, slammed closed before opening again, more forcefully with each repetition.

Dahlia snapped up Oscar's hat before it could be drafted into the poltergeist's activity and clutched it to her bosom.

The entire kitchen rattled around them as Oscar scooped Dahlia up and made a very fast beeline for the hallway. As soon as they had left the kitchen, it all stopped. Dahlia glanced over his shoulder at the room and found it in complete disarray. The chairs were stacked haphazardly on the table, and the cabinet doors hung off their hinges; at least two now lay on the floor. And the refrigerator and freezer doors stood open.

"We need to get to the others right now," Dahlia said. "Put me down, Oscar. The staircase is too narrow for you to carry me."

"Alright, but stay close. I want you in front of me on the stairs so I can catch you if anything happens." He placed his hand on her lower back and didn't move it until they reached the attic.

When they burst in, they found Mina and her trio of demons right at the top of the stairs.

"What happened?" Lilith asked.

"Poltergeist in the kitchen," Dahlia said. "And it had definitely seen that movie, stacking chairs and everything."

"We haven't had any encounters up here with the supernatural. Other than," Mina gestured at her three demons, "you know, the usual."

The doors in the hallway below the attic began to shake, doorknobs rattling.

"Maybe we should get out of here," Dahlia said.

Instead, Oscar pushed Dahlia toward her sister before turning and slamming the door to the attic closed. There was no lock, so Dahlia instinctively scanned the space for furniture. A mirror covered by a cloth, a chair with a broken wicker seat, an empty chest, and cardboard boxes full of junk were the only options. She took a step toward the chest, and Oscar moved to follow. They had only covered a foot or two before the door exploded, sending shards of wood across the attic.

Oscar flung himself over her, protecting her from the projectiles. She worried for Mina, but surely Lucifer would keep her from harm.

"Is my sister okay?" Dahlia asked Oscar, shouting over the noise of the furniture scraping across the wood floor. It circled them, moving in tighter, pressing them back together. Oscar and the others pushed Dahlia and Mina to the center and formed a tight circle around them.

Mina was bleeding.

Dahlia reached for her sister, cupping her face in her hand and examining the scratch along Mina's cheekbone. It wasn't deep. She didn't think it would need stitches.

"I'm okay," Mina said while managing a halfhearted smile.

"They shouldn't be able to hurt you," Dahlia said. "Not with Lucifer's protection."

"Unless these aren't demons," Mina said. "They must be human spirits."

Dahlia glanced up from where they crouched on the floor and caught a glimpse of Lucifer's face. He looked furious, but his eyes kept flicking back to Mina with concern.

"Can you command them, Lucifer?" Lilith asked. "It is kind of your domain."

"There's a barrier. I need time to get through it," he said.

"What you need is fewer distractions," Beelzebub said. "Let us get Mina and her sister out of here."

The room around them quieted. The furniture no longer moved. The air became preternaturally still.

"I don't think so," someone said, but Dahlia didn't recognize the voice. She clutched her sister's hand in her own. Mina tried to reassure Dahlia with a nod, but it didn't work. Whoever this new player was, Dahlia wanted nothing to do with them. Her suspicion that it was either Oscar's old boss or someone associated with him made her like their situation even less.

"Is this your doing?" Lucifer asked. "Call them off." His tone left no room for discussion. It was a command, one that tugged at Dahlia to obey, although she had no way to do so. Mina caught her eye, and she felt the compulsion fade away.

"Thank you, Satan, but no. Hell may be your domain, but I've been building mine here for a while." Dahlia still couldn't see this new demon, not aside from a pair of black boots that looked about three hundred years old.

"It's me you want," Oscar said.

"Ha, not hardly," the demon said. "I want your lady, though. First mother to a demon–human hybrid. I mean, I'd prefer the brat, but the mother will do for now."

"The fuck did he just say about my daughter?" Dahlia asked, and Mina had to hold her back.

"Don't engage," Mina whispered.

"Lucifer, what a smart bride you have. I'd happily take her too." The thump of his footfalls on the floor bounced around Dahlia's head. She had to get her sister out of here. And herself. And they had to find a way to murder this demon. She would not allow anything to threaten her daughter. "I'd love my own personal battery."

Lilith drew her sword. "Do you have a death wish, asshole?"

"Lilith, Lilith, Lilith. Fifteen hundred years ago I would have loved to let you peg me. Sadly you had no interest, so I moved on. But have you?"

"Go fuck yourself," Beelzebub growled. He took a step forward and popped the demon squarely in the jaw. Through the gap Beelzebub had created, Dahlia finally saw this demon.

He looked a bit like the grim reaper, his head and body made of nothing but bones. He was dressed in a flowing blouse, most of the ties at the throat undone, exposing his sternum and part of some ribs. His heeled boots covered his calves, and although she doubted there was meat beneath the leather, they curved around invisible muscle. A cloak hung loosely over his head and shoulders.

"What are you?" Dahlia asked before she could stop herself.

"Only humanity's worst nightmare."

"Change?" Mina asked. "No. That's not it. Humanity's greatest fear has got to be when a streaming service removes a show you were binge watching when you only have an episode left."

"Or when they cancel it before it gets a second season," Dahlia added. "Oh! On a cliffhanger."

"I tortured humans long enough to know that their worst fear is being humiliated," Beelzebub offered helpfully.

"No, that's just cis white men's worst fear," Lilith countered.

As they bantered around their increasingly frustrated adversary, they slowly moved, as a group, closer to the door.

The demon sighed with frustration. "I didn't say greatest fear. I said worst nightmare."

"Oh, sorry," Mina said. "My worst nightmare is the one where I forget that I'm enrolled in a class until right before the final, and I don't even know where the class is held."

"Oh, I have a variation on that one," Dahlia said. They were almost to the door now. Just a few more shuffles. They'd have to be quick, she suspected. He would realize what they were doing soon. "Only it's always an essay that's listed in the syllabus, but the professor hasn't brought it up since, like, the second week of school. And I don't know if she's still expecting it or not, and I'm not about to ask and potentially cause more work for us, but I'm also pretty sure if I fail to turn in the assignment, I won't graduate."

"Huh," the demon said. "I would think your worst nightmare would be your demon boyfriend abandoning you to raise your hellspawn alone."

"You'd think that, right? But turns out I have a really awesome support system. And my daughter may be a hellspawn, but she's also a product of love, and that's a hell of a lot more than you can say for yourself."

"You're going to regret that," he said and lunged through an opening that Beelzebub and Lilith had unwittingly left as they'd shifted to help get Mina to the doorway first.

Dahlia watched in slow motion as a skeletal hand reached for her wrist. It kept getting closer, but Dahlia couldn't move to escape it. She couldn't breathe.

But then she was out of its reach and her back rammed into Oscar's hard chest. His arms folded around her as he pivoted them toward the door.

Mina was standing where Dahlia had been, chin up, back straight, staring down the grim reaper. That hand of bones wrapped around her wrist instead. In a blink, they were gone.

Dahlia screamed, but Oscar wouldn't let go of her. He wouldn't let her go back for her sister. Instead, he took her downstairs and then outside. Then they were down the street and he was fumbling through her purse for her keys.

"We have to go back," she said, and she was sure that it was all she had been saying.

Oscar stopped his search and gripped her upper arms in his capable hands. "They've got her. Lucifer, Lilith, Beelzebub. They will stop at nothing to get your sister back, but we have got to protect our daughter."

"Tabitha," Dahlia gasped, ripping her purse from Oscar's hands and unlocking the car with the press of her hand to the door handle. "It's a key fob, Oscar. It works with proximity."

"I'm driving," he said.

"Like Hell you are."

Twenty-Four

T HE PRESS OF THE demon's fingers against Mina's skin
felt like dry ice, and she hissed, twisting her wrist
and pulling out of his grasp. Mina took a step back and
examined her arm. Not a mark. She shook it out to get rid
of the lingering sting, though.

They weren't in the attic anymore but another nondescript cave. Probably somewhere in Hell. She sighed and
rolled her eyes. Twice in two days. How annoying.

"So what's your plan, death dude?" Mina asked, crossing
her arms.

He stared at her blankly for a minute, snarled, and pushed
her against the nearest wall. She could see something shim-
mering over his left shoulder. Perhaps the portal he'd used.
No way Lucifer and the others wouldn't find a way through
it in a matter of minutes. At least, she hoped so. She had just
charged them all up a few times before this guy decided to
show.

"I may have meant to capture the other human, but you're
the better catch, really. My own personal battery pack."

"It's not like you can just plug into me, though. There is
a trick to it."

"Of course I know that. Even if I hadn't been keeping tabs on the new Zozo all these years, everyone in Hell knows how you work. Word spreads quite quickly."

"Does it really? Or is it just that so much time in Hell has passed compared to on Earth that the gossip has had plenty of time to spread?" She thought he narrowed his eyes at her, but she couldn't quite tell given the lack of tissue on his bony face.

"Either way, all I have to do is get you to come. Plenty of people have done it. Shouldn't be too hard."

"Oh, okay," Mina scoffed, "don't put in any effort. That will absolutely work for you."

"What kind of effort would you like?" When she didn't answer, he took a step closer. "Do I have your consent to try? I also know that bullshit is important to you."

She worried her lip between her teeth while she thought. Keeping him occupied while Luci and the others searched for her wasn't the worst idea. Who knows? Maybe this miserable asshole wasn't beyond her powers of orgasmic bliss.

"Okay," she said after a moment. "You have my permission to try."

"Good."

The elongated face of a spirit appeared out of thin air before Mina. Its screech pierced her eardrums, and she gasped as its anger became her own.

Skeletal hands broke free from the loose soil in the cave wall and wrapped around Mina's forearms, pulling her back fully against the wall. A radius and ulna bone banded around her middle, the attached hand wrapping around her side.

Mina flinched away from the ghost, but that only made it scream louder.

The demon chuckled. With a wave of his hand the ghost disappeared, but the skeletal bonds stayed very firmly in place. He lifted the front of her dress and tucked it around the arm bones to get it out of the way. With the tip of the distal phalanges of his forefinger, he traced along the seam of her panties from her hip across her thigh and down to her crotch, where he slipped under the gusset and tore, slicing away the fabric there. When the exposed bone grazed her skin, it didn't sting like she expected.

He didn't wait a moment before penetrating her with his knuckles. She was still wet from earlier, so it didn't hurt, but there wasn't anything pleasurable about it either.

Mina knew she should stay quiet about it. He wanted power from her so he stood a chance against her husband. If he kept on like this, he'd never get any. So not saying a peep was clearly the smartest move. Only then she'd be missing out on the opportunity to tease him. And he so desperately needed to be brought down a peg or two. So, instead of doing the smart thing, she laughed.

"What is so humorous?"

"Whatever it is you are doing."

"I thought I was pleasuring you." He pulled his arm back, shuffling his feet as if he had to stop himself from taking a step back as well.

"You started out strong, but then you completely skipped any stimulation to my vulva, dived right into my vagina. That's a rookie mistake."

"I don't understand. Isn't your vagina more sensitive?"

Don't tell him about the clitoris. Don't tell him about the clitoris. Don't tell him about the clitoris.

"You have to tease, build anticipation. And a lot of women can't come from penetration alone." She sighed at his blank expression. "Okay, do you have any hobbies? Do you like to play music? Watch sports?"

"Oh, I enjoy American football," he said.

"Okay, so when your team makes a touchdown, that's the best ever, right?"

"Traditionally, I believe that is why people watch. I, however, spectate for the head injuries, the trauma forever altering all those young brains. The violence, torment, and anger that will follow. It's intoxicating."

"Okay." Mina frowned. "I suppose it makes sense you'd feel that way. But the near misses add to your fun, right? If you just watched a clip show of people getting concussed without any context, would you enjoy it as much?"

"I suppose not." He scratched the side of his skull.

"Well, imagine that being concussed is the equivalent to having an orgasm. The journey to the orgasm is half the fun. And without the context of everything leading up to that orgasm, it would be meaningless. And, in a real world application, impossible to achieve."

He nodded.

"The other thing you have to understand—everyone's bodies are different. What works for one person doesn't work for the next. And even session to session, what worked before might not work again. You have to be adaptive. Watch for body language." When he didn't say anything in response, she added. "And you have to stay in control. At least with me. Most of the time."

"I don't—" he ground his teeth together. "I don't know how to do that."

"Stay in control?"

He scoffed at her. "No. The other thing."

"Watch my body language?"

He nodded.

"If you let go of one of my hands, I can demonstrate."

"This better not be a trick," he said as the hand released her right arm.

"It's not a trick, dude." She rolled her eyes and shook her head. "You're about to get a freebie." Massaging her breast in her hand, Mina rested her head against the wall and sighed. Her lips parted as she pinched her nipple between her fingers. "There are other places to stimulate as well." She released her breast so she could show him as she told him. "Behind the ear, under the jaw, along the neck. A gentle caress to the stomach or a graze along the hip. I can't reach, but the foot is very sensitive. And a caress along the calf or thigh on your way can be really effective."

Spreading her legs a little, she brought her fingers to her mound, rubbing the sensitive skin above her clit, stimulating it lightly as she did. She bit her lip as her body relaxed further. She ran her forefinger and ring finger along her labia.

He watched her intently as she continued to tease herself. Her breathing increased, and so did his.

Her middle finger dipped lower, rubbing her clit directly. Her gasp was audible. She increased her speed, her hips moving in tandem, then slipped her fingers down farther. Using the palm of her hand to continue to stimulate herself, she slipped two fingers into her pussy.

His eyes flicked between the hand working between her thighs and her face as her desire built.

"I can't remember the last time I wished I still had a dick," he mumbled quietly, but loud enough for her to hear.

And the thought of affecting him set her off. Bliss exploded in her nerve endings, her eyes closed tightly, and she couldn't hold back her moan. But she didn't stop her masturbation. Not until she had rung out as much pleasure as she could.

Slowly, her breathing returned to normal and she pulled her hand from between her thighs. When she opened her eyes, she gasped in surprise. The demon was no longer skeletal. He was covered in muscle and sinew, and, before her eyes, skin grew across his body.

She reached out to him. "Did I do this?" He was warm against her hand, which he grabbed and brought to his lips, closing them around her fingers and tasting her. His eyes shut as he hummed in appreciation.

He released her from the wall, and she stumbled into him. "Thank you for the lesson," he said, opening his eyes. They caught on the flesh on his own hand and widened in surprise. "What is this?" He touched his face.

"You're okay," Mina said, pressing both hands to his chest. She could feel his heart thump under her right palm. "I think you just changed into your human form."

"Impossible," he said.

"I mean, obviously not." She shrugged, a gentle smile lifting the corners of her mouth.

"I haven't had access to this form for," he shook his head, "a very long time." Cupping her jaw, he tipped her head back and kissed her. He pulled back just enough to speak, his lips brushing hers. "Thank you."

"Will you let the others in now?"

"Why would I?"

"You're still okay with kidnapping me?"

He nodded once.

"So not actually all that thankful," she said, tipping her head to the side and narrowing her eyes at him.

He started to speak but stopped to clutch at his temples. Three spirits, similar to the one he had called before, appeared in the cavern around them. They wailed and screeched, and the demon let go of his head so he could pull Mina against him.

"It's worse in this form," he yelled over the screaming. "The spirits don't like it when I remind them of the humanity they lost."

"But you deal with this on some level all the time?" Mina asked.

"The screaming ghosts?" He shrugged. "Yeah. It's part of the gig."

No wonder he was miserable. If he constantly had to listen to this, even with the volume turned down, it wasn't at all a surprise that he lashed out. Lied to Oz. Broke up Dahlia's family before it had even begun. And this power grab he was obviously attempting? Maybe he just needed someone to help him see an alternate path.

Even failing that, she had to drown out all this pain and anger somehow. She cupped his cheeks in her hands. "Look at me." He hesitated. "Please." She wanted to use his name, but she didn't know it.

Searching his face, she tried to find his name there. Maybe in his tanned skin, his silver eyes, or his dark hair. It looked almost violet in the dim light of the cave. And then she knew it, as if the universe had whispered it to her. His name. Of course.

"Adam," she said, "look at me." When their eyes met, something zapped between them, a physical spark, and he gasped. "You don't have to surround yourself in this. Let me show you."

He swallowed audibly as she untied his cloak and pushed it off his shoulders. The loose strings that held his shirt together were next. When she untucked his shirt from his trousers, he trembled.

"I was never the first man," he said as she unfastened his pants. She got on her knees to tend to the laces on his boots. "I was one of many. They made us in a batch. And she, she was also one of many."

"Eve?" Mina asked.

"There was never an Eve. No apple or serpent. No garden. That was a lie He told. A lie I believed for too long."

Mina helped him out of one boot then the other, tugging his pants off as well once his footwear was out of the way. She punctuated his nudity with a chaste kiss to his thigh.

"What happened to her? Not-Eve?" He helped her to stand.

"When she died, she was reincarnated. Like the rest of them. All except for me."

"Why not you?"

"Because I was the last," he answered. "Because someone needed to be remembered and to remember." He laughed. "But of course then I forgot."

He wasn't making much sense. But humans had been around for a while. Perhaps longer than scientists originally thought,

Mina had recently read. And his mind had been tampered with, memories lost and rewritten. Even though he'd reclaimed them, surely he still had healing to do.

She touched his stomach, tickling him lightly as she explored his skin.

"What are you planning, human?"

The ghosts had retreated as he'd talked. As if reclaiming his story allowed him to reclaim his power as well.

"I was hoping to give you a break from all that doom and gloom," she said, waving her hand where the spirits had been.

"And how did you plan on doing that?"

"It's not obvious?" Mina asked. "I stripped you naked. I'm touching your body. Do you like it?"

"Very much," he said. "But I don't deserve it."

"Who says?" She dragged her hands down his legs.

"I collect those souls, Mina. I've kept them of my own volition."

"Why?" She stepped toward him, rising up to kiss down his neck, nipping when she reached his shoulder.

"It is comfortable to have them."

She laughed. "That's not comfort. It's just what you've become accustomed to."

"Is that it?" he asked, wrapping his arm behind her back and pulling her flush against him. "Then let us see if what you have to offer gives me what I need." He kissed her, bending at the waist to take hold of the bottom of her dress, breaking the kiss only to pass the garment over her head.

He picked her up by her thighs, and she wrapped her legs around him. He thrust against her, running the length of his member along her. She squeezed her legs, leveraging herself so she could stimulate his sex with hers in return.

Adam lowered them to the ground, using his cloak as a blanket. He held himself above her and slowly looked her up and down. "Lucifer is a lucky being."

"Right now you're the lucky being." She propped herself up on an elbow and pressed her lips to his, wrapping her other arm around his neck and pulling him down on top of her. Mina found his erection. She encompassed it in her hand and stroked him lightly.

"I better pounce before my luck runs out." Pushing her flat on her back, he grasped her thighs and pressed her legs back, exposing her to his view. He slid into her in one smooth stroke. His groan of pleasure sent pure electricity up her spine, and she arched into him.

A perfectly manicured fingernail tapped Adam on the shoulder. He shrugged it off, but Mina laughed as she saw Lilith's face appear above his shoulder.

Lucifer lay down on his side next to them, his head propped up in his palm. "Hi there."

Twenty-Five

"F UCK!" ADAM SAID AS he rolled off Mina and away from her husband.

"You're looking better," Beelzebub said.

"I was going to switch back," Adam said, looking away from them sheepishly, "after."

"I suppose you needed a dick to fuck my wife," Luci said. He scooted closer to her and draped an arm over her naked body, and she turned into him.

"Luci?" she asked as she nuzzled against his chest.

"Yes, my love?"

"You interrupted us."

"Did I?" He brought his hand down on her ass cheek in a resounding smack, then smoothed the pain with a gentle rub.

"You did," she said, pressing back against his hand.

"I'm sorry." He lay flat on his back, pulling her with him. His deft fingers skillfully undid his pants, and he pulled out his cock. "Ride me." Mina didn't hesitate before climbing on top and taking him completely. Every time they fucked, it felt like coming home. His love surrounded her as she surrounded him. She may have met God before, but this was as close to divinity as she would ever be.

Beelzebub, Lilith, and Adam stared, transfixed by the sight of the two of them. Of Mina riding Lucifer. They moved together like sex was a dance they were born to perfect. Their hands found each other, and their fingers intertwined. He braced her with them, helping her find more leverage. To fuck him deeper.

All of her synapses wide awake, she forgot everything but him. His smell, the way he felt beneath her, inside her. How she wanted him forever.

He thrust into her, and her thoughts scattered. Sitting up, he wrapped himself around her, driving into her forcefully until she came, her muscles spasming around him, bringing him with her.

She gasped his name against his shoulder as he brushed her hair back and tucked it behind her ear.

"Do you feel better?"

"Yes," she said, "and no."

"No?"

"I wanted Adam to feel this post-orgasmic daze. He's constantly tormented. I thought a reprieve would do him good. Help break him out of his obsession with pain and anger." She peeked around Luci to see Adam standing naked against the cave wall. When his eyes met hers, he refused to look away. She beckoned him with an incline of her head, and he took a hesitant step forward.

"They outmatch me here," Adam said.

"Then why did you bring me to Hell in the first place?" Mina asked.

"To piss them off," Adam said. "I feed off any negative emotion, but anger has always been my favorite." He lifted his shoulders in a careless shrug.

"Do you still want to piss them off?" Mina asked.

Adam smirked. "Always."

"Do you still want what I'm offering?"

"I do."

"Then you'll apologize to my sister and to Oz," she said, purposely leaving their daughter out of it. She wouldn't even think her niece's name near him.

She plucked her dress from the ground and pulled it over her head, then stood, reaching out her hand to Luci. He used it to help himself up and swooped in for a quick kiss.

When Mina turned around to face Adam, she found him two paces in front of her. With another step, he closed the gap completely. He tipped her chin up with the knuckle of his forefinger until she was meeting his gaze. Luci's hands braced her hips, his heat warming her back.

"Thank you for the gift of these last few minutes, even if we did not get to finish what we started." His eyes flicked to Luci in a silent accusation before settling back on Mina. "But I won't apologize."

"Why not?" Mina asked. She had thought she was finally starting to reach him. He owed Oz and Dahlia an apology, but he owed it to himself too, so he could move on and become something more than the anguish he carried with him.

Maybe she had pushed him too much too quickly.

"Why should Oz have a happy ending?" Adam scowled as he dropped his arm and stepped back. He looked at Luci again. "You were right to stake your claim now. I would have tried to steal her away again, keep you from your happy ending as well."

⌒◇⌒

"What is with him?" Mina slammed the palm of her hand against the edge of the steering wheel with a frustrated grunt. They were stuck in traffic two exits from her family's home. "Ouch."

Luci took her hand in his own and pressed a gentle kiss to its side. Tingles spread down to her elbow. She giggled as her arm broke out in goosebumps. Her whole mood lightened, and she turned to smile at him. "Feeling better?" he asked, and she nodded.

"Thank you," she said. "I don't understand. Twice now, in a very short time, I might add, I've encountered demon-like beings and failed to win them over."

"You didn't fail," Lilith said. "Adam wanted to keep you."

"A lot of good that does our cause," Mina said, sighing.

"He might step up," Beelzebub said, "to protect you."

"Okay, so if my life is in imminent danger, he might show up. Are any of you planning to let it get that far?" Her eyes darted to catch a glimpse of Bellz and Lilith in the back seat via the rearview mirror.

"Of course not," Lilith said. She sounded annoyed that Mina had even asked.

"Then he's not much help, is he?"

"At least he's unlikely to get in our way, Mina," Luci said. "You did that. I think you can count it as a win."

"Am I being overly sensitive, or does it feel like you guys keep awarding me full credit for partial wins? Does this have anything to do with the fact that I haven't managed to get pregnant yet?"

"No," Luci said, his tone firm. "It has to do with the fact that you've done more to bolster our forces than any of us have ever done."

"But I can do more."

"Do you have something in mind?" Luci asked.

She did, or, she was starting to. Her mind kept thinking about the stadium where she'd first met Luci's family. He told her it had been filled with demons once upon a time, all of them loyal to him. She wanted that for him again. Even without the threat from God and his angels, she wanted Luci to be adored by the masses the way he was meant to be, the way she adored him.

"Do you think you could summon them all?" she asked, tipping her head to the side as she crept up behind the vehicle ahead of her, engaging the brake as she neared it.

"Them all?" Luci asked.

"Your legion," she said. "You have more power now than you did then. Hades made sure of that. Could you command them to return?"

"Of course," he said. "But Hell has always been about choice. I will not force them to follow me if they do not choose to do so willingly."

Mina shot him a soft smile. "But could you call them all together for a gathering? A dinner and a show, perhaps?"

"I believe I could manage that." He turned in the seat to face her. "I'm going to ask you this again, little human, and there will be consequences if you refuse to answer a second time. What do you have in mind?"

She licked her lips at the thought of his delightfully enticing threat. But this was too important to play games. "Call them to your stadium, and let your inner circle help you show them what I can provide. Besides, I have a theory about why I haven't been able to conceive yet, and this will help us test it."

"What's your theory?" Bellz asked.

"Getting Dahlia pregnant served Oz's primary objective, an extension of Adam's—it robbed her of a happy ending. At least, Adam thought it did." She peeked at Luci before returning her attention to the road. "Maybe we just need to manipulate fate into believing that getting me pregnant will help you perform your greatest purpose."

"And what's my greatest purpose?" Luci asked.

"Ruling Hell, of course," Mina said.

"Call all the horrors of Hell, let your generals get your human bride off a few times, and then impregnate her in front of them all," Bellz said, and heat rose in Mina's cheeks.

"That could work," Lilith said, scooting to the edge of her seat and popping her head over the console.

"It's going to be a nightmare trying to secure the stadium. We need time to prepare," Bellz said.

"We'll need to ask our new allies for help," Lilith said. "But I think it should be doable."

"When we get to my mother-in-law's house, start preparations," Luci said.

"Not to throw a wrench into my own idea or anything, but do we need to be worried about Adam striking out against my sister?" Mina asked. "That whole 'no happy endings' business is concerning, right?"

"We can split some resources, keep your family's home guarded. We'll just need to make sure your family stays put while we do what we need to in Hell."

"Okay, so they'll be under house arrest for, tops, a minute?" Mina asked.

"Does it sound to you two like she's questioning our prowess?" Luci asked.

"A little bit," Beelzebub said.

Mina watched Lilith shrug in the rearview mirror before traffic began moving again. "You do remember that time moves very differently in our two realms, yes?" Mina asked. "Clearly I was referencing that. I know you'd all keep me coming for days if I didn't need to stop for water, food, and sleep."

"You don't need any of that in Hell," Lilith said, reaching her hand out. Luci blocked her before she could touch Mina, though.

"She's driving, Lilith. Wait until we're home."

Twenty-Six

"YOU'RE SAFE!" DAHLIA flung her arms around her sister, hugging her tight. Mina squeezed back just as hard. Dahlia had been pacing the entire first floor waiting for Mina's return. Tabitha had retreated upstairs to play a game on her tablet, forgoing the large TV screen in the living room to escape her mother's annoying behavior. Oscar had plopped down at the bottom of the staircase where he could keep tabs on Dahlia while also guarding access to his daughter.

Luckily, Sandra was at a church function and missed all the chaos. If the sisters could shield their mother from her older daughter's misadventures, then they absolutely would. Sandra had been through enough without constantly worrying that Mina would fall prey to a demon.

Not that Lucifer would ever allow that to happen. Dahlia nodded to her brother-in-law in thanks, and he returned the gesture.

"What happened?" Dahlia asked, stepping back from her sister and allowing the rest of her party to enter the house. They piled into the dining room. Oscar stood in the doorway, one eye on the front door and the hallway between it and the stairs.

"I tried to get him to apologize to you two," Mina said, and Dahlia scrunched her forehead in confusion.

"Who?" she asked. "The original Zozo?"

"Yes. Although his name is Adam."

"That Adam?"

"Kind of," Mina said, her cheek twitching a bit.

"The story isn't like you've been told," Lilith said. "After creating me, Prometheus and his brother made a whole batch. I guess they felt they'd learned all they could from their failed first attempt."

"You're perfect," Mina said. "What more is there to learn?" Lilith winked at her, and Dahlia blushed, feeling like an intruder watching her sister flirt. She was seeing a glimpse of their private relationship, and, instinctively, she took a step closer to Oscar.

"Why would he apologize to us?" Oscar asked.

"Because he tore your family apart," Mina said.

"Yes, I understand why we deserve an apology. But why would he choose to apologize to us?" Oscar crossed his arms and leaned against the door frame, his hat hanging loosely from his fingers. "I've come to realize that he hates me. He enticed me with the promise of saying goodbye to my sister, but it was an illusion. By the time I'd figured it out, I'd sold my soul. He acted like a friend, settling me into his old role. Convinced me to trick humans the way he'd tricked me. Like I was doing them a favor or somethin'."

"Yeah, he definitely has a thing against anyone being happy," Mina said. "A real grump."

"Mina's worried that he will target you two," Lucifer said. "Are you okay if we arrange for some extra security for your home?"

Oscar grunted in agreement at the same time that he reached out his arm and snagged the belt loop on Dahlia's jeans, pulling her into him with the lightest tug. She didn't resist, falling against him.

"Where's Tabitha?" Mina asked.

"Upstairs on her tablet."

"Let's get her to come back downstairs," Oscar said. "I think we should have a game night."

"Tabitha!" Dahlia called upstairs.

"Yeah, Mom?" Tabitha yelled back.

"Come downstairs!" Mina scooted around them in the doorway and shouted from the bottom of the stairs.

"Okay, but there better be cookies," Tabitha said from the landing before clomping noisily down to the first floor.

"No cookies,"Mina said. "Is a game night okay, though?"

Tabitha pouted, crossing her arms, but begrudgingly made her way into the living room. Dahlia turned behind her to see which demons were joining them and laughed out loud when she saw Lucifer carrying a plate of freshly made cookies. He lifted a finger to his lips, but it was too late.

Tabitha had already seen them. "I have the best uncle ever!" Tabitha cheered, skipping around the living room. Lucifer placed the plate on the table.

Then Lilith pulled him aside, and he disappeared into the kitchen with her and Beelzebub. "What's that about?" Dahlia asked Mina.

"There's something I asked them to do. I don't think they'll be staying. Although, I'd prefer they do until we can get some friendly demons to keep watch over you three."

"How long until I'm calling them my siblings-in-law?" Dahlia asked.

"What?" Mina blushed. "Are we that obvious?"

"You've never been one for monogamy. There was never a single love triangle in any of the media we consumed growing up that you understood."

"Well, yeah. They're dumb. Just be a throuple."

"That's what I mean," Dahlia said. "If you ended up in a monogamous relationship, you wouldn't be you."

"I'm not sure how we're going to work it out. Luci's my guy. First and forever."

"So you're taking it slow."

"I also need them to figure out their first and forevers. Alastor and Lilith are clearly meant to be. And Beelzebub and Sindy are obviously sweet on each other. I don't want to get in the way of those relationships or overly complicate matters. So, for now, we play. We love each other, but no official commitments have been made."

"You mean aside from standing against Heaven together?"

"Yeah, aside from that pretty serious commitment." Mina bit her lip.

"You'll figure it out," Dahlia said, watching as Tabitha and Oscar reviewed video and board game options.

"How do you know that?"

"You're my big sister. You can do anything."

Mina shook her head. "You're the one who can do anything." She put her arm around Dahlia's shoulder and kissed her cheek before stepping away to join Oscar and Tabitha. "What are we playing?"

"Oscar wants to pull out the old console games."

"What old console?" Mina asked.

"The PlayStation, I think," Tabitha said. "He wants to play some racing game. There are modern racing games, Dad."

Dahlia's heart pinched to hear her daughter call Oscar that, just like it did every time these last few months. It would never get old.

"There was a game your mother liked to play when we first met. I never got to play it with her."

"Those old games are only two player. We won't all be able to play."

"We used to just rotate players, Tabitha." Mina hunched over and pretended to walk with a cane. "Back in my day."

"Did somebody turn my wife into an old lady while I was gone?" Lucifer asked. He scooped Mina up into his arms and she giggled in surprise.

Dahlia watched from her spot on the couch, hiding a yawn in her sleeve. She gave herself about a twenty percent chance of making it through game night without falling asleep on Oscar's shoulder. This had the potential to be an absolutely perfect night. You know, aside from her sister being kidnapped and the threat of attack from an asshole demon.

Dahlia groggily rubbed her eyes and stretched out her legs. She was on the couch, a throw pillow under her head. The room was dark except for the light coming from the flat screen where the menu of a racing game illuminated the room in red and purple.

Where was everyone?

She sat up, slowly registering that the kitchen light was on. She turned off the TV and went to investigate.

Oscar stood in front of the sink. His feet were bare, but he still wore his jeans and an undershirt.

"Did everyone go to bed?" Dahlia asked.

"Yessum," Oscar said. "I was just about to carry you up, darlin'."

She wrapped her arms around his middle and leaned against his back. "Are you worried about Zozo?"

"A bit," he said. "Mina's demons are taking turns keeping watch on Tabitha's room tonight." He sounded like he had more to say but cut himself off.

"What is it?" She stood on her toes and found the exposed skin on his neck with her lips.

"It's just odd coming back into Tabitha's life and finding that she already has everything she could possibly need. A full, loving family. Protectors across three realms."

"She needs you. You were always the missing puzzle piece for her," Dahlia said, pulling on his arm to get him to face her. "I ached for her, the hole in her heart that you left behind. And I've done my best to fill it, with my mother and sister's help, but it was never enough. Not truly."

He sighed. "I either hate myself for not being there for her or despise myself for being superfluous."

"Oscar, no." Dahlia rose higher, cupping his face in both of her palms. "None of it was your fault. She loves you, and you are here now for her to love. We'll make up for lost time."

He crushed her to him, his mouth finding hers, his hand wrinkling the fabric of her shirt. The back of her legs hit the kitchen table as he lifted her and set her on it. She spread them and he stepped into the unoccupied space, pressing close to her.

"I had you in one kitchen this morning. Should we bookend the day with a tryst in this one?" he rumbled against her collarbone.

"I think we should probably go up to my room," she said. "Anyone could walk in."

"I don't think they will. And Lilith or Beelzebub is pacing the hallway upstairs. We probably have more privacy down here."

Dahlia wrapped her legs around Oscar's waist and, using her arms braced on the table for leverage, thrust against him. "In that case." Through her jeans and his, she could only feel the general shape of him, but it was enough to tell that he was hard for her.

Oscar folded over her, brushing her hair aside so he could trail kisses under her jaw and along her neck. He pulled back to look at her, but something caught his attention behind her. He went rigid, pulling her from the table and shoving her behind him.

"What is it?" Dahlia asked. The fingers of one hand tugged at the back of his shirt, either to reassure herself that he wasn't leaving her or let him know that she hadn't left. She couldn't be certain herself.

"Zozo is here."

"What?" Dahlia shuffled backward, urging Oscar to do the same with an insistent yank on his flannel. "We need to get upstairs, alert the others, and get to our daughter."

"Stay within reach of me, Dahlia, until we are out of the kitchen. Then run as fast as you can upstairs. I'll be right behind you."

She backed through the archway that led into the living room, then turned and dashed to the stairs. When she reached the bottom, she almost ran right into Beelzebub's chest. With two large hands on her shoulders, he steadied her.

"I know he's here. I'm going to confront him. He shouldn't be able to get into the house."

"Do you want backup?" Oscar asked.

"I've got it, and Tabitha is asking for you both."

Oscar overtook Dahlia on the stairs and slammed into Tabitha's door. Dahlia was surprised he didn't wrench the door from its hinges, he threw it open with such force.

Tabitha sat up in her bed clutching a pillow to her chest, with Mina sitting beside her rubbing her back. "Mom! Dad!" Tabitha pushed the pillow aside and got up onto her knees to greet her parents. They joined her on the bed, and Mina moved to stand in the open doorway, acting as their guard.

Dahlia embraced her daughter, and Tabitha collapsed against her. "It's okay. We're here. You're safe." Oscar enfolded them both in his arms.

"I don't know, Mom. That guy is really angry."

"He's always angry," Mina said from the doorway, peeking her head out of the room.

Dahlia didn't know where Lucifer or Lilith were, but she suspected they were keeping watch on Beelzebub or guarding Sandra. "Where's your husband?"

"Keeping tabs on the situation."

A howling started outside Tabitha's window. It almost sounded like the wind, except for the human quality of its pitch. It ebbed and flowed along the side of the house as if looking for weak points.

Dahlia tightened her hold on Tabitha as Mina systematically turned off all the lights upstairs before moving to the window and pulling open the curtains.

Oscar let go of Tabitha and Dahlia. He jumped off the bed and flung himself between Mina and the window. "Get away. It's not safe. He could see you."

"That's why I turned off the lights."

"He's a demon, Mina," Oscar said. "He can see you in the dark just fine."

Mina peered around Oscar's shoulder, still trying to glimpse outside. "I think he's in the front yard anyway."

Oscar tugged the curtains closed. "That phantom we heard probably shares his consciousness. If it comes back, it's as good as him seeing you."

"Maybe we should go in the bathroom," Tabitha said, pointing to the Jack and Jill. "There aren't any windows in there."

Something large thumped into the window, making the pane rattle in an unsettling way. "What was that?" Mina asked, stepping toward the window again.

"Stop," Oscar said. "You three go in the bathroom, and then I'll check." He glared at Mina until she nodded.

"Is Grandma safe?" Tabitha asked.

"Lilith is with her," Mina said. "She was sleeping soundly." Tabitha and Dahlia wasted no more time entering the bathroom. Mina closed the door after stepping in behind them.

Tabitha crawled right into the bathtub with a throw she'd pulled from the foot of her bed and curled up into a ball.

Dahlia perched on the side of the tub, and Mina plopped down on the toilet seat lid.

"I'm sorry this night turned out like this," Mina said. "I mean, I would have felt worse about it before I found out that you brought a demon into this family first." Mina smirked at her sister, and Dahlia couldn't suppress the laugh that bubbled up.

"It had been a pretty perfect night, too." Dahlia sighed.

"You fell asleep almost right away, Mom," Tabitha said, yawning into her knee.

"Because I was content being surrounded by family. Your laughter soothed me to sleep."

Loud bangs were coming from all over the house. They could hear them against the window in Tabitha and Dahlia's rooms. But they weren't just hitting glass. The thuds against the brick siding were denser.

"What are they?" Dahlia asked. "Rocks?"

The entire house shook from one large boom, as if whatever was being thrown at the house hit every spot all at once. The bathroom door opened, and Sandra rushed inside. Lilith followed her in, closing the door once more.

"What's going on?" Mina asked.

"He's trying to get in," Lilith said, rolling her eyes.

"Using what?" Dahlia asked.

"Birds," Tabitha and Lilith said together. A chill ran down Dahlia's spine.

Everything remained quiet for a time as Tabitha made space in the tub for her Grandmother to join her. She'd brought her own blanket, and they looked like they were sharing a plush bath. Too bad Dahlia's phone was still in the living room. It would have made a cute picture, except for the metal faucet sitting ominously behind Sandra's head.

Lilith must have seen it too, because she briefly left the room only to return with two pillows. She tucked them into each end of the bathtub.

"Thank you," Tabitha said, and Lilith kissed her head.

A buzzing started, and Dahlia assumed they were from whatever new attack Zozo had thought up. They didn't hear any more thumps. From the bathroom, all they could make out was an insect-like buzz. Incessant this time, without a moment of peace.

"This is giving me the worst headache." Sandra rubbed her temples.

"Lilith," Mina said, standing up. "What can I do?"

Lilith nodded to the other door, and Mina turned on her heel and left the bathroom.

"Where's Aunt Mina going?" Tabitha asked.

"To help," Lilith said simply.

Twenty-Seven

MINA DID HER BEST to block out the sound of the awful buzzing filling the entire house. She did her best to forget that her family was currently in peril, that they were depending on her to give Bellz, Lilith, Oz, and Luci the power boost needed to send this asshole back to Hell.

Instead she focused on Luci's strong hands leaving dimples in her thighs as he held her in place on her old bed. His forked tongue worked her clit from two sides before slipping inside her and flicking against her g-spot. His nose brushed against her lust button, and when she tried to thrust against him, he pressed her down harder into the bed.

Per his instructions, she held her wrists above her head, each clasped in the hand of the other, binding herself for him with her own willpower and the motivation of his future praise.

He worked his tongue farther into her, bringing one hand down from her thigh to spread her labia. Involuntarily, Mina wrapped her now-free leg around his head, and he let her writhe against his face.

Luci rubbed her labia, bringing his fingertips closer to her clit. When he reached her pleasure center, he pinched it roughly. She came, her hips rolling against him as she rode it out, and he drove her through it, refusing to back off until one climax became two. Her thigh defied restraint, and Luci gave up, opting instead to press a finger against her anus. A third orgasm hit her by surprise and she released her arms so she could press them against her mouth to muffle her scream.

"Good girl," Luci said, standing up from his spot on the floor.

"Was it enough?"

"Most likely," he said, but he stripped out of his pants and climbed onto the bed between her spread legs. "But let's just make sure." He slid into her in a single thrust, and she clasped her arms around his broad shoulders. His eyes closed as he attempted to regain some control, his struggle clear as day.

"Let go," she whispered against his ear. "You've made me come three times. You can let go."

"I don't want to hurt you." Cupping her face in his hands, he met her gaze, letting her see the galaxies spinning away in his green eyes.

"I see you, Lucifer, my morning star. I loved you for longer than I can remember. You. The fallen angel. The king of demons." She pressed a hand to his chest. "I love your heart, and your vision for the future."

"Our vision," he interrupted, and she couldn't help but smile.

"And that. That thing you do where you never discount my feelings or my contributions. Fuck, that's intoxicating." She kissed him then, deeply, but she didn't linger, biting his bottom lip as she pulled away. "I can handle the beast that's inside of you. More than that. I crave it. Do your worst, Satan." She nipped at his jaw. "Do your worst, husband." Then she brought his earlobe into her mouth and ran the edge of her human teeth against his godlike flesh, once, twice, before laying her head back on the pillow.

He wasted not a moment more, driving into her with an unpredictable, erratic rhythm. His pitch-black wings sprouted from his back and spread wide above them. She whimpered as he thickened inside her. The hardness of him pressed against her internal walls with a newfound resilience. When he pulled back, something stabbed at her g-spot with teasing pokes, but when he thrust forward, rounded ridges rubbed against it.

She trembled beneath him. Unable to match his movements, and putty at the new sensations, all she could do was take everything he was giving her. With a breath, she whispered his name. Not once did he break eye contact. Not until her eyes rolled back and her delirium hit its apex, back arching, toes curling. And she could feel the energy of it around them. It fueled him, pushing him into his own crisis. His demon seed filled her, seeping out from around him as he slammed into her one last time, vibrating from his spine as his orgasm rolled on.

When she opened her eyes, he gently caressed her cheek. "Are you okay?" he asked with that look in his eye once more, the scared one, like he was terrified he'd ruined everything.

"I'm infinitely better than okay. That was amazing." She wiggled underneath him. "Let me see your cock. It felt very different."

He chuckled and rolled off her, gesturing crudely at his groin. "Have at it."

It was still erect and beautiful, but it looked nothing like normal. The majority of it was the same shade of black as his wings. And it was covered in red ridges, rounded on the top and spiked on the bottom. "Is this your demon cock? Have you been keeping *this* from me?" She dragged her palm along its length, then ran the back of her fingers against each ridge.

"I didn't want to hurt you, and we've never needed it. I've never needed it. Until you told me to let go, I didn't even really feel like it was my cock but a perversion of my true form."

"Luci, nothing about you is a perversion."

"Once upon a time, I liked to think that everything about me was."

"Mm," she rolled on her side, running a fingernail around his belly button. His tummy jumped and rolled as he tried and failed to hold in his laughter. "You're perfect in my eyes. Do you worry about the rest?"

"Not particularly."

She pursed her lips. "Except for your friends who need our help."

"I think that last burst topped them off nicely. I doubt they need our help."

"It's too quiet," she said, straining to hear the sound of a continued assault, but there was nothing.

Luci sat up. Swinging his legs over the edge of the bed, he went to the window and peeked out. "Get dressed," he said, dropping the curtain and heading straight for the door. "They've captured him."

"What?" Mina bolted upright and watched her husband open the door, walk through it, and close it behind him. She scrambled to get off the bed and get her clothes back on. A shower would have to wait. It was only when she glanced back at the bed that she saw the giant stain left from Luci's cum.

She caught up to Luci at the front door. "We owe my mom a new mattress," she said as she slid her hand into his.

"What do you mean you owe me a mattress?" Sandra said, emerging from the front study.

"What are you doing down here?" Mina asked.

"Tabitha and I are watching the show from the study window." She nodded to the room she had just left. "If whatever happened to the bed has anything to do with giving me more grandbabies, then I don't care."

"We'll replace it," Luci said. "No problem." He tugged on Mina's hand. "Let's get out there."

Outside, they found Beelzebub holding Adam firmly in place from behind, his arms immobilized behind his back. Lilith pressed a blade against the tip of Adam's chin as he plastered a stare to the green lawn.

"What do you want us to do with him?" Lilith asked.

"I suppose we could kill him," Luci said. "It would probably be a mercy, the way he's chosen to live his life."

"Remember that my niece is watching," Mina said.

"My bride seems to think we should allow him to live."

"What do you think, Adam?" Mina asked, her voice loud and clear in the night air.

Lilith lowered her blade and grabbed Adam by the hair, pulling his head up. He said nothing and stared at the air three inches from his face.

Mina dropped Luci's hand and took several steps forward until she occupied the spot in which he was staring. "You don't have to surround yourself in pain. You don't have to despair."

Twenty-Eight

D AHLIA CLUTCHED THE ARM Oscar had wrapped around her waist. They looked out of the dining room window at the front lawn as Beelzebub and Lilith confronted Zozo. When the first rush of power had filled the house, Oscar and Lilith had suggested they all come downstairs so Lilith could provide backup for Beelzebub. She'd gone outside after the third rush.

It was obvious when the power surges happened because Oscar would inhale sharply, and Lilith's eyes had glowed for a moment.

As Lilith and Beelzebub circled Zozo, Oscar's grip tightened on her. His legs gave out, and he inadvertently pulled her down with him so they both ended up on the floor, tangled together.

"Are you okay?" Dahlia asked, twisting in his arms.

He only grunted in return, nodding his head to the window that was now behind her. She turned and gasped, finding that Beelzebub and Lilith had apprehended Zozo. How had she missed it? Her back had been turned for a second.

"How did they do that?"

"Mina," Oscar said. "That was the biggest one yet."

"What are they going to do with him?" Dahlia asked. Tabitha and Sandra were in the office across the entryway, watching all of this unfold. Currently, Beelzebub and Lilith were being as gentle as they could be. Zozo's arms were held behind his back. The knife Lilith wielded would definitely do some damage if she wanted it to, but she held it loosely at Zozo's chin. Even though the threat was clear, she had not yet caused him harm.

Why did Dahlia care? This demon had ripped Oscar away from her, kept him from being Tabitha's father, and kidnapped Mina. He didn't deserve her concern. He certainly hadn't earned her forgiveness. He didn't even want it.

"I suspect they'll follow Lucifer's lead."

"He's not usually in the business of murdering his own kind, right?"

"What? Of course he is. There have been countless skirmishes since Mina came to Hell the first time, even some minor wars, and they weren't bloodless."

She heard Lucifer and Mina in the entryway, but they immediately pushed through the front door and joined the other two on the lawn. Dahlia's heart rate sped up, and she got up on her knees to get a better view.

"Why does that terrify me? They can't kill him, Oscar."

"They absolutely can kill him," he replied. Anger laced his words.

"Well, for one thing, our daughter is watching. Secondly, I don't fucking know, but I feel like he's ours." She used the window ledge to pull herself up.

"To kill?" Oscar followed her to standing. "I can get behind that."

"No. Ours," Dahlia said, "our responsibility. His pain is ours to soothe."

"What are you talkin' about darlin'?"

"I can't explain it, but I can't allow them to harm him." She stormed out of the dining room and gripped the handle of the front door.

"Dahlia, wait," Oscar called after her, but she kept going, ripping the door open and dashing toward the group and the demon who had tried to ruin everything. Her sister's words traveled to her, and she sighed with relief. Mina was trying to reason with him. They hadn't resolved to kill him. Not yet. She had time, and she slowed her steps.

Dahlia took up the spot next to her sister as Mina asked, "Why the obsession with happy endings, Zozo? Why do you want to destroy ours?"

"There's no such thing." His words were clipped as if it pained him to speak them.

"You're partially right," Mina said, lifting onto her toes and inching closer to him. "There's no such thing as an easy happy ending. You have to keep fighting. And sometimes what you thought you were fighting for was wrong, and you end up with something different. But happiness is always attainable if you're willing to work for it."

"Your story isn't over, Zozo," Oscar said. He placed a protective hand on Dahlia's shoulder from where he stood behind her, and a part of her relaxed.

"You can find your happy ending with us," Dahlia said. She reached out and brushed a piece of hair from Zozo's forehead.

His nod was so slight it was almost imperceptible, but Lilith and Bellz released him and immediately stepped back. Zozo bent over into a ball. His shoulders rocked with sobs. Mina fell across him first, wrapping herself around him. Then Dahlia and Oscar embraced him too.

"You haven't said you're sorry yet," Tabitha said as she approached from the house, the front door standing open. "For what you did to us." Zozo looked up at her from between the arms of those he had wronged. Tabitha bent over so they were face to face. "But we forgive you."

He cried harder. Tabitha gave his head a pat and his sobs stuttered to a stop. Even after he had sat up, his diaphragm leapt erratically, making it hard for him to breathe.

Lucifer stood above them. "Why don't you come inside, Adam? Or do you prefer Zozo?"

The demon shrugged. "Either is fine."

"Aunt Mina, you'll have to come up with a nickname for him," Tabitha said.

"Hey," Bellz protested, "those nicknames are earned."

"Why don't you come up with a nickname, Tabby?" Mina suggested.

"No," Zozo hiccuped, his words ragged. "No, thank you. No new names. I've tarnished enough of them."

"If you change your mind, I'll pull out the brainstorming notebook." Tabitha popped up to her feet and dashed back into the house.

Twenty-Nine

DAHLIA HANDED ZOZO—OR ADAM, she supposed—a hot mug of tea before pulling the quilt from the back of the couch and wrapping it around his shoulders. He was still shaking, and her gut clenched at the thought that he might be in shock.

She had sent Tabitha straight to bed upon entering the house; it was way past even Dahlia's bedtime. Then she set upon getting water boiling for their unexpected guest. Mina had looked exhausted too, and so she'd told her older sister to also get some rest. They could deal with most of this in the morning. Adam just needed a little help settling in for the night, and he definitely didn't need a large crowd hovering over him to do that.

Sandra had made up the pullout sofa in the front office for him so he'd have his own room for the night. But Dahlia was a little uncertain of leaving him alone just yet. Oscar watched from the door, his brow furrowed in concern. For her or for Adam, she wasn't sure. But she doubted that she could convince Oscar to leave even if she wanted him too. Which she most certainly did not.

She looked up at him, giving him a small smile as Adam stared at the steam rising from the mug clutched in his hands.

"Do you need anything else? There's a bathroom just on the other side of the stairs. If you get hungry, feel free to eat anything in the kitchen. It's a little bare right now. We'll go shopping tomorrow. Let me know if you want us to pick up anything specific for you."

"Why are you being so nice to me?" Adam asked.

"Well, you seem to be in a lot of pain. You have so much healing to do. I believe in second chances, but you aren't going to make much use of one until you get through what you're dealing with. You can't do it alone, whether you're Adam or Zozo."

"I'm not even sure if I want a second chance," he said.

"But that's exactly what I mean. If you can't make that decision yet, it just means you aren't ready to. Let us help you get there, and then you can cross that bridge."

"Or burn it," Oscar said from the doorway. Dahlia affectionately rolled her eyes.

"Ignore him." She placed a reassuring hand on Adam's shoulder, but he flinched and she removed it.

"No," Adam said. "It's nice to know that both options are still available."

Oscar took two steps into the room and glowered down at Adam. "If you hurt anyone in this house while you are here, I will make sure you live to regret it for eternity."

Adam looked like he was about to challenge that remark, but when he met Oscar's gaze, he only nodded and bowed his head.

"I think he knows he's outmatched, Oscar."

"Doesn't hurt to remind him." Oscar held out a hand to Dahlia, and she took it.

"We're right upstairs. First door to the right of the landing. Let us know if you need anything." Slipping into the hall behind Oscar, Dahlia softly closed the door. Then, as quietly as they could, they ascended the stairs and entered Dahlia's bedroom.

"Are we stupid letting him stay here without so much as a guard?" Dahlia asked. "I want to believe in him, and I don't think it's a good idea for him to see me questioning him, but between you and me, I need to ask."

"He's not unguarded," Oscar said. "Lucifer trapped him in the study."

"Oh." Dahlia gasped, her eyes getting wide. "So I just made a total ass of myself telling him where the bathroom was and to make use of the kitchen." She put her hands on her hips and shook her head. "Someone could have told me."

"He's a demon, darlin'. He doesn't need a bathroom or food."

She plopped down onto the bed. "Well, now I feel like even more of an ass."

"I'm sure he appreciated your attempt at hospitality."

"Or he thought I was mocking him."

"You brought him tea." Oscar shrugged, removing his hat and placing it on the top of the dresser.

Dahlia rolled her eyes. "That he won't even drink?"

"He might. It isn't poison. Besides, I'm sure he's happy to have something to warm his hands."

She threw herself back onto the bed, arms above her head, and let out a loud sigh. "Fuck. I don't even know why I care. He's a bastard who stole years from us. He deserves to rot in his own pain for that alone."

"We aren't the only people whose lives he's destroyed." Oscar sat at the end of the bed and yanked off his boots. Grabbing a pillow with her right hand, she pulled it to her face and let out a scream. Oscar crawled up the bed and lay on his side beside her. When she slackened her tension on the pillow, he pulled up a corner and peeked in at her. "You doing alright?"

"No," Dahlia said. "I'm conflicted. But at least our baby is safe."

"Can we go sneak into her room and watch her sleep?" Oscar asked, biting his bottom lip. "Please. Just this once."

"Okay," Dahlia said, tossing the pillow to the side. "But only because this night went so sideways."

After shutting off all the lights in her bedroom and unplugging the night-light in the bathroom that bridged her room and her daughter's, Dahlia and Oscar opened the door from the bathroom into Tabitha's room just enough to peer through the gap.

Tabitha lay on her side spooning a stuffed animal. Her breaths came regularly, and she looked relaxed. Once Dahlia's heart had calmed a bit with the reassurance that her baby was just fine, she tapped on Oscar's chest to signal that they should go back.

But they hadn't determined a code before starting this venture, so he misunderstood. As a result, when she stepped back, he moved forward, and they crashed into each other and collectively tumbled into the door jam, sending the door flying into Tabitha's desk.

Immediately, Tabitha woke up, sitting up straight, and flicking on the lamp on her bedside table. "Mom? Dad? What are you doing here? Is everything okay?"

"Sorry, sweetheart," Dahlia said, righting herself. Oscar helped to steady her once she had found her feet again. "We were just checking on you."

"It's my fault," Oscar said. "I asked your mom if we could watch you sleep for a little bit. I didn't get to do it when you were younger, so I took advantage of her distressed state tonight so she'd say yes."

"Oh, is that what you were doing?" Dahlia turned to him and glared. When he threw up his hands in surrender, she giggled.

Tabitha crawled out of her bed, clinging to her stuffed animal. It was the orangutan Mina bought for her the first time they went to the zoo. "Can I sleep with you tonight?"

Dahlia sighed. Tabitha hadn't asked to sleep with her for four years. As much as it had been a relief when the bed-sharing had stopped, Dahlia still found herself missing it. Mourning that her daughter was growing up at the same time that she celebrated each new milestone. But it had always been that way, the bittersweet nature of parenting. "Yes, but just this once."

Back in Dahlia's room—she did have the bigger bed, after all—Tabitha immediately claimed a spot on the left side of the bed. Dahlia brushed her teeth and changed into pajamas. As she passed Oscar on her way out of the bathroom, they quickly squeezed hands. Dahlia crawled into the middle of the bed and tucked a very sleepy Tabitha against her, leaving the right side free for Oscar. A few minutes later, he wrapped himself around Dahlia and she fell into a deep sleep.

Thirty

MINA KNOCKED ON THE study door in a syncopated rhythm and waited. Dahlia and Tabitha had left early that morning for work and a friend's house, respectively. Sandra was in the backyard working on her garden and had plans to get lunch with a youth leader from church. So Mina had asked for everyone to meet here so they could talk about Adam and plan for the gathering she had proposed.

It was going to be a long day, and she wouldn't be able to focus on any of it if she didn't check in to make sure Adam had made it through the night. She rapped her knuckles against the wood again. "Adam?"

The hinges groaned as she opened the door, and Mina almost groaned right alongside it.

"You're still alive," she said as she took him in. His eyes were gaunt, his nasal bone a little too pronounced. Actually, he looked a little skeletal all over. "Do you need another boost of power?"

Adam shrugged. He stood from the pullout and took two steps closer, meeting her at the door. "I don't deserve it."

"Okay, so you'll just scare my mother half to death?" Mina put a hand on her hip.

"I'll just stay out of sight." Another shrug.

"You aren't staying here looking like death," Mina said. "No way I'm letting you give my niece nightmares."

"Then have your husband move me somewhere else." Adam closed the door in her face.

Mina was still grumbling about it when she found Luci in the living room.

"I assume that the new roommate is doing well?"

"No. Nope. Uh–uh. Not even a little bit."

"What are we going to do with him?" Luci asked, chuckling softly as he pulled Mina into a hug.

"He's losing his human form again already."

"I'm surprised it is just now starting to fade. He expended a lot of energy last night."

"He refused my offer for a boost."

"He what?" Luci looked her over. "How could anyone turn down such an offer?" His eyes roamed over every inch of her and filled with Hellfire. "Would you like me to remind you what he's missing?"

Mina laughed. "Michael and Kathryn are coming over in about," she glanced at the clock on the wall, "fifteen minutes."

"Sindy, Alastor, and the others will be here then, too."

"So you have a quarter hour to soothe my ego," Mina said, smirking at him.

He gripped her by the hips and pulled her against him. His mouth descended on hers, and he devoured her in a soul-searing kiss. She took a step backward, and he followed. Clumsily, they made their way to the downstairs bathroom, and Mina locked them in.

Seconds later, Luci had propped her up on the nearest piece of furniture. She had to hold herself in place to keep from slipping into the pedestal sink.

"This is an interesting way to restrain you," Luci said. "You can't let go of the sink, or you'll fall in."

"Luci, my arms are going to give out when you make me orgasm. This is a horrible idea." But he wasn't listening. He peppered her flesh with kisses, lifting her tank top to expose her bare breasts and pulling up her skirt. His fingers found their way underneath her panties, and he explored the valley between her thighs.

"I'll catch you." He got down on his knees and ripped off her panties. His mouth clamped around her clit, his tongue flicking against her most sensitive flesh. Using three fingers, he fucked her, hard and fast. Like the night before, he held nothing back. As she was right on the brink, he slipped his pinkie inside her as well.

"Luci, I can't hold on." After another forceful thrust of his hand, she came. Her arms went rigid in the height of her pleasure, but as soon as that wave began to recede, they trembled with effort. But before she could collapse, Luci swept her off the sink and set her on the ground in front of him. He clutched her to him, letting her lean against him until her breathing returned to normal.

"Did that jog your memory?" Luci asked.

"Huh?"

"I was reminding you."

"I'm sorry. That orgasm. Wow." She looked up at him through hooded eyes. "Were you stretching me out for later?"

The corner of his mouth twitched. "There's something I didn't tell you last night."

She narrowed her eyes at him. "Why are you still keeping things from me?"

A smile made of pure evil widened his mouth and creased his eyes. And a deep-rooted longing pierced Mina's heart, zinging through her core. She would never stop wanting this man, her demon. "Last night, my cock was in its correct form, but not its correct size."

"How big are we talking, Luci?"

"Bigger than Alastor."

She sucked in her lips and bit down before puffing out her cheeks and exhaling. "I need my panties."

Her whole body was still shaking when the doorbell rang. The fresh memory of what he had done to her on that bathroom sink and the anticipation of what he still had to offer played on repeat in her mind. Damn it, she wanted him, and she was going to have to sit through this meeting before she could do anything about it.

When she opened the door, Kathryn didn't wait a moment before springing a hug on her. "I missed you," her human friend squealed.

"I missed you, too."

"You didn't say it was Adam who was here," Michael said as he pushed past them and into the house. "Adam," he called.

"He's in the study," Mina said, pointing her thumb at the closed door behind her. Michael wasted no time opening the study and walking in. "Crap." Mina followed.

Adam sat at the edge of the bed staring at his hand. The skeletal qualities in his face and body were gone, leaving healthy muscle and skin. He looked up as Michael knelt in front of him.

"Adam," Michael said. "We lost track of you centuries ago."

"A millennia and a half, at least," Adam said, voice flat and devoid of all emotion.

Mina swallowed and crossed her arms, the motion enough to snag Adam's attention. "I told you I didn't want this." He held up his hand.

"It wasn't for you," Mina said.

"How did you even have time? I just turned you down," Adam said.

"I'm sure if you give it a few days, you'll go back to being the grim reaper," Mina said.

"What is she talking about, Adam?" Michael asked.

"He'd lost his human form until he used me as a battery yesterday. After he'd burned through all that power trying to break into my family home last night, he started to lose it again."

"What have you been doing since we last met?" Michael stood up and took a step back. He scanned his old friend's face, assessing. "You're infected with tormented spirits."

Adam sat in silence, refusing to even acknowledge Michael's presence.

"Come on," Mina urged. "Let's let him rest. We can go talk in the living room." Mina reached for Michael's hand, and he let her lead him from the room.

Oz happily sat in one of the two armchairs, and Michael and Kathryn shared the loveseat as closely as possible without touching, while Mina and her lovers crowded around the couch, choosing to be close together. Mina sat on Luci's lap, with Lilith perched on the arm of the couch to their left. Beelzebub claimed the spot on their right and tugged on Mina's legs until they were draped across his lap and she was leaning against Lilith's side. Alastor sat on the opposite side of Bellz, and Sindy sat on the floor between Bellz' legs.

Sindy and Mina had shared a long hug when she had arrived with the other demons. Sindy had burrowed her nose into the crook of Mina's neck and gripped her tight, whispering unneeded apologies for missing all the drama.

"I missed this," Mina said, only loud enough for those on the couch to hear. Lilith put her hand on Mina's shoulder, and Mina placed her own on top of it and squeezed.

"What are we going to do with Adam?" Oz pronounced the name like it was poison on his tongue. Michael flinched.

"You said he was infested," Mina said, focusing on Michael. "Maybe let's start there."

"He's been collecting them," Oz said. "Since long before he collected me."

"What do you mean?" Michael asked, scooting to the edge of the cushion and propping his elbows on his knees, all the while being oh-so careful not to accidentally brush Kathryn.

"He used spirit boards to pull in those who were grieving or full of anger, lost souls who were looking for a connection to their living loved ones. He fed off their confusion and longing. He trapped them. They didn't infect him. He invited them in."

Mina's stomach tightened, and she wished that Dahlia were here. Dahlia should be here.

"He let me believe he had my sister, let her talk to me, and told me the only way he would release her was if I sold my soul to him. I then became the next Zozo so he could go on to pursue better opportunities."

"That's how you became a demon," Mina said.

"Yes, ma'am."

A thought crossed Mina's mind, and she turned to Luci. "Has it always been Oz? Has he always been Tabitha's father?"

Luci peered at Oz, turning his head to the side. "I think so. I've never met him in person before, Tabitha's father. But he does resemble the man I've seen in a portrait several lifetimes back."

"My deciding to fight for us isn't the only thing that's different this time, then," she said.

"I suppose not, but I don't understand what that has to do with anything," Luci said.

"It just makes it all feel more destined."

"You're worrying again that we're playing right into His hands," Luci concluded, and Mina nodded.

"His motivation has never been clear to me." Mina shook her head, trying to get back on track. "But we need to focus on the problems at hand. We have no control over God or His will. All we can control is what we do."

"So what *do* we do?" Kathryn asked. "I'm definitely out of my element here, but can you exorcise ghosts from a demon?"

"Adam isn't strictly a demon," Lilith said. "He's become more demon-like through his actions and the distortion of his morals over time, but he's also still a First Human."

"Technically a second human, Lilith. You were first," Mina said.

Lilith waved the suggestion away. "I said goodbye to my humanity when I was cast out. But Adam never officially did."

"Wait. Can he actually release souls?" Sindy asked.

Oz nodded. "This is why I don't trust him. He's playing along just until he can escape."

"Or he's been trapped in this torment of his own making for so long that he doesn't have the courage to break out," Beelzebub said.

"It's not courage he's lacking. It's faith," Alastor said. "Faith that the world outside his own is better."

"The devil you know," Mina said.

"So how do we give him faith?" Kathryn asked. She'd been silent, staring at Michael intently while they answered her question.

"He needs time to adjust," Luci said. "We need to show him that he can trust us. And we continue powering him up, despite what he says he wants."

"Luci," Mina said sharply. "Without his consent?"

"We're keeping him alive so that he can make a decision while in his right mind about what he wants to do. It's fine," Lilith said.

"I suppose that's true."

"Are you going to do it now?" Kathryn asked. "An orgy? That's how Mina feeds you all, right?"

Mina let out a cackle. "Why? Do you want to join us?"

Kathryn shook her head. "No, but I'd like to watch." She turned to Michael. "If that's okay with you."

"Well, that depends. Will you touch me?" Kathryn nodded and Michael inhaled deeply. "And will you let me touch you?"

"Maybe."

"I have no objections," Michael declared quickly.

"I'm not sure that this is the best place to keep him," Mina said.

"I agree," Oz said. "I'd feel much more comfortable with helping Adam if he were far away from my family."

"There is that, but I'm also worried about our family walking in on us when we're trying to, um, reinvigorate his will to live. Today they aren't expected back for a few hours, but usually there are people in and out of here all the time," Mina said.

"He can stay in my penthouse," Michael said.

"Or mine," Kathryn said.

"No," Michael said. "He's not staying with a human. Even one as fierce as you."

"I think that sounds like a fine idea," Luci said. "So I'll move Adam to Michael's condo, and we'll stop by regularly to get him whatever he needs."

"With that settled, let's talk about the gather—" Mina started but Kathryn cut her off.

"Wait, we aren't getting a free show right now?"

"I'm sorry. We have more to talk about," Mina said. "After, though, I promise. Just as soon as we get Adam moved."

"Fine," Kathryn said, pulling out her phone. "I have work I need to do anyway."

"No," Bellz said. "I think we can give them a little show now. You said your family won't walk in on us today. Don't you agree, Luci?"

"Absolutely," Luci said.

"We'll need to multitask," Alastor said.

"What?" Mina asked as Lilith, pulling Mina's arms behind her back, held her in place with one hand and brushed her hair off her shoulders and away from her neck.

"Oh." Kathryn's eyes widened and she patted Michael's leg in her excitement. Her phone lay discarded on the floor in front of the loveseat, completely forgotten.

Oscar cleared his throat and rose from his chair. "I'm going to go keep Adam company. No offense, but Mina's basically my sister now." Shortly after he left the room, Mina heard the door to the front study open and close.

Bellz pushed one of Mina's legs off of the couch and, wrapping his hand around the ankle of the other and pulling her leg out and up to rest against his chest, held her open.

"What resources do we need for our gathering?" Sindy asked. "Do we need to serve food? Or are we mostly concerned about security?"

Luci pushed Mina's skirt up and out of his way then traced words like "mine," "star," and "troublemaker" on the skin of her inner thigh with the tip of his finger. "Of course we'll be feeding them. Mina will be the food."

Lilith snapped her jaw right next to Mina's ear, who jumped in surprise then giggled when Lilith nibbled on her shoulder.

"I meant do you want a buffet before or after the main event," Sindy said, rolling her eyes playfully.

Luci shook his head as he dipped a finger underneath the elastic of Mina's panties, tickling the crease of her leg. "I want them hungry before we start, and they'll definitely leave satisfied. No need to worry about refreshments."

"You think I'll be enough?" Mina asked.

Instead of answering, Luci brushed a knuckle along her labia.

Swallowing her whimper, Mina pushed her point forward. "Being a good leader means anticipating your people's needs before they do, right? Is it really enough to just provide them with a show? At least provide beverages. They might be parched afterward."

Luci wet the end of a finger with Mina's juices, teasing her entrance.

"Are you often parched when we're finished?" Lilith asked Luci.

In response, Luci removed his hand from Mina's underwear and brought his finger to his mouth, sampling her with his tongue. "I have other ways of quenching my thirst."

Mina was riveted. She was afraid to blink and miss one moment of Luci's tongue flicking against his skin. The smile that spread across his face, pure villainy. She gulped at the desires she saw dance along the irises of his eyes.

"Not everyone you invite will have your level of access to me, correct?" Mina asked. "My orgasm will be the only interactive part for them?"

Luci glanced to Bellz beside him. "You have a good grasp on her?"

Bellz nodded as his grip tightened on her ankle. He moved his free hand to just above the knee of her braced leg to hold it tight.

Once again sliding three fingers underneath the elastic of Mina's panties, Luci tugged with a grunt, and the fabric fell apart. He flung it toward the loveseat, and Kathryn squealed when Michael caught it, climbing over him to get it. He held it just out of reach, so she retaliated by tickling his sides.

He wiggled, squirming so much that he tumbled from the loveseat, twisting at the last moment to keep from taking Kathryn with him. "This isn't fair, Kathryn. I can't touch you."

"Unfair? You still have her panties."

At this point, they had the full attention of the entire room. Luci lazily rubbed Mina's folds, and she arched into him, but even they watched the flirtation happening between the most recently fallen angel and his human love.

Michael opened his fist and smiled. "Hey, look at that. I do. I'll give them to you. For a price."

Thirty-One

KATHRYN ROSE TO HER knees on the couch and peered down at him. She bit the side of her bottom lip. "You can touch me," she said. He didn't smile, but Mina could see the happiness in his eyes. They practically lit up the entire room.

He got to his knees as well and shuffled toward Kathryn on the upholstery. His hands hovered over her hips, not yet coming into contact with her. Mina's ruined panties dangling from his middle finger. "Are you sure?"

Kathryn nodded.

"Verbally, if you please," Michael said.

"Touch me, Michael." And he did. His hands braced her hips as he tugged her forward, brushing his cheek against her breast. Kathryn snatched the panties then wrapped her arms around him, but first turned his head so his eyes were on the couch again.

"Fuck, they're distracting," Lilith whispered.

"We'll never finish our meeting at this rate," Sindy muttered.

"I'll organize something with our top allies when I'm back in Hell," Alastor said. "Don't worry about it. Let's just enjoy this."

Mina glanced over at the green demon. He'd been so quiet that she'd almost forgotten he was there. Her eyes fell to his cock. He'd tugged it free of his slacks at some point, and he was stroking it nonchalantly. It had been a bit since Mina had last seen him fully erect. She'd forgotten just how impressive he was. She looked it up and down once more before looking toward Luci. His smirk told her that he knew what she was thinking; but if Luci was even larger, how could he ever possibly fit? Mina gulped, and Luci's smirk turned more reassuring.

"We'll get you there," he whispered against her temple and slipped two fingers into her. His thumb brushed her clit, lightly at first, and then with more force. When she was on the edge of an orgasm, Luci pushed in a third finger. The added girth set her off, and her vagina pulsed around him.

When Mina's senses returned, she found everyone looking at her. Sindy had moved between Alastor's legs, and she was happily licking the length of him. Lilith pulled Mina's tank top above her breasts. She wasn't wearing a bra, and Lilith took full advantage, palming one breast in her hand.

Michael had removed Kathryn's top altogether, and his hand had disappeared beneath the cup of her bra. Mina could see the rise and fall of his knuckles as he kneaded Kathryn's breast.

Bellz sat frozen, eyes locked on Luci's hand as it worked between Mina's legs.

"Help me stretch her, Beelzebub," Luci demanded. He removed his third finger, then moved the two remaining to the side, pulling her open for Bellz. Bellz sucked on two digits before inserting them alongside Luci's. Together they alternated between pulling against her walls and pressing down against her perineum.

"What are you planning, Luci?" Lilith asked.

"Should I tell them?" Luci asked Mina. She nodded her head, gasping as Lilith brought one hand down to pinch her clit.

"Mina's going to take my demon cock," Luci said.

"You can't be serious," Alastor said. "You're larger than I am."

"Just a little," Luci said.

"I would break her," Alastor said, and Sindy punctuated his point by failing to wrap her lips around the head of his dick.

"Not if we prepare her adequately," Luci said.

"We're all going to fist you today, little human," Lilith said, running a manicured fingernail along the length of Mina's clitoral hood.

"Today and every day until the gathering," Luci said. He tried to slip another finger into her, but only managed to the first knuckle. "Would you like to be first, Lilith?"

"Alastor, Sindy, off the couch. Bellz, Luci, turn her and hold her between you," Lilith said as she released Mina and stood up from her perch on the couch's arm. Everyone complied immediately. After sliding the coffee table closer to the TV, giving Lilith more room to maneuver, Alastor sat on an armchair and pulled Sindy onto his knee.

As Mina stood awkwardly to the side, her knees still shaky, the anticipation of feeling Lilith's hand inside her zinging along her skin, Beelzebub and Lucifer rearranged themselves on the couch. They left a space in the middle for her, and Luci waved her over. With some slight pressure on her hip, Luci guided Mina until she was perched on the very edge of the couch. Luci braced her with an arm around her middle. With his other arm, he pulled her left leg up and over his lap. Bellz did the same to the right. He sat a bit farther back, settling into the cushion, but caressed her calf so she knew he was still within reach in case she needed him.

"Perfect," Lilith said, kneeling between Mina's spread legs. "Keep your hands on Lucifer and Beelzebub at all times, Mina." When Mina put her hand on Bellz' thigh, he snatched it up and brought it to his lips for a chaste kiss, then settled their clasped hands against his body. He would help her follow Lilith's instructions. She placed her other hand on top of the one Luci was using to hold her leg out of the way.

Lilith nodded her approval and then brushed the backs of her fingers along Mina's vulva, flicked her clit, and dragged her knuckles back down. Rubbing along Mina's folds, Lilith moistened her digits. With a heightened focus that made Mina flush, Lilith expertly stretched her until Mina could easily handle all four fingers. Lilith used her thumb to stimulate Mina's clit as she fucked her, and Mina struggled to stay put, willing her hips to remain still. When she inevitably failed, Luci and Bellz helped hold her in place.

"Almost there," Lilith said. She pulled her hand out just enough to tuck her thumb against her palm. "Ready?"

"Yes, Lilith."

"Good girl," Lilith said. She pushed, spinning her wrist to press her knuckles against Mina's entrance until they were past her opening and inside her. Another little push and only Lilith's wrist was visible. Lilith rose up and pressed her forehead against Mina's. She watched the human intently, breathing with her. "How do you feel?"

"Your hand is inside me. We are on Earth, and your hand is inside me. I feel fucking fantastic, Lilith." Lilith responded by kissing Mina and pulling her hand back to its widest spot before forcing it back inside. "Oh, fuck," Mina's head dropped back against Luci's chest, and she could feel his chuckle rumble through her.

Lilith dropped down to her heels once more, giving the others in the room the ability to see what she was doing. She picked up her pace gradually, slipping out a bit more or a bit less with each thrust. Her knuckles made contact with that sensitive spot inside Mina as often as possible. And Mina was crumbling. The mindfuck of being stretched this way while her husband and his best friend presented her like an offering only heightened her pleasure. And then she couldn't keep herself together anymore, and she was coming on those knuckles.

"We've got you," Luci said, gripping her tighter. And Bellz placed kisses all over her hand and arm.

"Sindy," Bellz bellowed. "Here, now." Only delaying long enough to kiss Alastor's cheek, Sindy promptly bounced over. "Take my spot," he said, inclining his head toward the couch as he slipped out from under Mina's leg.

"Do you want to be next, Beelzebub?" Lilith asked as she slowly removed her hand from Mina's cunt.

"Yes," he said, kneeling next to her on the carpet.

Lilith grasped Bellz' forearm and raised it for Mina to examine. "Do you think you can handle this?" Mina only nodded, her attention monopolized by Lilith's fingers, glistening in her juices, as they wrapped around Bellz.

"You're soaked," Sindy said. She chose to sit closer to Mina, her arm brushing Luci and her upper body providing a bit of support to Mina's as well. Trusting the position of her hip to keep Mina's leg open, Sindy dipped her hand to Mina's pussy and masturbated her vigorously. "What?" Sindy asked as everyone turned to look at her. "We have to keep her wet if she's going to take Beelzebub's giant hand."

"Do you know from experience, my lovely Sindy?" Lilith asked, tilting her head to the side.

"Uh-huh, sure do," Sindy said, blushing and ducking her head.

"I'm glad you have some experience at this," Lilith said. She stood abruptly, knocking Bellz' hand away and stalking toward Alastor. She draped herself across the green demon's lap and offered him her fingers. "Get every last drop, Alastor." She met his gaze. "I mean it." His eyes twinkled as he began to lick her clean.

Bellz shuffled forward, and he inserted two fingers from each hand into Mina. She only had enough time to notice that Kathryn and Michael were snuggled together, lightly petting one another as they sat in awe of all that was happening around them, before the feeling of Bellz' fingers moving inside her prevented her from absorbing anything else.

All that existed was her and him and the solid wall of warmth behind her. When he added a third finger from each hand, her focus narrowed further. "Bellz," she whimpered, and he smirked.

After another moment or so of stretching her, he removed the fingers from one hand. While Sindy continued to work Mina's clit, Bellz added his pinky from the hand that remained. He then lifted Mina's chin with his free hand, forcing her to look into his eyes. He held her head in place while he tucked his thumb in just as Lilith had. He fucked her up to his knuckles, turning his hand over and pressing his fingertips into her g-spot before fucking her again.

"It's so big," Mina murmured. She was in shock watching it slowly disappear into her. His was much more substantial than Lilith's. He filled her so well, and his hand wasn't even completely seated in her yet.

Luci nibbled on her ear. His tongue darted out to lick against that sensitive spot right beneath it, and goosebumps pebbled all over her body. Then Bellz pushed past his knuckles, and he was completely inside her.

"Fuck, Mina," Luci said. "You are so sexy." She gushed at his words.

Bellz removed his hand almost immediately. He put both his hands together and penetrated her with eight fingers, working them in and out. And she couldn't hold back. She moaned loudly as her hips jerkily rutted onto his hands. "Please," she whimpered, repeating that single word and the name of her tormentor.

"Come, Mina. Fuck yourself on my hands, and come," Bellz commanded, and she was powerless to resist him.

Thirty-Two

S INDY TUGGED MINA'S SKIRT and tank top back into place. Not a super easy task given that Mina was currently curled up against Beelzebub's chest. "Do you want a blanket?" Sindy asked quietly. When Mina only shivered in answer, Sindy glanced to Beelzebub, who must have nodded because Mina felt her back encased in warm fleece.

She tried to tell them that she was okay, just a little over-whelmed, but no words came. Luci sat down beside her, a warm cup of tea in his hands. He held it out to her, but she couldn't move a muscle. Instead, he brought it to her lips and helped her drink. He read the words she couldn't vocalize in her eyes and physically relaxed.

"She's just overstimulated," Luci said to Bellz. He placed a hand on his friend's shoulder, and, when Bellz leaned against him, Luci happily supported both his and her weight. Mina mumbled happily at being close to both of them.

"Hey, so, Adam is pretty agitated," Michael said. "Oscar is keeping an eye on him, but we definitely don't need to pump any more energy his direction right now."

"That's fine," Luci said, rubbing Mina's upper back. "She's not up for more right now, either."

"Can we move him?" Kathryn asked.

"I don't think we should just yet," Michael said, pacing the floor in front of the couch. The coffee table still sat where it had been moved earlier, making the space feel bigger.

"Mina's family will be home in a few hours. I'm hopeful we'll be able to get it done before then," Beelzebub said before he pressed a kiss to the crown of Mina's head.

"Nap?" Mina managed.

"Let's get you upstairs," Luci said as Beelzebub lifted her in his arms. They brought her to her old room. Luci pulled down the bedding so Bellz could place Mina in the center of the bed. Then they each took a side of the bed and trapped her between them.

She didn't mind. It was cozy and warm. She had almost everything she needed right here.

Almost.

"Lilith?"

"She's with the others downstairs," Bellz said from behind her, his breath tickling the back of her neck.

"Cleaning up and guarding Adam," Luci said. "Sindy and Alastor went back to Hell. We can't all be gone for too long."

Her heart ached to hear they had already left. She missed them both terribly.

"Not yet," Bellz said. "But this plan of yours, Mina, it has the potential to change a lot of things."

Mina tried to nod, but she couldn't keep the command in her brain long enough to actually execute it. Parts of her mind were firing rapidly, but the connections weren't being picked up. Thoughts, both meaningful and useless, flittered away into nothing before she could fully grasp them. Eventually she gave in and let sleep take her.

A clap of thunder startled her awake. Obviously a storm had rolled in, but that fact didn't help Mina feel less disoriented. The light in the room was darker than it should be. She couldn't have slept for more than an hour and a half, yet it felt like a whole day had gone by. When she glanced at the clock, it was only 3:30.

She nuzzled against Luci. She was half on him, her leg draped over his, her head on his chest. And Bellz spooned her lower half, his head on her hip.

"I think we need to do this for Adam," she thought out loud.

"Fuck him until he's catatonic for a few hours?" Bellz asked, turning his head so he could bite Mina's side.

"The aftercare cuddles," she clarified. "These moments are just as precious to me as the orgasms, if not more so. Maybe he needs to know that it's not all just a high from sex."

"I doubt he'll be too receptive to Bellz and me crawling into bed with him." Luci chuckled a little.

"Maybe I should try it just with me then?" Mina asked.

"I don't want you near him alone," Bellz growled. "I don't trust he won't try and take you for himself."

Mina sighed. "Sometimes I feel like everything we do is just cleaning up after God's messes."

"Well, that's because it's true," Bellz said. "God is one fucking great mess-maker."

"It doesn't make sense. If He was Prometheus, shouldn't He be better at this? Shouldn't He be able to see the consequences of His actions?"

Luci shrugged. "I think he put that mantle aside a long time ago. He became something different, or something happened to forge Him into someone different. He has different strengths and weaknesses now."

"It's exhausting, being His maid."

"But we aren't just cleaning messes," Luci said. "We're building something new. Something better. At least, we have to hope we are. Otherwise, what's the point? I might as well snag you and your family and hide out in the deepest reaches of Hell until the end of eternity. Fuck what happens to humanity or any other being in this Godforsaken universe of ours."

"There's an idea," Mina said. "But I think it might be hard to fit all the people we keep adding to our family and friends."

"Hell's a big place," Bellz said.

Mina shook her head. "I haven't quite given up on that whole dumb-hope thing, I suppose. But it is good to know we have a backup plan."

"Would you like a shower?" Luci asked.

"I'm not convinced my legs will hold me for that long."

"A bath, then," Luci said, nodding to Bellz.

"Honestly, I would rather go home. Take a bath in my own bathroom. Put on some pajamas and watch a rom-com with a few of my favorite demons."

"What about Adam?" Bellz asked.

Mina let out a huff of air. "I can't fix him if my tank is empty."

"Okay," Luci said. "You're our priority."

"What needs to happen to move Adam before my family gets back? That's the priority. I'm a close second, though."

"I'll transport Adam with Oscar, Michael, and Lilith," Bellz said. "You two go home and take that bath. I'll join you when it's done."

Thirty-Three

DAHLIA TAPPED HER FOOT as she watched the numbers on Michael's private elevator tick up. She'd never been inside a penthouse before. He had the whole floor to himself.

"Does God pay for this place?" Dahlia muttered to herself. Would He still foot the bill, or would Michael lose it when he failed to pay the property tax on it? Oscar had made small investments early on that had turned into a very large nest egg. It was possible that Michael had done the same. If not, maybe Kathryn would keep him from the fate of losing his home, or they could move in together. If the texts Oscar had sent her while she was at work were any indication, Kathryn and Michael were getting pretty close.

And Dahlia was happy for them. Kathryn had seen more than enough hardship for one lifetime. She deserved an angel who would follow her every command.

The elevator announced her arrival with a ding as the doors parted. She stepped onto the marble floors and immediately found Oscar in her path.

"What are you doing here?" he asked, crossing his arms.

"You aren't the only person I text during my day," she said, stepping around him.

"I supported moving Adam to keep him away from you."
Oscar extended his arm, blocking her again.

"Oscar." Dahlia used her mom voice. "Stop it."

"Why are you here?"

"Mina told me you guys got a little carried away."

"No. I had nothing to do with that." Oscar shook his head.
"I'm not doing that anymore. Not with your sister."

Dahlia smiled at him. "Can only handle one Cadere sister at
a time, huh?"

"I only have eyes for one Cadere sister. Only one of you has
ever had my heart and soul. And, as much as I care for your
sister, it was never her."

"You're sweet." She rose up on tiptoe, the heels of her feet
escaping from her pumps, and pressed a kiss to his cheek.
Firmly back in her shoes, she attempted to ease past Oscar once
more.

But, of course, he stopped her with a hand on her waist. "I'm
still not clear on why you are here."

"To give Adam his aftercare. Mina is a bit preoccupied with
her own, but I thought she had a point that he needed some
basic affection instead of more sex energy. I thought I'd help
her out." She placed her hand over his. "You should join me."

"You want my snuggles, little lady?" He tipped his hat in her
direction.

"Always."

Michael had set Adam up in his guest room. It was a large
space, which, given the size of the rest of the place, was hardly
a surprise. Adam and Michael lounged on the queen-size bed,
console controllers in their hands. The TV across from them
sat on a low dresser.

"This is quite the setup," Dahlia said. "You are all forbidden from telling my daughter about this."

Michael beamed at her. "You'll never guess who got me into gaming."

Dahlia kicked off her shoes and awkwardly sat on the edge of the bed before scooting closer to Adam, who barely acknowledged her with a flick of his eyes before the game held his full attention once more. Her pencil skirt didn't allow her a full range of motion, and she wished she had taken the time to go home and change.

"Who got you into gaming?" Oscar asked. He waved a hand at the TV. "I assume that's what this all is?"

"It's no fun if you don't guess," Michael grumbled.

"I think the time for games is over," Dahlia said, holding her hand out for Adam's controller. "You have a guest, and you're being rude."

"Okay, Mom," Michael said, his laughter filling the room.

"She's right," Oscar said.

"I know. I just couldn't resist," Michael said, pressing a series of buttons and turning off the gaming system.

Adam sighed and held his controller out for Dahlia with a lazy flick of his wrist. "Thank you," she said as she took it and placed it on the bedside table.

Adam turned his head to look at her. His eyes narrowed. "You look really uncomfortable."

"I'm less uncomfortable than I've been all day," she said with a wiggle of her toes, "now that I'm out of those pumps."

"But you still aren't comfortable."

"I rushed over here," Dahlia said. "I was worried about you."

"For fuck's sake, why?" Adam asked, leaning back against the headboard next to her.

"Oscar said you were a little twitchy after Mina did her thing."

"'Her thing?'" Adam raised a brow. "That's a euphemism for orgasm, I take it?"

"Yeah, she is my sister, you know?"

"So?" Adam asked, shrugging.

"We don't mix sex with blood relations, Adam. Humans, I mean."

"That has not always been true."

"Ew." Dahlia shook her head to banish the thought.

"Okay, so not your thing." Adam shifted closer to her. "What is your thing, human? Seducing the man who broke apart your family before it could even start?"

Dahlia flicked his shoulder. "Joke's on you. I'm not here to seduce you."

"Then why are you here?"

She blinked at him, waiting for him to make a guess. When he failed to provide even the simplest hypothesis, she laughed. "Snuggles. Duh."

Michael left the bed. "I'm monogamous with Kathryn right now, snuggles and all, but I will leave you to it."

"What about Mina?" Adam asked. "I thought you said she helped you after God gave you a dick?"

Dahlia's eyes widened, and she could see Michael blush from across the room. "We've agreed to only enjoy Mina together." He bowed his head as he slipped by Oscar in the doorway. Oscar stopped him for a moment, just long enough to ask something, but Dahlia couldn't hear what was said because Adam took that moment to challenge her.

"What exactly do you hope to accomplish?"

Dahlia leaned toward him, tucking her arm around his and placing her chin on his shoulder. She smiled when he subconsciously nuzzled her breasts with his bicep. "For some people, happy endings mean a never-ending supply of orgasms. For others, it means quiet time with family or friends. I want to show you that side. The soft, calm one."

"I like the soft bit," Adam mumbled, eyes darting to her breasts.

"Uh-huh." Dahlia rolled her eyes. "All we are doing is cuddling. I am not my sister. There's only ever been one man I was attracted to immediately." She inclined her head toward Oscar.

"Really?" Oscar asked.

"The only other people I've been attracted to, I had to have an emotional connection first. I realize now that I already had that emotional connection with Oscar, since he's fathered my daughter in past lives."

"What?" Adam asked.

"Do you not know how it works? We are reincarnated about every hundred years."

"So Lucifer can find Mina again," Adam said. "I knew that. I didn't realize that you and your family were also part of that."

"There were ripples, I guess, when Mina and Lucifer fell in love," Dahlia said. "We've all been caught in them by now. I think it will only get worse, but hopefully for the better."

"A confusing yet optimistic view."

"Confusing because it is optimistic or because of the contradictory way I worded it?"

"Both, I suppose."

"Sorry. My brain tends to stop language-ing well after a full day of work."

"Obviously," Adam snorted, and the corner's of Dahlia's mouth ticked upward.

Michael briefly made an appearance from the hallway. He thrust a bundle of clothing into Oscar's hands and then retreated.

"You aren't so bad when you aren't ruining lives, did you know that?" Dahlia asked.

Oscar didn't give Adam time to respond—if he even wanted to, which Dahlia doubted. "I had Michael scrounge up some pajamas for you," Oscar said, handing the clothing to Dahlia. Dahlia held them up to examine: a white, ribbed tank top and a pair of boxers covered in soccer balls. "Go get comfortable. I'll keep Adam company."

Dahlia hesitated for a second before making her way toward the en suite bathroom. "Be nice," she requested of them both before slipping into the tiled room and closing the door. The clothes fit surprisingly well. The tank top was a little tight across the chest, but her breasts looked amazing in it. The white fabric did nothing to cover her dark nipples. Briefly, she thought about redonning her bra, but if the top was tight now, her bra would only make it impossibly snug.

She shrugged at her reflection. Oscar would enjoy it, and Adam could deal.

When Dahlia emerged from the bedroom, she found Adam and Oscar reclining on opposite sides of the bed. "Did you leave the middle for me?" she asked. Oscar's eyes grew wide as he took her in. With curves on full display and plenty of exposed flesh, she wasn't surprised by his expression.

"I should have looked over those clothes before I just handed them over to you." Oscar leapt from the bed, grabbed a throw off the bench under the window, and wrapped her up in it.

"What are you doing?"

"Protecting your modesty."

"From Adam?"

"Yes?" Oscar tilted his head to the side. "You think I'm being silly."

"And a little misogynistic, if I'm being honest. But also slightly adorable." Oscar sighed but stepped aside. There was a glint in Adam's eye, and he was watching Dahlia intently.

"With the three of us, it's a little warm in here for a blanket," Adam said.

"True," Dahlia said. "But we are only cuddling. I'm just putting that out there again."

"I think we could convince her to change her mind, Oz. What do you say? Team up for old time's sake?"

Dahlia realized she was blushing, and not just because she was embarrassed. She clutched the edge of the blanket and shuffled her feet, glancing shyly at Oscar.

He waggled his eyebrows at her. "Darlin', it's not really aftercare without the sex first."

"You just rushed to cover me up, and you are now suggesting a threesome?"

"I've always been a bad influence on him," Adam said. He had risen to his knees on the bed, and his intimidating presence towered over them where they stood between the bed and the window. The desire in his eyes was intoxicating.

"This is such a bad idea," Dahlia said as she let the throw fall.

Oscar held his hand out to help her climb onto the bed. "We'll go slow. Won't we, Adam?"

"Of course. Only what the lady desires." He took up Dahlia's other hand and brought her knuckles to his lips and placed a kiss on each one.

Oscar pressed up behind her, his hands slipping under her top and exploring her supple flesh. "I love how soft you are," he said into her neck. He made his way up her body until he reached her breasts. Her nipples pebbled between his fingers. "Your hard nipples." He bit her earlobe, and she arched into his palms.

After Oscar dropped one hand to her tummy, tracing teasing circles around her belly button, Adam bent forward, taking Dahlia's nipple into his mouth and sucking on it through her top. She gripped the back of his head and surprised herself when a moan slipped past her lips. When he finally released her, the white fabric was completely transparent where his mouth had been, and he groaned at the sight of her.

Oscar, who had been kissing along her neck and shoulder, stopped to tug the tank top off of her. Dahlia shook her head, wondering why they had even bothered getting her pajamas.

"I want to trace my hands over every last curve," Adam said as his eyes roamed over her torso before meeting her gaze. "Would you allow me to do so?"

Dahlia swallowed. "Yes, please." Oscar braced her body with his own as Adam reached out tentatively, tickling her skin with his fingertips. Her flesh raised with goosebumps as he made good on his word, touching her from collarbone to hipbone.

"I was right to be jealous of you," Adam said to Oscar.

"Correct." Oscar nodded. "Doesn't make what you did any better, though."

"I know I can't make it up to you—either of you," Adam said. "But I can make you feel good, Dahlia."

Oscar pulled Dahlia back against him, turning them so they were lying along the bed. He spooned her and slipped a hand underneath the waistband of the boxers she was wearing. She'd opted to leave her panties on, and Oscar growled in frustration at the unexpected obstacle. "Adam, be a pal for once, and help me remove these boxers."

Adam happily obliged as Oscar pressed his middle finger against Dahlia's center. The tip of his finger pressed the gusset against her entrance while the length worked its way into her slit. She was wet, and her moisture seeped into her panties, causing the fabric to cling to her every ridge and valley.

Adam was staring, and when Oscar noticed, he pulled Dahlia's upper leg up and over his own legs, spreading her so Adam could see more clearly.

"May I kiss you, human?" Adam asked.

"Yes," Dahlia said.

"And you, Oz?" Adam's voice wavered a bit.

"Not a fucking chance, buddy," Oscar said.

Dahlia twisted to look at Oscar. "Do we need to stop this? I thought you were on board, but if you aren't comfortable, then it's a no for me as well."

"No," Oscar said. "That's not the problem. I want to do this with you. I want him to worship you until he's finally repaid a little of the harm he caused. It will take the rest of your human lifetime, at least, but he owes you." Oscar turned his attention to Adam. "You need to serve her. Devote your entire being to making her happy. And then maybe, just maybe, I'll give you my forgiveness. But you will not kiss me until you have redeemed yourself."

"That's fair," Adam said.

"One little kink with this plan, though," Dahlia said. "I've never been dominant in the bedroom."

"You can be a bit of a power bottom," Oscar said, "like when I've got you really worked up, and you flip the tables on me. Gets me hard just thinking about it."

"That doesn't change the fact that I don't know what to do with a submissive."

Adam's eyes lit up. "Oz will command me until you do so on your own, Dahlia. I will serve you both."

"Your loyalty will be to her first and foremost," Oscar demanded.

"From now until the end of days," Adam promised.

"Then get to work. I want to see our lady's breasts glistening from all the attention you give them."

Adam immediately followed orders, kissing and licking every inch of Dahlia's breasts. When he got to her nipples, he hardened them with a pinch before sucking them into his mouth.

Oscar masturbated her through her panties before peeling the scrap of fabric to the side and attacking her clit with the pad of a finger. Every time she approached her peak, he'd stop abruptly. He'd never kept her at the top of the cliff for so long before, never teased her so relentlessly.

"What are you doing, Oscar?" She whimpered after he'd edged her three times in a row.

"Trying to coax out that power bottom I promised Adam."

"Fuck," she said as he once again brought her to the brink only to pull back at the last possible second. "Adam, on your back."

"Yes, ma'am," Adam said, rolling over obediently.

Dahlia pushed Oscar's hand aside and peeled off her panties. Then she straddled Adam's face, lowering herself until her pussy was right above him. "Do I need to tell you what to do now?" Dahlia asked, biting her bottom lip and blushing. Giving him specific instructions might be beyond her. Oscar always knew just how to lick and nip at her to turn her into mush.

Adam's hands wrapped around her hips, holding her in place while he tilted his head and pulled one large lip between his own.

Dahlia bent forward and, with two hands, braced herself on the headboard. She tilted her hips back, and Adam lost her labia but made up for it by pressing the flat of his tongue against her. "Fuck me, Oscar. Fuck my while Adam licks me."

Oscar straddled Adam's legs and lined his erect cock up with Dahlia's slick entrance. She tried to picture what he saw—her quim dripping arousal over Adam's chin while his mouth worked furiously to please her. Her center open wide, begging to be filled with Oscar's hard cock.

"Please, Oscar. Make me come on Adam's face. Make him drink us both."

"No condom?" he asked. They'd talked that morning and decided that while they weren't ready to actively try for a baby, they felt safe enough dropping down to one mode of birth control.

"No condom," she agreed.

"As you wish, darlin'." Oscar grunted as he pressed into her, and Dahlia gasped at the way he parted her, how warm he felt without a barrier. At the same time that her tension built, a part of her also relaxed. As if Oscar's dick was the exact piece that she had been missing, the thing she'd been longing for without realizing just how incomplete she was whenever she went without for too long.

He stretched her exquisitely as he slowly worked into her until his hips met her bottom. His hands roamed over her backside before one moved over Adam's hand. He slipped his fingers between Adam's where they clutched Dahlia and squeezed, pressing into both of them. It was all the warning he gave before thrusting into her with abandon. The headboard banged into the wall with each forceful rocking of his hips.

Adam's tongue pressed against Dahlia's clit, lubricating it before he flicked at it, then nipped.

Dahlia tried to stay in place, to not move against Oscar so that she didn't interfere with the decadent pleasure Adam was serving up, but she failed to keep herself from pressing her hips forward into Adam. When he responded by sucking on her with an intensity she couldn't have even imagined, she came. And came. And came.

Oscar grunted into her, his hips speeding as his own crisis approached. And then he emptied himself into her. For a moment, she relished the thought that his seed filled her, seed that had once impregnated her and could do so again if not for the birth control she'd started when she realized that Oscar would be a permanent fixture in her life.

Dahlia rested her head against her arms, panting heavily as she engaged her muscles, milking all of Oscar's cum.

"Get ready," he said, giving another squeeze to both Adam and Dahlia with his hand. "Don't you dare move, Adam. Not until I tell you to."

Slowly, Oscar pulled out of Dahlia. Quick as lightning, he adjusted Dahlia's hips and pressed her down over Adam's mouth.

"Use that tongue, Adam. Lap up all of my cum, and make her come again."

Adam slipped his tongue into Dahlia. He worked it against her inner walls, her g-spot. He hooked it around the globs of semen Oscar had left behind and pulled their combined fluids into his mouth. Happily, he gulped them down.

Throughout it all, Adam kept Dahlia coming.

When Adam and Oscar were both satisfied with the job Adam had done, they eased an exhausted Dahlia onto her side. Oscar curled around her while Adam pulled her head onto his chest.

"I'm sorry," Adam whispered once they'd all caught their breath. "I don't deserve any of this. You should both run as far away from me as you can." He swallowed. "Tomorrow. Run tomorrow. I don't deserve this night, but I find that I'm still selfish enough to ask for it."

"Adam, do you ever think that by denying everyone else their happiness, you were really just hurting yourself?"

"I suppose so. I thought I'd already lost my chance at a happy ending. That I'd put all these other fuckers out of their misery by hastening along their own inevitable sorrow."

Dahlia shook her head. "That's terrible logic. If happiness is doomed from the outset, shouldn't you soak it up for as long as possible?"

"That's what I intend to do tonight," Adam said. "And in the morning, I'll accept my fate. Gracefully, this time."

"But it doesn't have to be that way, Adam," Oscar said. "That's what Dahlia is trying to say. You can stick around. Find joy with us for as long as you can. It might not last forever, but it can definitely last longer than one fucking night."

"Okay," Adam said.

"Sleep now?" Dahlia asked, kicking the comforter away from them and onto the floor. "How does Mina do this? It is so hot."

Thirty-Four

D AHLIA FELT THE BED move then heard the door to the bedroom open and close. She glanced over at the clock on the bedside table. It was the middle of the night. Drowsily, she curled up tighter against Oscar and tried to go back to sleep. She needed to be up early tomorrow to run errands before she had to be at church.

Funny, to have the most erotic experience of her life and then be expected to appear as though nothing about her had fundamentally shifted, all while wearing her Sunday best and listening to a sermon that had a greater than fifty percent chance of making her feel like a filthy heathen. Maybe she could skip it.

With a sigh, Dahlia lifted her head. No way she would get any shut eye without checking in on where Adam went. As she shuffled to the edge of the bed, Oscar's head popped up from his pillow.

"Everything alright, darlin'?"

"Adam disappeared a few minutes ago, and, as you pointed out to me, he probably isn't getting a glass of water."

"You're worried about him?"

She nodded, sitting up and pulling her knees to her chest. "What he did with us was fairly intense, and there has to be a lot of unpacking to do. Yesterday, he wanted to ruin our happiness, and tonight we invited him into our private life, our relationship, and at least one of our bodies. He was an active participant tonight in something that he has told himself for centuries he hates. That has to be a mindfuck."

"I see your point." Oscar sat up, too, and tucked a piece of hair behind her ear. It had to be an absolute disaster, all full of tangles and knots.

"Then there's the thing where you had him eat your cum out of me. Does that somehow mirror his responsibility in what he did to our family? Removing the substance that could get me pregnant at your command, is that a physical way of demanding his apology? Or is it repeating history but this time within our control?"

"I don't think you need to write a doctorate on what we did. I asked him to do that because I thought it would be hot, and I was pretty sure that he'd agree."

"Oh, maybe he had to go somewhere else to take care of himself. He didn't come, right?"

"He didn't want to come, Dahlia," Oscar said. "You are really spiraling on this. Why don't we just go look for him so you can talk to him?"

Dahlia exhaled and dropped her head back against the headboard. "You make some valid points." Then she turned to look at him, her head at an awkward angle. "Will you come with me?" She didn't wait for his answer before scooting off the bed.

"Gladly." He pulled the throw from the foot of the bed as he rounded it and tucked it around her. Beating her to the door, he held it open.

As soon as they were in the hallway, they heard a shriek. At first, it sounded like a single voice, but as they made their way down the hall, Dahlia picked out multiple voices, layered tightly on top of one another. She reached for Oscar's hand, and he clasped hers tightly.

When they made it to the living room, they found Michael standing in front of the floor-to-ceiling, sliding-glass doors that led to a balcony. He held two steaming mugs in his hands, and as they approached him, he turned and wordlessly handed them over.

Dahlia brought the beverage to her nose and inhaled—chamomile tea. She looked up and caught sight of Adam on the balcony. Reaching above his head, face tipped up to take in the sky, streams of spirits ignited from his hands in a constant flow of colors. Dahlia gasped.

"He's releasing the spirits," Oscar said in awe.

"He is," Michael said.

The shrieks were coming from the souls in a cacophony of emotions. Laughter, fear, joy, anguish, all mixed together in a discordant yet lovely symphony. But Dahlia couldn't help her brain from spiraling to the worst-case scenario.

"Should we be concerned? Is he setting poltergeists loose on the city? Is there someone we should call for that?"

Michael chuckled. "So far, none of them have stuck around."

"He's most likely holding on to the worst of them," Oscar suggested.

"How long has he been at this?" Dahlia asked.

"Ten minutes," Michael said. "He's going to be exhausted when he's done. I'll make more tea."

Dahlia slid open the large door and stepped out into the cold night air. She didn't dare get too close, but she felt wrong leaving Adam to do this by himself. Oscar followed her, keeping his free hand clasped in hers.

After a few moments, the stream subsided, and Adam lowered his arms then fell to the painted concrete with a gasp. Dahlia rushed forward, leaving her mug on an end table on the way, and pulled Adam into her arms. "Are you okay?" she whispered against his dark hair. His skin and muscle faded to nothing, but still she held him.

"I'm fine," he grumbled.

"You are not fine," Dahlia said. "You've gone all skeletal again."

He lifted his hand and laughed. "Took more energy than I had expected."

Oscar gripped Adam by the elbows and helped him find his feet. "That was a lot of power you were holding on to."

"They're gone now, finding their way to their afterlife," Adam said.

"So, no lingering messes for us to deal with? There won't be an influx of hauntings around town?"

Adam shook his head. "I never kept a soul who would do more damage on their own. Being tied to the mortal realm when they'd have rather moved on was what made them so powerful. Plus, I've always enjoyed a little chaos. Can't have that if I'm holding onto the truly angry spirits who'd willingly keep themselves shackled all on their own."

"Good. I mean, not good. Kind of awful, actually. But helpful in this exact scenario," Dahlia said. "Why don't we go back inside, enjoy some tea, and see about getting some rest."

"And, Adam, maybe go to Luci and Mina's little get-together in the Hell realm, yeah?" Oscar suggested. "Word on the street, she'll help replenish some of that energy you lost."

"At least I don't have to worry about scaring your daughter in the meantime," Adam said, leading the way back inside.

Thirty-Five

M INA COULD HEAR THE roar of conversation below her. She stood on a dais suspended above the arena, the seclusion providing a little tranquility before the storm that was to come. Mina's wrists and ankles were adorned with golden cuffs. A jewel-encrusted collar enclosed her throat, and a small tiara sat atop her head. She wore nothing else.

Sindy's calming touch brushed her lower back. "Are you about ready?"

"Yes," Mina said, taking one more deep, cleansing breath before she accepted Sindy's help getting into her gold cage. Luci had insisted that even playing the part of his slave, she would be treated like a queen.

On her hands and knees, Mina's body lined up perfectly for Sindy to clip the cuffs to the restraints on the bars. Sindy secured a strap to each side of the cage, pulling it underneath Mina's hips to help support her. The fabric was soft against her naked skin, but strong enough that she could relax her hips a bit while remaining at the right height. Another swing-like support was added to her rib cage right below her breasts.

The brush of Sindy's fingertips against Mina's ankles as she pulled them into place and secured them sent shivers up Mina's spine.

"You're beautiful, Mina," Sindy said, pressing a kiss to the curve of her ass. She ran her hands along Mina's inner thighs. Mina knew that Sindy was perched on a stool behind the cage so she'd be comfortable while initiating today's game.

Luci's voice boomed, and the audience quieted immediately. He welcomed and thanked them for answering his summons, as if they'd had a choice. Mina hoped this gamble paid off. He'd expended a lot of energy to pull the underworld together. It would be disastrous if she failed.

"You won't fail," Sindy said, reading Mina's mind. "We won't let you." Sindy used a squirt bottle to cover Mina's backside in a lube. She pressed two fingers to either side of Mina's clit, but didn't touch it. Then she slid her digits back along Mina's vulva, pulling at her sensitive flesh. "You're already so wet."

"You did just spritz me," Mina said.

"Not here," Sindy said, prodding Mina's entrance. "This is all you." The demoness slipped two fingers into her as Luci's voice once more filled the arena.

"I've prepared a treat for you all. Please, sit back, relax, partake in the refreshments, and enjoy the show."

For a heartbeat, there was only silence. Then the churning of chains started as the dais lowered until it was level with the stadium floor. Mina kept her eyes trained on that floor. Even if it hadn't been part of the show, the one she had dreamed up with the help of her demon lovers, Mina would have been reluctant to look up and meet the gaze of so many enemies—no, potential allies. The excuse to stay in her role was a blessing.

Sindy stood up behind Mina. She was wearing a strap-on with a medium-sized phallus. Something big enough to get

Mina started, but the real stretching would come later. Sindy fucked into Mina at an angle, making sure to give the crowd a good view but sacrificing a small amount of Mina's pleasure. The hope was to rile up the audience without getting Mina anywhere near orgasm. The demon hoard would have to wait a little while longer for that.

The dais slowly turned, giving everyone in the audience the ability to see the action from all angles. And Mina sighed in relief when she caught sight of Luci's shiny dress shoes. He was dressed to kill in a navy blue suit, so dark it almost looked black. She had seen him an hour ago, right before their guests began to arrive and she and Sindy had to get into place, so she knew he wore a tie covered in stars. Their stars.

He had cupped her face and kissed her sweetly, telling her he loved her before he had let her leave his side.

Now he sat in his throne, as gaudy as her cage and adornments. A smaller throne was next to his, but it was empty. Alastor, Beelzebub, and Lilith stood in places of respect behind him. She dared to look up just enough to see them all. Their postures were relaxed, but their faces betrayed their arousal. And she knew then that they'd see her through this.

Sindy pulled out of her, reaching down to caress Mina again, rubbing her fingers along Mina's swollen flesh before slipping three fingers inside. A fourth soon followed, but not her thumb. Sindy used that to finally touch Mina's clit. And Mina had to curl her toes to keep from coming.

"Not yet, human," Luci bellowed, and the audience laughed.

Fuck. Mina had to close her eyes and concentrate. He'd only made it worse.

"Let me help, my lord," Lilith said, approaching the dais. She held a flogger limply at her side, brushing it over Luci's lap as she passed.

"Please do," Luci said, his tone flippant.

After unclipping the top of the cage and removing it, giving her access to Mina's back and butt, Lilith brought the flogger down across Mina's shoulders in a soft caress. It thudded against her on the next hit. Slowly, Lilith worked her way down Mina's back, stopping to pay special attention to her lower back and ass. Through it all, Sindy continued to work her hand into Mina, eventually tucking her thumb into her palm and striving to fit her entire hand into Mina's tight cunt.

"See how much of your hand you can fit in too, Lilith. Then we'll let the poor woman come." Luci's voice filled the space and sent a thrill of fear down her spine. He referred to her so casually, as if they hadn't fractured their very essence to fit one another, to knit their lives together for eternity.

Mina took a slow, calming breath, counting her exhale silently in her mind.

Lilith draped the flogger across the smallest point of Mina's back and knelt next to Sindy. With care, she added her fingers to Sindy's hand, slipping them beside it before pulling to the side to stretch Mina further. When they thought Mina was ready, Sindy pulled her hand back, cupping her fingers against Lilith's. Together they pushed forward to the point that the last set of their knuckles met her opening.

"Breathe," Lilith instructed, and Mina repeated her calming breath from before. When they pushed again, their hands successfully docked inside her. Mina trembled at the fullness.

But they weren't done. One of them stimulated her clit while the other rubbed along her labia.

"Come now," Luci demanded. Mina had no choice but to obey him. She'd been holding back for what felt like an eternity, and her bonds rattled against the bars. "Good girl," he said, and an aftershock rippled through her. "Very good."

As Sindy and Lilith removed themselves from her now-gaping orifice, the air in the stadium changed. The power of it caressed her like another lover.

Lilith whispered into her ear, "They're straining in their seats to get more of you. Every pair of eyes in this place is riveted to you. You have their attention. Will you give them more?" When Mina nodded, Lilith smiled and ran a hand down her back. She removed the flogger, then held a hand out for Sindy, and together they left Mina on the dais alone.

She shuddered in anticipation of what Bellz had planned for her next. They'd only sketched out the loosest plan together. He preferred to leave her guessing.

Thirty-Six

BEELZEBUB STEPPED ONTO THE dais, his footfalls strong and assured. The confidence he oozed soothed Mina's nerves like a balm. Yet her anticipation heightened. He stopped behind her, his palm lightly brushing against her rear. If he weren't so calculated all the time, she would have thought the touch happened accidentally.

"Lilith barely warmed you up," Bellz said just loud enough that only Mina could hear him. "Would you like a little more impact play? Or should I jump to exploring your holes?" He didn't wait for a response before pressing the tip of a finger against her anus. "I'm not actually sure I can wait to be inside you."

Earlier, before she had gotten into her spot with Sindy, Bellz had pulled her aside just to hold her. It had been a long hug, and when Sindy had come over to take Mina away, Bellz had pulled her into the embrace as well.

"You made me jealous of Sindy, Mina. Sindy. My Sindy." He removed his fingertip, then turned his hand so the pads of his fingers stroked her from asshole to clit. He brought them back and plunged three into her cunt.

For a moment, he brought his thumb to his palm and wet it inside her pussy. But then he was pressing it against her ass, sinking it into her there. "It was very confusing for me. Sindy was gorgeous in that strap-on. I wanted her, but then she started fucking you, and I was overwhelmed with jealousy too."

He shook his three fingers and thumb, fucking against her instead of into her. "I've decided that you'll both have to make it up to me later."

"Do you think that's how you're making Luci feel now?" Mina asked softly. She didn't dare break the illusion of the show, but she also couldn't pass up the opportunity to connect with Bellz when he was being so open with her.

"I'll ask him," Bellz said as he maneuvered the stool into place with his free hand. He sat down, leaned forward, and bit into the cheek of her butt.

Mina gasped loudly in surprise.

"I'm not keeping you in this cage much longer. Got something else planned. But I want you to come for me first. Give them all a small taste of you."

He vibrated his whole arm, pressing down on her with his thumb while oscillating his fingers against her g-spot. Her orgasm started, but he didn't relent. And when she squirted all over his hand, his sleeve, and the pant of his suit, he chuckled.

Removing his hand, he brought it up against her clit in three hard smacks. Then he slipped his fingers into her again and, using the same technique, pulled another come out of her.

The audience roared their approval. Feet pounded against the stands, and Bellz grabbed the back of her head, fisting her ponytail and pressing her head down.

"They are demanding more," Bellz told her. "But not rushing the stage just yet." As he continued to hold her head in place, he brought his hand down between her cheeks, the sting of it smarted against her sensitive skin. But then he wasn't touching her anymore, and instead he was unhooking her cuffs from the cage.

He pulled her upright, turning her so her back was to his front. He clasped the base of her throat, just beneath her collar, in one hand and wrapped the other around her waist. Still she kept her gaze down, focusing on the perfectly tied laces of his black dress shoes. They'd all dressed their best tonight.

But the audience didn't care. She knew they were watching as Bellz held her in place, and he let them look.

"Good girl," Bellz said. "They like what they see. Soon Luci will have you, and he'll take you as his queen and command that you acknowledge them. But until then, you're just ours, as you have been for millennia."

He cupped her breast, kneading her as he worked his way to the tip. His fingers closed around the base of her nipple and pinched hard enough to make her gasp. "Lucifer had jewels made for these as well. Would you like to wear them?"

After a nod from Mina, Bellz pulled a nipple clamp from his pocket. Gold, of course, and decorated with emeralds that reminded Mina of Luci's eyes. Bellz clipped the clamp in place, then moved in front of her, pressing her back a step or two. "Arms up," he commanded. Her wrists made contact with a padded surface, and her cuffs clicked as the magnet inside them activated. She relaxed her arms, but they remained in place.

"Perfect." He tickled down her sides. Lowering his head, he took her other nipple in his mouth to prepare it before attaching the second clamp, a perfect twin to the first. Kneeling before her, he spread her legs, and her ankle cuffs snapped into place. "One more." Bellz leaned forward, sucking her clit.

He placed a clamp there as well, and then Bellz wrapped straps that held more clamps around Mina's thighs, using them to pull back her outer labia, exposing her sex completely. Then he got to work fitting his hand inside her, fucking her with it, stretching her to take even more. When he had her almost where he wanted her, he stepped, snapped his fingers at Lilith, and caught the flogger the demoness tossed him.

With a flick of his wrist, he brought the leather tails up between her legs, expertly missing her clit. But the clamps holding her labia were knocked away by the force of the hit. Systematically, he hit every bit of her body, but he left her clit and nipples for last. Right as she thought she would break, waiting for the pain of it so much worse than the reality of what she would actually feel when the blood came rushing back to her most vulnerable bits, he put her out of her misery. Bringing the flogger up between her lips so the ends of the tails caressed her labia and at the last moment flicking the clamp off of her nub. Then with a criss-cross motion, he hit both nipples.

She cried and sagged forward, but he was there, bracing her body with his own, whispering kindnesses into her ear, reminding her of his undying devotion. Her breath returned, and he pressed a kiss to her brow before falling to his knees once more and filling her with his fist. The orgasm shattered her.

And this time, the demons did rise. They would have stormed the stage, but an invisible force kept them at bay.

Lucifer stood from his throne. "Be calm!" And they were, returning to their seats. Luci had commanded her attention as well, and she watched in a trance as he retook his seat. "We aren't done."

Bellz grasped Mina's chin and forced her to look at him. "I've got you. So does he, but stay here with me. Alastor and Lilith will be joining us now." He pressed his lips to hers in a searing kiss. "I hope you can handle it."

Thirty-Seven

"WHY ARE YOU BRINGING me here?" Dahlia asked as she stared up at the home Oscar had purchased, the one that Adam had infested. "On our date night?"

"I thought it might be nice to actually see it all. You can help me decide what to do with it, darlin'," Oscar said, tugging on her hand and leading her to the front door. "Pick out which room you want for Tabitha."

"Are you asking us to move in with you?"

"I'm pretty much living with you now, but this would be our own place. We could build a home together." He unlocked the door and pushed it open, ushering her inside. "Maybe we could also build us more of a family." Dahlia turned to look at him, taking a step back. The rim of his hat blocked his face, so she couldn't see his expression.

"You mean like Mina's doing? Do you want to invite Adam to be our third? Because, and I can't believe I'm saying this, but maybe. Once Tabitha graduates and no longer lives with us."

"That's not what I meant." Oscar removed his hat and placed it on a hook by the door. He still avoided making eye contact for another moment, running his hands through his hair and straightening his button-up.

"Oh?" Dahlia asked. She drew a blank for about half a second before it dawned on her. "Ooh. You mean more kids."

Absentmindedly, she covered her lower abdomen. It had been more than thirteen years since she'd been pregnant, but she still remembered how it felt when Tabitha kicked her. For those nine months, everywhere she went, she had someone to talk to. Even in her darkest moments, before she knew she'd have Mina and Sandra's undying love and support, facing the thought of single parenthood, the fear of going through childbirth alone, she'd at least had her little nugget.

Could she do it again, now? Plenty of women had children in their early thirties, but she'd already done it and thought she'd be through before she was forty.

"I lost you," Oscar said, cupping her cheek. When she focused on his face, she found his brow furrowed, his lips twisted in concern. "Reckon you could have all those thoughts out loud?"

Dahlia sighed and sat down on the stairs. Oscar quickly joined her, wrapping her up in his arms and tucking her close.

"I just never thought that having more children would ever even be an option. I probably would have gotten my tubes tied if I'd thought anyone would have the ability to turn my head, but I was so busy with raising Tabitha and building my career that I never got around to it."

"Alright," Oscar said. "I always thought I'd have a big family, but that was when I was human. Once I became a demon, I put all that aside. Having Tabitha, having you," he paused, his eyes scanning her face, "It's enough."

"Just give me time to think about it," Dahlia said. "It's not a no. Not yet." She smirked at him. "It might be a yes. I have a lot of fond memories of the newborn days. Most of it is probably lies, sleep-deprivation-fueled lies, but still. A little bundle of warmth snoring softly on my chest. Needing me for everything.

"But on the other hand, ugh, needing me for everything. It's a lot of work. You lose a bit of yourself for a while. Luckily I had my mom and my sister supporting me while I went to school, got my degree; so, not feeling like my own person, it didn't last too long. And this time I'd have you.

"So, maybe. My answer is maybe."

Oscar rested his chin on top of Dahlia's head. "I really mean it, Dahlia. No pressure. Whatever form our family takes, it will be perfect. I love you."

"I love you, too." Dahlia bumped her shoulder into him.

"But I volunteer for all the diaper duty."

Dahlia laughed, imagining him changing ten diapers a day. No way she'd make him do that all alone. That was a lot of work for anyone.

"I've never asked you," she said, a thought occurring to her. "Why is it that you can be on Earth whenever you want? Mina went through all that trouble summoning Lucifer and the others before their soul bond."

She felt him shrug behind her. "I've always been based on Earth. Just like Zozo. We specialize in spirits, or what humans believe to be spirits. It's easier if we stay stationed here. Although, now that I know more about Zozo—I mean, Adam—it makes a lot of sense. He was a human once, too. There's a lot I never did question. Didn't seem like having the answers would make much of a difference, anyhow."

"We can ask him, next time we see him." Dahlia grabbed a hold of the banister and pulled herself up. "Come on. Let's go check out upstairs."

"Wait, darlin'. There's one more thing I'd like to ask you."

"Oh, sure." Dahlia paused on the stairs, peering back at him. "What's up?"

He came up onto one knee. The position looked a little awkward on the stairs, and it put him quite a bit below her.

"What are you doing?" she asked, eyes wide, mouth agape.

"Dahlia Cadere, will you marry me?" He pulled a square box out of his pocket and opened it. The ring was an antique, and as beautiful as it was simple.

Dahlia gasped. Her heart sped up, equal parts excitement and anxiety. "Oscar, how?"

"How?" That handsome brow of his wrinkled in confusion. "I bought it years ago from the estate sale after my parents died. It was my mother's, and she wanted me to have it. For my bride. For you, I hope. If you'll have me?" He held the ring up higher.

"That's lovely, but it isn't what I meant. How are we supposed to get married? What does that mean? Your human identity has been dead for a hundred years, so it's not like we can get married in the eyes of the law. And I'm not particularly religious. Your mom was Catholic. Do you want me to convert so we can get married in the church?"

"What? No." Oscar closed the ring box. "I guess I just thought it could mean whatever we wanted it to mean."

"And what do you want it to mean, Oscar?"

"A commitment to each other. To our family. A promise that you're my one and only."

"Except for when we invite Adam to play?" Dahlia asked, lifting an eyebrow with a chuckle.

"It's different between the two of us. At least, it is for me. Even if we share other partners, there's only one person I want to spend the rest of my eternity with and tell all my secrets to. It's you, Dahlia.

"I don't know where I fit in this new world Lucifer and Mina are bound to create, or what my role will be. But I do know that I want you by my side while I figure it out. When I look to the future, all I see is you and Tabitha."

"Oscar." Dahlia's bottom lip trembled and she stepped down until she was level with him. "Oh, Oscar." She wrapped her arms around him and buried her face against his neck. "Yes, I'll marry you."

"Phew, you had me worried there."

"I just wanted a clearer picture of what I was saying yes to." She kissed the soft bit of skin beneath his ear, his stubble chafing against her cheek. "I do have one condition, though."

"What's that?" He stiffened in her arms.

"I want to do it properly." She pulled back so she could see him. "Mina and Luci bound their souls to one another. That's what I want."

His eyes widened.

"Too much of a commitment?"

"No." Oscar shook his head. "I am absolutely in, darlin', but we're going to need help for that."

"Whose help do we need?" Dahlia worried her bottom lip.

"Your brother-in-law's."

"Oh," Dahlia relaxed. "That won't be a problem."

Thirty-Eight

G ENTLE fingers brushed a rogue strand of hair from Mina's forehead as the magnets holding her arms in place deactivated. Lilith. Mina leaned into her touch, but lost her balance, taking a step or two before stumbling.

Alastor's large limbs came around her, lifting her off her feet. "You doing okay?" he asked, deep voice pitched low. In response, Mina rested her head against his chest. She could feel his pecs rumble as he chuckled. "It won't be too much longer," Alastor said, before turning to Bellz. "I think you broke her."

"She just needs a minute," Bellz said, nodding toward something behind Alastor that Mina couldn't see.

"Let's move this along, fellas," Lilith said. "I'm not sure the crowd is going to give us a minute."

Alastor placed Mina on a padded surface. She put her palm down and felt its leathery texture. It was red, and barely larger than a bench.

Lilith gave Mina a once-over before shooting her a wink and a half-smile. Then her attention turned to Alastor. "Lose the pants."

"Make me," he said. Lilith glared, and Alastor shrugged, turning away from her to hide his smirk. But he followed her orders.

"Now get under Mina," Lilith said. Once again, Alastor picked Mina up and sat up. This time he settled her on his lap, her back to his chest. He turned her so her legs were draped over his, leaving her exposed to the audience once more. Lilith stepped between their spread legs and knelt. She brushed Mina's inner thighs with her fingers then Alastor's.

He was already rock hard, his monstrously large dick standing to attention between Mina's legs, when Lilith rolled a condom onto him.

"Lay back, Alastor, and, Mina, turn around," Lilith instructed, and Bellz held out a hand to help Mina stabilize herself as she obeyed. They were all being so gentle with her, giving her the breather she needed, but she knew what was coming next. And her clit throbbed at the thought. "Bend over, Mina."

Bellz rubbed her lower back before bringing his hands down over her ass and spreading her cheeks. Lilith inhaled deeply with desire. Bellz pressed the tips of four fingers and one thumb against her vaginal entrance. He had no trouble working his hand into her this time. Lilith slipped a few fingers in next to his hand, pulling up and stretching her again until she could fit her hand alongside Bellz'.

"I think she's ready," Lilith said. Their hands retreated, and Mina moaned at the emptiness. "Hold on there, love. Soon my Alastor will fill you." But that sentence already filled Mina up. Lilith claiming Alastor, after all this time. She could only assume that meant that Alastor had finally allowed her to claim him.

Bellz and Lilith spritzed her and Alastor with more lube until they and the bench beneath them were drenched. Then Bellz grabbed Mina across her chest and under her arms and pulled her up. "We're going to fuck you onto his cock," he whispered.

"Don't move, Alastor," Lilith said as she prodded Mina with the tip of him. Tip was an understatement. It alone covered her entire vulva. Lilith tapped Mina's clit with him, and it felt like being poked with a battering ram. A battering ram that would soon be inside her. A battering ram that was smaller than Lucifer's.

Fuck. What had she gotten herself into? She bit her bottom lip and clenched her eyes closed in anticipation.

Lilith moved Alastor's cock down, notching him into her expanded opening. Once they were aligned, Bellz pushed down on Mina, forcing her onto Alastor. She gasped as his cock pushed against her inner walls, spreading her wider than before. The sting was exquisite, and Mina curled her toes and clenched her fists, trying to hold in the pleasure, let it mingle with the pain.

Slowly, Lilith and Bellz collaborated to fill Mina with Alastor's girth. There was no hope that she'd take his full length. Soon he was as deep as he could go, and when Mina heard him whimper, she reached out and clumsily brushed his jaw with her fingers. They held still for a moment, letting Mina adjust.

But only for a moment. Then Mina couldn't wait any longer, and she began to move up and down on him, fucking herself with him. Lilith and Bellz followed her lead, helping her keep the pace she'd set.

Bellz snuck a hand underneath Mina and circled her clit with two fingers. She never had a chance to defend herself against the cataclysm that slammed through her, a fast wave that rippled through the stadium.

"Stop now," he said, adjusting his position beside her so he could see her face. "Lilith is going to prep you for Luci. Keep your eyes on me, and breathe." He tucked a loose strand of hair behind her ear as Alastor caressed her lower back with one hand.

Mina winced a little as cold lube hit her ass, rolling down toward her vagina. She felt pressure against her perineum.

"That's only one finger," Bellz said. "She'll keep adding more until she can do to Alastor's dick what she did to my hand." Mina breathed through each new finger as Bellz signaled to Lilith when it was time to continue.

Lilith's hand finally fit around Alastor's rod, and Mina had never felt anything like it. It hurt, and she wanted more. But she couldn't bring herself to move. All she could do was focus on the air entering and leaving her lungs and plead for more in soft whimpers.

Lilith and Alastor began to move, fucking Mina in tandem. Mina could feel the knuckles of Lilith's hand with each thrust. Alastor moaned below her. Soon, Lilith was pushing in up to her wrist on every rep as Bellz continued to work Mina's clit.

She came again, her pussy clamping down so hard Mina feared she'd break completely.

"Oh, fuck," Alastor muttered. "I'm going to come."

Lilith removed her hand as Bellz pulled Mina up and off of Alastor's cock. Lilith took off Alastor's condom and helped Bellz settle Mina between Alastor's legs so she sat on the ground, her face lifted up at the green demon. He erupted, shooting his ejaculate all over her chest. Lilith spread it over Mina's breasts while Bellz scooped up a bit and fed it to her.

"Move," Lucifer said from behind them. He'd stepped on the dais. As one, Lilith, Alastor, and Bellz retreated, finding seats in their spots behind the thrones.

He stared down at her with those green eyes of his, pupils so dilated Mina could barely make out the pigment. She collapsed to the floor underneath his gaze, and he stepped closer, towering over her.

"You're mine now."

Thirty-Nine

T HE AIR AROUND THEM shimmered as everything on the dais changed. The bench, the rack, all of it gone with the flick of Lucifer's strong wrist. In one breath, Mina sat on her knees, nothing but the hard ground beneath her. In the next, she was sliding on a sea of satin, pillows cushioning her knees, ropes wrapping themselves through the cuffs on her wrists and ankles. They pulled her onto her back, spreading her wide for her demon husband. Laying her out like a sacrifice on the altar they'd built together.

Only, they didn't build it like this. This final scene was supposed to be hard, fast. The crescendo of what the others had built up before. But Luci got down on his limbs and crawled to her. When he reached her foot, he lifted it and placed a gentle kiss on her instep.

She wanted to ask him what he was doing. She distinctly remembered telling him that when his time came, he was supposed to take her savagely. Her words exactly: "Just fuck a baby into me."

This wasn't the plan. For a second, she panicked that it would all crumble, that his tenderness for her would be seen as a weakness, and her mind raced to find a solution. There had to be a way to goad him into playing the role they had planned.

But then she caught his eye, and the love she saw there stole the breath from her lungs. No way would she get in the way of letting him love her any way he wanted to. Not with him looking at her like that.

His hands were warm as they caressed up her leg, but when he got to the top of her thighs, he moved his hands to her hips and squeezed. He kneaded her flesh there before sliding his hands up her sides, slowly, reverently, like he was savoring every moment he had the privilege of touching her.

He didn't touch her breasts, either, but continued past them, lightly tickling over her collarbone before cupping her cheeks in both palms. Then he leaned forward and gently brushed his lips against hers. Mouthing that he loved her, so that only she could feel it.

"Touch me, Lucifer, please," she said, pulling on the satin ties holding her.

"Is that all you want, human?" He traced the curve of her armpit, and she squirmed.

"I want to feel your demon cock inside me."

He moaned against the curve of her breast. "Is that your deepest wish?" He licked one nipple then sucked on it, pulling it between his teeth and biting down.

"To have you deep inside me? Your cum even deeper, until your DNA is literally in my blood? That's probably my deepest wish." She moaned as he used two fingertips to trace her labia majora. "But what do I have to give you in return? You already have my soul."

"I want to watch your belly swell with our child," he said before circling her clit. "I want you to be the mother of my children."

"Deal," she said.

Luci pulled back and squatted between her spread legs. The position gave her her first glimpse of his full demonic penis. It was covered in black and red bumps and ridges. The ridges were pointed towards the base. She remembered the sting she had felt every time he pulled out to thrust again, and she gasped. He was bigger now.

The audience roared at her reaction, misinterpreting her arousal for fear, and she knew then that they'd assumed Lucifer had been toying with her. Softening her up, just to destroy her and give them all the show they'd assumed they'd be witnessing.

"Ready?" Luci asked.

"Fuck yes." Mina wiggled her hips in desperation. He brought the head of his cock to her vulva, swiping it along her, picking up her natural lubricant along with what was left behind from Lilith, Bellz, and Sindy. She focused on her breathing, and he docked at her entrance.

When he started to push into her, though, she didn't feel any pain. Only pure pleasure. Her eyes fluttered closed as he bottomed out, his hips abutting her thighs. He was completely inside her.

"Mina." Luci's voice sounded panicked, and her eyes snapped open. His brow was furrowed in concern, and he cupped the side of her head, brushing her temple with his thumb. "Are you alright?"

"Fuck, Luci. You feel so good. Fuck me. Please, fuck me." To punctuate her request, she tilted her pelvis toward him.

He groaned, pulling back before thrusting forward. His rhythm remained slow at first as he analyzed her reactions.

Every nerve ending sparked to life until there was more pleasure than Mina. And all she could do was chase it. She cursed her bounds, wanting to touch Luci, wrap her legs around his ass, and encourage that glorious cock even deeper.

The thought had hardly left her mind before the satin untied itself, and she clutched her lover close. Writhing into him, taking more of his cock. She was begging. For more. Harder. And he obliged. Until her muscles were clamping around his dick, and the ecstasy was filling her up and pouring out of her.

After the first orgasm crested, another soon followed. They stacked on top of each other in a never-ending loop, coaxing Lucifer's orgasm. And he exploded inside her, filling her fuller than her pleasure. And somehow, even though it had felt impossible only seconds before, she came one more time.

Once they could both function, Luci scooped her up into his arms, lifting her and removing her from the dais. Bringing her before the twin thrones, Luci stopped in his tracks and just stared at them.

Mina hadn't been paying much attention, but when her senses expanded beyond the two of them, she noticed how quiet the stadium had become. She glanced up and found the demons in stunned silence. Truthfully, Luci and Mina had made love more than fucked, and she hoped they weren't disappointed. That they wouldn't demand retribution.

Luci continued to stare at the thrones, unmoving.

"What is it?" she whispered.

"This is wrong," he said, peering down at her, a slight frown on his lips.

She reached up and stroked his chin lovingly. He looked away from her and grunted. Taking two steps toward the smaller throne, he lifted a foot and rested it against it. Then he kicked it over. As it hit the floor, it broke apart into dust and dissipated.

Facing away from the remaining throne, his throne, Luci lowered them both onto it. Then, in a loud and clear voice he said, "Our queen, Mina, painter of stars, bringer of hope."

Mina had to keep from wincing as the audience roared its approval, the sound deafening. Each demon in the stands stood together, and then they knelt as one.

To mask Mina's gasp, Luci wrapped his hand around her throat, pulling her against him. She arched her back, shoving her tits out. A hush descended as if everyone collectively held their breaths. Palpable anticipation filled the air.

Luci bit Mina's earlobe, tugging gently. "Sindy, Lilith, Alastor, please go pick one lucky audience member each." He spread her legs wide, lifting each one and placing it over the arm of the throne. "If they can make their new queen come in a timely manner, they'll be invited to join us for an intimate after party."

They left quickly to follow orders as Lucifer's hand roamed along Mina's body. Her skin tingled, prickling with each stroke.

"Bellz, show them how it's done," Lucifer commanded.

"Gladly." Bellz fell to his knees before them.

Forty

W HEN CONSCIOUSNESS RETURNED TO Mina, she found herself in a pile of limbs. A large green torso rose and fell underneath her head, and Lilith's arm draped over her waist. Sindy had curled between her legs, her head resting on Mina's thigh. Mina lifted her head, glancing around. Bellz slept on the couch across the room. The winning demons had only been allowed to stay for three hours of the after party, at which point the after-after party had relocated to Luci and Mina's cavern rooms for one last, very sloppy round. They had all collapsed in their bed, which wasn't as large as Bellz'. Mina assumed that's why Bellz had moved.

But where was Luci? She bit her bottom lip at the thought of navigating her way off the bed without waking everyone else up.

Gently, she removed Lilith's arm, then scooted up the bed as far as she could while simultaneously nudging Sindy onto Alastor's leg. Then she stood up and used the headboard to step over Lilith's sleeping form before landing softly on the rug beneath the bed. She held her breath as she glanced back, sighing with relief when no one stirred.

Still wary of disturbing her lovers, Mina tiptoed to the bathroom. When she found it was empty, she opened the door to

Luci's sex room but discovered nothing. Turning around, Mina walked back out into the main room. When she neared the couch, Bellz nodded to her, lifting one hand from his chest with a half-hearted wave. The edge of Mina's mouth lifted in a smile, and she blew him a kiss before heading out of the cavern, not bothering to find clothing.

Luci was nowhere in the long tunnel that led to the very large cavern where he had found her over a year ago. Once she exited into that cavern, it didn't take her long to find him, naked as she was.

"Luci," Mina called as she neared him, and he turned and smiled at her. But he looked a little tired. "You okay?" she asked as she approached him, reaching up to brush her hand against his cheek.

He leaned into her palm and nodded. "Yeah. I'm okay."

"Then why are you here, sweating with the magma?" The air was oppressive, and Mina tugged on his arm, encouraging him back toward their cooler rooms. "Is it technically magma? I feel like Hell is definitely beneath the earth, so it can't be lava, right?"

"We aren't below the earth, Mina. This is a different plane of existence."

"Hm, good point. I did know that. So, lava then?"

Luci chuckled, stopping her when they reached the mouth of the cave that would lead back to the others.

"I successfully distracted myself from hearing your answer, my prince of darkness."

"You did at that." Luci took in a deep breath, letting it out all at once. "I was just thinking. No, that's not right. I think I was mourning, actually."

"Mourning what?" Mina worried her lip. "Your child-free existence? Are you having second thoughts about becoming a father?"

"No, absolutely not."

Mina grasped both his hands in hers. "You can tell me anything, Lucifer Cadere."

"I'm mourning having you to myself."

"I was with you, what, a day before you started sharing me with the others, Luci."

"They don't count. They're family. They've been a part of this, a part of us, from almost the beginning. No, it's sharing you with my legion."

"The legion that you just got back?"

"Yes," Luci smiled at her. "I'm pleased about that. It is finally all coming together, but I can't help but feel like we've concluded a chapter. And I don't know what comes next."

"Our family comes next. We've got all of Hell's forces to protect us now. Whatever Heaven throws at us, we can handle it."

"You truly believe that?" Luci asked, pulling her into his arms. He nuzzled her hair.

"I have to, Luci."

He pressed a kiss to her temple. "You will always be my hope."

They stood a moment in silence while Luci processed what they had just discussed and Mina reminisced about seeing him here in this spot for the first time. His pale skin had reflected all the red around him. He was her breath of fresh air then, as he was now.

His forehead creased as she regained his focus. "Did you give me your last name?"

"Well, you don't have one, so I can't take yours."

A smile spread across his face, igniting joy in his eyes. "I love it." She pressed closer to him, burying her nose in his scent.

"Would you like to go back to bed?" Mina pulled back to look at him. "Actually, I'm not sure how we'll fit in that bed, but I bet if we ask nicely, Bellz will share the couch with us."

"There's no way all three of us will fit on that couch."

"Not feeling energetic enough yet to conjure us a bigger one?"

Luci hummed before bending at the knee to grip Mina under hers. He lifted her and pressed her against the rock next to the mouth of the cave, placing her ass on a small boulder that jutted out from the wall. "Another little boost from you wouldn't hurt."

He held her knee up with one hand while the other slipped between her legs. Expertly finding her clit, he quickly brought her to her peak. "Please, Luci," she begged as his hand dropped away. "Don't stop there."

"What do you want, human?"

"Fuck me, please, Luci."

"I haven't prepared you yet," he said as she nudged the head of his penis against her opening.

"You don't have to, Luci," she said, tilting her head to the side. "Didn't you feel it before? You fit me like you belong inside me."

"Of course I felt that, Mina. I always feel that. But you felt it too?"

"Yes. Your demon cock, it felt different. Fuller. The pain was more exquisite. Well, it had the same edge that pain brings, but, honestly, it only felt good. I want it again, Luci."

"Then you'll have it again. As often as you require." He thrust into her with one forceful drive of his hips. She felt herself open for him. "Fuck, you feel divine."

"Divine?" Mina laughed, then gasped as her pussy clenched around him. She tipped her head back against the wall, struggling to keep her eyes open and on Luci.

He held her throat in his hand, lifting her chin with his thumb and forefinger. "Stay with me, my love." He pulled back, then pushed forward again, rocking into her. And she kept her eyes on his as he fucked her against the rock even when she came apart around him and he filled her full of his seed.

Luci carried Mina back to their rooms, and Bellz happily made space for them on the couch, especially after Luci made it big enough for all three of them. Mina thought it looked suspiciously like the one in Bellz' dungeon, only covered in blue fabric instead of black leather.

They wrapped themselves around her. Mina's head rested on Luci's chest, while Bellz spooned her. He sleepily tugged her against him before whispering, "Luci, regretting your decision to share her with more of us?"

"Mhm," Luci said. "A completely rational emotion, don't you think?"

"Absolutely," Bellz said. "I'm pretty pissed it came to this."

"You both like sharing me, admit it. You loved watching those random demons have their way with me."

"Two of them kind of sucked at it," Bellz grumbled, and Mina laughed. It was true. Of the three winners, only one of them had been able to make Mina come unassisted. But they'd all been invited back to the after party anyway, and the other two had shown some improvement.

"Not all demons are sex gods," Mina said. "I just got lucky with you."

"Luck had nothing to do with it. I would never have picked an inner circle that couldn't fuck," Luci said.

"Fuck and fight," Bellz said.

"The second one is less important, though," Luci said, his speech slurring a bit with sleepiness. His breathing slowed, and Mina knew he was nearing slumber.

Two years ago, if someone had asked Mina if she thought demons slept, she would have told them that demons weren't real. Now she knew that they didn't sleep often. Rarely did they need it. But a fuck fest was the surest way to wipe a demon out. Like being sleepy after a full meal.

"I love you both," Mina said before succumbing as well.

Forty-One

D AHLIA RECEIVED A TEXT from her sister letting her know they were back on Earth and that everything had gone well. Dahlia replied with a request to talk to Lucifer and Mina but only got the snoring emoji in response. She showed Oscar. He was sitting on the couch with Tabitha, watching some adventure show that tied into a dinosaur movie franchise.

"I guess they'll call us when they wake up," Oscar said, shrugging. "We have time."

Dahlia plopped down beside them.

"Time for what?" Tabitha asked, and Dahlia cursed herself silently for thinking Tabitha was engrossed with the TV.

Oscar shot Dahlia a questioning look, shrugging and lifting his eyebrows. She shook her head before nodding. "Your mother and I are planning to get married," Oscar said.

"Married?" Tabitha bounced in place before turning on the couch to face them, her show all but forgotten. "That's so exciting! Can I be a bridesmaid? Wait! How is that going to work? Are you just going to have a ceremony that won't be legally binding?"

Oscar chuckled. "She's definitely your daughter."

"We're going to ask your Uncle Luci for help combining our souls."

"Oh," Tabitha said, sitting back into the cushions. "That's a commitment."

"What's wrong?" Dahlia asked, reaching across Oscar to grab her daughter's hand.

"It's just, I think Mina pulled herself from the cycle by doing that with Luci. They are tied together, including their lifespans. And now you're going to too. But what about me? What about Grandma? Will we still cycle without you?" Tabitha's eyes shone with unshed tears.

"No, darlin'," Oscar said, "you were born out of the cycle. You're half demon."

"What does that mean?" Dahlia asked.

"Lucifer told me shortly after we revealed your parentage, Tabitha. Half of your DNA being demon is enough to make you immortal. Your mother and I marrying means that we'll be together indefinitely."

"What about Grandma?"

Sandra appeared behind them, a plate full of brownies in her hands. "What about me?"

"Oscar and Mom are going to get married, and I'm supposedly immortal because Oscar's my dad, and that means that none of us will die. But you're still mortal, Grandma." Tabitha managed to get the words out before bursting into tears.

Sandra slid the plate of brownies onto the coffee table and scooped her granddaughter into her arms. "Sweetheart, it's okay." Sandra shushed her, rocking her gently back and forth. "I don't want to live forever. I'll be more than content finally getting to spend my afterlife with your grandpa."

"I don't want to lose you," Tabitha said between sobs.

"You aren't going to lose me any time soon," Sandra said. "And even once I'm gone, I'll still always be with you."

"You mean memories and stuff."

"Sure, but I'm also in your genes. No escaping that." Sandra pressed a kiss to Tabitha's head. "Now, what do you mean Oscar's your dad?"

"I'm sorry, Mom," Dahlia said. "I should have told you sooner. I met Oscar via a spirit board the summer after high school. We had a short affair before he disappeared—completely not his doing, by the way—and I ended up pregnant."

"You have nothing to be sorry for," Sandra said. "That was a lot for you all to process, I'm sure. I'm glad you are telling me now."

"Are you sure you aren't angry?" Dahlia asked.

"No," Sandra said. "You getting married to Tabitha's father is happy news. Am I allowed to throw a party for this one? Your sister still hasn't made good on her promise."

"Maybe we can do a shared party," Dahlia suggested. "From what little I know about the ceremony, we are going to want to keep it to as few people as possible."

"You better at least give me a heads up before it happens so we can celebrate right away," Sandra said, patting her daughter on the knee.

"So no bridesmaids," Tabitha said, drying her eyes on her sleeve.

"No. I'm sorry," Dahlia said.

"You can give a toast at the party," Oscar said. Tabitha leaned over, crashing into Oscar's side. The top of her head collided with his jaw, and he winced, but she didn't seem to notice.

"Thanks, Dad."

He smiled and wrapped an arm around her. "I'll never get enough of hearing you say that."

"What? 'Thanks'?" Tabitha asked.

"No. 'Dad.'"

Dahlia wiped a tear from the corner of her eye and laid her head down on Oscar's other shoulder.

"This dinosaur show is still on the air?" Sandra asked.

"It's streaming, Grandma," Tabitha said. "The last season just dropped."

"I don't know what 'dropped' means," Sandra said.

"It means that all the episodes of the season became available," Dahlia said.

"Well, in this case it does. But sometimes they just drop one episode a week. It's so lame when they do that," Tabitha said. "Like, do they want us to binge watch or not?"

"Yes, I can imagine how having to wait an entire week in between episodes would be rough," Sandra said, rolling her eyes. "Can you imagine if they forced you to watch commercials?"

"Yuck!" Tabitha screeched.

"Commercial breaks were kind of the best. Gave you time to go to the bathroom, refresh your snacks, or read," Dahlia said.

"You all grew up with moving pictures that just appear in your house," Oscar said. "You complain about the silliest things."

Dahlia looked at Oscar, blinked, then laughed. "Sometimes I forget how old you are. You look younger than me."

"I do not," Oscar said. "My body may have been younger than yours is now when I sold my soul and stopped aging, but life was harder back then. Look at these crow's feet." He pointed to his eyes, but he was squinting to make any minuscule wrinkles he might have had more pronounced.

"It's sweet that you would lie like that to make me feel better." Dahlia gave Oscar a quick peck on the cheek.

"I could probably figure out a way to get you back the body you had when we first met, if you wanted."

"Absolutely not. I earned this body." Dahlia pushed away from him and wrapped her arms around herself. "Would you want that?"

"No. Of course not. You're perfect." Oscar's brow wrinkled. "I didn't mean it like that."

Sandra glanced over at them. "Why don't you two go have some alone time upstairs. Tabitha and I will let you know if these kids manage to get off this island. Although I doubt it. Gilligan will just mess it up for them again."

"Grandma, what? Who's Gilligan?"

Oscar stood up first, offering his hand to Dahlia. She hesitated just the slightest amount before taking it. Once they were upstairs and Dahlia had shut the door, Oscar fell to his knees and wrapped his arms around her middle. "I loved the body you had at eighteen, but I love this body even more."

"And why is that?" Dahlia asked, clasping his jaw in both palms and tilting his head back, forcing him to look her in the eye.

"I could say that it's because it's the body that grew and nurtured our daughter. That this body is the result of you giving birth to her, breastfeeding her, and providing for her. But that wouldn't be the deeper reason."

"It wouldn't?" Dahlia asked.

"No. I love this body because it's the one I get to hold on to. This time, I don't have to go. I get to go to sleep with you in my arms and wake up with you sprawled all over me."

"I do not," Dahlia said, snorting a laugh.

"You do. You're a total bed hog. But I love it. And if your body changes—"

"It's going to change, Oscar. That's what human bodies do."

"We don't know that for sure. I reckon there's a chance you stop aging after we bind our souls together. But if it does keep changing, I'll keep continuing to love it best because it means that I get to spend my life with you. Finally. Also, your curves are sexy as fuck."

"Get up and kiss me."

He stood and kissed her senseless, backing her up to the bed. "Darlin', are you sure we have time for this?" He didn't wait for an answer before working his hand underneath her shirt, taking his time to touch every inch of her stomach and waist before reaching for her breasts. He traced his fingers along her tits, memorizing each stretch mark, savoring all of her, putting his words into action.

"It's a school night, so we have about an hour and a half before Tabitha comes to bed." She bit her bottom lip as she pulled off her top. "We have time."

"Not as much time as I would like," Oscar said. "But I'll make do." After Dahlia undid her jeans, he helped pull them off. He took hold of her hips, lifted her effortlessly, and tossed her onto the bed. Then he climbed on top of her.

"Why aren't you undressing?" Dahlia asked as she untucked his button-up.

"I want to focus on you," Oscar said, shrugging.

"But I want your dick," Dahlia said, unhooking his belt and then unbuttoning his pants. "In my hand, in my mouth, in my pussy."

"You make it impossible to say no to you." Oscar got off the bed and stripped. Dahlia thrust her hips up so she could work her panties past her butt. Then Oscar grabbed them and pulled them off the rest of the way. She'd taken her bra off when she'd gotten home from work. They were both naked, and Dahlia couldn't help but pant at the sight of her cowboy demon, his perfectly sculpted body forged not in a gym but through ranch tending.

Dahlia would never get tired of being able to see him, even if he hadn't looked like a god. "You're way out of my league," Dahlia said.

"Dahlia, you are the most beautiful woman I have ever met." He grasped her hips in his hands and pulled her toward the end of the bed. Kneeling between her legs, he spread her wide with his shoulders and the petals of her pussy with his fingers. "Every inch of you is gorgeous."

He teased her clit with his tongue, then licked each labia. Dahlia's hips lifted from the mattress of their own volition, and Oscar chuckled. Closing his lips around her clit, he hummed against her, sending sparks down to her toes.

He placed one finger at her entrance and pressed into her the tiniest bit. "You feel so good, even on just the tip of my finger."

"Oscar, please. I can't handle all this teasing." It hadn't escaped her that he'd put himself in a position where she couldn't reach him. She needed him on the bed. "Please, Oscar."

"What do you want?" He pushed his finger into her completely. "More of this?" He fucked her with it. Deep strokes, all the way out, then all the way back in. But it wasn't enough.

"I want you in reach, dammit."

"Do you, now?" He grabbed her hand and placed it on his head. "I'm right here." Lowering his head, he brought his lips around her clit once more.

"Fucking fuck, Oscar, give me your dick."

"My, my, Dahlia, you're swearing like a cowboy on his first cattle drive. It's a little out of character." His tongue flicked against her, but he didn't break eye contact.

"I need you inside me." She buried her fingers in his hair and tugged. Placing his hands on either side of her hips, he pushed himself up. Then he hooked her legs around his waist and seated his cock inside her with a series of deepening thrusts. Dahlia gasped at the intrusion, her muscles flexing against him as she welcomed his girth.

They worked together, pumping their hips in tandem, bringing each other closer to crisis. It slammed into her first, and she clawed at his back, biting down on his shoulder to keep from being heard by the entire household. He followed her over the cliff a moment later.

Dahlia barely gave him the chance to finish before she had tossed him off of her and climbed between his legs. She wrapped her mouth around him, tasting his cum and hers. He whimpered beneath her, but she didn't stop even when she'd cleaned his cock completely.

"Dahlia, please, it's too much," he said.

She pulled off him then. "I just wanted to make you beg, and you didn't give me the opportunity to taste you beforehand."

He encouraged her up the bed and pulled her into his arms. Rubbing her back in soothing circles, he told her how much he loved her in a hushed voice.

"Shower with me?" Dahlia asked. "We've got enough time for somewhat leisurely aftercare."

"Let's do it, darlin'."

Forty-Two

DAHLIA FLIPPED OFF THE water as Oscar reached around the shower curtain and grabbed her towel. He made sure she was warm and cozy before grabbing his own. Then he hopped onto the bathmat and helped her step over the high rim of the bathtub.

He brought the edge of his towel up and wiped away a bit of water on her nose. A delighted giggle bubbled out of her, and she returned his gesture with a kiss. They brushed their teeth next to one another, making silly faces in the mirror, before shuffling into Dahlia's bedroom to find clothes.

They'd barely put on pajamas when Lucifer appeared in their bedroom. Dahlia jumped backward, grabbed a throw pillow from the floor by the bed, and tossed it at him. It bounced ineffectually off his chest, and he guffawed.

"I'm sorry," Lucifer said. "I did not mean to surprise you."

"Then use the front door," Dahlia said. "Or at least text."

"I will do that next time." Lucifer stooped over to pick up the pillow and handed it back to Dahlia. "Mina said you needed me."

"Could have been a phone call," Dahlia said, shrugging.

"I might be feeling a little antsy," Lucifer said, "since we regained my legion."

"Earlier tonight?" Dahlia asked. Oscar grunted and sat down on the bed. He hooked an arm around Dahlia and pulled her down next to him.

"We were in Hell for about a week," Lucifer said. "I've had longer to adjust."

"And yet," Dahlia said, smirking at him.

"Yeah," Lucifer said. "I might also be anxious about whether the second half of Mina's plan worked. The part where we hoped I succeeded in impregnating her."

"Please, no details," Dahlia said, holding up a hand. "But I hope it worked, too."

Lucifer chuckled. He plopped down on her desk chair. "What is it you two need? If you could make it an impossible task that is also highly important to get my mind off of things, I'd be eternally grateful."

"We want to get married," Oscar said.

"Congratulations," Lucifer said. "But why do you need me for that?"

"We want to get married the way you married my sister," Dahlia clarified.

"Oh," Lucifer said. "I can help you with that. It might be a little difficult as an observer. You have to orgasm simultaneously, and at the exact same instant I have to pull your souls from your body and merge them, split them, and give them back to you."

"Uhhh," Dahlia said, her brain shorting out a bit at the idea that her brother-in-law was going to have to not just see her orgasm, but also take out her soul, reconfigure it, and return it.

Oscar's arm tightened around her. "There's no other way? Could you teach me how to do it?"

"No. It's something I got from Hades. That level of soul manipulation is unique to me." Lucifer tapped his finger on his chin while Dahlia took a deep breath, bracing herself before she vocalized the decision she'd made. And then he went and changed the parameters.

"It might take some practice," he added. "I may have to ask for another go. If I'm at all unsure, I won't risk damaging either of your souls."

"We need a practice run?" Dahlia asked.

"I can make sure we come at the same time, darlin', no problem."

"It's not that. It's making sure Lucifer knows when we're coming," Dahlia said. "The exact second? That's going to be hard."

"Well, for one thing, we can announce it. That will help," Oscar said.

"I should be able to tell," Lucifer said. "Mina's orgasms might be more potent, by a large magnitude, but all orgasms produce energy. It should be pretty easy to time it correctly. Although it might be a good idea to do a test run."

Dahlia buried her face in her hands. "You mean you're going to have to watch us do it more than once." She groaned with dread.

"I wish there was another way," Lucifer said.

"We need to talk to Mina," Dahlia said. "She needs to be on board with this. We aren't doing anything that she's uncomfortable with."

"We aren't going to do anything you aren't comfortable with either, Dahlia," Oscar said. "There could be another way to accomplish our goal."

"No," Dahlia said. "That will take time, time I'm not willing to lose. Unless Mina pulls the cord, I'm in. Besides, you've seen my sister orgasm. It's probably only fair that he sees me."

"Consent most definitely does not work that way," Lucifer said. "Tit for tat is only valid if it's agreed upon beforehand or during, I guess. I would never let anyone compel you to do something you don't want to do, sister, just to balance the scales."

"Thank you, Luci," Dahlia said, using her brother-in-law's nickname for the first time.

His eyes sparkled with glee.

"I'm really fighting the urge to defend myself, here," Oscar said.

"Why?" Dahlia asked.

"I didn't know she was your sister at the time. I wasn't myself, either. Not after I lost you," Oscar said.

"Oh, sweetheart, I know all that. Mina helped you get out of your funk, then she led you to me, and I finished the job."

Oscar leaned down and pressed his lips to hers. "You did."

There was a knock on the door. "Can I come in?" Mina asked, her voice muffled through the wood.

"Yes, please do," Dahlia said. "I didn't know you were here. I want to talk to you, too."

"I wanted to be close to family when we got back from Hell." Mina peeked her head in the door, her eyes widening when they landed on her husband. "Is this where you ran off to?"

"Sorry," Lucifer said. "I should have told you where I was going, but I couldn't bring myself to disturb you."

"How long have you been here?" Mina asked.

"Half an hour?" Lucifer guessed, shrugging.

"I couldn't have been asleep that long after you'd left, then," Mina said, moving to sit with Lucifer after he patted his lap. "What is it that you need, Dahlia?"

"They want to get married, Mina, the same way we did," Lucifer said, saving Dahlia the embarrassment of having to explain. "Which means I'd have to be in the room while they have sex. Maybe more than once."

"Why more than once?" Mina asked, her head whipping around so she could gape at her husband.

"To ensure we get the timing right. I don't want to make a mistake when both of their souls are on the line. We might not need it, but, just in case we do, I want us all prepared."

Mina's head bobbed slowly. "That makes sense." She playfully hit Lucifer's arm with the back of her hand, which, of course, he immediately caught and kissed. "Don't mess up my sister's soul."

"So, you're okay with it?" Dahlia asked. "If you aren't, we'll find another way."

"I'm honestly more than okay with it. I trust Luci to respect boundaries and stay professional. And if this means you'll share Oscar's lifespan, then I won't have to lose you." Mina bounced off of Luci's lap and made a beeline for the door. "I'll go take Mom and Tabby out for late-night ice cream to distract them."

"What?" Dahlia clutched at her pajama top. "We aren't doing this tonight." She looked at Oscar, then at Mina. "Are we?"

Mina's hand dropped from the door handle. "Oh, sorry. Did I get ahead of myself?"

"We didn't wait." Lucifer shrugged. "But we did have more pressing reasons not to."

"It's okay if you need more time, darlin'. There's no rush," Oscar said, brushing a kiss against the curve of her shoulder.

"It's just my nerves about being watched," Dahlia said. "But, really, this is a lot more low-key than the night we shared with Adam."

"You slept with Adam?" Mina asked, eyes wide.

Dahlia tucked a piece of hair behind her ear. "Um, yeah. I guess I forgot to tell you about that."

"When you went over to check in on him for me? I didn't expect you to take over my usual role, too." Mina crossed her arms and chewed on her bottom lip. "I'm sorry."

"Don't be sorry," Dahlia said. "It was fun. We actually made plans to do it again." She sighed, sagging a bit against Oscar before changing the subject. "We need to get moving if we're going to do this tonight. That ice cream shop is open late, but not all night."

Mina gave a fake salute. "On it." She closed the door behind her a second later.

With the three of them alone, Dahlia's pulse sped. This was really happening. She was about to have sex with her fiancé while her brother-in-law watched. It sounded like the plot to a bad porno. Taking a deep breath, Dahlia reminded herself that they weren't recording this for the internet. She trusted Lucifer. He wouldn't surprise her by joining in during a vulnerable moment.

"Are you sure about this, Dahlia?" Lucifer asked.

"Yes," she said, "I am."

"You can change your mind at any time," he continued. "You get the slightest bit uncomfortable, just say the word, and I'll leave. That goes for you, too, Oscar."

"Thanks, Lucifer," Oscar said. "I don't know how to repay you."

"You don't need to worry about that. We're family. We don't keep score." Lucifer smiled. "Would you like me to give you two a few minutes to get started?"

"Are we starting with our practice run?" Dahlia asked.

"We can consider it practice if you want, but if I manage to line it up just right, I won't hesitate. Is that okay?" Lucifer asked.

Dahlia glanced at Oscar and found his answer in his eyes. "We trust you," she said.

With a final nod, Lucifer left the room.

Oscar moved faster than she could track, pivoting them so that she was on her back beneath him. He hovered over her, his eyes roaming over the curves of her body. His tongue slipped over his lips at the sight of an exposed strip of her bare tummy. Dahlia gasped when he caressed her there before pushing her shirt up, exposing her up to her collarbone.

"Would you like to keep this on?" he asked, lifting her top just the slightest bit higher. "Preserve some modesty?"

She shook her head, pulling the article of clothing off herself. "Just cover me with your body. You'll protect my modesty, right?" She wiggled out of her pajama bottoms. She hadn't bothered with underwear after their shower.

"If that's what you wish," he said, pressing his body against hers. He slipped a hand between their bodies, working his hand against her core until she helplessly spread her legs and thrust her hips up to meet him. She was on the edge in no time, but he backed off.

She whimpered while he chuckled.

"I promise I'm not trying to frustrate you into taking control this time," he said.

"I know. Circumstances being what they are, probably better to save my orgasm for the right moment, especially since it won't be my first of the night."

Oscar nuzzled into the crook of her neck and moaned. He pinched one outer labia between two fingers and tugged, bringing Dahlia right back to the edge. She wrapped one leg around him, encouraging his hips down against her pelvis. Brushing her hands against his ass, she tucked her fingers into the waistband of his bottoms and pulled them down just far enough to free his hardness. She grasped him in one hand, pumping him.

"I'm not so sure that's a good idea. I'm already about to burst."

Dahlia brought the head of his cock to her entrance, and he drove forward. She wrapped her arms around his torso, and he covered her breasts with his chest. They rocked against each other, and every movement sent blasts of pleasure through her body.

Oscar's thrusts became more erratic, and he grabbed her thighs, pulling them up and around him, angling her so he could penetrate her deeper, hitting all the right spots in just the right way. The hand he'd kept between them rubbed against her clit.

"Oh, Oscar, I'm going to come," Dahlia said, louder than she'd meant to.

"Fuck, yes, darlin', come for me," Oscar said. She did, tightening around him and triggering his orgasm as well.

At the height of her pleasure, Dahlia's chest seized in pain. It felt like the air had been knocked out of her. She dug her fingers into Oscar's back, trying to gain purchase as the room filled with colored light, one half purple and the other brick-red.

Above her, Oscar looked just as panicked as Dahlia felt. But he was searching her face, trying to determine if she was okay. She could tell he was more concerned with her well-being than his own. Even though she wanted to reassure him, she couldn't utter a word.

Then the lights mixed and swirled, becoming a beautiful hue of magenta before splitting and slamming into both Oscar and Dahlia. In a moment, Dahlia could breathe again, and she loosened her hold on Oscar. He pulled her against him, and she felt the reassuring rise and fall of his chest.

"Success," Lucifer said behind them. "I commend you both on your timeliness. I believe I just heard Mina returning. I'll go down and run interference while you two newlyweds, um, bask in your wedded bliss."

Dahlia heard the door shut. "When did he even come back in? Did you hear him?"

Oscar chuckled. "We did it, darlin'."

"Can you hand me my t-shirt," Dahlia said, gently pressing her hand against Oscar's chest until he rolled off of her.

He scooped up her top and handed it to her in one smooth motion, his focus never wavering from her. "Are you okay?" he asked as she hastily pulled the shirt over her head. "Already grapplin' with regrets?"

"No," Dahlia said. "I mean, a little. That really hurt. Did I die? It felt like I died." She rested her back against the headboard and then pulled her knees to her chest. Placing her head on

354 SUSAN BETH COLE

her knees, she pulled herself in. "It was terrifying. I just need a minute."

"A minute alone?"

She shook her head.

Scooting next to her, Oscar draped an arm over her and set his head on top of hers.

"It was worth it," she whispered.

"That's a relief." They sat together for a while, fingers as intertwined as their souls. Slowly, it became obvious that this overwhelming feeling, so large it was truly troublesome to process, was utter and complete joy.

"I think, Oscar, that I've never been happier, and it is the single most terrifying feeling I have ever experienced."

He lifted his head, then brought a finger below her chin and tipped her head up so he could find her eyes with his own. "I promise to do everything in my power to ensure that you never need to be scared of joy again. I will protect it with my eternal life."

Her heart swelled. "I want to protect yours, too."

Their lips met and tongues danced. They kissed for what felt like an eternity, and, when they finally parted, a bit out of breath, Dahlia found that she was ready to face her family.

"My mom is going to be so pissed," Dahlia said.

Epilogue

L UCI AND MINA STOOD in the mostly unfurnished parlor of Oscar and Dahlia's future home. What it lacked in chairs, it made up for in party decorations. Sandra had covered every wall with banners, pictures of Mina and Dahlia as children, and more recent photos of her daughters with their husbands. Streamers were draped across every doorway.

Dahlia hadn't even put up a fight when Sandra demanded that she be allowed to throw them a joint party celebrating their nuptials. Mina couldn't blame her sister, though. She would never forget the anger on her mother's face seven months ago when Dahlia and Oscar came downstairs that night, still firmly entrenched in their afterglow. She was beyond pissed.

"You fucking did this to me, too?" Sandra had growled. Dahlia and Oscar had grimaced and quickly acquiesced to all of Sandra's demands.

"There were supposed to be chairs," Dahlia said, coming up behind them. She was wearing an ivory sheath wedding gown. Every inch of it covered in lace. She looked beautiful. "But the vendor screwed up. You should have heard how loud Mom got on the phone with them."

Mina's hand brushed the satin of her tea-length wedding dress as she cupped her rounded belly. The dress was nothing like the gown she'd worn to the family gathering she'd thrown with Luci after they'd eloped. But she could easily pee on her own in this one, and it flattered her baby bump.

A lack of chairs was definitely going to be a problem. She was okay standing for now, but she would have to get creative long before the party was over. She looked down at the hardwood beneath her feet. It would take at least two people to help her up if she had to resort to sitting on the floor.

Luci followed her train of thought. "Don't worry, love. I will make you a chair long before it comes to that."

"Oh," Dahlia said, a grin spreading across her face. "You could just conjure up some chairs for us now. Before any guests arrive?"

Luci sighed, then flicked his wrists. Chairs and even a table or two for gifts and goodies appeared in the space. "How's that?"

Sandra chose that moment to swoop into the room. "Where did all this come from? Did the vendor come through?"

"No, Mom. Luci did this," Mina said.

"I'm going to go find Oscar," Dahlia said, hurrying off.

"This is incredible," Sandra said. "Thank you, Son. Giving me grandbabies and chairs. You're just incredible." She stood on tiptoes and pressed a kiss to the Prince of Hell's cheek.

"You're welcome," Luci said, blushing. Mina failed to hide her giggle.

"How are you doing?" Sandra said, turning to her daughter. "You are bigger every day. Why don't you sit down."

"I'm okay, Mom," Mina said.

"You are carrying quite the load," Sandra said. "Promise you'll take it easy tonight."

"I promise, Mom," Mina said.

"Good," Sandra said. Her hand hovered near Mina's belly. "Can I touch you?" She waited for Mina to nod before placing her hand on her daughter. "Have they been moving a lot today?"

"A little this morning," Luci said. "I got to feel them. Finally."

"They've been very shy around their father." Mina smiled up at her husband, noting his worried expression. "They'll warm up to you. You're very lovable."

"Am I?" Luci's lopsided grin hit Mina right in the core. Her heart started to race, and desire sprouted. Pregnancy had supercharged her already strong libido. Maybe they could sneak away without anyone noticing. Surely no one would wander up into the attic. Some ropes might still be up there.

She bit her bottom lip, and Luci watched every movement. His eyes darted to the door, and she dipped her head slightly in what she hoped was subtle agreement.

Sandra, unfortunately, did not miss any of what was happening between them. "Nope. No way. I know your hormones are hard to ignore, but you two are not allowed to disappear until after the cupcakes have been served." Sandra gasped. "They moved!" Mina felt it too. On her left side.

"That's the boy," Mina said.

"If you'd tell us the names you've picked out, we could stop reducing them to their sexes," Sandra said.

Luci chuckled. "We have to agree on names first."

"I thought you'd decided," Sandra said.

"Yeah, I had second thoughts." Mina shrugged. "It's fine. We have time."

"You two settle in. Stake your claim on a chair now, Mina." Sandra said. "Guests will be here any minute."

Somehow, they managed to make it to cupcakes without sneaking off completely. There was a moment when she'd gone to get more ice from the freezer and Luci had pulled her into the pantry for a too-brief makeout session. And the time when he'd pushed her back into the bathroom after her third pee of the evening. He'd put his hand under the layers of her skirt and touched her expertly until she came. Instead of taking the edge off, however, it only fired her up more.

Someone handed them cupcakes. Dahlia and Oscar next to them were also given the dessert. The photographers were posed with cameras drawn and ready. It had been one of Sandra's stipulations that they feed each other cake.

Mina loaded up a fork with a small bite of cupcake that had the perfect ratio of cake to icing. She held it up as Luci held a full cupcake in his hands. Was he just going to shove the whole thing in her face? She narrowed her eyes at him. His sparkled with mischief.

As one, they moved toward each other. Mina lifted the fork to his lips and watched raptly as his mouth closed around the prongs.

He brought the cupcake to her mouth and stopped until she opened her mouth. Then he helped angle the cake so she could take a sizable bite. Her lips brushed his fingertips, and he shuddered, his throat bobbing as he gulped.

They maintained eye contact as they chewed and swallowed. A small dollop of icing remained on Luci's thumb. She stopped him from wiping it away on his napkin by clutching his wrist in her hand and bringing his thumb to her mouth, cleaning him with a flick of her tongue.

The sugar from the dessert and the earlier lemonade made its way to the babies, and they started a dance party. "Oh, wow," Mina said, clutching her abdomen.

"Are you okay?" Luci asked, moving her to the nearest chair and helping her down into it.

In response, Mina grabbed his hands and placed them on her belly. The twins kept moving. "Do you feel them?"

"Oh, wow," Luci said, echoing Mina's earlier reaction. He looked up at her, tears in his eyes. "We did it."

Mina leaned forward, resting her forehead against his. He cupped the side of her neck and kissed her.

Acknowledgements

A huge thank you to all my readers. I hope you enjoyed seeing Mina & Luci and Dahlia & Oscar get their Happily Ever Afters. There's one more novel in the Paradise Ours series, but I have a lot of novellas planned. So many novellas. It might be too many, but I keep falling in love with these side characters, and I want them all to find love and happiness. I hope you'll join me on those journeys as well.

A special thank you to everyone who shared their love for The Little Death. Your support means the world to me.

Thank you to my husband and my children for inspiring me and supporting me as I follow my dream.

Thank you to my beta readers and to my copy-editor, Jenny. This book would not be the polished piece of literature it is today without your hard work and expertise.

Thank you Meowlayn for bringing my characters to life with your beautiful cover art. I couldn't ask for a better experience working with an artist for the first time. The work you've done for The Little Death and The Quickening is beyond my wildest imaginings.

I also wanted to express my gratitude for the Friday night movie crew—Matt, Robby, Tansy, Aaron, Alissa, and Jacob—for cheering me on and helping me unwind after a long week. I'm sorry, Matt, that no one lost their head in this book. People did get head, and I hope that makes up for it.

A big thank you to the authors out there who inspire me—go read their books next: Maya Maitea, Rebekah Weatherspoon, Kayla Grosse, Tasha L. Harrison, Celestine Martin, Farah Rochon, Nenia Campbell, Liana De la Rosa, Kimberly Lemming, and Jasper Hyde, among so many others.

About the author

Susan Beth Cole has a BA in English. She largely grew up in the mountains around Leadville, Colorado and worked six and a half years as a bookseller for an independent bookstore in Boulder, Colorado. When she's not writing, she's reading, watching anime, or playing Final Fantasy XIV. She lives in Longmont, Colorado with her werewolf of a husband, two kids, and a bunch of pets.

Also by Susan Beth Cole

Paradise Ours

The Little Death